Praise for *Wonders of the Invisible World*

"A casket full of wonders. I think each story is my favorite, until I read the next. McKillip has the true mythopoeic imagination. Here lies the border between our world and that of Faerie."
—P. C. Hodgell, author of the Kencyrath series

"One of the true wise women of fantasy literature, Patricia McKillip is a writer to treasure. This brilliant new collection puts on display the audacity, the warmth, the intelligence and depth of her huge and magnificent talent."
—Peter Straub, author of *Ghost Story* and *A Dark Matter*

"I read—and re-rea[...]ls me that fantasy is worth writing."
—Stephen R. Donaldson, author of The Chronicles of Thomas Covenant

"McKillip skillfully knits disparate threads into a rewardingly rich and satisfying story."
—*Amazon.com*

"McKillip's name is the first that comes to mind when I'm asked whom I read myself, whom I'd recommend that others read, and who still makes me shake my grizzled head and say, 'Damn, I wish I'd done that!'"
—Peter S. Beagle, author of *The Last Unicorn*

WONDERS OF THE INVISIBLE WORLD
PATRICIA A. McKILLIP

Introduction copyright © 2012 by Charles de Lint

Interior and cover design by Elizabeth Story
Cover art copyright © 1998 by Thomas Canty

Tachyon Publications
1459 18th Street #139
San Francisco, CA 94107
www.tachyonpublications.com

Series Editor: Jacob Weisman
Project Editor: Jill Roberts

ISBN 13: 978-1-61696-087-2
ISBN 10: 1-61696-087-6

Printed in the United States by Worzalla
First Edition: 2012
9 8 7 6 5 4 3 2 1

All stories copyright © by Patricia A.
McKillip

"Wonders of the Invisible World"
copyright © 1995. First published in
Full Spectrum 5, edited by Jennifer
Hershey, Tom Dupree, and Janna
Silverstein (Bantam Spectra: New
York).

"Out of the Woods" copyright ©
2004. First published in Flights: Ex-
treme Visions of Fantasy, edited by Al
Sarrantonio (Roc: New York).

"The Kelpie" copyright © 2005. First
published in The Fair Folk, edited by
Marvin Kaye (Science Fiction Book
Club: Garden City, New York).

WONDERS OF THE INVISIBLE WORLD
PATRICIA A. MCKILLIP

Tachyon
San Francisco

For Dave, to whom most of these old tales will be new

CONTENTS

INTRODUCTION
Charles de Lint

If you want to know who Patricia McKillip is, just read her stories. Really, all we need to know about the creative individuals who fill our lives with their poetry, prose, music and art is waiting for us right there in the work itself.

But we're always curious, aren't we? When something moves us we want—almost *need*—to know more about the individual who was able to wake such a reaction in us.

It can be a double-edged sword, of course. Sometimes the person is everything we hoped they would be, with a heart beating in their chest as big and generous as we imagined. Their eyes are so clear and wise that it seems utterly appropriate that they give us a more profound experience of the world's mysteries.

Other times, the person is so *wrong* in terms of how we imagined them that we can no longer engage in their art in the same way that once we did.

It's a curious thing, but even when we know that it might turn out badly, we still walk into the riddle that is the artist whose work we admire so much, hoping for the best.

The truth is, more often than not, despite their spark of genius, these artists are not unlike you or me—a mix of good and bad, patient and intolerant, welcoming and private—all in varying degrees. And of course we're all different, depending on the day and situation in which we find ourselves.

So I can't tell you who the *real* Patricia McKillip is. All I can tell you is who she is to me.

Like most of you, I first met her in the pages of one of her books. For me, it was *The Forgotten Beasts of Eld.* I remember it was the Avon paperback edition that came out in the mid-seventies, which means I've been reading her for around thirty-five years.

I adored that book. Then *The Riddle-Master of Hed* came out a year or so later and I became completely smitten. When I went looking for more by her, I was surprised to discover that her novels came out first in hardcover as young adult books, then were reprinted as adult paperbacks. I tracked them all down and, to this day, I always pick up her new books.

If you're reading this, you know why: they're just so damned good. She's one of the few writers I've read who hasn't written a bad book. I don't think she has it in her.

For all that I love the secondary world novels for which she is best known, my favourite book of hers is probably *Stepping from the Shadows*, a standalone contemporary book that contains the *idea* of fantasy more than the actual trappings. (Note to self: it's time to reread that book.)

The first time I actually met Pat was at one of the New England World Fantasy Conventions where I asked her to sign my advance reading copy of that self-same *Stepping from the Shadows*. I remember her being soft-spoken and charming—and a little aghast that I'd bought an expensive ARC in the dealer's room, when I already owned a copy of the book. But I didn't have the hardcover with me, and I really wanted a personalized book to bring home and treasure.

And ever since, I continue to see her at World Fantasy Conventions whenever we both happen to attend. Through the years these cons have become the only place where I can spend time with people I don't normally get to see. Writers, artists, editors and readers from different parts of the continent (and the world!) gather in a hotel in some major city to...well, mostly sit around in the hotel bar and schmooze with each other.

One particular afternoon in one of those hotel bars remains a fond memory for me: sitting around a large round table with Pat, Terri

Windling and Midori Snyder as we went through a big stack of Brian Froud's art, choosing the pieces that would appear in the books we would write for a series called "Brian Froud's Faerielands." Sadly, only two of the books came out in their planned illustrated form: my *The Wild Wood* and Pat's lovely *Something Rich and Strange*.

I'm not sure why the series was cancelled. Terri's *The Wood Wife* and Midori's *Hannah's Garden* were published—how could two such fine books not be published?—but it would have been so much nicer to have the illustrated quartet all be available as originally intended, resplendent with Brian's art. In another world, I'm sure that happened. We're simply not privy to it.

What I remember most of that afternoon as we were choosing the art was how there were no arguments, gentle or otherwise. We each just kept picking the illustrations we wanted and there was no overlap. We delighted in each other's choices, but were completely satisfied with what we got for our own books.

And that's how I know Pat outside of her stories. Every time I've seen her at a World Fantasy Convention she remains soft-spoken and charming, gracious and articulate. And a little shy, too. Or is that me, still smitten with one of my literary heroes after all these years?

If you need to know more, turn to the reprint of her 2004 WisCon Guest of Honor speech at the end of this collection, which will give you a taste of her life outside of her books.

Though really, as I said earlier, you're best off to dive right into the stories collected here. They might surprise you because she doesn't always write the gentle fantasies with which she's usually associated. Her contemporary settings (which can have a little bit of a darker edge) are a perfect contrast to her gentler fantasies; she does both so very well.

—Charles de Lint
Ottawa, Canada
Spring 2012

WONDERS OF THE INVISIBLE WORLD

I AM THE ANGEL sent to Cotton Mather. It took me some time to get his attention. He lay on the floor with his eyes closed; he prayed fervently, sometimes murmuring, sometimes shouting. Apparently the household was used to it. I heard footsteps pass his study door; a woman—his wife Abigail?—called to someone: "If your throat is no better tomorrow, we'll have Phillip pee in a cup for you to gargle." From the way the house smelled, Phillip didn't bother much with cups. Cotton Mather smelled of smoke and sweat and wet wool. Winter had come early. The sky was black, the ground was white, the wind pinched like a witch and whined like a starving dog. There was no color in the landscape and no mercy. Cotton Mather prayed to see the invisible world.

He wanted an angel.

"O Lord," he said, in desperate, hoarse, weary cadences, like a sick child talking itself to sleep. "Thou hast given angelic visions to Thy innocent children to defend them from their demons. Remember Thy humble servant, who prostrates himself in the dust, vile worm that I am, forsaking food and comfort and sleep, in humble hope that Thou might bestow upon Thy humble servant the blessing and hope at this harsh and evil time: a glimpse of Thy shadow, a flicker of light in Thine eye, a single word from Thy mouth. Show me Thy messengers of good who fly between the visible and invisible worlds. Grant me, O God, a vision."

I cleared my throat a little. He didn't open his eyes. The fire was dying down. I wondered who replenished it, and if the sight of Mather's bright, winged creature would surprise anyone, with all the witches, devils and demented goldfinches perched on rafters all over New England. The firelight spilling across the wide planks glowed

14

just beyond his outstretched hand. He lay in dim lights and fluttering shadows, in the long, long night of history, when no one could ever see clearly after sunset, and witches and angels and living dreams trembled just beyond the fire.

"Grant me, O God, a vision."

I was standing in front of his nose. He was lost in days of fasting and desire, trying to conjure an angel out of his head. According to his writings, what he expected to see was the generic white male with wings growing out of his shoulders, fair-haired, permanently beardless, wearing a long white nightgown and a gold dinner plate on his head. This was what intrigued Durham, and why he had hired me: he couldn't believe that both good and evil in the Puritan imagination could be so banal.

But I was what Mather wanted: something as colorless and pure as the snow that lay like the hand of God over the earth, harsh, exacting, unambiguous. Fire, their salvation against the cold, was red and belonged to Hell.

"O Lord."

It was the faintest of whispers. He was staring at my feet.

They were bare and shining and getting chilled. The ring of diamonds in my halo contained controls for light, for holograms like my wings, a map disc, a local-history disc in case I got totally bewildered by events, and a recorder disc that had caught the sudden stammer in Mather's last word. He had asked for an angel; he got an angel. I wished he would quit staring at my feet and throw another log on the fire.

He straightened slowly, pushing himself off the floor while his eyes traveled upward. He was scarcely thirty at the time of the trials; he resembled his father at that age more than the familiar Pelham portrait of Mather in his sixties, soberly dressed, with a wig like a cream puff on his head, and a firm, resigned mouth. The young Mather had long dark hair, a spare, handsome, clean-shaven face, searching, credulous eyes. His eyes reached my face finally, cringing a little, as if he half expected a demon's red, leering face attached to the angel's body. But he found what he expected. He began to cry.

He cried silently, so I could speak. His writings are mute about much of the angel's conversation. Mostly it predicted Mather's success as a writer, great reviews and spectacular sales in America and Europe. I greeted him, gave him the message from God, quoted Ezekiel, and then got down to business. By then he had stopped crying, wiped his face with his dusty sleeve and cheered up at the prospect of fame.

"There are troubled children," I said, "who have seen me."

"They speak of you in their misery," he said gratefully. "You give them strength against evil."

"Their afflictions are terrible."

"Yes," he whispered.

"You have observed their torments."

"Yes."

"You have taken them into your home, borne witness to their complaints, tried to help them cast out their tormentors."

"I have tried."

"You have wrestled with the invisible world."

"Yes."

We weren't getting very far. He still knelt on the hard floor, as he had done for hours, perhaps days; he could see me more clearly than he had seen anything in the dark in his life. He had forgotten the fire. I tried to be patient. Good angels were beyond temperament, even while at war with angels who had disgraced themselves by exhibiting human characteristics. But the floorboards were getting very cold.

"You have felt the invisible chains about them," I prodded. "The invisible, hellish things moving beneath their bedclothes."

"The children cannot seem to stand my books," he said a little querulously, with a worried frown. "My writing sends them into convulsions. At the mere act of opening my books, they fall down as dead upon the floor. Yet how can I lead them gently back to God's truth if the truth acts with such violence against them?"

"It is not against them," I reminded him, "but against the devil, who," I added, inspired, "takes many shapes."

He nodded, and became voluble. "Last week he took the shape of thieves who stole three sermons from me. And of a rat—or something like a hellish rat—we could feel in the air, but not see."

"A rat."

"And sometimes a bird, a yellow bird, the children say—they see it perched on the fingers of those they name witches."

"And since they say it, it is so."

He nodded gravely. "God made nothing more innocent than children."

I let that pass. I was his delusion, and if I had truly been sent to him from God, then God and Mather agreed on everything.

"Have they—" this was Durham's suggestion "—not yet seen the devil in the shape of a black horse who spews fire between its teeth, and is ridden by three witches, each more beautiful than the last?"

He stared at me, then caught himself imagining the witches and blinked. "No," he breathed. "No one has seen such a thing. Though the Shape of Goody Bishop in her scarlet bodice and her lace had been seen over the beds of honest married men."

"What did she do to them?"

"She hovered. She haunted them. For this and more she was hanged."

For wearing a color and inciting the imagination, she was hanged. I refrained from commenting that since her Shape had done the hovering, it was her Shape that should have been hanged. But it was almost worth my researcher's license. "In God's justice," I said piously, "her soul dwells." I had almost forgotten the fire; this dreary, crazed, malicious atmosphere was more chilling than the cold.

"She had a witchmark," Mather added. "The witch's teat." His eyes were wide, marveling; he had conjured witches as well as angels out of his imagination. I suppose it was easier, in that harsh world, to make demons out of your neighbors, with their imperfections, tempers, rheumy eyes, missing teeth, irritating habits and smells, than to find angelic beauty in them. But I wasn't there to judge Mather. I could hear Durham's intense voice: Imagination. Imagery. I want to know what they pulled out of their heads. They invented their devil, but all they could do was make him talk like a bird? Don't bother with a moral viewpoint. I want to know what Mather saw. This was the man who believed that thunder was caused by the sulfurous farts of decaying vegetation. Why? Don't ask me why. You're a researcher. Go research.

Research the imagination. It was as obsolete as the appendix in most adults, except for those in whom, like the appendix, it became inflamed for no reason. Durham's curiosity seemed as aberrated as Mather's; they both craved visions. But in his world, Durham could afford the luxury of being crazed. In this world, only the crazed, the adolescent girls, the trial judges, Mather himself, were sane.

I was taking a moral viewpoint. But Mather was still talking, and the recorder was catching his views, not mine. I had asked Durham once, after an exasperating journey to some crowded, airless, fly-infested temple covered with phallic symbols to appear as a goddess, to stop hiring me; the Central Research Computer had obviously got its records mixed when it recommended me to him. Our historical viewpoints were thoroughly incompatible. "No, they're not," he had said obnoxiously, and refused to elaborate. He paid well. He paid very well. So here I was, in frozen colonial New England, listening to Cotton Mather talk about brooms.

"The witches ride them," he said, still wide-eyed. "Sometimes three to a besom. To their foul Witches' Sabbaths."

Their foul Sabbaths, he elaborated, consisted of witches gathering in some boggy pasture where the demons talked with the voices of frogs, listening to a fiendish sermon, drinking blood, and plotting to bring back pagan customs like dancing around a Maypole. I wondered if, being an angel of God, I was supposed to know all this already, and if Mather would wonder later why I had listened. Durham and I had argued about this, about the ethics and legalities of me pretending to be Mather's delusion.

"What's the problem?" he had asked. "You think the real angel is going to show up later?"

Mather was still speaking, in a feverish trance caused most likely by too much fasting, prayer and mental agitation. Evil eyes, he was talking about, and "things" that were hairy all over. They apparently caused neighbors to blame one another for dead pigs, wagons stuck in potholes, sickness, lust and deadly boredom. I was getting bored myself, by then, and thoroughly depressed. Children's fingers had pointed at random, and wherever they pointed, they created a witch. So much for the imagination. It was malignant here, an instrument of cruelty and death.

"He did not speak to the court, neither to defend his innocence nor confess his guilt," Mather was saying solemnly. "He was a stubborn old man. They piled stones upon him until his tongue stuck out and he died. But he never spoke. They had already hanged his wife. He spoke well enough then, accusing her."

I had heard enough.

"God protect the innocent," I said, and surprised myself, for it was a prayer to something. I added, more gently, for Mather, blinking out of his trance, looked worried, as if I had accused him, "Be comforted. God will give you strength to bear all tribulations in these dark times. Be patient and faithful, and in the fullness of time, you will be rewarded with the truth of your life."

Not standard Puritan dogma, but all he heard was "reward" and "truth." I raised my hand in blessing. He flung himself down to kiss the floor at my feet. I activated the controls in my halo and went home.

Durham was waiting for me at the Researchers' Terminus. I pulled the recorder disc out of my halo, fed it to the computer, and then stepped out of the warp chamber. While the computer analyzed my recording to see if I had broken any of one thousand, five hundred and sixty-three regulations, I took off my robe and my blond hair and dumped them and my halo into Durham's arms.

"Well?" he said, not impatient, just intent, not even seeing me as I pulled a skirt and tunic over my head. I was still cold, and worried about my researcher's license, which the computer would refuse to return if I had violated history. Durham had eyes like Cotton Mather's, I saw for the first time: dark, burning, but with a suggestion of humor in them. "What did you find? Speak to me, Nici."

"Nothing," I said shortly. "You're out several million credits for nothing. It was a completely dreary bit of history, not without heroism but entirely without poetry. And if I've lost my license because of this—I'm not even sure I understand what you're trying to do."

"I'm researching for a history of imaginative thought."

Durham was always researching unreadable subjects. "Starting when?" I asked tersely, pulling on a boot. "The cave paintings at Lascaux?"

"No art," he said. "More speculative than that. Less formal. Closer to chaos." He smiled, reading my mind. "Like me."

"You're a disturbed man, Durham. You should have your unconscious scanned."

"I like it the way it is: a bubbling little morass of unpredictable metaphors."

"They aren't unpredictable," I said. "They're completely predictable. Everything imaginable is accessible, and everything accessible has been imagined by the Virtual computer, which has already researched every kind of imaginative thought since the first bison got painted on a rock. That way nothing like what happened in Cotton Mather's time can happen to us. So—"

"*Wonders of the Invisible World,*" Durham interrupted. He hadn't heard a word. "It's a book by Mather. He was talking about angels and demons. We would think of the invisible in terms of atomic particles. Both are unseen yet named, and immensely powerful—"

"Oh, stop. You're mixing atoms and angels. One exists, the other doesn't."

"That's what I'm trying to get at, Nici—the point where existence is totally immaterial, where the passion, the belief in something creates a situation completely ruled by the will to believe."

"That's insanity."

He smiled again, cheerfully. He tended to change his appearance according to what he was researching; he wore a shimmering bodysuit that showed all his muscles, and milk-white hair. Except for the bulky build of his face and the irreverence in his eyes, he might have been Mather's angel. My more androgynous face worked better. "Maybe," he said. "But I find the desire, the passion, coupled with the accompanying imagery, fascinating."

"You are a throwback," I muttered. "You belong to some barbaric age when people imagined things to kill each other for." The computer flashed a light; I breathed a sigh of relief. Durham got his tape, and the computer's analysis; I retrieved my license.

"Next time—" Durham began.

"There won't be a next time." I headed for the door. "I'm sick of appearing as twisted pieces of people's imagination. And one of these days I'm going to find myself in court."

"But you do it so well," he said softly. "You even convince the Terminus computer."

I glared at him. "Just leave me alone."

"All right," he said imperturbedly. "Don't call me, I'll call you."

I was tired, but I took the tube-walk home, to get the blood moving in my feet, and to see some light and color after that bleak, dangerous world. The moving walkway, encased in its clear tube, wound up into the air, balanced on its centipede escalator and station legs. I could see the gleaming city domes stretch like a long cluster of soap bubbles toward the afternoon sun, and I wondered that somewhere within the layers of time in this place there was a small port town on the edge of a vast, unexplored continent where Mather had flung himself down on his floorboards and prayed an angel out of himself.

He could see an angel here without praying for it. He could be an angel. He could soar into the eye of God if he wanted, on wings of gold and light. He could reach out, even in the tube-walk, punch in a credit number, plug into his implant or his wrist controls, and activate the screen above his head. He could have any reality on the menu, or any reality he could dream up, since everything imagined and imaginable and every combination of it had been programmed into the Virtual computer. And then he could walk out of the station into his living room and change the world all over again.

I had to unplug Brock when I got home; he had fallen asleep at the terminal. He opened heavy eyelids and yawned.

"Hi, Matrix."

"Don't call me that," I said mechanically. He grinned fleetingly and nestled deeper into the bubble-chair. I sat down on the couch and pulled my boots off again. It was warm, in this time; I finally felt it. Brock asked,

"What were you?"

Even he knew Durham that well. "An angel."

"What's that?"

"Look it up."

He touched the controls on his wrist absently. He was a calm child, with blue, clinical eyes and angelic hair that didn't come from me. He sprouted wings and a halo suddenly, and grunted. "What's it for?"

"It talks to God."

"What God?"

"In God We Trust. That God."

He grunted again. "Pre-Real."

I nodded, leaned back tiredly, and watched him, wondering how much longer he would be neat, attentive, curious, polite, before he shaved his head, studded his scalp and eyebrows with jewels and implants, got eye-implants that held no expression whatsoever, inserted a CD player into his earlobe, and never called me Matrix again. Maybe he would go live with his father. I hadn't seen him since Brock was born, but Brock knew exactly who he was, where he was, what he did. Speculation was unnecessary, except for aberrants like Durham.

The outercom signaled; half a dozen faces appeared onscreen: Brock's friends who lived in the station complex. They trooped in, settled themselves around Brock, and plugged into their wrists. They were playing an adventure game, a sort of space-chase, where they were intergalactic thieves raiding alien zoos of rare animals and selling them to illegal restaurants. The computer played the team of highly trained intergalactic space-patrollers. The thieves were constantly falling into black holes, getting burnt up speeding too fast into strange atmospheres, and ambushed by the wily patrollers. One of them, Indra, tried to outwit the computer by coming up with the most bizarre alien species she could imagine; the computer always gave her the images she wanted. I watched for a while. Then an image came into my head, of an old man in a field watching his neighbors pile stones on him until he could no longer breathe.

I got up, went into my office, and called Durham.

"I could have stopped it," I said tersely. He was silent, not because he didn't know what I was talking about, but because he did. "I was an angel from God. I could have changed the message."

"You wouldn't have come back," he said simply. It was true. I would have been abandoned there, powerless, a beardless youth with breasts in a long robe raving about the future, who would have become just one more witch for the children to condemn. He added, "You're a researcher. Researchers don't get emotional about history. There's nothing left of that time but some old bones in a museum from where they dug them up to build a station complex. A gravestone with an angel on it, a little face with staring eyes, and a pair of cupid wings. What's to mope about? I put a bonus in your account. Go spend it somewhere."

"How much?"

He was silent again, his eyes narrowed slightly. "Not enough for you to go back. Go get drunk, Nici. This is not you."

"I'm haunted," I whispered, I thought too softly for him to hear. He shook his head, not impatiently.

"The worst was over by then, anyway. Heroics are forbidden to researchers. You know that. The angel Mather dreamed up only told him what he wanted to hear. Tell him anything else and he'd call you a demon and refuse to listen. You know all this. Why are you taking this personally? You didn't take being a goddess in that Hindu temple personally. Thank God," he added with an obnoxious chuckle. I grunted at him morosely and got rid of his face.

I found a vegetable bar in the kitchen, and wandered back into the living room. The space-thieves were sneaking around a zoo on the planet Hublatt. They were all imaging animals onscreen while their characters studied the specimens. "We're looking for a Yewsalope,"

Brock said intently. "Its eyeballs are poisonous, but if you cook them just right they look like boiled eggs to whoever you're trying to poison."

The animals were garish in their barred cells: purple, orange, cinnamon, polka-dotted, striped. There were walking narwhales, a rhinoceros horn with feet and eyes, something like an octopus made out of elephant trunks, an amorphous green blob that constantly changed shape.

"How will you know a Yewsalope when you see it?" I asked, fascinated with their color combinations, their imagery. Brock shrugged slightly.

"We'll know."

A new animal appeared in an empty cage: a tall, two-legged creature with long golden hair and wings made of feathers or light. It held on to the bars with its hands, looking sadly out. I blinked.

"You have an angel in your zoo."

I heard Brock's breath. Indra frowned. "It could fly out. Why doesn't it fly? Whose is it? Anyway, this zoo is only for animals. This looks like some species of human. It's illegal," she said, fastidiously for a thief, "on Hublatt."

"It's an angel," Brock said.

"What's an angel? Is it yours?"

Brock shook his head. They all shook their heads, eyes onscreen, wanting to move on. But the image lingered: a beautiful, melancholy figure, half human, half light, trapped and powerless behind its bars.

"Why doesn't it just fly?" Indra breathed. "It could just fly. Brock—"

"It's not mine," Brock insisted. And then he looked at me, his eyes wide, so calm and blue that it took me a moment to transfer my attention from their color to what they were asking.

I stared at the angel, and felt the bars under my hands. I swallowed, seeing what it saw: the long, dark night of history that it was powerless to change, to illumine, because it was powerless to speak except to lie.

"Matrix?" Brock whispered. I closed my eyes.

"Don't call me that."

When I opened my eyes, the angel had disappeared.

OUT OF THE WOODS

THE SCHOLAR CAME TO LIVE in the old cottage in the woods one spring.

Leta didn't know he was there until Dylan told her of the man's request. Dylan, who worked with wood, cut and sold it, mended it, built with it, whittled it into toothpicks when he had nothing better to do, found the scholar under a bush, digging up henbane. From which, Dylan concluded, the young man was possibly dotty, possibly magical, but, from the look of him, basically harmless.

"He wants a housekeeper," he told Leta. "Someone to look after him during the day. Cook, wash, sew, dust, straighten. Buy his food, talk to peddlers, that sort of thing. You'd go there in the mornings, come back after his supper."

Leta rolled her eyes at her brawny, comely husband over the washtub as she pummeled dirt out of his shirts. She was a tall, wiry young woman with her yellow hair in a braid. Not as pretty or as bright as some, but strong and steady as a good horse, was how her mother had put it when Dylan came courting her.

"Then who's to do it around here?" she asked mildly, being of placid disposition.

Dylan shrugged, wood chips from a stick of kindling curling under his knife edge, for he had no more pressing work. "It'll get done," he said. He sent a couple more feathery chips floating to his feet, then added, "Earn a little money for us. Buy some finery for yourself. Ribbon for your cap. Shoe buckle."

She glanced down at her scuffed, work-worn clogs. Shoes, she thought with sudden longing. And so the next day she went to the river's edge and then took the path downriver to the scholar's cottage.

She'd known the ancient woman who had died there the year before.

The cottage needed care; flowers and moss sprouted from its thatch; the old garden was a tangle of vegetables, herbs and weeds. The cottage stood in a little clearing surrounded by great oak and ash, near the river and not far from the road that ran from one end of the wood to the other. The scholar met her at the door as though he expected her.

He was a slight, bony young man with pale thinning hair and gray eyes that seemed to look at her, through her and beyond her, all at the same time. He reminded Leta of something newly hatched, awkward, its down still damp and all askew. He smiled vaguely, opened the door wider, inviting her in even before she explained herself, as though he already knew.

"Dylan sent me," she said, then gazed with astonishment at the pillars and piles of books, scrolls, papers everywhere, even in the rafters. The cauldron hanging over the cold grate was filthy. She could see a half-eaten loaf on a shelf in the open cupboard; a mouse was busily dealing with the other half. There were cobwebs everywhere, and unwashed cups, odd implements she could not name tossed on the colorful, wrinkled puddles of clothes on the floor. As she stood gaping, an old, wizened sausage tumbled out of the rafters, fell at her feet.

She jumped. The scholar picked up the sausage. "I was wondering what to have for breakfast." He put it into his pocket. "You'd be Leta, then?"

"Yes, sir."

"You can call me Ansley. My great-grandmother left me this cottage when she died. Did you know her?"

"Oh, yes. Everyone did."

"I've been away in the city, studying. I decided to bring my studies here, where I can think without distractions. I want to be a great mage."

"Oh?"

"It is an arduous endeavor, which is why I'll have no time for—" He gestured.

She nodded. "I suppose when you've become a mage, all you'll have to do is snap your fingers or something."

His brows rose; clearly, he had never considered the use of magic for housework. "Or something," he agreed doubtfully. "You can see for yourself what I need you for."

"Oh, yes."

He indicated the vast, beautifully carved table in a corner under a circular window from which the sunny river could be seen. Or could have been seen, but for the teetering pile of books blocking the view. Ansley must have brought the table with him. She wondered how he had gotten the massive thing through the door. Magic, maybe; it must be good for something.

"You can clear up any clutter in the place but that," he told her. "That must never be disturbed."

"What about the moldy rind of cheese on top of the books?"

He drew breath, held it. "No," he said finally, decisively. "Nothing on the table must be touched. I expect to be there most of the time anyway, learning spells and translating the ancient secrets in manuscripts. When," he asked a trifle anxiously, "can you start?"

She considered the various needs of her own husband and house, then yielded to his pleading eyes. "Now," she said. "I suppose you want some food in the place."

He nodded eagerly, reaching for his purse. "All I ask," he told her, shaking coins into her hand, "is not to be bothered. I'll pay whatever you ask for that. My father did well with the tavern he owned; I did even better when I sold it after he died. Just come and go and do whatever needs to be done. Can you manage that?"

"Of course," she said stolidly, pocketing the coins for a trip to the market in the village at the edge of the woods. "I do it all the time."

She spent long days at the cottage, for the scholar paid scant attention to time and often kept his nose in his books past sunset despite the wonderful smells coming out of his pots. Dylan grumbled, but the scholar paid very well, and didn't mind Leta taking leave in the late afternoons to fix Dylan's supper and tend for an hour to her own house before she went back to work. She cooked, scrubbed, weeded and washed, got a cat for the mice and fed it too, swept and mended, and even wiped the grime off the windows, though the scholar never bothered looking out. Dylan worked hard, as well, building cupboards and bedsteads for the villagers, chopping trees into cartloads of wood to sell in the market for winter. Some days, she heard his ax from dawn to dusk. On market days, when he lingered in the village tavern, she rarely saw his face until one or the other of them crawled wearily into bed late at night.

"We never talk anymore," she murmured once, surprisedly, to the dark when the warm, sweaty, grunting shape that was Dylan pushed under the bedclothes beside her. "We just work and sleep, work and sleep."

He mumbled something that sounded like "What else is there?" Then he rolled away from her and began to snore.

One day when Ansley had gone down to the river to hunt for the details of some spell, Leta made a few furtive passes with her broom at the dust under his worktable. Her eye fell upon a spiral of gold on a page in an open book. She stopped sweeping, studied it. A golden letter, it looked like, surrounded by swirls of gold in a frame of crimson. All that richness, she marveled, for a letter. All that beauty. How could a simple letter, this undistinguished one that also began her name, be so cherished, given such loving attention?

"One little letter," she whispered, and her thoughts strayed to earlier times, when Dylan gave her wildflowers and sweets from the market. She sighed. They were always so tired now, and she was growing thinner from so much work. They had more money, it was true. But she had no time to spend it, even on shoes, and Dylan never thought of bringing her home a ribbon or a bit of lace when he went to the village. And here was this letter, doing nothing more than being the first in a line of them, adorned in red and gold for no other reason than that it was itself—

She touched her eyes, laughed ruefully at herself, thinking, I'm jealous of a letter.

Someone knocked at the door.

She opened it, expecting Dylan, or a neighbor, or a tinker—anyone except the man who stood there.

She felt herself gaping, but could not stop. She could only think crazily of the letter again: how this man too must have come from some place where people as well as words carried such beauty about them. The young man wore a tunic of shimmering links of pure silver over black leather trousers and a pair of fine, supple boots. His cloak was deep blue-black, the color of his eyes. His crisp dark curls shone like blackbirds' wings. He was young, but something, perhaps the long, jeweled sword he wore, made both Dylan and Ansley seem much younger. His lean, grave face hinted of a world beyond the wood that not even the scholar had seen.

"I beg your pardon," he said gently, "for troubling you." Leta closed her mouth. "I'm looking for a certain palace of which I've heard rumors all my life. It is surrounded by a deadly ring of thorns, and many men have lost their lives attempting to break through that ensorceled circle to rescue the sleeping princess within. Have you heard of it?"

"I—" Leta said, and stuck there, slack-jawed again. "I—I—"

Behind the man, his followers, rugged and plainly dressed, glanced at one another. That look, less courteous than the young man's, cleared Leta's head a bit.

"I haven't," she brought out finally. "But the man I work for is a—is trying to be—a mage; he knows a thousand things I don't."

"Then may I speak with him?"

"He's out—" She gestured, saw the broom still in her hand and hid it hastily behind her. "Down by the river, catching toads."

"Toads."

"For his—his magic."

She heard the faint snort. One of the followers pretended to be watching a crow fly; the other breathed, "My lord, perhaps we should ask farther down the road."

"We'll ride to the river," the young lord said, and turned to mount his horse again. He bowed graciously to Leta from his saddle. "Thank you. We are grateful."

Blinking at the light spangling off his harness and jewels, she watched him ride through the trees and toward the water. Then, slowly, she sat down, stunned and witless with wonder, until she heard Ansley's voice as he walked through the doorway and around her.

"I found five," he announced excitedly, putting a muddy bucket on his table. "One of them is pure white!"

"Did you see—?" Her voice didn't come. She was sitting on the floor, she realized then, with the broom across her knees. "Did you see the—? Them?"

"Who?" he asked absently, picking toads out of the bucket and setting them on his papers.

"The traveler. I sent him to talk to you." She hesitated, finally said the word. "I think he is a prince. He is looking for a palace surrounded by thorns, with a sleeping princess inside."

"Oh, him. No. I mean yes, but no I couldn't help him. I had no idea what he was talking about. Come here and look at this white one. You can do so many things with the white toads."

She had to wait a long time before Dylan came home, but she stayed awake so that she could tell him. As he clambered into bed, breathing a gust of beer at her, she said breathlessly, "I saw a prince today. On his way to rescue a princess."

He laughed and hiccuped at the same time. "And I saw the Queen of the Fairies. Did you happen to spot my knife too? I set it down yesterday when I was whittling, and it must have strolled away."

"Dylan—"

He kissed her temple. "You're dreaming, love. No princes here."

The days lengthened. Hawthorn blossoms blew everywhere like snow, leaving green behind. The massive oaks covered their tangled boughs with leaves. An early summer storm thundered through the woods one afternoon. Leta, who had just spread Ansley's washing to dry on the hawthorn bushes around the cottage, heard the sudden snarl of wind, felt a cold, hard drop of rain on her mouth. She sighed. The clothes were wet anyway; but for the wild wind that might steal them, she could have left them out. She began to gather them back into her basket.

She heard voices.

They sounded like wind at first, one high, pure, one pitched low, rumbling. They didn't seem human, which made Leta duck warily behind a bush. But their words were human enough, which made her strain her ears to listen. It was, she thought bewilderedly, like hearing what the winds had to say for themselves.

"Come into my arms and sleep, my lord," the higher voice crooned. "You have lived a long and adventurous life; you may rest now for a while."

"No," the deeper voice protested, half-laughing, half-longing, Leta thought. "It's not time for me to sleep, yet. There are things I still must teach you."

"What things, my heart?"

"How to understand the language of beetles, how to spin with spindrift, what lies hidden in the deepest place in the ocean and how to bring it up to light."

"Sleep a little. Teach me when you wake again."

"No, not yet."

"Sleep."

Leta crept closer to the voices. The rain pattered down now, great, fat drops the trees could not stop. Through the blur of rain and soughing winds stirring up the bracken, she saw two figures beneath an oak. They seemed completely unaware of the storm, as if they belonged to some enchanted world. The woman's long, fiery, rippling hair did not notice the wind, nor did the man's gray-white beard. He sat cradled in the oak roots, leaning back against the trunk. His face looked as harsh and weathered, as ancient and enduring as the wood. The woman stood over him, close enough for him to touch, which he did now and then, his hand caressing the back of her knee, coaxing it to bend. They were both richly dressed, he in a long, silvery robe flecked with tiny jewels like points of light along the sleeves, the hem. She wore silk the deepest green of summer, the secret green of trees who have taken in all the light they can hold, and feel, somewhere within them, summer's end. His eyes were half-closed. Hers were very wide as she stared down at him: pale amber encircling vivid points of black.

Leta froze. She did not dare move, lest those terrible eyes lift from his and search her out behind the bush with Ansley's trousers flapping on it.

"Sleep," the woman murmured again, her voice like a lightly dancing brook, like the sough of wind in reeds. "Sleep."

His hand dropped from her knee. He made an effort, half lifting his eyelids. His eyes were silver, metallic like a knife blade.

"Not yet, my sweet Nimue. Not yet."

"Sleep."

He closed his eyes.

There was a crack as though the world had been torn apart. Then came the thunder. Leta screamed as she felt it roll over her, through her, and down beneath her into the earth. The ancient oak, split through its heart, trailing limbs like shattered bone, loosed sudden, dancing streams of fire. Rain fell then in vast sheets as silvery as the sleeper's eyes. Leta couldn't see anything; she was drenched in a moment and sinking rapidly into a puddle. Rising, she glimpsed the light shining from the cottage windows. She stumbled out of the mysterious world toward it; wind blew her back through the scholar's door, then slammed the door behind her.

"I saw—I saw—" she panted.

But she did not know what she saw. Ansley, his attention caught at last by something outside his books—the thunder, maybe, or the lake she was making on his floor—looked a little pale in the gloom.

"You saw what?"

But she had only pieces to give him, nothing whole, nothing coherent. "I saw his eyes close. And then lightning struck the oak."

Ansley moved then. "Oh, I hope it won't topple onto my roof."

"His eyes closed—they were like metal—she put him to sleep with her eyes—"

"Show me the tree."

She led him eagerly through the rain. It had slowed a little; the storm was moving on. Somewhere else in the wood strange things were happening; the magic here had come and gone.

They stood looking at the broken heart of the oak, its wood still smoldering, its snapped boughs sagging, shifting dangerously in the wind. Only a stand of gnarled trunk was left, where the sleeper had been sitting.

"Come away," Ansley said uneasily. "Those limbs may still fall."

"But I saw two people—"

"They had sense enough to run, it seems; there are no bodies here. Just," he added, "a lot of wet clothes among the bushes. What exactly were those two doing?"

"They're your clothes."

"Oh."

She lingered, trying to find some shred of mystery left in the rain, some magic smoldering with the wood. "He closed his eyes," she whispered, "and lightning struck the oak."

"Well, he must have opened them fast enough then," Ansley said. "Come back into the house. Leave the laundry; you can finish all that later." His voice brightened as he wandered back through the dripping trees. "This will send the toads out to sun...."

She did not even try to tell Dylan, for if the young scholar with all his books saw no magic, how could he?

Days passed, one very like the next. She cooked, washed, weeded in the garden. Flowers she had rescued from wild vines bloomed and faded; she picked herbs and beans and summer squashes. The scholar studied. One day the house was full of bats, the next full of crows. Another day he made everything disappear, including himself. Leta stepped, startled, into an empty cottage. Not a thing in it, not even a stray spider. Then she saw the scholar's sheepish smile forming in the air; the rest of his possessions followed slowly. She stared at him, speechless. He cleared his throat.

"I must have mistranslated a word or two in that spell."

"You might have translated some of the clutter out of the door while you were at it," she said. What had reappeared was as chaotic as ever. She could not imagine what he did at nights while she was at home. Invented whirlwinds, or made his pots and clothes dance in midair until they dropped, it looked like.

"Think of magic as an untamed creature," he suggested, opening a book while he rained crumbs on the floor chewing a crust he had found on his table. "I am learning ways to impose my will upon it, while it fights me with all its cunning for its freedom."

"It sounds like your garden," she murmured, tracking down her gardening basket, which was not on the peg where she hung it, but, for some reason, on a shelf, in the frying pan. The scholar made an absent noise, not really hearing her; she had gotten used to that. She went outside to pull up onions for soup. She listened for Dylan's ax while she dug; he had said he was cutting wood that day. But she didn't hear it, just the river and the birds and the breeze among the leaves.

He must have gone deeper than usual into the woods, she thought. But she felt the little frown between her brows growing tighter and tighter at his silence. For no reason her throat grew tight too, hurt her suddenly. Maybe she had misunderstood; maybe he had gone into the village to sell wood instead. That made the ache in her throat sharper. His eyes and voice were absent, those days. He looked at her, but hardly saw her; he kissed her now and then, brief, chuckling kisses that you'd give to a child. He had never gone to the village so often without her before; he had never wanted to go without her, before...

She asked him tentatively that night, as he rolled into bed in a cloud of beer fumes and wood smoke, "Will you take me with you, next time?"

He patted her shoulder, his eyes already closed. "You need your rest, working so hard for two houses. Anyway, it's nothing; I just have a quick drink and a listen to the fiddling, then I'm home to you."

"But it's so late."

He gave her another pat. "Is it? Then best get to sleep."

He snored; she stared, wide-eyed, back at the night.

She scarcely noticed when the leaves first began to turn. Suddenly there were mushrooms and berries and nuts to gather, and apples all over the little twisty apple tree in her own garden. The days were growing shorter, even while there seemed so much more to do. She pulled out winter garments to mend where the moths had chewed; she replenished supplies of soap and candles. Her hands were always red; her hair, it seemed, always slightly damp with steam from something. The leaves grew gold, began to fall, crackle underfoot as she walked from one house to the other and back again. She scarcely saw the two men: the scholar hunched over a book with his back to her, her husband always calling good-bye as he went to chop or sell or build. Well, they scarcely saw her either, she thought tiredly; that was the way of it.

She stayed into evening at the scholar's one day, darning his winter cloak while the stew she had made of carrots and potatoes and leeks bubbled over the fire. He was at his table, staring into what looked like a glass ball filled with swirling iridescent fires. He was murmuring to it; if it answered him, she didn't hear.

At least not for some time. When she began to hear the strange, crazed disturbance beneath the wind rattling at the door, she thought at first that the sound came from within the globe. Her needle paused. The noise seemed to be coming closer: a disturbing confusion of dogs barking, horns, faint bells, shouting, bracken and fallen limbs crackling under the pounding of many hooves. She stared at the glass ball, which was hardly bigger than the scholar's fist. Surely such an uproar couldn't be coming from that?

The wind shrieked suddenly. The door shook on its hinges. She froze, midstitch. The door sprang open as if someone had kicked it. All the confusion in the night seemed to be on the scholar's doorstep and about to roil into his cottage.

She leaped to her feet, terrified, and clung to the door, trying to force it shut against the wind. A dark current was passing the house: something huge and nameless, bewildering until her eyes began to find the shapes in the night. They appeared at random, lit by fires that seemed to stream from the nostrils of black horses galloping past her. The flames illumined great hounds with eyes like coals, upraised sword blades like broken pieces of lightning, cowled faces, harnesses strung with madly clamoring bells.

She stared, unable to move. One of the hooded faces turned toward her as his enormous horse, its hooves sparking fire, cleared her potato rows. The rider's face was gaunt, bony, his hair in many long braids, their ends secured around clattering bones. He wore a crown of gold; its great jewel reflected fire the color of a splash of blood. White moons in the rider's eye sockets flashed at Leta; he opened his jaws wide like a wolf and laughed.

She could not even scream, her voice was that shriveled with fear. She could only squeak. Then the door was taken firmly out of her hands, closed against the night.

The scholar grumbled, returning to his work, "I couldn't hear a thing with all that racket. Are you still here? Take a lamp with you when you go home."

She went home late, terrified at every step, every whine of wind and crackle of branch. Her cold hands woke Dylan as she hugged him close in their bed for warmth and comfort. He raised his head, breathing something that may have been a name, and maybe not. Then his voice came clear.

"You're late." He did not sound worried or angry, only sleepy. "Your hands are ice."

"Dylan, there was something wicked in the woods tonight."

"What?"

"I don't know—riders, dark riders, on horses with flaming breath—I heard horns, as if they were hunting—"

"Nobody hunts in the dark."

"Didn't you hear it?"

"No."

"Were you even here?" she asked incredulously. He turned away from her, settled himself again.

"Of course. You weren't, though, so I went to bed."

"You could have come to fetch me," she whispered. "You could have brought a lamp."

"What?"

"You could have wondered."

"Go to sleep," he murmured. "Sleep."

Winter, she thought as she walked to the scholar's cottage the next morning. There wouldn't be so much work then, with the snow flying. No gardens to tend, no trees to chop, with their wood damp and iron-clad. She and Dylan would see more of one another, then. She'd settle the scholar and come home before dark; they'd have long evenings together beside the fire. Leaves whirled around her. The brightly colored autumn squashes were almost the last things still unpicked in the garden, besides the root vegetables. One breath of frost, and the herbs would be gone, along with most of the green in the world.

"You'll need wood for winter," she reminded the scholar. "I'll have Dylan bring you some."

He grunted absently. She sighed a little, watching him, as she tied on her apron.

I've grown invisible, she thought.

Later, she caught herself longing for winter, and didn't know whether to laugh or cry.

Dylan stacked the scholar's wood under the eaves. The squashes grew fat as the garden withered around them. The air smelled of rain and sweet wood smoke. Now and then the sky turned blue; fish jumped into sunlight; the world cast a glance back at the season it had left. On one of those rare days Leta spread the washing on the bushes to dry. Drawn to the shattered oak, she left her basket and walked through the brush to look at it, search for some sign that she had truly seen—whatever she had seen.

The great, gnarled stump, so thick that two or maybe three of her might have ringed it with her arms, stood just taller than her head. Only this lower, rooted piece of trunk was left intact, though lightning had seared a black stain on it like a scar. It stood dreaming in the sunlight, revealing nothing of its secrets. Just big enough, she thought, to draw a man inside it, if one had fallen asleep against it. In spring, living shoots would rise like his dreams out of the trunk, crown it with leaves, this still-living heart big enough to hide a sleeping mage....

Something moving down the river caught her eyes.

She went through the trees toward it, unable to see clearly what it was. An empty boat, it seemed, caught in the current, but that didn't explain its odd shape, and the hints of color about it, the drift of cloth that was not sail.

She ran down the river path a ways to get ahead of it, so that she could see it clearly as it passed. It seemed a fine, delicate thing, with its upraised prow carved into a spiral and gilded. The rest of it, except for a thin line of gold all around it, was painted black. Some airy fabric caught on the wind, drifted above it, and then fell back into the boat. Now the cloth was blue, now satiny green. Now colors teased at her: intricately embroidered scenes she could not quite make out, on a longer drift of linen. She waited, puzzled, for the boat to reach her.

She saw the face within and caught her breath.

It was a young woman. She lay in the boat as though she slept, her sleeves, her skirt, the tapestry work in her hands picked up by passing breezes, then loosed again. Her hair, the color of the dying leaves, was carefully coiled and pinned with gold. Leta started to call to her. Words stopped before they began. That lovely face, skin white as whitest birch, held nothing now: no words, no expressions, no more movement than a stone. She had nothing left to tell Leta but her silence.

The boat glided past. Golden oak leaves dropped gently down onto the still figure, as though the trees watched with Leta. She felt sorrow grow in her throat like an apple, a toad, a jewel. It would not come out in tears or words or any other shape. It kept growing, growing, while she moved because she still could—walk and speak and tell and even, with a reason, smile—down the river path. She followed the boat, not knowing where it was going, or what she was mourning, beginning to run after a while when the currents quickened and the trees thinned, and the high slender towers of a distant city gleamed in the light of the waning day.

The Kelpie

Ned met Emma Slade at her brother Adrian's new lodgings, the night Bram Wilding brought the monkey and it set fire to the veils in which Euphemia Bunce was posing for Adrian's painting. Ned had come to the party with some friends who knew Adrian, and had been invited to help him celebrate his new studio. Drink in hand, trying to remember people's names in the lively, disorganized gathering, Ned watched Bram catch the monkey with one elegant hand and, with the other, dump a vase full of water and drooping lilies—a prop for the painting—onto the flaming veils, which were now down around Miss Bunce's ankles. There had not been much under them. The model, a flame-haired stunner with a body the color of fresh cream, grabbed the tapestry covering the piano and wrapped herself in it, spitting some choice language at Bram. He threw back his head and laughed. She picked up the candle the monkey had dropped on her veils and flung it at him. Then Adrian's housekeeper, cooing soothingly, bundled a cloak over her and drew her away to dress.

Ned spotted a familiar face, with a beard like a hedgehog sprouting from its chin. The face belonged to a tall, vigorous poet by the name of Linley Coombe.

"What did she call him?" Ned asked, raising his voice above the din.

"Ah, Bonham. I didn't know you were acquainted with Adrian."

"I'm not; I followed some friends here. A clabber-brained—something?"

"A clabber-brained jabbernowl," Linley said, relishing the syllables.

"Meaning?"

"Pretty much what he is," a young woman commented tartly, "bringing a monkey into this jungle."

Hers was another recognizable face, Ned saw with pleasure: the lovely Sophie Burden, another model. He had painted her a year earlier as Cassandra prophesying some dire event in the marketplace and being ignored. With her storm-gray eyes and long black hair, she made a marvelous doom-laden figure, barefoot among the cabbages while lightning flashed above her. Now she smiled at him cheerfully. "Hello, Mr. Bonham. Have you got me hung yet?"

"I'm touching up the painting for the spring exhibit. You look wonderful, but the cabbages seem strangely lurid under the lightning."

"Lurid cabbages," Coombe murmured with delight, then eyed Sophie quizzically. "Was that a note of disparagement I heard toward the incomparable Wilding? I thought all his models fell in love with him."

She made a wry face, flashing the dimples that kept plaguing Ned at odd moments as he painted the dour Cassandra. "He's careless of people," she said briefly, and did not elaborate.

The monkey had escaped from Bram's hold. A tiny, golden, spidery-limbed creature, it was sitting on the mantelpiece now, chattering at the party. Some very fine pieces of blue and white pottery stood near it. Ned wondered how long it would be before the little monkey started heaving them across the room. Someone else had foreseen disaster, and was moving through the crush toward the monkey. Ned watched her. She was very tall; it made her movements somewhat tentative, uncertain, as though she didn't quite know what disorders her rangy limbs might cause. Like a wood-nymph at a tea party, he thought. She scooped up the monkey easily with her long fingers and turned, looking for its owner. Ned saw her face and blinked. She really was a nymph, he thought dazedly. Or one of the minor goddesses, a forgotten sister or daughter of one of those deities who attract all the attention and cast their relatives into obscurity. Obviously she had gotten lost on her way to some ethereal gathering; here she was, minding a monkey in an artist's rackety studio instead.

"Who is that?"

"Which?" Linley Coombe asked.

"Which? Which, indeed! That fair-haired young Amazon carrying the monkey."

"Oh. That's Miss Emma Slade, Adrian's sister."

They watched her ease back through the crowd with that odd, cautious manner, as though she walked on water but didn't understand by what grace.

"Coltish," Coombe commented.

"She probably grew tall very fast," Sophie said shrewdly. "Country living might do that to a girl. All that fresh air and rambles across the cow pastures. She only just came to the city recently to help Adrian get organized. I've heard Adrian's encouraging her to paint."

"I'd love to paint her," Ned said fervently.

Sophie flung him a mischievous glance. "Maybe she'd like to paint you."

Miss Emma Slade resembled her brother Adrian, Ned thought. Both had curly golden hair and wide-set eyes beneath broad, untroubled foreheads. He couldn't see the color of her eyes; they were lowered, intent on the monkey. Then, as he watched, they lifted, turned to gaze at someone. It was Bram Wilding, Ned saw, come to take his monkey from her. Their eyes were at a level. His, dark as a horse's, seemed transfixed by the airy azure of hers.

Ned, who had opened his mouth to ask Coombe for an introduction, closed it. As usual, Bram had wasted no time getting acquainted with the charming newcomer. His paintings had power and discipline; his reputation grew daily, it seemed. He would ask her to pose and who would resist? Slightly older than the roisterous young men in Adrian's circle, he had an aura of experience and was, with his black flowing locks and profile like a Greek statue that had been lightly toasted by the sun, remarkably handsome. Some said devilishly so. Ned could claim his own amount of manly attributes: muscles where they were needed, nutmeg curls, hazel eyes, an open, modest demeanor often sought after by his painter friends when they needed someone to pose for the friend of the dying knight, or the rejected suitor.

He found the poet's hand on his shoulder. "Have you met Adrian yet?"

He shook his head. "The friends I came with pointed him out, and then we all got distracted by the fire."

Coombe grinned at the memory. "Come with me. Why should Bram have all the fun?"

Adrian was found sitting on a crate of unpacked books, opening a bottle of wine. He recognized Ned's name, and, to Ned's delight, even remembered where he'd seen it.

"You painted that marvelous landscape with the white owl and the full moon shining over the snow: *Winter Solstice*," he said, rising to grasp Ned's hand. "I wished I had thought of it first."

"I would like to have done your *Last Roman Soldier Standing Watch on Hadrian's Wall*."

Adrian shook his head, drawing the cork out of the bottle. "No, you wouldn't. It rained every single day while I was painting the wall, and when it wasn't raining, the mosquitoes surrounded me in droves. Most miserable experience I've ever had. I came home with a massive cold and painted the soldier in my studio, between sneezes. Where's your glass?" Ned held it out; Adrian refilled it, then turned to Coombe. "I hope you brought some poetry to read."

"An epic," Coombe assured him.

"Oh, good. I thought we might scatter some of these crates around, since there won't be enough chairs. Ah, there you are, Buncie." He reached quickly for another glass, peering at his model, who had reappeared. She was dressed now, and, but for her reddened eyes, a bit more composed. "Are you all right? You didn't get hurt, did you?"

"I hate your Mr. Wilding," Miss Bunce said between her teeth.

"Try to forgive him; he's not entirely right in the head. I won't make you work any longer tonight." He gestured toward a long plank table painted cherry red, on which the housekeeper was piling platters and bowls of cold meats and fruits, pies and puddings and punch. "Have a sausage. Mr. Coombe is going to read to us soon." He cast an upraised brow at Sophie. "Perhaps you and Miss Bunce should corner a

comfortable place to sit before all the chairs get taken. Nelly," he called
to his housekeeper, a wiry young woman with a cheerful face and a
good deal of energy, "I just remembered all those cushions—Where
were they last seen?"

"You shoved them all in a cupboard, Mr. Slade."

"Well, we'll just shove them out again, and line them up along the
walls. I'll ask my sister to play the piano while everyone's filling a plate.
That'll quiet them down. Where is she?" he asked, standing on the crate
to peer over the crowd. "Emma? Coombe, have you—"

"When last seen," the poet said drily, "she was speaking to Bram
Wilding."

Adrian closed his mouth over a toneless "Mmm." He stepped off
the crate, added briskly, without elaborating, "Well."

"I can help you with the cushions," Ned offered, "if you'll tell me
where they're hiding."

"That cupboard by the door, I think. Thank you." He paused, his
eyes flicking over the crowd again. "Ah. There's Emma in a corner,
showing Wilding her drawings."

He vanished into the crush, and Ned went to set the cushions free.

The new lodgings were on Carmion Street, in an apartment building
on a corner; it had an oblique view of the river if you stood at the right
window. The building was a staid brick block with large windows tidily
painted white and unadorned with fripperies. The fripperies had all
followed Adrian in, it seemed. They lay scattered everywhere: brilliant
carpets and shawls he'd picked up on the streets, ancient tiles, pieces of
costume to use as props for his paintings, plates and cups, bulky chairs,
a horsehair sofa, massive chests and sideboards, even the odd piece of armor and broken statuary. It looked, Ned thought, like the sorting room
in a museum basement. Paintings leaned against the walls. Ned recognized a few of them from exhibits, or visits to other friends' studios.
The chaos, he noted as he opened the cupboard, extended into the next
room as well, and was even strewn all over the massive, canopied bed.

He found a stack of round, oversized cushions covered with faded
crewelwork. Wedged into a square cupboard, they resisted Ned's efforts

until one popped out near the middle of the stack, exuding a puff of antique dust. What exactly they had been intended for, Ned could not imagine. He began strewing them hither and yon, which became easier as the party gathered around the table, leaving him some bare floor. People, plates and cups in hand, wandered back and sat upon them as soon as he dropped them. Adrian appeared beside him suddenly while he wrestled with another.

"Here we are," he said cheerfully, taking the cushion out of Ned's arms after he staggered back from the tug-of-war with the cupboard.

"It's like dancing with a drunken costermonger," Ned muttered. "What were these in their previous lives?" He hauled out another cushion and turned to find himself face to face with the nymph.

He blinked at her, startled, wondering how Adrian had turned into his sister. Then Adrian rejoined them, dusting his hands.

"You must meet my sister," he declared. "Emma, this is Edward Bonham, who painted that wonderfully chilly painting with the owl in it."

"Oh yes." She spoke, Ned thought dazedly, as she walked: carefully and delicately, as though she had just turned from a graceful poplar into a woman and was uncertain about the effects she might have on people. "I loved that painting, Mr. Bonham." There was an unnymphlike smile in her eyes, perhaps left by the wake of his costermonger comment.

"You should show him your drawings," Adrian suggested, hauling the last cushion out, and giving it a hearty shove with one boot to an empty spot along the wall.

"I've just been showing them to Mr. Wilding," she told them. "He said that technically I show promise, but that thus far passion seems to have eluded me. He offered to give me a lesson or two." Adrian's mouth opened abruptly; she continued with unruffled composure, "I told him that I understood what he meant, but that true passion in painting could only be expressed by true mastery of technique; without it passion looked sentimental, trite, and in the end ridiculous."

Adrian grinned. "Good for you. What did he say?"

"That most women painters should confine themselves to watercolors, since they have not the breadth of soul to express the fullness and complexity of oils, though he had seen one or two come close enough to counterfeit it."

Adrian rolled his eyes. "What did you say to that?"

"That I would do my best to prove him wrong," she answered simply. "And then the monkey had an accident on his hair and he went off to wash."

Ned loosed an inelegant guffaw. A corner of Emma's long mouth crooked up. "What are your thoughts on the breadth of a woman's soul, Mr. Bonham?"

"I think," he said fervently, "I could travel a lifetime in one and never see the half of it."

She regarded him silently for a heartbeat, out of eyes the color of a fine summer day, and in that moment he caught his first astonished glimpse of the undiscovered country that was theirs.

Adrian cleared his throat. His sister looked suddenly dazed, herself, as though she had forgotten where she was.

"Come and eat," Adrian said, smiling. "Then you can show Bonham your drawings."

Emma played the piano after supper while the party, clustered into little groups on cushions and crates, argued intensely about the nature of Art, or languished, satiated, over their coffee and listened to Emma. She scarcely heard what her fingers were doing. She was still lost in that little moment when she had looked into Mr. Bonham's hazelnut eyes and seen her future. They say it happens that way sometimes, she thought, amazed. I just never thought it would happen now. I never thought that it would actually happen, only that it was always something to be expected, to hope for, never that it would suddenly happen and I would be wondering: What happens next?

Then Mr. Bonham drifted over and smiled at her. She smiled back. That was what happened next. He lingered to listen; she played, simply content with his nearness. There was nothing extraordinary about his looks; there were half-a-dozen young men in the room, including her brother and the irritating Mr. Wilding, she would have chosen over

Ned to pose for the hero of her painting. True eye-stoppers, they were. But hers had stopped at a boyish face with a determined jawline and a sweet, diffident expression, behind which a busy, talented brain conceived pictures like the simple mystery of that winter night, and crafted them with a great deal of ability. She had come to the city to learn to paint; perhaps she could learn something from him.

Perhaps that was next.

She was trying to conceive a painting around him, idly wondering which role might suit him best, when Adrian came up to her. She softened her playing, lifted her brows at him questioningly.

"Emma, this is Marianne Cameron. She wants to ask you to pose for her, but she is too shy."

The young woman in question snorted at the idea, making Adrian laugh. She was short and stocky, with frizzy, sandy hair and truly lovely violet eyes. Her pale lavender dress, sensibly and elegantly plain, suited those eyes.

"You," she said to Emma, "are the most beautiful thing in this room, with the possible exception of Bram Wilding, who can't be bothered to pose for anyone. Several of us rent a room on Tidewater Street; we'd love you to come and pose for us. Adrian says you paint, too. If you like, we can make a space for you to work. It's a bit quieter than this place; we don't have monkeys and poets swinging from the rafters there."

"Speaking of which," Adrian murmured, "I wonder where that monkey has gotten to?"

"Us?" Emma asked.

"We women," Marianne said briskly. "We have made our own band of painters, and we refuse to be convinced of our inferiority. We learn from one another. Would you like to come and see?"

"Oh, yes," Emma said instantly. "I would very much." She remembered Adrian then; her eyes slid to him. "That is—I came to help Adrian get settled—"

"Go ahead," Adrian urged. "We both must work; we can deal with this clutter in the evenings."

"Good!" Marianne said with satisfaction. "I'll come for you tomorrow at noon then. We work all day, but the afternoon light is best."

"Miss Cameron paints quite well," Adrian said, propping himself against the piano as Marianne moved away. "She has even had one or two paintings exhibited: *Love Lies Bleeding* and *Undine*—that one has marvelous watery lights in it."

"It's strange," Emma sighed. "I always feel such a great country gawk, and here I am to be painted."

"You're as far from a gawk as anyone can get without turning into something completely mythical."

She smiled affectionately at her brother. "You didn't say such things when we were younger."

"I don't recall that I was ever less than perfectly well behaved."

"You called me a she-giant once and warned that I would never stop growing; I'd be tall as a barn by the time I was twenty, and there would be nobody big enough to marry me."

"I'm sure I never said any such thing, and anyway you were probably taller than me, then, which as your older brother I found completely unacceptable. Now I'm taller, so I can be magnanimous." He straightened, glancing at the party; the noise level had ratcheted upward considerably when Emma stopped playing. "We'd better have Coombe read now that Nelly has finished clattering plates. I do wonder where that monkey is; I hope it isn't burning up the beds."

"I'll go and look," Emma said, and slipped through the crowd as Adrian began describing the unutterable delight yet to come: an epic of epic proportions by the brilliant Linley Coombe on the subject of— what was the subject again? Emma heard them all laugh at something the poet said as she opened the kitchen door.

The kitchen, along with the small dark rooms attached to it, was the domain of Nelly and the cook, Mrs. Dyce. Nelly, who had a thoroughly practical and unflappable nature, was Adrian's treasure; she could conjure beds out of books and floorboards for any number of unexpected guests, he said, and she did the work of five servants without turning a hair. Now the housekeeper was being scullery-maid, helping Mrs. Dyce with the mountain of dirty dishes. Earlier that day, Emma had helped her unpack the crates, dust furniture for the party, find silverware and candlesticks and lamps among the boxes, and summon food and wine for an unknown number of guests, all before she vanished into the kitchen to help Mrs. Dyce cook the elaborate supper.

Mrs. Dyce, a gaunt, mournful woman who could turn out a fragrant shepherd's pie with one hand while she was wiping away a tear for her dead husband with the other, only sighed and shook her head at the notion of monkeys in the kitchen.

Nelly wiped her hands on her apron, said calmly, "I'll have a look, Miss."

She took a lamp into the inner sanctums of bedchamber and pantry, while Emma checked the high shelves and cupboards.

"I don't see it, Miss Emma," Nelly said, reappearing. "Maybe Mr. Wilding shut it up in a cupboard after it set Miss Bunce on fire."

"I doubt that Mr. Wilding would think of doing anything so sensible."

"You may be right, Miss. But one can hope."

"One can, indeed, hope. I'll ask him."

But, reluctant to put herself again under that powerful, discomfiting gaze, she looked first into Adrian's bedroom, expecting she might find the little monkey curled up and napping among the sheets. Her lamplight, sliding over the room, revealed only its familiar chaos. Finally she glanced into the room, hardly bigger than the pantry, where she slept.

No monkey.

She turned back into the hallway, perplexed, and jumped. Bram Wilding stood in her lamplight with the golden monkey on his shoulder reaching for the lamp.

She moved it hastily. "Mr. Wilding. You startled me."

"You were looking for me."

"I was looking for your monkey."

"Ah. Well, I've come in search of you. Please forgive my earlier rudeness, Miss Slade; the last thing I would want is to discourage you or anyone from painting. The truth is that I am so distracted by you that any amount of idiocy can come out of my mouth without me hearing a word of it. From the moment I saw you, I knew I must paint you. I see you as the great, doomed Celtic Queen Boudicca, in silk and fur and armor, with her long fair hair flying free as she faces her conquerors, knowing that she will lose the final battle but ready to fight until she can no more for her lost realm. Will you pose for me?"

"I'm sorry, Mr. Wilding," she said with relief. "I've already promised Marianne Cameron that I would pose for her—"

"Put her off."

"Tomorrow."

He was silent. The monkey chattered at her, wanting her flame, its great eyes filled with it. Bram's dark eyes seemed impenetrable; light could not reach past them.

"I'll talk to her," he said finally.

"Mr. Wilding, I wish you wouldn't. She has offered me a place to paint. I want to go there."

He only smiled cheerfully. "I'm sure you will be welcome in any case, Miss Slade."

There was a step behind Bram. She lifted the lamp higher and caught Ned Bonham's face in her light. She gazed at him a moment, smiling upon him and wondering how his face, which she had never seen before that night, could give her so much pleasure.

"Miss Slade," he said, smiling back.

"Mr. Bonham."

"I see you found the monkey."

Bram Wilding, who must have felt invisible, moved abruptly. His face, which until then seemed genial and imperturbable, had grown masklike; Emma could not guess at his thoughts.

"You might say it found me."

"We are all found," Bram said lightly, moving ahead of them into shadow. "I suppose we must go and hear Coombe read. What is the subject this time?"

"A mortal straying into the realm of Faery and how he gets himself out again—something like that."

"I didn't think you could," Emma said. "Aren't you lost forever if you wander out of the world?"

"It depends, I think, on how you actually got there. If you're taken by a water sprite, an undine, or by La Belle Dame Sans Merci, you're sunk. But others have found a way to freedom—Thomas the Rhymer, for instance, and Tam Lin."

They were walking more and more slowly, Emma realized. Bram Wilding had already vanished back into the party. Light and Linley Coombe's sonorous voice spilled through the studio doors Wilding had left open.

> *Through mists and reeds he ran,*
> *Through water gray as cloud*
> *And air that grasped him with unseen hands,*
> *And clung closer than a shroud.*

They stopped before they reached the doors. Their eyes met above the lamp in Emma's hand. She searched, curious, hoping to find the reflection of her strange feelings in his eyes.

He said softly, huskily, "Miss Slade, I don't mean to offend, but I've never—I've never felt this way before about anyone. As though all my life I have been on my way to meet you."

A smile seemed to shine through her as though she had swallowed the lamplight. "Oh, yes," she whispered. "Yes. I feel it, too."

"Do you?" he whispered back with an amazed laugh. "Isn't it strange? We hardly know each other."

"I suppose that's what comes next."

"What?"

"Getting to know one another," she answered. "For example, you should know that my second name is Sophronia."

"Really? Emma Sophronia?"

"After my mother's great aunt."

"Well," he said, drawing breath. "It won't be easy, but I think I can bear it. Mine's Eustace."

"Edward Eustace Bonham. How terribly respectable."

"I try to live above it."

> *Until at last he saw the day*
> *Green and gold around him spread,*
> *The timeless, changeless land of Fay,*
> *And he was seized with mortal dread.*
> *"Would I were with the dead instead,"*
> *he cried, then saw the Fairy Queen.*

"Any other dreadful secrets?" he asked.

"I once threw an aspidistra at Adrian."

"Did you hit him?"

"Yes."

"Good shot. I'm sure he deserved it."

"And you?"

"I suppose you should know," he said reluctantly, "that I can never be that romantic figure, the struggling artist in the garret, much as I wish I could deceive you. I was an only child, and my father died several years ago, leaving me more money than is good for anyone, a house in the city, and another on a lake in the north country."

"Oh," she said, amazed. "Mr. Bonham, how have you managed to stay unattached?"

"How have you?" he countered, "looking the way you do, like a young goddess who got stranded among mortals?"

She felt her cheeks warm. "Really? I always see myself as such a hobbledehoy of a girl. Fashionable young women are supposed to look delicate and spiritual. That's hard to do when you're nearly as tall as most men. In the country, I have a reputation for being eccentric. I wander around in a pair of big rubber boots and a huge hat, carrying my easel and paints. I bribed the milkmaid to pose for me dressed in ribbons and lace among the sheep, and the old gardener to wear a cloak and a tunic and pose as a druid on top of a ruined tower. He never heard the end of that."

And oh, she was as fair as fair
Can be, with hair spun out of gold
And emerald eyes without a cloud or care,
Just a smile to make the mortal bold
And walk into her lair. She said,
"Come into my bower and tarry with me..."

"Miss Slade."

"Yes, Mr. Bonham?"

"Should I ask you to marry me now, or would you like me to wait a bit?"

She felt no great surprise, only a deepening of the strange peace she felt upon first looking into his eyes. "I suppose," she said reluctantly, "you should wait, otherwise people will think we are completely frivolous. Perhaps you should invite me for a walk in the park instead. Tomorrow afternoon when I finish posing for Miss Cameron. There should be time before dark."

"Do you think I am frivolous?"

"No," she said quickly, surprised. "How can you ask that? You must know that my heart has already answered you."

He started to speak, did not, only held her eyes and she felt the warmth of the smile on his lips like a phantom kiss.

She scarcely slept after the party had broken up in the early hours of the morning, and the house finally quieted. It was difficult, she discovered, to smile and sleep at the same time. When she heard the housekeeper stirring, she rose and dressed, went into the kitchen to ask for a cup of tea.

"You're up early, Miss," Nelly said.

"I thought I would do some unpacking, rid our lives of a few more crates."

"It will be nice not to have to walk around them. I'll give you a hand as soon as I tidy up from the party."

Mrs. Dyce produced Scotch eggs and cold ham and toast; after breakfast they worked so hard that when Marianne Cameron rang the bell at noon, most of the books had been unpacked and shelved, and Adrian's collection of oddities and props had found places to reside that were not the floor or his bed. He had come out of his room at midmorning, helped them pile empty crates and hang paintings. By the time Miss Bunce came to pose and he began to paint, there was an empty island of polished floorboards around his easel.

"I'll get the door," Emma told Nelly, whose arms were full of costumes out of a crate that needed to be folded and put away. "It'll be Miss Cameron, come for me."

But, opening the door, she found Bram Wilding instead.

Surprised, she glanced behind him down the hall, hearing bells striking noon all through the city.

"Good day, Miss Slade," he said. "I have good news. I was able to persuade Miss Cameron to let me paint you first."

She stared at him, still bewildered by the unwelcome sight of his face instead of the one she expected.

"How?" she asked incredulously.

"I offered to speak to a gallery owner who exhibits my work about doing an exhibit of work by the women's studio. Miss Cameron found my suggestion irresistible."

Emma found his suggestion awoke a childish impulse in her to stamp her foot at him. "I wished," she said coldly, "to pose for her."

"And I wish you to pose for me."

"Do you always get your wishes, Mr. Wilding?"

"In this case, I believe I do. I don't see why I should bother to persuade the gallery owner to hang an exhibit of little-known, though possibly talented, women painters if you do not pose for me."

She opened her mouth, stood wordless a moment, too astonished to speak. Then her eyes narrowed. "Mr. Wilding," she said softly, "I believe this is what they call blackmail."

"Do they?" he said indifferently. "Well, no matter, as long as I can have my Boudicca. I'll just step in and let Adrian know where you're going. Join me when you're ready."

Ned painted feverishly all day in his own comfortable studio on the top floor of his house. He had enlarged and added windows on all sides of the studio; he could see the river to the east, city to the north and south, and the park to the west, where, when the sun came to roost like a great genial bird on the top branches of the trees, he intended to be strolling with Miss Emma Sophronia Slade. Or, as would be as soon as respectably possible, Mrs. Emma Bonham.

He whistled while he tinkered with a painting that he never seemed to get right. He had been working on it for several years, shutting it away in exasperation when he got tired of reaching his limitations. The subject was along the lines of Linley Coombe's poem: a man lost in a wood and glimpsing in a fall of sunlight the Fairy Queen and her court riding toward him. The figures emerging through the light could barely be seen; some of them he conceived as only half human, figures of twig and bark on horseback, with faces of animals, perhaps, or exotic birds. The look on the man's face, of astonishment tinged with dawning horror as he realized he had walked out of the world, never seemed convincing. Most of the time he looked simply pained, as though berries he had eaten earlier were beginning to make themselves known. The fairy figures were no less difficult; color had to be suggested rather than shown, and the strange faces, part human, part fox or bluebird, were extraordinarily elusive.

A good thing, he reminded himself, I'm not doing this for a living.

At last the sun sank within an inch of the trees in the park. Shafts of lovely, dusty-gold fairy light fell between the branches, gilded the grass below. It was one of those spring days that revealed how much more ease and warmth and loveliness there was to come. A perfect mellow dusk for a first walk into the future. He cleaned and put things away quickly, slipped on his coat and went around the block to Adrian's apartment.

Adrian, who was in the midst of paying Euphemia Bunce, received Ned with pleasure and without surprise.

"Come at the same time tomorrow, Buncie," he requested. "Maybe

I can finish those veils and we can start on the platter you're holding. Ned, I don't suppose you would let me borrow your head. You've got exactly that combination of innocence and strength in your face that I need."

"Doesn't sound like it helped me much if my head winds up on a platter."

"You can bask in the company of Miss Bunce and me for a couple of weeks. And Mrs. Dyce's cooking."

"Might Miss Slade be basking with us?" He glanced around. "Has she returned from the women's studio? We had plans to walk."

"Oh." Adrian's amiable smile diminished slightly. "I'm afraid she's been snared by Wilding."

"What?"

"He apparently talked Miss Cameron into letting my sister pose for him first. That's what he told me, at any rate. I doubt that's the full story. But we'll have to wait for Emma to tell us the rest. She should be here soon." He folded Miss Bunce into her shawl. "Tomorrow morning, then, Buncie."

"That Mr. Wilding is a mischief-maker," she said tersely. "I'd keep your eye on him."

"I will do just that with both eyes," Adrian promised, opening the door for her.

"Thank you, Mr. Slade. Goodnight, Mr.—Bonham, was it?" She flashed him a smile. "I hope your head will join us."

"So that's what she was doing in those veils," Ned murmured. "Salome dancing about with the severed head. I wondered. Do you suppose the public will appreciate it?"

"They will appreciate Miss Bunce. And your guileless and saintly head, cut so tragically short from its body, will affect them deeply, I'm sure. There won't be a dry eye at the exhibit." He was cleaning his brushes with a great deal of energy, glancing down at the street now and then.

Ned paced a step or two, then stopped and said simply, "Where is Wilding's studio? I'll go and meet her there."

"Yes," Adrian said emphatically. "Good idea. It's straight down Summer Street beside the river, a yellowish villa-ish sort of thing with red tiles on the roof. You can't miss it."

Even if he had missed the eye-catching villa at the corner of Summer Street and River Road, the monkey chattering at him on the wall beside the gate would have alerted him to Wilding's domain. The monkey wore a thin gold chain around its neck, long enough for it to reach the ground, but too short for it to do more than climb back up. Ned opened the gate cautiously, wondering what other wildlife roamed Wilding's garden.

The only wildlife he found on the other side of the wall was Emma and Bram Wilding, walking together toward the gate.

"Ah, Bonham," Wilding said, with a faint smile in his eyes. "How good of you to come and visit me. Miss Slade is just leaving."

Ned looked at her. She had colored at the sight of him, but other than a trifle embarrassed, she seemed quite pleased to see him.

"I'm sorry I can't stay," he told Wilding with satisfaction. "I have an appointment to escort Miss Slade through the park."

"So she told me when I tried to persuade her to accept some supper. Another time, perhaps, Miss Slade. I will see you tomorrow at noon?"

"Unless my brother needs—"

"Now, Miss Slade," Wilding interrupted gently. "We discussed this. I need my Boudicca. I will be more grateful than you can imagine for your time."

"I would be happy to join you, Miss Slade," Ned offered. "I would like to see Mr. Wilding's work."

"Oh, yes—"

"Alas, I find it difficult to work when I'm watched. You understand, Mr. Bonham."

"Perfectly," Ned assured him, watching the monkey rise on the wall behind Wilding and fling what looked like a chestnut from last autumn's crop at Wilding's head. It bounced off its target with a satisfying thump.

"Mr. Wilding," Emma said, her hands flying to her mouth. Her voice wobbled. "Are you hurt?"

Wilding turned briefly to stare at the monkey as he rubbed his head. "Perfectly fine, I assure you." He added, his eyes on Ned, "I should tell you that there are occasionally creatures in the garden who might be dangerous if surprised. I need to know exactly when my guests are coming or leaving so that I can have them put away. You were fortunate that I'd already done so before you came in. Didn't Slade tell you?"

"He did not," Ned answered, surprised. "Perhaps he thought I would find Miss Slade on the street."

He offered his arm to Emma, whose face had lost expression.

"Miss Slade," Wilding said with his charming smile.

"Goodnight, Mr. Wilding," she said perfunctorily, and went through the gate without a backward glance. "I don't believe in his dangerous animals," she whispered when the gate closed behind them. "I think he just said that to keep you away."

"Why—"

"Mr. Bonham, do you know where Marianne Cameron's studio is?"

"Yes, I do."

"Will you please take me there now?"

"Not the park?" he said wistfully.

"I'm sorry." Her fingers tightened a little on his arm; she added ruefully, "I know none of this makes much sense. But when I speak to Miss Cameron, you'll understand."

The women's studio, which Ned had visited several times, was the second floor of an old warehouse along River Road. Ned smelled paints and turpentine, mold and the lingering odors of mud flats as they climbed the creaky flight of stairs. The stairs ended at a long sweep of floorboard beneath unpainted rafters. Light came from tall windows overlooking the river, inset where doors had once opened in midair for goods to be grappled and winched up for storage off boats in the full tide below. Older windows on the other side gathered the morning light. The vast room was filled with easels, canvases, paints and paper, stools with stained smocks hanging over them. The painters had vanished into the fading light; only Marianne was there, lighting lamps to continue her work.

She looked stricken when she saw Emma, and came to her quickly. "Oh, Miss Slade, I do apologize. It was an offer I couldn't refuse. I'm so glad you came here. Hello, Mr. Bonham. Have a stool."

"Hello, Miss Cameron." He sat, looking at them puzzledly. "I wish someone would explain what I've missed."

"Mr. Wilding—" Emma began.

"I invited Miss Slade to pose for us—"

"And then Mr. Wilding begged me to pose for him, and I refused because I had promised Miss Cameron, and anyway I wanted to come here and paint—He knew that, and yet he found a way to sabotage our plans."

Miss Cameron's broad face flushed. "He offered us an exhibit, Mr. Bonham. A promise to talk to the owner of a new gallery about a women's show. If we let him have Miss Slade first."

"Will he keep his promise?" Emma asked grimly.

"As long as he gets what he wants, he will. I felt dreadful giving you up like that, but—it was too much to refuse. I've been trying for years to get someone to agree to exhibit us. And he paints wonderfully well; you'll be pleased with what he makes of you."

Emma sighed. "But I have to endure his company for hours. I thoroughly dislike him. I didn't know why at first, but now I do."

"Has he been rude to you?" Ned asked abruptly. "If he has, he'll be wearing his painting around his neck."

"No. He hasn't. I just feel a bit trapped."

"And so you have been, and I've been complicit in your entrapment," Miss Cameron said ruefully. "How can I make it up to you? Can you find time to come and paint with us? I won't charge you for studio space; you can come and go as you please, and see what the rest of us are doing."

"Yes," Emma said emphatically. "That's why I came to talk to you. I would love a corner here to work in. I feel underfoot at my brother's, and his friends, though terribly interesting, are so terribly distracting. I could paint here in the mornings, then pose for Mr. Wilding in the afternoons..." Her voice trailed away; Ned found her blue eyes on his face as though she had sensed his sudden pang of distress. She was silent a moment, conjecturing; then she added softly, "And in the evenings, Mr. Bonham, you and I can draw one another."

He said, his odd heartache gone, "I can think of nothing I would like better. Well, actually I can, but that will wait until the fullness of time."

Miss Cameron eyed them speculatively. "I see you have outplayed us all, Mr. Bonham," she murmured. "Even the paragon, Mr. Wilding."

"I was the more fortunate," he admitted. "Speaking of posing, your brother wants my head for Salome's platter. Shall I give it to him?"

"What a wonderful idea," Emma said, laughing. "Yes, I think you should indulge my brother. You can get to know him better and meet all of his disreputable friends."

"And what is Mr. Wilding making out of you?" Marianne asked her curiously.

"I am Queen Boudicca, about to plunge into my last battle."

"I wouldn't have pictured you as a warrior queen," Marianne said thoughtfully. "May Queen, maybe, or Queen of the Fairies, something with a lot of flowers."

"Mr. Wilding prefers to set me off with a musty bearskin rug over my shoulders. He claims he shot it in some wilderness or another. Oh, and he says he must put a horse in the painting as well, as soon as he finds the right one."

She was looking at Ned speculatively as she spoke. So, he realized uneasily, was Miss Cameron.

"Perhaps," Marianne mused slowly, "when your brother is finished with him."

"Yes. As what, do you think?"

"Something with dignity," Ned pleaded, envisioning himself barelegged on a pedestal with a bow in his hand, dressed fetchingly as Cupid, the object of intense and critical female scrutiny.

"The young knight errant, going forth into the world to rescue maidens and do battle with wicked knights who look like Wilding?"

"Can't I be evil? Just once?"

"Can't you settle for being triumphant?" Emma asked with such affection and trust in her eyes that he could only be grateful for his fate.

He bowed his head and acquiesced.

"For you."

Emma found herself whirling through her days like a leaf in a sluice. In the mornings, she went to Marianne's studio, where she had set up her easel. She drew whatever caught her eye in the endless supply of still life on the studio's shelves, which held everything from old boots to exotic draperies and vases in which dried grasses, seed pods, and flowers purloined from the park could be arranged. Occasionally, as she worked, someone would come to sketch her. She scarcely noticed. Sometimes she herself drifted through the room, watching the other women work in ink and watercolor, pencil and oil. She confined herself to sketching for a while, to improve her technique. Miss Cameron moved among them now and then, gently suggesting, never criticizing. She was in the midst of an oil, mostly whites and grays and browns, of the river beyond the window, beneath lowering sky, and the boats and ships that moved ceaselessly along it, the buildings on the far shore, and the stone bridge in the distance, tiny figures crossing it the only flecks of brightness in the painting.

While Emma drew, she let her thoughts wander about, searching for a compelling subject to paint. Something simple, she wanted, like Ned's solstice or Marianne's river. But with a human face in it, drawing the viewer's eye and kindling emotions. Whether the face was male or female, mortal or mythical, and what emotions it should evoke, Emma could not decide. She was content for the moment just to be in the company of painters, watching and learning from them, her mind an open door to inspiration, not knowing what face it would wear when it finally came knocking.

Somewhere around midday, the contentment would fray. Mr. Wilding would enter her thoughts and refuse to go away. Finally time would force her to put away pencil and paper, take off her smock, and say goodbye to Miss Cameron, who always looked a little guilty when she left.

"Don't fret," Emma told her. "When Mr. Wilding procures the exhibit for us, I'll be in it, too. That will make up for everything."

She would return to her brother's for one of Mrs. Dyce's excellent and very informal lunches: Adrian fed anyone who happened to be there. Invariably, he and Ned would make her laugh. And then Ned would walk with her through the streets to Wilding's villa.

Sometimes Mr. Wilding met her at the gate; more often it was a silent, wraithlike servant whose eyes would dart nervously about the garden as he escorted her to the house. He carried a roughhewn walking stick carved out of a tree limb; the polished burl at the top looked formidable.

Curious, she commented on it once; he answered briefly, "In case they left one out of their cages, Miss."

"One what?" she said incredulously.

He rasped his prickly white chin. "Can't rightly say, can I, Miss? Whatever they are, he gets them from far away."

"Are they like the monkey? Or more like big cats?"

"Big," he conceded. "That they are. But I wouldn't say either monkey or cat. More like—like—Well, I couldn't say that either, Miss, since I've never seen anything like them in my life. Not even at the zoological gardens, where I have been a time or two in my youth."

She was silent, willing to doubt they were real, but disturbed by the thought that Wilding was terrifying his servants with mythological monsters.

Mr. Wilding only laughed when she expressed her doubts. "Do you think I've conjured up a garden full of harpies and manticores? Of course they're real. Most are harmless, though they might not look it. Most would run from old Fender."

"Most?"

"I'm very careful," he assured her. "I value my friends too much to want them eaten by beasts."

Friends by the dozens might come to visit, but never, it seemed, while he was working. At mid-afternoon the villa was as still as though it stood in one of the countries whose houses it emulated: the ones that drowsed in heat and light and came alive at night. Mr. Wilding himself painted silently much of the time. From what Emma saw of the painting, it could become a masterwork. Each hair on the bearskin hanging across her shoulders was meticulously recorded by a brush as fine as an eyelash; as a whole the painted pelt, thick and glossy, made her want to run her hand over it, feel its softness.

Her own face emerging out of the canvas slowly, like a figure from a mist, astonished her. It was fierce and lovely, nothing tentative about it that she could recognize.

"That doesn't look like me at all," she protested.

He smiled tightly. "Oh, yes, it does. When you look at me."

"Really?"

"You dislike me, Miss Slade. Your face is quite expressive. Luckily, Boudicca didn't like her enemies, either; that makes you perfect."

Her eyes narrowed. "Did you do that deliberately, Mr. Wilding? Make me dislike you for this?"

"No," he said, surprised. "Turn your head again; you're out of position. I want very much for you to like me. A little more. Lift your chin. Stare me down. Because I think you are the most beautiful woman I have ever seen in my life, and one of the most intelligent and interesting. I hoped—Chin up, Miss Slade; I have come to steal your realm and slay your people. I hoped you would confess to some truer feeling about me."

"Truer," she said through rigid jaws.

"You are afraid of me because you are drawn to me. That makes you dislike me. So you turn to the much safer and predictable Mr. Bonham."

Her jaw dropped; so did her spear-arm. "Mr. Wilding—"

"You asked, Miss Slade," he said evenly. "Chin up, spear up. Remember the exhibit."

"You take advantage, Mr. Wilding!"

"No, no. You, after all, have the spear; you can throw it at me any time. I tell you what is in my heart. Can you blame me for that?"

He left her wordless. She could only stare at him as he requested, at once furious and vulnerable, willing to skewer him yet unable to move, while he touched her constantly with his eyes, and his brush stroked every hair on her head and every contour of her body.

Toward the end of the session, when she was drained, angry, and thoroughly confused, he would tell her some improbable yet fascinating story about how he had acquired one or another of his animals. One had been found floating in the middle of the sea, surrounded by the flotsam of a sunken ship, alone in a rowboat but for a litter of fishbones and a bloody pair of boots. Explorers had come across another on a tropical island; it had chased them up a tree, then settled into a vigil among the roots, waiting for them to fall one by one like coconuts. Such things colored her weary thoughts, painted bright images; imagining them, she forgot that she had been angry.

So when Ned, waiting at the gate, saw them across the garden, she and Mr. Wilding would seem to be amiably chatting like friends and her smile might seem for him rather than in expectation of Mr. Bonham's face. Even this, Wilding used as a weapon, she knew. The truth lay in his painting: the warrior queen fighting her strong-willed adversary over a realm to which he had no claim.

The evenings belonged to Ned.

Tired and content in his company, she had little to say on their walk to Adrian's apartment. She didn't encourage questions; she might inadvertently tell him something that would make her posing for Mr. Wilding impossible, and ruin all expectations of the prized exhibit. I must go through this, she told herself adamantly. I will have my reward.

So she kept her comments light, asked about Ned's painting day, about his posing with Miss Bunce, and which of her brother's friends he had met that day.

"Valentine DeMorgan," he answered with awe one evening. "He wears a cloak lined with purple satin, and yellow gloves. He keeps in one pocket a slim volume of his poems, all of which are so dreadfully sweet you could stir them into your tea." Or: "Eugene Frith, the reformed pickpocket turned bookseller. He taught himself to read, Adrian said. And now he is an expert on rare editions. Your brother must know half the city."

But she did not fool his painter's eye, which caught the troubled expressions on her face at odd moments, and the faint lines and shadows left by her never-ending days.

"You're tired," he told her one evening after a few weeks of the inflexible routine.

"A little," she confessed.

"Has Wilding been—"

"No," she said quickly. "He wants his painting too much to drive me away."

"Or do you want that exhibit too much?" he guessed shrewdly.

"He's working very fast," she temporized. "And his painting will be wonderful. I have been working hard, but that part of my day will come to an end." She smiled at him brightly. "Then I can pose for you, if you like."

He didn't answer her tactless suggestion, just gazed at her, frowning a little. They were sitting in a comfortable corner of Adrian's studio; Ned was sketching her as she leaned back in her chair, too weary herself to draw. Beyond their little lamp-lit world, Adrian and Linley Coombe, Miss Bunce and Marwood Stokes, another painter who had brought a couple of friends with him, sat around the table cracking nuts and drinking and telling stories. Their laughter rolled across the room, but somehow didn't disturb what lay within the intimate circle of light.

"I know," Ned said abruptly. "I'll take you up north for a rest. To my house on the lake. It's lovely there, this time of year."

She stared at him. "But we can't just go away together, as if we were—as if we were—"

"We are," he said simply, "in our hearts. Anyway, I'm not suggesting that. We'll take your brother with us. Slade!" he called abruptly, turning toward the merry group. "Let's take our paints north to my lake house for a week or two. Your sister needs a rest. The scenery is amazing, and we can live on fat salmon and grouse. The house is big enough for everyone."

Adrian, who had reached an affectionate understanding with his wine, raised his glass promptly. "Brilliant. Coombe can come and catch fish for us. And Stokes here can shoot. But—"

"No," Emma said firmly, raising her voice. "No, no, no. I can't go now."

"But we won't invite Wilding," Adrian finished, then peered at her. "No?"

"I can't go now. Please." She straightened, nearly took Ned's hand, stopped herself. "I would love to go," she told him softly. "But I'd rather do it when I can truly relax and not have any worries. Anything complicated," she amended quickly, "like the exhibit or Mr. Wilding's painting to come back to."

"All right," Ned agreed reluctantly. Their hands and fingers and knees were very close as they leaned in their chairs towards one another. The company around the table watched them owlishly. "But promise to tell me the moment you change your mind."

"I will."

At the oddly silent table, someone hiccuped. "Slade," Stokes said excitedly. "What is this we're seeing? Can it be—"

"Mr. Stokes, I forbid you to mention my sister's name in the company of other gentlemen."

"Her name will not leave my lips, on my solemn oath," Stokes said earnestly, hiccuping again. "But are we to understand that this—this goddess and this young painter of the most exciting potential—"

"No," Adrian said firmly. "We are to understand nothing of the sort until we are given permission to understand it. Fill your glass and be quiet. Coombe is going to recite all nine hundred lines of his latest masterpiece."

"You look tired," Marianne Cameron said brusquely a few days later, as Emma arranged two pears from Mrs. Dyce's pantry and a bunch of wildflowers from the park on a platter. "You're too pale, and there are smudges under your eyes. You'll make yourself ill. Go home and put your feet up. Or go and buy yourself a bonnet. Get some sunlight."

Emma shook her head. "Don't worry," she said absently, trying the pears in different positions. "I think this needs something else... What do you think?"

"You've got ovals and circles and horizontal lines," Marianne said, gazing at it, and forgot her advice. "You need a vertical. How about a candlestick? Or your brushes in a cup?"

"My brushes. The very thing. A bouquet of brushes in a jar."

She drew contentedly until noonday sun spangled the river with light, and Mr. Wilding's face insinuated itself into her thoughts.

"You've got interesting shadows under your eyes," Mr. Wilding commented that afternoon as, in bearskin and tunic, she took her position. "They make you look even more heroic and doomed. Perhaps I'll use them... Has your brother been keeping you awake with his late hours?"

"I haven't been sleeping well. But Adrian is never less than thoughtful."

"You mustn't get ill. Perhaps you should stop going to Miss Cameron's studio until I finish my painting."

"I will be fine," Emma said stolidly, shifting her grip on the spear until it balanced properly. "I have no intention of giving up my studio time."

He reached out, gently shifted hair away from her eyes. "Your hair has such lovely shades of saffron in it. Perhaps I'll take forever with this painting," he added. "What I weave by day I will unravel by night, like Penelope... Miss Slade, you look positively horrified. Where has your fighting spirit gone?"

"I hope you are joking, Mr. Wilding."

"Perhaps," he said lightly. "Perhaps not. I don't intend to stop seeing you." Her hand tightened on the spear. "That's better. The hawk's glare rather than the hare's stare of terror."

Emma didn't answer. He painted a while, mercifully silent. Her thoughts strayed to Mr. Bonham. Edward, she thought fondly, remembering his face in the lamplight as he sketched her. Edward Eustace. My Ned.

"Perhaps your sleep is troubled by foreboding," Wilding commented after a while. "No, don't answer. Don't move an eyelash. Foreboding of the future. A house full of caterwauling children, a husband who, no matter how good his intentions, cannot, for the sake of his own art, put your work before his needs. You are equals now. But marriage has a way of altering the scales. He will tend to his art. You will tend to everything else." His eyes flicked to her frozen face. "You think I am cruel. I am only thinking of you."

"I can't imagine why," she said sharply. "You have told me that no matter what I do, my art will be inferior."

"I did not say that," he answered calmly. "I said that most female painters lack depth. Surely not all. But I can't know what your art might become."

"No."

"Don't speak. And neither will you know, if you marry. You simply won't have time. What is regarded as novel and intriguing and perhaps is important in you now will be looked upon as irrelevant when you have a household and a husband to look after. I'd think very hard about those things, if I were a woman. Don't speak. I'm doing your mouth." He concentrated on it for a while, then went on smoothly, "I never wanted children around. Noisy, messy, ignorant little barbarians who must be taught the slightest thing... Nor do I need a wife to make myself seem respectable. What I have longed for is a companion. An equal, in wit and temperament and of course in beauty. Free to indulge herself in whatever she might consider important. She would not need my permission to do as she pleased because legally I would have no claim on her. Consider that, Miss Slade."

She did, straightening so suddenly with a whirl of spearhead that he blinked. "Mr. Wilding," she said icily, her voice trembling, "what kind of monster are you, trapping me and then tormenting me?"

He raised his brows, gazed at her perplexedly for a moment. Then he put down his brush. "I think, Miss Slade, that I will send you home early today. You must be very tired to be imagining such things. Tell your brother that you need a good night's sleep. Forego the studio in the morning just this once. Try to come back refreshed tomorrow."

"Mr. Wilding—".

"It's all right. I've just given you some things to think about, that's all. They may seem a bit confusing now, but they're worth examining. Get dressed. I'll walk you out and send you home in my carriage. Fender had an unfortunate encounter in the garden this morning; it will be a while before he'll be up and about."

Emma flung open Adrian's studio door and said tersely to the group of startled faces—Ned, Euphemia Bunce, and Adrian—around his easel, "Mr. Bonham, I have changed my mind. I really do need to get away. Can we leave for your house in the north as soon as possible?"

Ned didn't ask questions. He didn't dare. There was tension in his beloved's voice and in her movements that told him simply to do what must be done as quickly as possible. He sent word to his caretaker and housekeeper in the north to prepare for a full house, perused the train schedules, and started packing. Beneath his alarm for her, he was delighted, and afraid that if he delayed or discussed her reasons for the abrupt decision, she might change her mind again. Long hours rambling through the country was what she needed: sun and rain on her face, work whenever she wanted, laughter in the evenings, fish out of the rivers, fresh cream and strawberries, and long, peaceful, dreamless sleeps.

Two days later, when the train to the north country began to move out of the station, Ned saw the tension suddenly melt out of Emma like something palpable. She turned to look at him with wonder. Around her, friends and her brother and their older female cousin Winifred, whose art lay in her embroidery threads, chatted and laughed. Aisles and racks were piled with their luggage, as well as baskets of provisions, sketchbooks to record the journey, blankets, books and a great trunk full of the paraphernalia of their art.

"We're moving," she said incredulously. "I thought it wouldn't be possible. Something would happen to prevent it."

"Is Wilding that difficult?" he asked her, appalled.

She thought, watching the city flow past her, before she answered.

"He is playing a game to make me feel like Boudicca. But, unlike her, I will win. I just needed to retreat for a week or two." She smiled at him, the shadows like bruises under her eyes. He could not find a smile to give back to her.

"You will not go there again," he said flatly. "I will explain that to Mr. Wilding."

Her smile faded; he glimpsed a look in her eyes that Wilding must have put there: fierce and inflexible.

"You will not fight my battles for me," she said softly. "If I can't fight for myself and my art, then what kind of an artist can I be? Only what you will permit me to be."

He blinked at her, startled at this stranger's face. Then he thought about what she said, and answered haltingly, "I think I understand. This is that important to you."

"Yes."

"More important than me or Wilding."

Her face softened; she touched his hand, held it unexpectedly. "No. As important as you. The only important thing about Wilding is what we will get from him when this is finished."

He opened her fingers, let his own explore her long bones and warm, softer skin, roughened here and there by a callous from her pencil, or by scrubbing to remove dried paint. Though their hands were tucked neatly out of sight beneath her skirt, he felt that warmth against his lips, as though longing, for an instant, had made it so.

"Miss Slade," he said huskily.

"Mr. Bonham?"

"Will you please marry me so that I might have the privilege of putting my arms around you?"

She nodded, sighing audibly. Then she added quickly, "I mean no. I mean not yet. Soon. I meant that—I dearly wish you could. How long have we known each other?"

"One month, three weeks, four days and some odd hours. Surely that's long enough."

"Surely it must be," she agreed, "in some countries. You would bring my father half a dozen cows and he would give you his blessing and me. If he were still alive."

"If I had any cows. Perhaps I should offer some to Adrian."

"Perhaps that would be proper."

"How soon," he begged, "is soon?"

"Not soon enough." She held her breath, thinking, then looked at him helplessly. "Do you think two months might be considered within the pale of propriety?"

"Miss Slade, may I remind you that as an artist you are already beyond the pale?"

She laughed breathlessly, a sound he had heard only rarely during the past weeks.

"Then when two months have passed since the night we met you may ask me again, and I will answer with all my heart."

"Well, then," he said, clasping her fingers gently in both hands and smiling mistily down at them. "That's settled. I'll start collecting some shaggy northern cattle from the hills the moment we get there."

The lake house, a great square four stories high, was built of stone as gray as the water. It stood alone near the edge of the water, its lawns and gardens surrounded on all sides by wild shrubs, gorse and heather, and juniper twisted by the winds. A stony hill rose behind it, hiding the village on the other side. The road that wound up and over the hill from the village to the house was an ancient thing; stones runneled with archaic letters and odd staring faces appeared out of the shrubbery now and then as though they watched all who journeyed along the road.

"What are those peculiar stones?" Winifred wondered. She was a paler version of Adrian and Emma, rather tall and bony without Emma's grace, her hair more sandy than gold. But she shared their even temperament and fearless interest in unusual things.

"No one really knows," Ned answered. "The locals have various tales about them: they mark graves, or once gave directions to travelers, or even that they're doorposts into fairyland."

"Really?" Coombe said. "How wonderful. I intend to see if they work. If I vanish, you'll know where I've gone."

"You'd better not," Adrian told him. "You're in charge of catching our fish."

"My caretakers, Mr. and Mrs. Noakes, know a lot of local tales. Mrs. Noakes is housekeeper and cook; she can do uncanny things with a grouse. Mr. Noakes tends the gardens and keeps the house from falling down. Sometimes I think they're as old as it is. They're its household gods."

The crowd, smelling hot bread and savory meat as soon as Noakes opened the door to the rattle of wagons, seemed willing to worship. Mrs. Noakes, round as an egg with a crown of gray braids, greeted them all calmly, unperturbed by the numbers. She dispatched them to various rooms, pointing directions with the wooden spoon in her hand. Noakes, a burly old man with eyebrows like moth wings, began hauling their baggage upstairs.

"You gave us short notice," he remarked to Ned. "But Mrs. Noakes managed to air out the rooms and find beds for everyone. You came just in time for the strawberries in the garden. I've checked the boats; they're both sound, and all the fishing gear is in order. Word is that the sky should clear up soon; all the signs are there, they say, though I couldn't tell that myself."

"You are a paragon, Noakes. I'm sorry we didn't give you much time to prepare. We made up our minds very suddenly."

His eyes, gray as the stone walls around them, crinkled with a smile. "It's good for the house to be full, makes it feel young again."

Inside, the house was as simple as its outer lines suggested. The whitewashed rooms were large and full of light; windows and doors were framed with solid oak; thresholds were worn and polished with age. The odd unframed oil or strip of embroidery hung here and there; beyond that, only the views of water and blooming heather and rocky hills adorned the rooms. The party spent some time exploring, watching the sunset out of different windows, exclaiming over the solitude, the colors, the potential for their brushes. A herd of wild ponies galloping through the gorse rendered them nearly incoherent.

Then the last piece of luggage found its place, the sun vanished, and they clattered down the stairs to supper.

Afterwards, they rearranged the vast drawing room, pulled chairs and couches and cushions taken from other rooms as close to the enormous fireplace as possible. They took turns reading out of ancient volumes they had discovered around the house: obscure poetry, a farmer's journal, a collection of local folktales. Marwood Stokes, who had a fine and fruity voice, was reading about a pesky household hobgoblin whose tricks could drive people to leave their homes, and who would pack itself in among their possessions and follow them along to the next, when someone pounded at the door.

Ned, half-listening, heard Noakes's footsteps on the flagstones, and then a brief exchange. Then the drawing room opened and there stood Bram Wilding, smiling genially upon them.

"Sorry I'm late."

They all stared at him wordlessly. Then Adrian threw a cushion at him. "You weren't invited, Wilding. Go away."

"I know," he said imperturbably. "I've got a room in the village. But I couldn't let you have all the fun without me. Nor did I want my Boudicca out of sight, though I promise—" He held up his hand as Ned and Adrian protested vigorously and incomprehensibly at once. "I promise I won't ask her to work as long as she is here." He looked at her; she sat motionless in an old rocking chair, her face colorless and expressionless. "May I stay?" he asked her. "I only came to paint a landscape."

She shifted slightly, let her hand slip beneath the chair arm to rest lightly on Ned's shoulder, where he sat on a cushion beside her. "Here I am not Boudicca," she said softly. "I am Emma Slade, whom you barely know. You are my brother Adrian's friend; it is of no interest to me if you stay or go."

"Oh, Adrian, let him stay," Winifred, who hardly knew him, said kindly. "He has come so far. And country darkness is so—dark."

Adrian cocked a brow at Bram. "If my sister says you go, you go. Is that agreed?"

Wilding bowed his head, added cheerfully, "I brought gifts of appeasement from the city. Bottles of brandy, baskets of fruit, and Valentine DeMorgan's latest book of poetry, fresh from the press."

They all exclaimed at that. "Produce it," Coombe demanded. "Read and prove your worthiness."

Mrs. Noakes put her head through the doorway. "Pardon me, Mr. Bonham, am I to make up another bed?"

"Mr. Wilding has a room in the village," Ned said firmly.

"Oh, dear. Mr. Noakes misunderstood and sent the wagon on its way back to the village. Should he wait up, then, to take Mr. Wilding back?"

Ned sighed. "He's liable to be waiting all night." He hesitated a moment, then said tersely to Wilding, who was trying to look meek and penitent and not succeeding well at either, "You can stay tonight, if Mrs. Noakes can find you a bed."

"There's a narrow bed in an attic room," Mrs. Noakes suggested doubtfully. "It leaks in the rain."

"That sounds perfect."

"You are too kind," Wilding murmured.

"I," Emma said, rising abruptly, "think I will say goodnight. I'm very tired. Come with me, Winifred?"

Her cousin joined her with a rather wistful glance back at the party and the fascinating newcomer. He smiled cordially at them, then stretched out on the carpet in front of the fire as the door closed behind them, and promptly began to read about a young woman wasting away from a broken heart as the violets He had given her withered before her eyes in their vase, a poem of such sweet and lugubrious melancholy that Wilding had most of the party weeping with laughter within a dozen lines. Adrian, sipping port and watching Wilding, did not find him amusing; nor did Ned.

But there was nothing to be done that night, and Emma, he reminded himself, might prefer to find her own ways of dealing with Wilding in the light of day.

Ned rose early, trying to be quiet as he gathered his sketchbook and watercolors and boots and took them all downstairs. As always,

Mrs. Noakes was earlier; the sideboard was laden with hot tea and scones, boiled eggs, smoked salmon and sausages, and strawberries from the garden.

As Ned stood in his stockings, drinking scalding tea and eating a sausage with his fingers, the door opened and delighted him with the unexpected vision of Emma.

"I heard someone creep past my door, and looked to see who it was," she said. "I hoped it might be you."

She brought her sketchbook down as well, her pencil case and a broad, well-weathered hat. He happily poured her tea, brought it to her as she sat.

"I'm going down to the lake to see what I can make of the water and those rocky hills in the distance," he said.

"Oh, good. I'll come with you."

"Yes."

"We could take a boat," she suggested eagerly. "Row out onto the water and draw. Shall we?" She rose, began filling the pockets of her painting smock with scones, strawberries wrapped in a napkin, and a couple of eggs. "Let's go now before anyone else is up; the sun is rising and it's so beautiful out there now."

"All right," he said, managing to gulp tea and put his boots on at the same time. Like children trying to be quiet, they only succeeded in dropping things and snorting with laughter as they made their way out of the house into the morning.

A low mist still hung over the lake, obscuring the water, but the clouds were fraying above their heads, and sunlight broke through from behind the hills, illumining the jagged slopes. Raindrops sparkled on every tree branch and grass blade. The air smelled of strawberries and bracken. Ned took deep, exuberant breaths of it as they made their way across the lawn toward the water. In the boathouse, someone moved. Noakes, Ned saw, as the old man raised a hand; he had probably brought the fishing gear down.

Emma came to a sudden stop, gripping Ned. "I saw something," she breathed.

"That's just Noakes."

"No, something in the mist—something white moving across the water."

"A wild swan, maybe."

"Maybe." She started moving again, her long strides free and confident, he saw, when she was in the open. Sunlight touched her hair, turned it into an aura of gold around her face, and his breath caught. Entranced, he stood still, watching her move across the morning. Missing him, she turned, laughing, walking backwards and beckoning him on.

Then her face changed, became guarded, inexpressive; he guessed at what she had seen behind him and sighed.

He turned. Wilding, his own steps lithe and quick, was gaining on them. He, too, had a sketchbook under his arm, a pencil case in his pocket.

"Good morning," he called cheerfully.

"It was," Ned muttered. Emma had already started on her way again, firmly ignoring the interloper. She went down the path to the boathouse, causing Wilding to ask promptly when he caught up with Ned, "Are you rowing out? What a splendid idea." He clapped Ned lightly, irritatingly on the shoulder, his eyes following Emma. "Thanks for the bed, by the way. Creaky thing; my feet hung over the end. But amusing." He had continued his brisk walk before he finished talking, leaving Ned in his wake. "I just need a word with Miss Slade—"

"Wilding!" Ned protested, hurrying after him. "She came here to rest."

"I know," Wilding called soothingly over his shoulder. "I know. Miss Slade!"

She didn't answer. She had nearly reached the lake, where the mist, beginning to burn off, revealed reeds near the boathouse, a strip of water, and a flock of baby ducks paddling after their mother. Ned, flushed and angry, caught up with Wilding, nearly plowing into him as Wilding stopped abruptly.

"Look at that," he said breathlessly.

Nick, seeing for the moment only Wilding's excellently tailored back, stepped aside and looked over his shoulder.

A horse as white as the mist stood on the shoreline. Emma had seen it, too; she walked toward it slowly, one hand outstretched. Ned heard her speaking to it, half-laughing, half-crooning, and remembered the country girl she was, raised among all kinds of creatures and not likely to be afraid of a wild pony.

It looked quite a bit bigger than the local hill ponies; Ned wondered if it had escaped from someone's pasture. It stood very still, watching Emma come, mist snorting out of its nostrils. It looked like a hunter, Ned guessed, realizing how big it was as Emma, his rangy goddess, moved closer to it.

"It's perfect," Wilding whispered.

"What?"

"I wanted a horse just like that to put behind Boudicca."

"Good. You've found it. You paint it while Miss Slade and I go rowing."

"No, I need her—" He started walking again, calling, "Miss Slade!"

She shook her head as though at a midge. The horse nuzzled her fingers; she stepped closer, running her hands along its mane. Wilding, hurrying so quickly he was nearly running, cried her name again.

"Miss Slade!"

She glanced at him finally, her face set and colorless. Then someone else shouted—Noakes, who never raised his voice. She gripped the thick mane, pulled herself up as she must have done countless times as a child, riding the placid farm horses bareback, with an eye-catching flash of knee above her boot before she settled her skirts.

The horse gathered its muscles, turned, and leaped so cleanly into the mist over the lake that Ned did not hear a sound from the water, and the hatchling ducks floated serenely by, undisturbed. The silence seemed to spread over the world, through Ned's heart; he couldn't find a word, a sound, for what he had seen. Beside him, Wilding was as still; he didn't breathe.

Only Noakes made noises, dropping something with a clatter, calling incoherently and puffing as he ran out of the boathouse. He stared at the quiet water and cried again, a shocked, harsh noise. Ned moved then, trembling, stumbling, his heart trying to outrace him as he reached the boathouse.

"Noakes—" he said, gripping the old man. "Noakes—"

"What was—What happened?" Wilding demanded raggedly.

"We must go out there—You take one boat, Noakes, we'll take the other—Hurry!"

"No time to hurry," Noakes said, wiping his twitching face. "No place to hurry to. Never," he added in a whisper, "saw that before in my long life. Heard about them but never thought I'd live to see one."

"One what?" Ned cried.

"Kelpie," Noakes said. He wiped at his brow, trembling, too; his cap fell on the ground. "I'm sorry, lad."

"Kelpie—What's a kelpie?" Ned asked wildly.

"What you saw. That white horse. A water sprite. No mercy in them. They lure you onto their backs with their beauty, they carry you into the water, and then—and that's the end."

"What end?" Wilding asked sharply.

The old eyes, gray as the water, gazed back at Ned with a sheen of tears over them. "In all the tales I ever heard, you drown."

Emma, after the first gasp of shock from the horse's sudden plunge into the cold water, was holding her breath. They were going down, she realized, down and down, deeper than the shallows of the lake had any right to be. She had slid off the horse's back, but her fingers were still locked into its mane. Water weeds trailed past her, and schools of startled fish. The horse, which was behaving like no horse she had ever met in her life, dragged her ruthlessly. It galloped in water effortlessly; she was as buffeted, roiling around its body, as she would have been on land. Sometimes, flung over its outstretched head, she glimpsed a black, wicked eye, a widened nostril, its great muscular neck snaked out, teeth bared. It shook its head now and then, trying to loosen her grip, she thought; she only clung tighter, her lungs on fire, her eyes strained open, round and staring like a fish's, unable not to look at what could not be possible.

If I must breathe, so must it, was her only coherent thought; she clung to that as well, ignoring all the implications of the horse's magic. Beneath that thought lay a confused impulse, a fragment from some fairy tale or another, the only thing shaken to the surface of her mind as the monstrous horse surged into impossible depths and she twisted in the water like an eel clamped to a writhing fish.

Don't let go.

And then the pain spilled through her, burst out of her until it must have filled the world, for she felt nothing else, not water nor motion nor the coarse mane, long and wet as sea grass, in her fingers. She closed her eyes at last, and drowned in pain.

She woke again, at which she felt vaguely surprised. Drenched and limp as a bundle of beached sea kelp, she lay on sand in what must have been the bottom of the world. A hollow of rock rose around her; a cave, holding air like a bubble. Beyond it, she saw the gray-green glimmer of water, shadowy things moving among trailing weeds.

The great horse loomed over her, its long white head with its onyx eyes and great dark nostrils swooping down as though to bite. Its mouth stopped an inch from her cheek. It only scented her, once, fastidiously, as though it were uncertain what she was.

"Am I dead?" she asked. Her voice had no more strength than a tendril of water moss.

"You should be," its eye told her, or its thoughts; she couldn't tell exactly where the voice came from.

She sat up slowly, pulling herself together in piecemeal fashion, bone by bone off the fine white sand. It crusted her hair, her clothes; she tasted it on her lips. The horse backed, stood watching her motionlessly. She saw a glimmering, moving reflection in its eye, and turned stiffly; her bones might have been there for centuries, they felt that creaky.

A man entered the cave. Some manlike creature, at any rate, if not truly mortal. His skin seemed opalescent, wavery gray-green, like the water; his green hair floated like sea-grass around his head. He wore a coronet of gold and pearl and darkly gleaming mother-of-pearl. In his tall grace and beauty, in his eyes the shade of blue-black nacre, he bore a startling resemblance to Bram Wilding.

She sighed. "Out of the frying pan…" she whispered. Her throat hurt, as though she had tried to scream under water. "Who are you?"

He gave her a look she couldn't fathom before he spoke. "You are in my realm," he answered, a lilt in his voice like the lap of waves against the shore. "This water is my kingdom."

"How do you understand me?" she asked with wonder.

"I am as old as this water. I have been hearing the sounds that mortals make since before they learned to speak."

"What happens now?"

He gave a very human shrug. "I have no idea." She stared at him. "No one has ever ridden my kelpie and lived."

"I'm still alive?"

"So it seems."

"I wasn't sure. I feel as though I have gotten lost in someone else's dream. Why did the kelpie come to kill me?"

"It's the way of things," he answered simply. "To ride the kelpie is to drown."

"But I didn't."

"No."

She thought a moment; her mind felt heavy, sluggish with water, thoughts as elusive as minnows. "You could," she suggested finally, "have the kelpie take me back."

He scratched a brow with a green thumbnail; a tiny snail drifted out. "I could just leave you in here; you would die eventually. But the kelpie kills, not I. Perhaps you were not meant to die. Every other mortal dragged underwater lets go of the kelpie to swim. It swims too deep, too quickly; they can never reach the surface again before they drown. But you would not let go."

"I think I got my tales confused," she answered fuzzily.

"Are there rules for such things?" the lake king asked curiously. "What happens in other tales at times like this?"

She tried to remember. Her childhood seemed very distant, on the far side of the boundary between water and air, stone and light. Inspiration struck; she felt absurdly pleased. "We might bargain," she told him. "You could ask me for something in return for my life."

He grunted. "What could you possibly have that I might want?"

She felt into the pockets of her smock, came up with a soggy handkerchief, some crumbled charcoal, sand, an unfortunate carp, a few crushed strawberries. "Oh," she breathed, a sudden flame searing her throat.

"What is that?" the lake king asked.

"It was part of our breakfast."

"No. Not that in your hand. That in your voice, your eye."

She blinked and it fell. "A tear," she told him. "I just remembered how happy we were, running out into the morning. We were going to row onto the lake, eat scones and strawberries, paint the world. And then Wilding came. And then the kelpie. And now here I am, and Mr. Bonham might as well be on the moon for all we can see of one another." She wiped away another tear. "He must think I am dead. In no conceivable circumstances would it occur to him that I might be sitting in a cave under water talking to the king of the lake."

The king came to kneel beside her, his eyes like the kelpie's, wild and alien, as he studied her.

"You have words I don't know," he said. "I hear them in your voice. What are they?"

"Sorrow," she told him, her voice trembling. "Joy. Eagerness. Dislike. Astonishment. Anger. Love."

"Are they valuable?"

"As air."

He was silent, his strange eyes fixed on her, his beautiful underwater face so like and unlike Wilding's it made her want to laugh and weep with rage: even there, that far beyond the known world, she could not get away from him.

"Give me those words," the lake king said, "and I will send you back."

She gazed at him mutely, wondering at the extraordinary demand; it was as though a trout had asked her to define joy. Slowly, haltingly, having no other way but words in that underwater world to explain such things, she began a tale. She started with her brother, and then Bram Wilding came into it, and then painting, and Boudicca, and the women's studio, and Edward Eustace Bonham, and how he and she had so unexpectedly fallen together into the depths of a word. All that had made her understand the words the lake king had heard in her voice, she told him, having no idea how much he understood, and not daring to hope that they might be worth more to him than a handful of pretty pebbles she might have picked up on the shore and lightly tossed into his realm.

On the shore, the assembled houseparty stared numbly across the water. They had spent the morning rowing frantically over the lake, searching for any sign of Emma. Noakes had summoned villagers, who carried more boats over the hill on their wagons. Ned had refused to come in until the oars slipped out of his aching hands, and one of the villagers pulled him and his boat ashore. Adrian tried to persuade him to rest. But he could only pace along the water's edge, tormented by visions of Emma floating among the reeds in a lonely, distant stretch of shoreline.

Adrian, his eyes reddened, his face white and set with shock, kept asking reasonably, "How could she possibly have been taken by a kelpie? It's not real. How could it be real? These things belong in tales and paintings, not in life. We imagine them! They have no power over us."

"Yes, they do," Wilding finally said. "They have power. They force art out of us."

His imperturbable composure had not only been shaken; it had dissolved. He looked as stunned and wretched as any of them; for once in his life he had not a tactless word to say. He had very little to say, Ned noticed dimly. He was just there, whenever a hand was needed to push a boat out, when a trek to one cove or another was planned, when Coombe, searching the murky water under the boathouse, came defeated to shore and needed a blanket.

What Wilding said to Adrian worked its way finally into Ned's thoughts. Winifred came among them with a tray of mugs and fresh tea. He took one, warmed his hands and took a burning sip. Then he looked at Wilding. "What we paint is real. That's what you're saying?"

"You saw," Wilding reminded him inarguably.

He shook his head, took another swallow. "I never thought such things were real," he said huskily. "But if we—if we see these realms and paint them, then why can't we—why should we not be able to find our way into them? Find their doorways, cross their borders? Why can't we?" Wilding didn't answer. Ned turned his eyes back to the lake. He was gathering strength to resume his search, along the shore or on the water or in it, any way he could.

"We can't breathe water," Wilding said gently. "That's the boundary we can't cross."

"Neither can horses," Ned reminded him. "Yet nobody saw the kelpie come back up for air."

"It's a symbol," Adrian said heavily. "Kelpie means death. That's what Noakes said." He dropped his hand on Ned's shoulder, left it there a moment. On the lake, in shallower waters, the villagers had dropped grappling hooks. So far they had pulled up only weeds.

"If it's only a symbol, then how could it kill Emma?" His voice shook, and then his face; he turned blindly away from them, staring at the stony hills. "There must be a way," he whispered when he could. "There must be a way in. Those standing stones—doorposts, they're said to be—All those tales of people coming and going, taken and then finding their way back—"

"It's never anyone you or I know," Adrian said, "who finds their way back out of fairyland. It's always someone in a tale."

"This time it's Emma," Ned said fiercely. "Where there's a way in, there must be a way out. I'm going to find it." He dropped his cup on the grass, went towards the water. All the boats were in use. But they were no good anyway, he thought. They only sat on the surface of the water, keeping you safe and ignorant. How to find the place where tale becomes truth... He pulled off his shoes, felt the water on his feet, and then around his knees. And then, before he could reach the depths and glide beneath the surface, seek out the true kingdom of water, someone caught at him, pulled him back.

It was Wilding. Ned broke free of him, stumbled back. Wilding lost his balance, splashed down among the reeds.

"All this is your fault!" Ned shouted at him furiously. "You hounded her—you drove her up here, and even then you couldn't leave her alone, you had to come here yourself and drive her away from you again—she rode that kelpie to get away from you!"

"I know." Wilding was shivering in the water. His face, without its mask of arrogance and irony, was nearly unrecognizable. "Do you think," he asked Ned huskily, "that I will ever forgive myself? But the kelpie didn't come for me or you. You won't find it this way."

"I might," Ned said stubbornly, wading out again. "I can swim so close to death I might see its white mane and its black eye. I'll ride that kelpie then, and I will never let it go until it shows me where it has taken Emma. We paint such things because it's safe—we see them without danger—Our canvas is the boundary between worlds."

"It's all we know of them," Wilding said. "All we can ever know. Emma is gone."

"Emma—"

There was a sudden roil in the placid surface of the lake in front of them. Water streamed upward, splashed everywhere. Some said later they glimpsed in the bright jets raining back into the lake, a mane as white as spume, a spindrift tail, hooves like opalescent shell, eyes blacker than the nothing between stars. All anyone saw for certain as the strange eddy calmed, was someone swimming away from it toward the shore.

Ned, waist deep in the water, knew then that a heart could break with joy as well as grief, and twice in the same day.

He dove into the water and swam to meet her.

Later, they curled together under blankets on a sofa beside the great hearth, their wet heads close, their hands clasped. The group had sat around them mutely listening to Emma tell her tale. Then, in the face of such intimacy, the gathering broke up to marvel with one another, to eat and drink, to wander off and stare at the surface of the quiet lake, or up the hillside to gaze at the ancient stones. Then they strayed back to marvel again at Emma and ask for the tale again.

Adrian finally asked the obvious. "Are you planning to marry my sister, Mr. Bonham, or merely trifle with her affections?" They laughed at him. He reached out, his eyes widening with remembered pain and wonder, and lightly touched Emma's drying hair. "No one," he breathed, "will believe this. I still don't."

"No," Emma said. "They won't. But now I have a use for Mr. Wilding."

Wilding, who had been hovering at the door, unable to come in or go away, asked her hesitantly, "What is that?"

She gestured to him; he came to the fire, held out his hands to it. He hadn't changed his clothes, Ned saw; water moss and mud and bits of lake grass clung to his damp suit. Emma regarded him thoughtfully, without a trace of trouble in her eyes.

"I have bargained for my life with the king of the lake and won. Surely I can do the same with you."

"You don't have to," he answered painfully. "I won't ask you to pose again."

"But I will," she said. "And in return, I want you to pose for me."

He was silent, not in protest, Ned saw, but perplexed. He inclined his head. "Yes, of course. Anything. But—as what? A very great fool?"

"No. As the king of the lake. He looked exactly like you," she sighed. "It wasn't funny," she told Adrian, who had loosed a bark of laughter. "It was, in fact, extremely annoying to think that Mr. Wilding's might be the last face I saw in my life."

"I'm sure it was," Wilding said ruefully.

"And I'll paint the kelpie beside you: that's another face I'll never forget for as long as I live. I intend to hang you, Mr. Wilding, in the women's exhibit." She turned to Ned then, as though she felt his pang of uncertainty, his resignation: never the hero, always the squire, the spear-bearer. She took his hands, held them very tightly. "You will be in it, too," she told him softly. "The man on the lake shore waiting beyond hope. The one to whom I will always find my way back."

He smiled, stroking her damp mermaid's hair, and wondered briefly how many worlds she might chance into, how often he might have to wait in terror and wonder at the edge of the unknown. But it would not matter, he decided. As long as she wanted, he would be there waiting.

HUNTER'S MOON

THEY WERE LOST. There was no other word for it. Dawn, trudging glumly through the interminable trees, tried to think of a word that wasn't so definite, that might have an out. Ewan had been quiet for some time. He had stopped kicking over rocks to find creepy-crawlies and shaking hard little apples out of gnarly branches onto his head and yelling at her to comelookathis! Now he just walked, his head ducked between his shoulders, both hands stuffed into his pockets. He was trying not to reach for her hand, Dawn knew, trying not to admit he was afraid.

Lost. Misplaced. Missing. Gone astray. They were in that peculiar place where lost things went, the one people meant when they said, "Where in the world did I put that?" She was stuck with her baby brother in that world. It was gray with twilight, hilly and full of trees, and they seemed to be the only people in it. The leaves had begun to fall. Ewan had stopped doing that, too: shuffling through piles of them, throwing up crackling clouds of red and gold and brown. Dawn huffed a sigh, knowing that he expected her to rescue them. She hadn't wanted to take him with her in the first place. She had followed him aimlessly through the afternoon while he ran from one excitement to the next, splashing across streams and chasing squirrels. Now he was tired and dirty and hungry, and it was up to her to find their way home.

Trouble was, home wasn't even home. Here in these strange mountains, which weren't green, but high, rounded mounds of orange and yellow and silver, where rutted dirt roads ran everywhere and never seemed to get anywhere, and nobody seemed to use them anyway, she didn't know how to explain where Uncle Ridley's cabin was even if they did stumble across anyone to ask. It wasn't like this in the city. In the city there were street signs and phones and people everywhere. And lights everywhere, too: in the city not even night was dark.

A bramble came out of nowhere, hooked her jeans. She pulled free irritably. Something fell on her head, a sharp little thump, as though a tree had thrown a pebble at her.

"Ow!" She rubbed her head violently. Ewan looked at her and then at the ground. He took one hand out of his pocket and picked a small round thing out of the leaves.

"It's a nut." He looked up at her hopefully. "I'm starving."

She took it hastily. "Don't you dare."

"Why not? Eating nuts never hurt me."

"That's because you never ate the poisoned ones."

She threw it as hard as she could into some bushes. The bushes shook suddenly, flurried and thrumming with some kind of bizarre inner life. Dawn froze. A bird shot up out of the leaves, battering at the air with stubby wings. It was large and gray, with long, ungainly legs. It fell back to the ground and stalked nervously away, the weirdest bird that Dawn had ever seen.

"What is that?" Ewan whispered. He was tugging at her sweater, trying to crawl under it to hide.

"I don't know." Then she knew: she had seen that same bird on one of Uncle Ridley's bottles. "It's a turkey," she said, wonderingly. "Wild turkey."

"Where's its tail?" Ewan asked suspiciously; he was still young enough to color paper turkeys at school for window decorations at Thanksgiving.

"I guess the Pilgrims ate all the ones with tails." She twitched away from him. "Stop pulling at me. You're such a baby."

He let go of her, shoved his hands back into his pockets, walking beside her again in dignified silence. She sighed again, noiselessly. She was older by six years. She had held him on her lap and fed him, and helped him learn to read, and reamed into bullies with her backpack when they had him cornered in the schoolyard. But now that she had grown up, he still kept following her, wanting to be with her, though even he could see that she was too old, she didn't want her baby brother hanging around her reminding her that once she too had been small, noisy, helpless, and boring. She kicked idly at a fallen log; bark crumbled and fell. She had wanted a walk in the woods to get out of the cabin, away from Uncle Ridley's endless fish stories and her father trying to tie those little feathery things with hooks that looked like anything but flies. But she couldn't just be by herself, walking down a road to see where it went. Ewan had to come with her, filling the afternoon with his chattering, and leading them both astray.

"I'm so hungry," Ewan muttered, the first words he had spoken in some time. "I could eat Bambi."

"Bambi" was what their mother said their father had come to the mountains to hunt with his brother, who had run away from civilization to grow a bush on his chin and live like a wild man. Uncle Ridley had racks of guns on his cabin walls, and a stuffed moose head he had shot "up north." Painted wooden ducks swam across the stone mantelpiece above his fireplace. The room Ewan and their father shared was cluttered with tackle boxes, fishing poles, feathered hooks, reels, knives, handmade bows and arrows. Dawn slept on the couch in the front room underneath the weary, distant stare of the moose. Once, when she had watched the fire burn down late at night, an exploding ember had sparked a reflection of flame in the deep eyes, as though the animal had suddenly remembered life before Uncle Ridley had crossed his path.

A root tripped her; she came down hard on a step, caught her balance.

She stopped a moment, looking desperately around for something familiar. There was a farmhouse on the slope of the next hill, a tiny white cube at the edge of a stamp-sized green field. Bright trees at the edges of the field were blurring together, their colors fading in the dusk. The world was beginning to disappear. Dawn's nose was cold; so were her hands. She wore only jeans and her pale blue beaded sweater. The jeans were too tight to slide her fingers into her pockets, and her mother had been right about the sweater. Ridiculous, she had said, in the country, where there was no one to see her in it, and useless against the autumn chill.

"I think we're close," she told Ewan, who was old enough to know when she was lying, but sometimes young enough to believe her anyway.

"It's getting dark."

"Your point being?"

"Things come out in the dark, don't they? In the forests? Things with teeth? They get hungry, too."

"Only in movies," she answered recklessly. "If you see it in a movie, it isn't real."

He wasn't young enough to buy that. "What about elephants?" he demanded. "Elephants are real."

"How do you know?"

"And orcas—I saw one in the aquarium. And bats—"

"Oh, stop arguing," she snapped crossly. "Nothing in these woods is going to come out in the dark and eat you, so—"

He grabbed for her at the same time she grabbed for him at the sudden, high-pitched scream of terror that came from the depth of the wood. They clung together a moment, babbling.

"What was that?"

"What was that?"

"Somebody's getting eaten. I told you they come out now, I told you—"

"Who comes out?"

"Werewolves and vampires and witches—" Ewan dived against her with a gasp as something big crunched across the leaves toward them. Dawn, her hands icy, hugged him close and searched wildly around her for witches.

Someone said, "Owl."

She couldn't see him. She spun, dragging Ewan with her. A tree must have spoken. Or that bush with all the little berries on it. She turned again frantically. Maybe he was up a tree—

No. He was just there, standing at the edge of shadow under an immense tree with a tangle of branches and one leaf left to fall. He seemed to hover under the safety of the tree like the deer they had seen earlier: curious but wary, motionless, tensed to run, their alien eyes wide, liquid dark. So were his, under a lank flop of hair like the blazing end of a match. He didn't say anything else. He just looked at them until Dawn, staring back, remembered that he was the only human they had seen all afternoon and he might vanish like the deer if she startled him.

"Who," she said, her breath still ragged. "I thought owls said who."

"Screech owl," he answered and seemed to think that explained matters. His voice was gentle, unexpectedly deep, though he didn't look too much older than she.

Ewan was peeking out from under Dawn's elbow, sizing up the stranger. He pulled back from her a little, recovering dignity.

"We're lost," he admitted, now that they had been found. "We walked up a road after lunch, and then we saw some deer in the trees, and we tried to get closer to them but they ran, and we followed, and then we saw a stream with some rocks that you could walk across, and then after we crossed it, there were giant mushrooms everywhere, pink and gray and yellow, and that's where we saw the black and white squirrel."

The stranger's face changed in a way that fascinated Dawn. Its stillness remained, but something shifted beneath the surface to smile. His thoughts, maybe. Or his bones.

He let fall another word. "Skunk."

"I told you so," Dawn breathed.

"And then we followed—"

"My name is Dawn Chase," she interrupted Ewan, who was working his way through the entire afternoon. "This is my brother Ewan. We're staying with our uncle Ridley."

The young man's face went through another mysterious transformation. This time it seemed as though he had flowed away from himself, disappeared, leaving only a mask of himself behind. "Ridley Chase."

"You know him?"

He nodded. He took a step or two out of the trees and pointed. Dawn saw nothing but more trees, and a great gathering of shadows spilling down from the sky, riding across the world. She clasped her hands tightly.

"Please. I don't know where I am, or where I'm going. I never knew how dark a night could get until I came here. Can you take us back?"

He didn't answer, just turned and started walking. Dawn gazed after him uncertainly. Then she felt Ewan's damp, dirty hand grip hers, tug her forward, and she followed.

The moon rose just when it got so dark that the bright hair always just ahead of them seemed about to disappear. Dawn stopped, stunned. It was a storybook moon, immense, orange as a pumpkin, the face on it as clear as if it had been carved out of crystal. Surely it couldn't be the same little white thumbnail moon that she noticed now and then floating above the city, along with three stars and a dozen flashing airplane lights. This moon loomed over the planet like it had just been born, and she, Dawn Chase, was the first human to stand on two legs to look at it.

She felt Ewan pulling at her. "Come on. We're home."

Home under that moon? she thought confusedly. Home in what universe? He dragged her forward a step, and she saw the light beneath the moon, the lantern that Uncle Ridley had hung on the deer horns nailed above the cabin door.

She looked around, dazed like an animal with too much light. "Where's—where did he go?"

Ewan was running across the little clearing, halfway to the cabin. "Come on!" he shouted, and the door swung open. Uncle Ridley stuck his round, hairy face out, grinning at them. The old retriever at his knee barked wildly with excitement.

"There you are!" he shouted. "I knew you'd find your way back!"

"But we didn't," Dawn said, her eyes flickering through the moonlit trees. They cast moon shadows across the pale ground; the air had turned smoky with light. "There was someone—"

"I'm starving!" Ewan cried, trying to wriggle past the dog, who was trying to lick his face. "What's for supper?"

"Bambi!" Uncle Ridley answered exuberantly. That was enough to make the deer Dawn saw at the edge of the clearing sprint off with a flash of white tail. She stepped onto the porch, puzzled, still trying to find him. "Someone brought us home," she told Uncle Ridley, who was holding the door open for her.

"Who?"

"I don't know. He never said. He hardly talked at all. He looked—he was only a couple of years older than me, I think. He had really bright red hair."

"Sounds like a Hunter," Uncle Ridley said. "There are Hunters scattered all through these mountains, most of them redheads. Ryan, maybe. Or Oakley, more likely. He never uses one word when none will do."

"He didn't even let me thank him." She stopped at the threshold, her stomach sagging inside her like a leaky soccer ball at the smell of food. "Where's Dad?"

"He took the truck out to go searching for you. He was pretty worried. There's always some idiot in the woods who'll take a shot at anything that moves. He's probably lost himself now on all those back roads. I told him there's nothing out there to hurt you in the dark. Even the bears would run."

"Bears?"

"But it's best if you don't roam far from the cabin during hunting season. Come in before the bats do, and have some stew."

"It smells great."

He shut the door behind her. "Nothing like fresh venison. Shot it last week, four-pronged buck, near Hardscrabble Hollow."

"Venison?" she asked uncertainly, her throat closing the way it had when he talked about bears.

"Deer."

When she woke the next morning, she was alone. They had all gone hunting, she remembered, even the dog. Earlier, their whispers had half-wakened her. Coffee burbled; the wood stove door squeaked open and shut; bacon spattered in a pan, though it had to be the middle of the night.

"Shh," her father kept saying to Ewan, who was so excited that his whispers sounded like strangled shouts.

"Can I really shoot it?"

"Shh!"

Finally, they had all cleared out, and she had gone back to sleep. Now, the quiet cabin was filled with a shifting underwater light as leaves fell in a constant shower like colored rain past the windows. She lay on the couch watching them for a while, random thoughts blowing through her head. She could eat deer, she had found, especially if it was called venison. She hoped Ewan wouldn't kill anybody. He had never shot a rifle in his life. Uncle Ridley had invited her to come with them, but she didn't really want to be faced with the truth of the link between those wary, liquid eyes and what had smelled so irresistible in her bowl last night. The eyes in her memory changed subtly, became human. She shifted, suddenly finding possibilities in the coming day. She hadn't seen his face clearly in the dusk, just enough to make her curious. The stillness in it, the way it revealed expression without moving.... She sat up abruptly, combing her short, dark hair with her fingers. If she stayed in the clearing in front of the cabin, no one would mistake her for a deer, and maybe he would see her there.

She sat for a time on the lumpy ground in the clearing pretending to read, then for another stretch of time on a rock at the edge of the stream that ran past the side of the house, swatting at bugs and watching the falling leaves catch in the current and sail away. She was half asleep in the sagging wicker chair on the cabin porch, feeling the sun pushing down on her eyelids, when the boards thumped hollowly under her. She opened her eyes.

He didn't speak, just gave an abrupt little nod. Even close, she couldn't see the pupils in his eyes; they were that dark. Again she had the impression of expression just beneath the surface of his face, like a smile just before it happened. She straightened in the chair, blinking, then ruffled at her hair and smiled at him. His skin was the warm brown of old leaves, the muscles and tendons visible in his throat, around his mouth. The sun picked out strands of gold in his fiery hair.

"Ryan?" she guessed, remembering what Uncle Ridley had said. "Or is it Oakley?"

"Oakley," he said in his husky, gentle voice. "Oakley Hunter."

"Everyone's gone," she explained, in case he wondered, but he seemed to know; he hadn't even glanced through the screen door. He sat down on the edge of the porch, his movements quiet, neat, like an animal's.

"Dawn," he said softly, and she blinked again. No one had ever said her name that way; it seemed a word she hadn't heard before. "I stopped by to ask," he continued, surprising her farther by stringing an entire sentence together, "if you'd like to take a walk with me."

Her feet still felt yesterday in them, that endless hike, but she stood on them promptly without thinking twice. "Sure."

He didn't take her far, but it was far enough that she was lost within five minutes. This time she didn't care; she rambled contentedly beside him through the wood he knew, listening to him naming grackles and nuthatches, elderberries, yarrow, maples and birch and oak. She told him about the ungainly turkey; he told her the name of the nut she had thrown at it.

"They only fan their tails for courting," he explained. "Like peacocks."

"How long have you lived here?" she asked. "I mean, your family. You were born here, weren't you?"

He nodded. "There have been Hunters in these mountains for forever."

"Do they ever leave? Or are they all like you?" He turned his dark eyes at her, waiting for the rest of it; she felt the warmth of blood like light under her skin. "I mean—I can't see you taking off to live in the city." She paused, laughed a little. "I can't even see you buying a slice of pizza in the village deli."

"I've eaten pizza," he said mildly. "There are Hunters scattered all over the world." He took his eyes from her face then, but she still felt herself in his thoughts. He drew breath, took another step or two before he spoke. "Every year, in autumn, we have a big gathering. A family reunion. They've been coming for days, now. It begins tonight, when the full moon rises."

"I thought that was last night."

"It seemed that way, didn't it? But one side lacked a full arc. You had to look carefully."

"It was beautiful," she sighed. "That's all I saw."

She felt his eyes again, lingering on her face. "Yes."

"It doesn't seem possible that there could be that many people back here in the hills. Yesterday we didn't see anyone for hours, not even a car. Until we saw you."

"Oh, they're here," he said mildly. "Most of them live in a wood or a forest somewhere in the world. They're used to being quiet. Noise scares the animals and trees; we hate to see them suffer."

"Noise scares the trees?"

"Sure." She looked for his secret smile again, the one he kept hidden in his bones, but she missed it. "You can hear them chattering when they're scared. They get shot, too, along with deer and birds, in hunting season."

"Anything that moves," Dawn quoted, remembering what Uncle Ridley had said. It sounded like a fairy tale: the old trees aware and quaking at the hunters' guns, unable to run, their leaves trembling together, speaking. Oakley had led her into a different wood than yesterday's wood, she realized suddenly. She was seeing it out of his eyes now, a mysterious, unpredictable place where trees talked, and deer lived peacefully among the Hunters. She smiled, not believing, but willing to believe anything, as though she were Ewan's age again.

Oakley gave her his opaque glance. "What's funny?"

"Nothing," she said contentedly. "I like your wood. What do you do, all you Hunters, at the family gathering? Have a barbecue?" She winced at the word after she said it; given their love of animals it seemed unlikely.

But he only answered calmly, "Something like that. After the hunt." She stared at him incredulously; he shrugged a little. "We're Hunters; we hunt."

"At night?"

"Under the full moon. It's a family tradition."

"I thought you said you hated to see animals suffer."

"We don't hunt the animals. It's mostly symbolic."

"Oh."

"Then we have a feast. A big party. We build a fire and eat and drink and dance until the moon goes down."

She tried to imagine a symbolic hunt. "You mean like a game," she guessed. "A game of hunting."

"Yes." He paused; she saw the words gathering in his face, his eyes, before he spoke. "Sometimes we invite people we know. Or friends. We were thinking of maybe asking your uncle. Because he likes to hunt so much. You could come, too. Not to hunt, just to watch. You could stay for the party, watch the moon set with me. Would you like to come?"

She didn't answer, just felt the answer floating through her, a bubble of happiness, completely full, unable to contain a particle more of the sweet, golden air. They wandered on, up a slope, down an old, overgrown road into a dark wood, hemlock, he told her, where an underground stream had turned stones and fallen trunks above its path emerald green and velvety with moss.

She could hear water falling softly nearby. They lingered there, while Oakley showed her tiny mushrooms on the moss, ranked like soldiers, with bright scarlet caps.

"You didn't answer my question," he reminded her, and she looked at him, let him see the answer in her face.

"Yes," she said. Her voice sounded small, breathless among the listening trees. "I'd love to come."

The world exploded around her.

She screamed, not knowing what had happened, not understanding. A crack like lightning had split the air and then a deer leaped in front of her, so close she could smell its scents of musk and sulphur, so close it seemed immense, its hooves the size of open hands, its horns carrying tier upon tier of prongs, some flying banners of fire as though the lightning had struck it, and all of them, every prong, the color of molten gold. She saw its eyes as it passed, so dark she could not see the pupils, only the red flame burning deep in them.

She screamed again.

Then she saw three faces at the edge of the wood, all pallid as mushrooms, all staring at her. Behind her, she heard the great stag as it bounded from the moss onto dead leaves. And then nothing: the wood was silent. The stag left no other sound of its passage.

She heard her father shout her name.

They stumbled toward her, slipping on the moss, Uncle Ridley reaching out to take the rifle from Ewan as he began to run. She couldn't move for a moment; she couldn't understand why they were suddenly there, or where Oakley had gone, along with all the fairy magic of the little wood. Then she saw the stag again in her mind, crowned with gold, its huge flanks flowing past her as it leaped, its great hooves shining, and she began to shake.

Ewan reached her first, grabbing her around the waist, and then her father, holding her shoulders, his face drained, haggard.

"Are you all right?" he kept demanding. "Honey, are you all right?"

"I'm sorry," Ewan kept bellowing. "I'm sorry."

"We didn't see you," Uncle Ridley gasped. "That buck leaped and there you were behind it—thought my heart was going to jump out of me after it."

"What are you talking about?" she whispered, pleading, completely bewildered. "What are you saying?"

"How could you get so close to it? How could it have let you come that close? And didn't you think how dangerous that might be in hunting season?"

"It was Oak—" she said, still trembling, feeling a tear as cold as ice slide down her cheek. But how could it have been? Things tumbled in her head, then, bright images like windblown autumn leaves: Oakley under the tree, the deer watching at the edge of the wood, the great, silent gathering of Hunters under the full moon, Hunters who loved animals, who hated to see them suffer, who understood the language of trees. She saw Uncle Ridley among them, on foot with his gun, smiling cheerfully at all the Hunters around him, just another one of them, he would have thought. Until they began to hunt. "It was a Hunter," she said, shivering like a tree, tears dropping out of her like leaves.

They weren't listening to her; they were talking all at once, Ewan still shouting into her sweater, until she raised her voice finally, feeling on firmer ground now, though she could still feel the other wood, the otherworld, just beneath her feet. "I'm okay," she managed to make them hear. "I'm okay. Just tell me," she added in sudden fear, "which one of you shot at the deer?"

"It was standing there so quietly," Uncle Ridley explained. "Young buck, didn't hear us coming. Gave us a perfect shot at it. I couldn't take it; I've got my limit for the season. We all had it in our sights, but we let Ewan take the shot. Figured he'd miss, but your dad was ready to fire after that. So Ewan shot and missed and the deer jumped and we saw you."

Her father dropped his face in one hand, shook his head. "I came within an inch of shooting you. Your mother is going to kill me."

"So no one—so you won't go hunting again. Not this season. Uncle Ridley?"

"Not this season," he answered. "And not until I stop seeing you standing there behind anything I take aim at."

"Then it will be all right, I think," she said shakily, peeling Ewan's arms from around her. "Then I think you'll all be safe. Ewan. Stop crying. You didn't hurt me. You didn't even hurt—You didn't hurt anything." He raised his red, contorted, snail-tracked face. You rescued us, she thought, and took his hand, holding it tightly, as though she might lose her way again if she let go, and who knew in what ageless realm of gold and fire, of terror and beauty she might have found herself, among that gathering under the full moon?

Some day, she promised the invisible Hunter, I will come back and find out.

Still holding her brother's hand, she led them out of the wood.

OAK HILL

MARIS WROTE in her book:

"Dear Book, You are my record and my witness of the magic I learn in Bordertown. I have chosen you because you are silver and green, which seem to me magic colors, though I don't know why. Anyway, as soon as I learn some spells I will write them in you. As soon as I find Bordertown." Squatting on the dusty road, the blank book on her knee, she looked up at a distant growl of gears. She stuck her thumb out, hopefully. A woman in a pickup with a front seat full of what looked like the brawling body parts of fourteen children, all under six, gave Maris a haggard look and left her in a cloud of gold. Maris blinked dust out of her eyes, and picked up her pen again, which was also silver, with a green plume. "I hope to get there soon. That woman did not look as though she knew the way, nor does this road look like it knows the way to anything but worn-out farms and diners. But. You never know. That, I believe, is the first rule of magic."

She stopped there, pleased, and put the book and pen into her backpack.

Much later, after an endless ride in a slow truck towing a full hay-wagon that kept wanting to ramble off by itself into the fields, she sat in a diner at a truck stop just off the interstate and alternately chewed French fries and the end of her pen as she wrote. It was quite late; the nearest city, she guessed from the newspapers in the racks, seemed to be Oak Hill. From the size of the newspaper, there was a lot of it.

"Bordertown could be there. It could be anywhere," she wrote. "Which is just as well, since I have no idea where I am. Did I cross a state line in that hay-wagon? Anyway, it gives me some place to go toward. Oak Hill. It sounds magical, a great city within an ancient forest of oak overlooking the world." She paused, seeing it instead of the lights flashing in the dark along the interstate, instead of trucks grinding and snorting their way to the ranks of fuel pumps beside the diner. "But possibly it has no more to do with oaks than Los Angeles has to do with angels. Expect the unexpected. Which is another rule of magic. Except in this case, I think the expected is more—"

"You want something besides fries, hon?" the waitress asked her. The waitress was tall and big-boned, with a heavy, placid face and skin as clear and smooth as silk. Yes, Maris said silently, intensely, I want your skin. Your beautiful milky skin. I will give you anything for that.

"No," she said aloud. "Just another coke, please."

The waitress hovered. "It's kind of late, isn't it? For you to be out here by yourself?"

"My parents are over at the motel," Maris said glibly, "watching TV."

"Oh."

"I got hungry."

"Oh." She shifted weight, her expression unchanging. "Good thing you brought your backpack with you, to keep it safe. Never know about parents."

"It has my secrets in it," Maris explained. "I'm going to learn magic." That, she learned early, always made people fidget, forget to ask questions, find something interesting in the stuffed deer head, or the clock across the room. Another thing was her face, which made them uncomfortable, especially when she painted stars over the chronic mega-zits that built up like cinder cones over a smoldering beneath the surface. Her eyes were too close together, and a watery gray; her nose had grown a roller-coaster bump in the middle of it; her long hair, once white-blonde, had changed the past year or so into a murky, indeterminate shade between ash and mud. She had taken to dressing out of thrift shops to distract attention from her hopeless face: worn velvets, big hats with fake pearl necklaces looped along the brim, sequined tops that made her glitter like tinfoil on a bright day, long, tattered skirts of rich, warm colors that made her look mysterious, a gypsy, a fortune-teller, a woman who knew secrets she might part with for the right gift. Her mother said she looked like an explosion at a Halloween party. "People like you for yourself," her mother said. "Not what you look like. I mean—You know what I mean. Anyway. I love you."

The waitress seemed unfazed by magic; the word glanced off her benign expression without a ripple, as if it were something kids did, like dyeing their hair green, and then grew out of. "Well," she said. "I guess they'll know where to find you when they miss you."

"Nobody knows where to find me," Maris wrote a day or three days or a year later, her back against a cement wall, as if she had been driven there by the overwhelming noise of the city. Her fingers holding the pen were cold; she had been cold since she got to the city, though people slept outside without blankets, and the thin light passed through a windless shimmering of heat and dust. It made writing difficult, but at least the fear stayed in her fingers; so far it hadn't gone to her head. She paused to stare at a group of people on the other side of the street. They had just come out of a club; they wore black leather, black beads, black feathers in their long, pale, rippling hair. Their sunshades were tinted silver; they stared back at Maris out of insect eyes, and then began to laugh. She pushed back against the wall, as if she could make herself invisible. "Oak Hill has no oaks. Oak Hill has no trees. The truck driver said he knew where I should go, and he stopped in the middle of all this and said this is it. This is what? I asked. He said, This is the end of the line. I got out and he kept going. If this is the end of the line, then why did he keep going? You don't understand, I said. I am going to Bordertown to learn magic. This isn't Bordertown. This isn't where I want to go. And he said, Take a look at that. All I saw were some white-haired kids on fancy bikes. He said, Keep out of their way, and find a place to stay with your own kind; that's all I can tell you. Then I got out and he kept going." She paused again, watched a pair of bikers shouting at one another, both with one thigh-high leather boot dropped for balance in four inches of water pooling over a clogged drain, as they argued about who had splashed who. She returned her attention to her book. "This is not at all what I expected the unexpected to be like."

A shadow fell over her. She looked up into the most beautiful face she had ever seen.

Later, when she had time to think again, she wondered which she had seen first: the beauty that transfixed her and changed the way she thought about the word, so that it stretched itself, in an instant, to embrace even the noisy, unfeeling, vain and swaggering opposite sex; or, as her eyes rose instinctively to see her own reflection in his expression, the terrifying malevolence in his eyes.

She jumped, a faint squeak escaping her; she felt her shoulder blades hit the wall. "You," he said explosively.

She made another strangled noise.

"Get out of here. Find your own kind. If you have one. There must be some place for small, white mice to scutter together in this town. You are taking up space in my eyes that I require for other purposes, such as reading the graffiti on the wall behind you."

She stared at him, stunned by hatred, as if he had walked across the chaotic street just to slap her for existing. She recognized him then, by his thigh-high boots: one of the bikers who had been arguing in the puddle. His satin shirt, the same silvery-gray as his eyes, had a tide-line of water and dirt on the front. She wondered if he had eaten the other biker, or just froze him to death with his eyes.

She caught her breath suddenly, dizzily. I am here, she thought. This is the place. "You," she said, scarcely hearing herself. "You are not human."

He spat, just missing her shoe. "Why am I still seeing you?" he wondered.

"I came here because of you."

He was seeing her then, where before he had seen only what he was not. His eyes narrowed dangerously. "You are not worth the chase, ugly little mouse," he said softly. "You are not worth breath. But I will give you ten. Five breaths of terror, and five of flight, before I summon a pack of ferrets to catch the mouse. They like to play with mice, and there are very few places here to hide. One."

"I came here to learn magic."

He blinked, perhaps hoping she would disappear. "Two."

"I have a book to write the spells in." She showed him. "And a pen." She was babbling, she knew, wasting breath, but if he was all the magic she met in Bordertown, then he was all she had. "I'm not running away from anything, or anyone, and you're right, I am ugly, but that's not why I want to learn—"

"Three."

"So since you can't stand the sight of me, maybe there's someone you know who is blind, maybe, or doesn't care—And it's not even for me," she added desperately.

"Four."

"I mean, it's not so I can turn myself beautiful or something, at least I don't think it is, it's just that—"

"Five."

"It's what I want. How can I say what I want when I don't even know what magic is? The word for it is all I know, and you know all the rest. Teach me."

He was so still she didn't hear him breathe. Then he said very softly, "Run."

For a moment, they both wondered if she would. Then she heard the word itself, clear and simple, as if he had handed her a pebble. He had given her five more breaths; he had given her more than that; maybe the danger was not from him. Maybe he was teaching her the first step: How to listen. Or maybe, she thought as she hugged book and backpack to herself and scrambled to her feet, it was a word of advice, something to do with the sudden roar of bikes around the corner. She whirled, then turned back to look at him. "Thank you," she said, and saw his look of utter astonishment. Then she ran down the street, smelling the clogged drain, oil spills, exhaust, hearing laughter around her, burning like the hazy light. Dragons bellowed at her heels, followed her around corners, down alleys where rats and startled cats scurried for safety. She risked a single glance backward, out of curiosity, and found more of him, though younger, lithe and feral, their wild hair white as dandelion seed, their faces, like his, doors that opened and slammed at once, so that she could only glimpse something they would never let her enter. Their hatred was unambiguous and relentless. They would not let her go; they followed her through crowds and up steps, into abandoned buildings and out again, whooping and calling, barking like dogs, crying a name now and then, until they finally tired of playing, and on a busy street, where pedestrians, laughing and cursing, leaped out of their way, one shot forward among the crush to ride beside her.

He caught her arm; sobbing, her hair catching in her eyes, she tried to pull away. "Get on!" the biker hissed, and Maris, stumbling over her hem, tried desperately to see. The voice was a woman's. "Hurry!"

She had lost her backpack in some alley; but she still clutched her book and pen; even now, trying to hoist herself onto a moving bike, she refused to drop them. The bike picked up speed; hair flicking into Maris's eyes and mouth was dark. She spat it out, tightening her hold, the book and pen crammed between them. It was a long time before the voices of dragons behind them became the beat of her heart.

Later, under the light of a single bare bulb hanging down from a scruffy ceiling, she wrote, "Dear Book, I don't know where I am." She paused, hugging herself, staring down at the book. Her skirt was ripped, her feet blistered and bleeding from running in vintage patent leather shoes; her hair and face were grubby, her hands skinned from where she had slipped on garbage in an alley and skidded on cobblestones. She picked up the pen again, though it hurt to write. "You are all I have left of the other world. I lost everything else. This house is swarming with people. Most of them are my age. They came for so many reasons. Some of them are too scared of what they ran from to talk. Some of them are too angry. The house was an apartment building once, I think. There are stairs running everywhere. But a lot of the walls were torn down. Or maybe they just fell down. You can see plumbing pipes, and water stains all over. They gave me something to eat, and told me never, never go into that part of town again. But how can I not? I asked them where to go to learn magic. They just laughed. He didn't laugh. Trueblood. That's what they said he was. Elf. Beautiful and dangerous to humans. But he has something I want."

She paused again, glimpsing his face among the scattered, terrifying memories of the afternoon. Had he warned her about the bikers? Or had he called them? She wrote again, slowly, "I'll have to disguise myself somehow to go back there. They know my face."

The mysterious comings and goings in the house, she learned as days passed, had simple explanations; there was some order to the constant movement, the replacement of faces. Many of the kids had jobs; they played in bands, or made things to sell, like jewelry, or dyed clothes, out of what they found thrown out in the streets, or in cardboard boxes at thrift shops. Things filtered down to them from places that gave Maris a glimpse of a world beyond the bleak, crumbling buildings. Some—odd, bright feathers, dried leaves—hinted of the wood that Maris had guessed must be only a ghost, a memory of oak among the streets. Other things spoke of wealth: rich fabrics, tarnished rings, beads and buttons tossed casually away that bore elaborate carvings, or strange, woven designs, or even faces, sometimes, that seemed not quite human. "Where did you get this?" she asked constantly. "Where did this come from? What is this?" The answers were always vague, unsatisfying, and accompanied by the baffled expression that Maris seemed to inspire in people.

"Nobody understands why you're here," a girl who made colorful shirts out of scraps told her one day.

"I came to learn magic," Maris said; it seemed simple enough, and she had said it a hundred times.

"Why? Because of something that happened to you? Because of someone?" Maris gazed at her, baffled herself, then thought she understood.

"You mean because of the way I look? Because I'm ugly? Things happened to me because of that, and that's why I ran away to learn magic?"

"You're not—" the girl stopped, and started again. "No one that just comes here for—" She stopped again. "I mean—"

Maris scratched her head, wondered absently if she had fleas. "Maybe," she suggested, "I could understand what you mean if you tell me why you're here."

The girl's face, whose beauty she seemed always trying to deny, slammed shut like a door, the way the elven faces had, against Maris. Then, as she studied Maris's face, with its churning skin and angelfish eyes, Maris saw her open again, slowly, to show Maris things she kept hidden behind her eyes: fear, loathing, hope.

"You're not afraid," she said abruptly. "You're not afraid of—what you left behind. That's what makes you different."

Maris peered at her, between strands of untidy hair. "Maybe you could explain," she said tentatively. "Maybe you could tell me your name."

They sat for a long time on the bare mattress where Elaine sewed swatches of gaudy fabric into a sleeve while she talked. At supper, an endless parade wandered at will through the kitchen, most of it standing up to eat before parts broke off and disappeared, to be replaced by others, rattling crockery, sucking in stew, grunting to one another while they chewed. Maris, who helped cook, took a closer look at the faces around her. For days, they had seemed indistinguishable, all pale and thin, secretive, giving her strangers' stares if they looked at her at all. Few of them knew her name, though someone had given her a nickname. She had been called a lot of things, most of them having to do with fast food, or small, burrowing animals. But this one surprised her. Teacher, they called her, because she was always asking unanswerable questions. Teach.

Tonight she separated their faces, picked out things from their expressions, their eyes, put words to them: furtive, belligerent, sick, angry, scared. All of them were scared, she realized slowly. Even the ones who ignited at a skewed look, a word pitched wrong. They hit with their eyes, their fists, their voices. Nothing could come close to them; they were scared the worst.

"Dear Book," she wrote after supper. "I could not believe the things Elaine told me. She showed me her scars. She said I could not, no, there was no way, but I finally persuaded her: she is going to dye my hair with her cloth dyes, which she says are made of natural things, like nuts and berries. She knows someone who knows someone who finds those things and makes the dyes. She said she'd think about my face, which is easy to forget, but hard not to recognize, especially with all the living constellations on it. She told me not to talk about myself like that. Why shouldn't I? Everyone else does. Besides, that way I get to laugh first. She didn't understand that. Anyway, she knows someone else who makes masks out of feathers and painted cloth, but so far she's balking over that. She thinks it's too dangerous. But so is magic. I didn't know that before, but I know it now."

She woke in the dark, that night, hearing strange music. The house was pitch-black, as if the power had gone out again; a single streetlight, as yet unbroken, gave her an obscure perspective of shadowy stairs and corners as she moved through the house. The music drew her down, down, like a child's hand, innocent and coaxing, saying: Come look at this flower, come look at this pebble, this nut. She followed it without thinking, barefoot, her eyes barely open, trailing the torn lace of an old, sleeveless flapper's dress she wore to bed. Before she had gotten up, the moment she had heard the music, she had reached for her book and pen; she carried them without realizing it, without wondering what she would do with them on an empty city street in the middle of the night.

The door squealed when she opened it, but no one in the house called out. The gritty sidewalk was still warm. She saw no one playing anywhere; the music might have come from someone piping on the moon. She yawned, trying to open her eyes, see more clearly. It comes from the streets, she thought, entranced. All the water pipes and cables underground are playing themselves. The electricity is singing. She felt the vibrations through her feet, heard the music find its way into her blood. Then she heard herself humming random, unpredictable notes, like the patter of light rain. The city flowed away from her eyes in a sea-wave, a cluttered gray tumble of buildings and streets, with lamp lights spinning like starfish among them. It paused, and rolled toward her again, green this time and golden-brown, smelling not of stone but of earth.

She stood on the oak hill, surrounded by a vast wood. The trees were huge, old, towering over her, even while she saw through them into the distances they claimed. I am queen of the hill, she thought dreamily. Where is my face? She bent, still humming, and began to gather fallen leaves.

She found the oak leaves, the next morning, inside the pages of her book.

She shook them out slowly, staring. Around her she heard the heavy thump of feet finding the floor, a tea kettle shrieking in the kitchen, somebody running up a scale on an electric guitar, somebody else yelling in protest. She shifted a leaf, fitted one over another, another against them. Her skin prickled suddenly. She picked up the pen, wrote unsteadily on a blank page: "Thank you."

She borrowed thread from Elaine, to patch a skirt, she said, and spent the morning sewing leaves into a crude mask. The eye holes were tricky; they kept slipping away, no matter how much thread she used. Finally she threatened them with scissors if they did not let her see, and leaves opened under her needle to let the city in.

She tore a ribbon from her skirt to tie it with, and slid it back into her book. Elaine, sewing with feverish concentration on her mattress, scarcely looked up from her own work as Maris dropped the thread beside her. She grunted, and pushed a jar with her dirty, delicate bare foot towards Maris. "That dye I promised you."

"What color?"

Elaine shrugged. "Something. I'm not sure. It'll find its color from your hair."

It found no color at all, apparently, Maris saw when her hair dried. I look like I've been frightened to death, she thought, trying to flatten a silvery crackling cloud of spider web. All the mirrors in the house were cracked, warped, distressed. Like all the faces in them, she thought, wandering from one to another, trying to get a clearer image of herself.

She gave up finally, and borrowed clothes to go outside: a pair of torn jeans, a black T-shirt that said, "Yosemite National Park. Feed the wildlife in you." She went barefoot in case she had to run.

She was lost before she turned three corners. The ominous, sagging buildings all looked alike; strangers jostled her without seeing her. The city stank like an unwashed, unfed animal; it wailed and growled incessantly. There seemed no magic anywhere, nor any possibility of magic, ever in mortal time. There were no leaves anywhere, only stone and shadow and light too harsh to see through. Maris opened her book, found the mask quickly. She tied it on and breathed again. In disguise, she thought, you can be anyone. Anything. Then, chilled, she remembered what she was carrying.

But they don't have to be mine, she thought an instant later. I found them in the street. Someone must have dropped them, someone too much in a hurry to stop. She tangled the pen into the tangle of silver on her head, let the green plume dangle over her shoulder, and tucked the book under her arm. He hadn't noticed the closed book, probably, only the open book before she began to run.

Her skin prickled as she thought of him, part fear, part anticipation. How can I persuade him? she asked the book. Maybe I should give him something. If I ever find him again. If he even lets me talk before he calls the ferrets. Anyway, I don't have anything he would want. I don't even have anything he would want to look at.

Or is he expecting me?

She let the city pull her into itself, drifted with it deeper into its unknown heart.

Gradually she realized that people were staring at her, avoiding her, parting to let her pass, even those who wore fine, scrolled blades like pendants around their necks and masked their eyes with darkness. She was used to hastily averted eyes, even to the sudden silence that she seemed to inspire, at least among humans, before she passed and they thought she couldn't hear their jokes behind her back. But these were the ferrets, wild, magical creatures who had chased her, barking, through the streets; now they were stepping out of her way, their faces carefully expressionless. Can't they tell? she wondered. Can't they see? It's only me behind a mask of dying leaves and a T-shirt from Yosemite. They couldn't, apparently. She walked taller, took a longer, sweeping stride through them, refusing to think about what would happen when they did find out that it was only her.

She saw him finally, coming toward her down the sidewalk, and she stopped. He saw her at the same time; his face hardened. But it had masked itself against fear, she saw in wonder, not against her. He stepped around her carefully, hoping, it seemed, that she had not stopped for him. But she turned, looking up at him as he passed, holding his eyes, until he took a futile half-step, trapped in her gaze, and finally stood still.

He whispered, "Who are you?"

She swallowed sudden dryness, decided simply to answer his question. "Maris."

"Who do you want?"

"You."

He drew breath slowly. His skin was so pale it could not grow any whiter, but she saw the tension along his jaw. "What do you want from me?"

She swallowed again, feeling the closed book under her elbow pushing hard against her ribs, wondering how much power the mask she wore held over him, wondering if she had the courage to say what she wanted to say. But how else would she know who she was, in that moment, in his eyes? She answered finally, carefully, "I want you to say yes. To anything I ask."

"Yes."

"Good." She lifted her hand, pushed the mask up so that he could see her marred, sweaty human face. "Teach me magic."

He stared at her silently a moment longer. Then a shudder rippled through him, pushed words out. "Who are you?"

She opened her mouth, then stared back at him, suddenly perplexed. Maris, she had started to say, but she did not recognize this Maris, who had stopped a Trueblood in his tracks and made him ask her for her name. "I don't know," she said slowly, still astonished that he was not summoning his ferrets furiously out of gutter drains and broken windows. "Who are you afraid of?"

She heard his breath again; his face lost some of its rigidity. "I could not see your eyes," he said softly. "Or your face. Only leaves. You looked at me out of leaves as old as our world, and said you had come for me. Until now, I thought I was afraid of nothing." He paused again. "I seem to be afraid of you. Where did you get the leaves?"

"In a dream."

He nodded, unsurprised. "And you came back here to look for me. You aren't afraid of me, even after I drove you out of here."

Oh, yes, I am, she thought. Oh, yes. I would be just as afraid of the lightning bolt I caught in my hand. But I am the Maris who can catch a lightning bolt and still be alive and talking to it. "Why did the forest let me dream about it? Why did it give me leaves?"

He shook his head. "I have dreamed of it. But it has never let me take anything away with me." He touched the leaves above her eyes gently, tentatively. Then he asked, unexpectedly, "What happened to your hair?"

"It went white."

Again he nodded; such things happened, she guessed, in the old forest. "You look more like one of us."

"I was trying to disguise myself, so you wouldn't recognize me and chase me away again."

He shrugged slightly. "It wouldn't have mattered; all humans look alike to me. I would never have recognized you without the leaves."

"But you didn't know—"

"I recognized the magic in you," he said simply.

She felt her clenched hold on the book, on herself, loosen a little. Standing on the crowded, burning street with him, human in a place where borders merged, worlds touched and might explode or sing at any moment, she suddenly felt safe. "Then you will teach me."

His brows lifted slightly, ruefully; he looked for a moment almost human. "I said yes."

"Dear Book," she wrote in fear and triumph that night, on her stained mattress, while the old building stirred noisily around her. Sounds of hurrying boots and arguments cluttered the air; someone played a raucous ballad on a guitar; someone else played, very faintly, an older ballad on a pipe. "Today I did my first magic. I made one of the Trueblood see my human face and say my name. Maybe that's why we all have come here, with our scars and our secret faces. We want the ancient magic to recognize us. To welcome us home." She paused. Her pen descended, hesitated at a word, wrote again finally. "I'll write to my mother tomorrow. This is hardest for me to say. She was right."

THE FORTUNE-TELLER

MERLE SAW THE SILK trailing out from under the toothless pile of rags snoring in a muddy alley. She glanced around. Most in the busy marketplace were buried under hoods and shawls, eyes squinched against the drizzling rain. They paid her no attention. She knelt swiftly, tugged at the silk. Cards came with it; she felt them as she stuffed the plunder under her shawl and strode away. Oversize, they were, like her mother's cards, and knotted in threads spun by little worms on the far side of the world. The sleeping lump had probably stolen them herself, and there was no reason why Merle shouldn't have them instead. She, after all, wasn't wasting the day facedown in the mud. Fortune favored those who recognized her, and Merle had watched her mother read the cards often enough to know what to do with them.

She worked quickly and efficiently through the crowd, a tall, thin, unremarkable figure swathed against the rain like everyone, with only her eyes visible and wide open. Her long fingers caught the change rattling into a capacious coat pocket as its distracted owner bit into the sausage roll he had just purchased. Farther down among the stalls, she slid a lovely square of linen and lace, perfumed against the smells of the street, out of a lady's gloved fingers. The lady had stopped to laugh at a parrot inviting her to "Have a dance, luv, have a dance." Opening her bag to find the one-armed sailor a coin, she gave a sudden exclamation. Merle left her searching the cobbles for her lace, and disappeared back into the crush.

Another carelessly unguarded pocket in a great coat caught her eye, its shiny brass button dangling free of its loop and winking at her. She drew up close, dipped a hand in. Faster than thought another hand followed, closed around her fingers.

She drew a startled breath, gathered her wits and more breath in the next instant to raise an indignant and noisy complaint against the ruffian who had grabbed a poor, honest young girl going about her business.

Then she saw the face between the upraised coat collar and the hat. Her tirade whooshed into a laugh.

"Ansel! You gave me a moment, there."

He didn't look amused; his lean, comely face, his jade eyes were hard. "Someone will give you more than a moment," he warned, "if you don't stop this."

She shrugged that away, more interested in his clothes. "Where did you steal the coat?"

"I didn't. I'm a working man. I drive a carriage now. You—"

"I'm a working girl," she interrupted before he could get started.

"You're a thief."

"I'm a fortune-teller. Look. I even have cards now." She opened her cloak, gave him a glimpse of the cards in their silk tucked into her waistband. "I found them this morning."

He gave a sour laugh. "You stole them."

"Nobody else was using them."

"You said you were going to—"

"You know I can earn my way, telling fortunes. I've done it before. I told yours. Remember?" She shifted the shawl wrapped up under her almond-shaped eyes to remind him of the full lips and sweet, stark jawline beneath, a trifle wolfish, maybe, but then she was ravenous half the time. His own lips parted; his eyes grew vague with memory. "Remember? The day we met. You saw me and followed me to my tent; I told your fortune with tea leaves and coins made of candle wax. You stole bread and sausages and cheese for our supper. Now that I have cards, I can build a reputation like my mother had—at least when my father stayed in one place long enough."

"You told me," he reminded her softly, "that I'd meet a stranger with storm-gray eyes I'd follow forever. I thought, that night, I had."

She shrugged slightly. "You liked me well enough then. But you didn't stay forever."

"You promised me you'd stop this magpie life. I stopped, but you didn't."

"Now I can," she said, tightening her cloak around the cards again. But he only made a sound between a sigh and a groan, and stepped back impatiently.

"You'll never change."

"Come and see. You know where to find me."

"Wherever they lock you away, most likely, one of these days. You can't play your tricks on the world forever."

"I'll stop, I promise," she told him, half-laughing again. He shook his head wordlessly, turning away, and so did she, with another shrug. She had coins for a meal, lace to sell; she could spend some time studying the cards now. She made her way back to her tent, pocketing a stray meat pie from a baker's busy stall along the way. Why should she pay for what the world put in her way for free?

Her fortune-teller's tent was makeshift: an abandoned shell of a wagon on the edge of the marketplace. It had a broken axle and two barrels propping up the corners where the wheels were missing. A discarded sail nailed over the ribs kept it dry. Merle had brightened the inside with dyed muslin and sprigged lawn skirts she'd separated from their drying lines. Fine shawls with gold threads, ribbons, beads of crystal and jet, left unattended in carriages or dangling too far over a lady's arm, she'd appropriated from their careless owners. She picked apart the seams and wound the swaths around the wagon ribs to make a colorful cave of embroidery, lace, ribbons, flowing cloth. She collected candle ends wherever she found them, to scatter around her while she worked. The tent was guarded by an old raven she'd found protecting a blind beggar who had fallen dead in the street. She'd coaxed it to eat; it came home with her. It had a malevolent eye, a sharp beak, and a vocabulary of two words—"Help! Murder!"—which it loosed with an earsplitting squall when it was alone and faced with a stranger.

It greeted Merle with a rustle of wind and a faint, throaty chuckle. She lit candles and shared bits of the meat pie with the bird. Then she reached outside to hang her painted sign above the wagon steps, and draped a long, dark, beaded veil over her hair and shoulders. She unwrapped the cards.

The silk was snagged and frayed, with a spill of wine along one edge. The cards themselves were creased, flecked with candle wax, and so thumbed with use that some of the images were blurring. She began to lay them out.

Scarecrow. Old Woman. Sea. Gypsy Wagon.

She paused, studying them. It was an odd deck, not at all like her mother's with its bright paintings of cups and swords, kings and queens. Those had once belonged to Merle's great-grandmother; her mother cherished them, wrapped them in spotless silk and tucked them into a cedar and rosewood box between readings. These, well-drawn and colored despite their age, said nothing at all familiar. She laid out a few more and gazed at them, perplexed. There seemed to be a lot of crows. And what would a snake curled into a hoop and rolling itself down a road possibly signify?

The curtains trembled. Merle glimpsed fingers, pale and slender, heard whisperings outside on the steps. She drew the veil across her face. No sense in getting herself into unnecessary trouble if someone happened to recognize her. When the whispering didn't go away, she lit more candles around her and waited.

The curtains opened finally. Three young women, as neatly and fashionably dressed as they could afford, stared at her anxiously.

"Come in."

Something—the exotic veil, her deep voice, which made her sound older and possibly wiser than she was, the flames weaving a mystery of light and glittering dark around her—reassured them. They ducked under the canopy, seated themselves on pilfered carriage cushions, the golden-haired one in front, the other two behind. They spent a moment eyeing the fortune-teller, the cards she had gathered up again, the motionless raven, the drifts of silk and muslin above their heads.

The one in front spoke. "I need to know my fortune."

Merle, shuffling the deck, supposed that anyone with that pretty, tired, worried face probably needed all the good news she could get.

She named her price, and when the coin lay between them, she began to turn the cards, laying them into a pattern: the rainbow arc of life and fortune.

"Wolf. Sun. Old Woman. Well." Again, nothing was familiar; she had to guess at what they should be called, keeping her voice calm and certain, no matter what showed its face. "Spider. The Blind Man. The Masked Lovers." She hesitated briefly. Who on earth was this? A blue-eyed grinning skeleton with a full head of red-gold hair, cloaked in blue and crowned, rode a pitchfork with three blackbirds clinging to the tines. "Lady Death," she guessed wildly, and the young women made various distraught noises.

One suggested timidly, "Three of crows?" which made sense when Merle remembered the other crows in the deck.

But she answered smoothly, "When a card falls into the arc of life, it no longer belongs to a suit. Don't be afraid. She doesn't always signify death. Let's see what falls after her..." She turned another card, hoping it wasn't more crows. Pockmarked puddles came up; that was plain enough. "Rain." She turned the next and decided it would be the last: best to end with a cheerful face. "Fool." She put the deck down. "This is good. Very good."

"It is?" the young woman who had paid said incredulously. "But it says so little about love."

Love. Of course.

"Oh, but it says a great deal." Improvising rapidly, she led the rapt watchers through it, card by card. "Wolf, at the beginning of the arc, signifies a messenger. Sun is, of course, a fortuitous message. The Old Woman in conjunction with the Well is someone you will meet who will give you strength and power—that's the well water—to achieve your heart's desire. Spider may be good or bad. When it appears in the arc, it's the web that signifies, and here it means something well planned, successful."

And so on. She could chart a fortune through twigs and broken eggshells, if she had to. Where she saw a pattern, she could find a fortune. She'd learned that much from her mother before she'd escaped from her eternally traveling family to the city. Even she couldn't see a fortune in a tinker's wagon.

"But what about Lady Death?" the young woman whispered, mesmerized by the card. "Who will die?"

"In this arc," Merle explained glibly, "Lady Death signifies protection. She guards against misfortune, malice, bad influences. Rain follows her. A little stormy weather will hamper the lovers, but that is natural in the course of true love. In the end the Fool, who signifies the wisdom of innocence, will guide your heart to achieve its innermost dreams."

The young woman, whose mouth was hanging by now, closed it with a click of teeth. She sighed and began to smile; the faces behind her brightened. "So he will love me in spite of everything."

"So the cards have shown," Merle answered solemnly, sweeping them together and palming the coin at the same time. She wondered briefly what obstacles the cards had missed. The rival lover? The deluded husband? The betrayed wife? Lack of money to wed? Mismatched circumstances: she a seamstress, he a noble who had admired too closely the shape of her lips? Merle had a hunch that, under other eyes, the cards would have suggested a darker, more ambiguous future. But the young woman had paid for hope, and Merle had earned her pay.

You see? she told Ansel silently as the women went back into the rain. I have a profession, too. Soon, with these strange cards, I'll even have a reputation. Then I can afford to be honest.

Ansel came to her that night as she knew he would. In spite of himself, she guessed wryly, taking note of his dour, reluctant expression. But she knew tricks to make him smile, others to make him laugh, which he did at last, though he sobered up too soon after that.

"You've learned a few things on the street since I saw you last," he commented, rolling onto his back in her meager bed, and stroking her hair as she laid her cheek on his chest.

"Knowledge is free," she said contentedly.

"Is it?"

"At least I don't have to steal it. Don't—" she pleaded as he opened his mouth. "Don't go back to glowering at me. You like what I learned."

She felt him draw breath, but he didn't lecture. He didn't say anything, just smoothed her hair, drew it out across his chest to watch it gleam in the candlelight, onyx dark, raven dark, true black without a trace of color in it. He laughed a little, gently, as at a memory.

"You're growing so beautiful... All I could see of that the few months ago I met you was in your eyes. You were such a scrawny girl, all bones and sharp edges, and those huge eyes, the color of a mist that I wanted to walk through to see what I would find."

"And what did you find?"

He was silent again; she listened drowsily to his heartbeat. "Someone like me," he said finally. "Which was fine until I started not liking what I was... So I made myself into someone more to my liking."

Within the little cave he had made of her hair, her eyes opened. She felt a sudden, odd hollow inside her. As though he had tricked her, taken something from her that she didn't know she had until he showed her.

"So now you like me less," she said softly, and pulled herself over him until they were eye to eye in the dark fall of her hair. "But I'm going to make myself respectable with my cards."

"You stole them."

She laughed. "From some old biddy lying dead drunk in an alley. Besides, I'll hardly be the first to turn myself respectable with stolen goods. I didn't rob a bank, after all. They're only cards."

"Are they?" He eased out from under her and sat up, reaching for his trousers. "I've got to go. I'm stealing time, myself, from my job."

"Come tomorrow?"

He gave her a wide-eyed, almost startled look, as though she'd suggested leaping off a roof together, or rifling through his employer's house.

"I don't know." His face disappeared under his shirt. "I doubt that I'll have time." He reappeared. "You haven't heard a word I said."

"What word didn't I hear?" she demanded. "Tell me."

But he was withdrawing again, going away from her, even before he left the wagon.

She sighed, sitting on her pallet, naked and alone but for the raven, feeling again that strange hollow where something should have been but wasn't any longer.

"You'll come back," she whispered and reached abruptly for the cards in their stained silk to find him in her future. She shuffled them and dealt the arc: Old Woman, Spider, Rain, the Masked Lovers, Lady Death...

She gave a cry and flung the deck down. Candlelight glided across the Old Woman's raddled face; she seemed to smile up at Merle.

You stole a poor old woman's only means to earn a coin, the smile said. You stole her hope. And now you want to twist her cards, make them lie to you, show you how lovable you still are...

The raven rustled on its perch, made a sound like a soft chuckle. Merle gathered the cards together with icy, trembling fingers, wanting to cry, she felt, but not remembering how to start. She pulled on clothes, flung her cloak around her, and splashed barefoot into the rain, not sure where to find the old woman, only certain that until she returned the cards she could not change her future of webs and rain and fools and the Old Woman's knowing eyes.

JACK O'LANTERN

JENNY NEWLAND SAT PATIENTLY under the tree in her costume, waiting for the painter to summon her. Not far from her, in the sunlight, one of the village girls sneezed lavishly and drew the back of her wrist under her nose. A boy poked her; she demanded aggrievedly, "Well, what do you want me to do? Wipe me nose on me costume?" Jenny shifted her eyes; her clasped fingers tightened; her spine straightened. They were all dressed alike, the half-dozen young people around the tree, in what looked like tablecloths the innocuous pastels of tea cakes.

"Togas?" her father had suggested dubiously at the sight. "And Grecian robes for the young ladies? Pink, though? And pistachio...?" His voice had trailed away; at home, he would have gone off to consult his library. Here, amid the pretty thickets and pastures outside the village of Farnham, he could only watch and wonder.

He had commissioned the renowned painter Joshua Ryme to do a commemorative painting for Sarah's wedding. Naturally, she couldn't wear her bridal gown before the wedding; it was with the seamstress, having five hundred seed pearls attached to it by the frail, undernourished fingers of a dozen orphans who never saw the light of day. Such was the opinion of Sylvester Newland, who claimed the sibling territory midway between Sarah, seventeen, and Jenny, thirteen. It was a lot of leeway, those four years between child and adult, and he roamed obnoxiously in it, scattering his thoughts at will for no other reason than that he was allowed to have them.

"Men must make their way in the world," her mother had said gently when Jenny first complained about Sylvester's rackety ways. "Women must help and encourage them, and provide them with a peaceful haven from their daily struggle to make the world a better place."

Jenny, who had been struggling with a darning needle and wool and one of Sylvester's socks, stabbed herself and breathed incredulously, "For this I have left school?"

"Your governess will see that you receive the proper education to provide you with understanding and sympathy for your husband's work and conversation." Her mother's voice was still mild, but she spoke in that firm, sweet manner that would remain unshaken by all argument, like a great stone rising implacably out of buffeting waves, sea life clinging safely to every corner of it. "Besides, women are not strong, as you will find out soon enough. Their bodies are subject to the powerful forces of their natures." She hesitated; Jenny was silent, having heard rumors of the secret lives of women, and wondering if her mother would go into detail. She did, finally, but in such a delicate fashion that Jenny was left totally bewildered. Women were oysters carrying the pearls of life; their husbands opened them and poured into them the water of life, after which the pearls...turned into babies?

Later, after one of the pearls of life had finally irritated her inner oyster enough to draw blood, and she found herself on a daybed hugging a hot water bag, she began to realize what her mother had meant about powerful forces of nature. Sarah, tactfully quiet and kind, put a cup of tea on the table beside her.

"Thank you," Jenny said mournfully. "I think the oysters are clamping themselves shut inside me."

Sarah's solemn expression quivered away; she sat on the daybed beside Jenny. "Oh, did you get the oyster speech, too?"

She had grown amazingly stately overnight, it seemed to Jenny, with her lovely gowns and her fair hair coiled and scalloped like cream on an éclair. Sarah's skin was perfect ivory; her own was blotched and dotted with strange eruptions. Her hair, straight as a horse's tail and so heavy it flopped out of all but the toothiest pins, was neither ruddy chestnut nor true black, but some unromantic shade in between.

Reading Jenny's mind, which she did often, Sarah patted her hands. "Don't fret. You'll grow into yourself. And you have a fine start: your pale gray eyes with that dark hair will become stunning soon enough."

"For what?" Jenny asked intensely, searching her sister's face. The sudden luminousness of her beauty must partially be explained by Mr. Everett Woolidge, who had already spoken to Sarah's father, and was impatiently awaiting Sarah's eighteenth birthday. "Is love only about oysters and the water of life? What exactly was Mama trying to say?"

Sarah's smile had gone; she answered slowly, "I'm not sure yet, myself, though I'm very sure it has nothing to do with oysters."

"When you find out, will you tell me?"

"I promise. I'll take notes as it happens." Still a line tugged at her tranquil brows; she was not seeing Jenny, but the shadow of Mr. Woolidge, doing who knew what to her on her wedding bed. Then she added, reading Jenny's mind again, "There's nothing to fear, Mama says. You just lie still and think of the garden."

"The garden?"

"Something pleasant."

"That's all it took to make Sylvester? She must have been thinking about the plumbing, or boiled cabbage."

Sarah's smile flashed again; she ducked her head, looking guilty for a moment, as though she'd been caught giggling in the schoolroom. "Very likely." She pushed a strand of hair out of Jenny's face. "You should drink your tea; it'll soothe the pain."

Jenny stared up at her, fingers clenched, her whole body clenched, something tight and hot behind her eyes. "I'll miss you," she whispered. "Oh, I will miss you so. Sylvester just talks at me, and Mama—Mama cares only about him and Papa. You are the only one I can laugh with."

"I know." Sarah's voice, too, sounded husky, ragged. "Everett—he is kind and good, and of course ardent. But I've known you all your life. I can say things to you that I could never say to Mama—or even to Everett—" She paused, that faraway look again in her eyes, as though she were trying to see her own future. "I hope he and I will learn to talk to one another...Mama would say it's childish of me to want what I think to be in any way important to him; that's something I must grow out of, when I'm married."

"Talk to me," Jenny begged her. "Anytime. About anything."

Sarah nodded, caressing Jenny's hair again. "I'll send for you."

"Why must he take you so far away? Why?"

"It's only a half day on the train. And very pretty, Farnham is. We'll have long rides together, you and I, and walks, and country fairs. You'll see."

And Jenny did: the village where Mr. Woolidge had inherited his country home was charming, full of centuries-old cottages with thick stone walls, and hairy thatched roofs, and tiny windows set, with no order whatsoever, all anyhow in the walls. The artist, Mr. Ryme, had a summer house there as well. Jenny could see it on a distant knoll from where she sat under the chestnut tree. It was of butter-yellow stone with white trim, and the windows were where you expected them to be. But still it looked old, with its dark, crumbling garden wall, and the ancient twisted apple trees inside, and the wooden gate, open for so long it had grown into the earth. The artist's daughter Alexa was under the tree as well, along with four comely village children and Jenny. The village children with their rough voices and unkempt hair would have horrified Mama. Fortunately she had not come, due to undisclosed circumstances that Jenny suspected had to do with oysters and pearls. Sylvester was away at school; Mr. Ryme would add their faces to the painting later. The governess, Miss Lake, had accompanied Jenny, with some staunch idea of keeping up with her lessons. But in the mellow country air, she had relaxed and grown vague. She sat knitting under a willow, light and shadow dappling her thin, freckled face and angular body as the willow leaves swayed around her in the breeze.

The artist had positioned Jenny's father on one side of the little rocky brook winding through the grass. The wedding guests, mostly portrayed by villagers and friends of the painter, were arranged behind him. The wedding party itself would be painted advancing toward him on the other side of the water. A tiny bridge arching above some picturesque stones and green moss would signify the place where the lovers Cupid and Psyche would become man and wife. Papa wore a long tunic that covered all but one arm, over which a swag of purple was discreetly draped. He looked, with his long gold mustaches and full beard, more like a druid, Jenny thought, than a Grecian nobleman. He was smiling, enjoying himself, his eyes on Sarah as the artist fussed with the lilies in her hands. She wore an ivory robe; Mr. Woolidge, a very hairy Cupid, wore gold with a purple veil over his head. At the foot of the bridge, the artist's younger daughter, golden-haired and plump, just old enough to know how to stand still, carried a basket of violets, from which she would fling a handful of posies onto the bridge to ornament the couple's path.

Finally, the older children were summoned into position behind the pair. Mr. Ryme, having placed them, stood gazing narrowly at them, one finger rasping over his whiskers. He moved his hand finally and spoke.

"A lantern. We must have a lantern."

"Exactly!" Papa exclaimed, enlightened.

"Why, Father?" the artist's daughter Alexa asked, daring to voice the question in Jenny's head. She thought Mr. Ryme would ignore his daughter, or rebuke her for breaking her pose. But he took the question seriously, gazing at all of the children behind the bridal pair.

"Because Cupid made Psyche promise not to look upon him, even after they married. He came to her only at night. Psyche's sisters told her that she must have married some dreadful monster instead of a man. Such things happened routinely, it seems, in antiquity."

"He's visible enough now," one of the village boys commented diffidently, but inarguably, of Mr. Woolidge.

"Yes, he is," Mr. Ryme answered briskly. "We can't very well leave the groom out of his own wedding portrait, can we? That's why he is wearing that veil. He'll hold it out between himself and his bride, and turn his head so that only those viewing the painting will see his face."

"Oh, brilliant," Papa was heard to murmur across the bridge.

"Thank you. But let me continue with the lantern. One night, Psyche lit a lantern to see exactly what she had taken into her marriage bed. She was overjoyed to find the beautiful face of the son of Venus. But— profoundly moved by his godhood, perhaps—she trembled and spilled a drop of hot oil on him, waking him. In sorrow and anger with her for breaking her promise, he vanished out of her life. The lantern among the wedding party will remind the viewer of the rest of Psyche's story."

"What was the rest, Mr. Ryme?" a village girl demanded.

"She was forced to face her mother-in-law," Alexa answered instead, "who made Psyche complete various impossible tasks, including a trip to the Underworld, before the couple were united again. Isn't that right, Father?"

"Very good, Alexa," Mr. Ryme said, smiling at her. Jenny's eyes widened. She knew the tale as well as anyone, but if she had spoken, Papa would have scolded her for showing off her knowledge. And here was Alexa, with her curly red-gold hair and green eyes, not only lovely, but encouraged to reveal her education. Mr. Ryme held up his hand before anyone else could speak, his eyes, leaf green as his daughter's beneath his dark, shaggy brows, moving over them again.

"Who..." he murmured. "Ah. Of course, Jenny must hold it. Why you, Jenny?"

Behind him, Papa, prepared to answer, closed his mouth, composed his expression. Jenny gazed at Mr. Ryme, gathering courage, and answered finally, shyly, "Because I am the bride's sister. And I'm part of Psyche's story, as well, like the lantern."

"Good!" Mr. Ryme exclaimed. His daughter caught Jenny's eyes, smiled, and Jenny felt herself flush richly. The artist shifted her to the forefront of the scene and crooked her arm at her waist. "Pretend this is your lantern," he said, handing her a tin cup that smelled strongly of linseed oil from his paint box. "I'm sure there's something more appropriate in my studio. For now, I just need to sketch you all in position." He gestured to the dozen or so villagers and friends behind Mr. Newland. "Poses, please, everyone. Try to keep still. This won't take as long as you might think. When I've gotten you all down where I want you, we'll have a rest and explore the contents of the picnic baskets Mr. Woolidge and Mr. Newland so thoughtfully provided. I'll work with small groups after we eat; the rest of you can relax unless I need you, but don't vanish. Remember that you are all invited to supper at my cottage at the end of the day."

Jenny spent her breaks under the willow tree, practicing historical dates and French irregular verbs with Miss Lake, who seemed to have been recalled to her duties by the references to the classics. At the end of the day, Jenny was more than ready for the slow walk through the meadows in the long, tranquil dusk to the artist's cottage. There, everyone changed into their proper clothes, and partook of the hot meat pastries, bread and cheese and cold beef, fresh milk, ale, and great fruit-and-cream tarts arrayed on the long tables set up in the artist's garden.

Jenny took a place at the table with Sarah and Mr. Woolidge. Across from them sat Papa and Mr. Ryme, working through laden plates and frothy cups of ale.

"An energetic business, painting," Papa commented approvingly. "I hadn't realized how much wildlife is involved."

"It's always more challenging, working out of doors, and with large groups. It went very well today, I thought."

Jenny looked at the artist, a question hovering inside her. At home, she was expected to eat her meals silently and gracefully, speaking only when asked, and then as simply as possible. But her question wasn't simple; she barely knew how to phrase it. And this was more like a picnic, informal and friendly, everyone talking at once, and half the gathering sitting on the grass.

"Mr. Ryme," she said impulsively, "I have a question."

Her father stared at her with surprise. "Jenny," he chided, "you interrupted Mr. Ryme."

She blushed, mortified. "I'm so sorry—"

"It must be important, then," Mr. Ryme said gently. "What is it?"

"Psyche's sisters—when they told her she must have wedded a monster..." Her voice trailed. Papa was blinking at her. Mr. Ryme only nodded encouragingly. "Wouldn't she have known if that were so? Even in the dark, if something less than human were in bed with her—couldn't she tell? Without a lantern?"

She heard Mr. Woolidge cough on his beer, felt Sarah's quick tremor of emotion.

"Jenny," Papa said decisively, "that is a subject more fit for the schoolroom than the dinner table, and hardly suitable even there. I'm surprised you should have such thoughts, let alone express them."

"It is an interesting question, though," Mr. Ryme said quite seriously. "Don't you think? It goes to the heart of the story, which is not about whether Psyche married a monster—and, I think, Jenny is correct in assuming that she would have soon realized it—but about a broken promise. A betrayal of love. Don't you think so, Mr. Newland?"

But his eyes remained on Jenny as he diverted the conversation away from her; they smiled faintly, kindly. Papa began a lengthy answer, citing sources. Jenny felt Sarah's fingers close on her hand.

"I was wondering that, myself," she breathed.

Mr. Woolidge overheard.

"What?" he queried softly. "If you will find a monster in your wedding bed?"

"No, of course not," Sarah said with another tremor—of laughter, or surprise, or fear, Jenny couldn't tell. "What Jenny asked. Why Psyche could not tell, even in the dark, if her husband was not human."

"I assure you, you will find me entirely human," Mr. Woolidge promised. "You will not have to guess."

"I'm sure I won't," Sarah answered faintly.

Mr. Woolidge took a great bite out of his meat pie, his eyes on Sarah as he chewed. Jenny, disregarded, rose and slipped away from her father's critical eyes. She glimpsed Miss Lake watching her from the next table, beginning to gesture, but Jenny pretended not to see. Wandering through the apple trees with a meat pie in her hand, free to explore her own thoughts, she came across the artist's daughter under a tree with one of the village boys.

Jenny stopped uncertainly. Mama would have considered the boy unsuitable company, even for an artist's daughter, and would have instructed Jenny to greet them kindly and politely as she moved away. But she didn't move, and Alexa waved to her.

"Come and sit with us. Will's been telling me country stories."

Jenny glanced around; Miss Lake was safely hidden behind the apple leaves. She edged under the tree and sat, looking curiously at Will.

Something about him reminded her of a bird. He was very thin, with flighty golden hair and long, fine bones too near the surface of his skin. His eyes looked golden, like his hair. They seemed secretive, looking back at her, but not showing what they thought. He was perhaps her age, she guessed, though something subtle in his expression made him seem older.

He was chewing an apple from the tree; a napkin with crumbs of bread and cheese on it lay near him on the grass. Politely, he swallowed his bite and waited for Jenny to speak to him first. Jenny glanced questioningly at Alexa, whose own mouth was full.

She said finally, tentatively, "Country tales?"

"It was the lantern, miss." His voice was deep yet soft, with a faint country burr in it, like a bee buzzing in his throat, that was not unpleasant. "It reminded me of Jack."

"Jack?"

"O'Lantern. He carries a light across the marshes at night and teases you into following it, thinking it will lead you to fairyland, or treasure, or just safely across the ground. Then he puts the light out, and there you are, stranded in the dark in the middle of a marsh. Some call it elf fire, or fox fire."

"Or—?" Alexa prompted, with a sudden, teasing smile. The golden eyes slid to her, answering the smile.

"Will," he said. "Will o' the Wisp."

He bit into the apple again; Jenny sat motionless, listening to the crisp, solid crunch, almost tasting the sweet, cool juices. But these apples were half-wild, her eye told her, misshapen and probably wormy; you shouldn't just pick them out of the long grass or off the branch and eat them...

"My father painted a picture of us following the marsh fire," Alexa said. "Will held a lantern in the dark; I was with him as his sister. My father called the painting *Jack O'Lantern.*"

"What were you doing in the dark?" Jenny asked fuzzily, trying to untangle the real from the story.

"My father told us we were poor children, sent out to cut peat for a fire on a cruel winter's dusk. Dark came too fast; we got lost, and followed the Jack O'Lantern sprite, thinking it was someone who knew the path back."

"And what happened?"

Alexa shrugged slightly. "That's the thing about paintings. They only show you one moment of the tale; you have to guess at the rest of it. Do you want to see it? My father asked me to find a lantern for you in his studio; he won't mind if you come with me."

Jenny saw Miss Lake drifting about with a plate at the far end of the garden, glancing here and there, most likely for her charge. She stopped to speak to Sarah. Jenny swallowed the last of her meat pie.

"Yes," she said quickly. "I'd like that." It sounded wild and romantic, visiting an artist's studio, a place where paint turned into flame, and flame into the magic of fairyland. It was, her mother would have said, no place for a well-brought-up young girl, who might chance upon the disreputable, unsavory things that went on between artists and their models. Jenny couldn't imagine the distinguished Mr. Ryme doing unsavory things in his studio. But perhaps she could catch a glimpse there of what nebulous goings-on her mother was talking about when she said the word.

"You come, too, Will," Alexa added to him. "You don't often get a chance to see it."

"Is there a back door?" Jenny asked, her eye on Miss Lake, and Alexa flung her a mischievous glance.

"There is, indeed. Come this way."

They went around the apple trees, away from the noisy tables, where lanterns and torches, lit against insects and the dark, illumined faces against the shadowy nightfall, making even the villagers look mysterious, unpredictable. Alexa, carrying a candle, led them up a back staircase in the house. Jenny kept slowing to examine paintings hung along the stairs. In the flickering light, they were too vague to be seen: faces that looked not quite human, risings of stone that might have been high craggy peaks, or the ruined towers of an ancient castle.

Will stopped beside one of the small, ambiguous landscapes. "That's

Perdu Castle," he said. He sounded surprised. "On the other side of the marshes. There's stories about it, too: that it shifts around and you never find it if you're looking for it, only if you're not."

"Is that true?" Jenny demanded.

"True as elf fire," he answered gravely, looking at her out of his still eyes in a way that was neither familiar nor rude. As though, Jenny thought, he were simply interested in what she might be thinking. He was nicer than Sylvester, she realized suddenly, for all his dirty fingernails and patched trousers.

"When you saw it, were you looking for it?"

"Bit of both," he admitted. "I was pretending not to while I searched for it. But I was surprised when I found it. I wonder if Mr. Ryme knew it was there before he painted it."

"Of course he did," Alexa said with a laugh. "Great heaps of stone don't shift themselves around; it's people who get lost. My father paints romantic visions, but there's nothing romantic about carrying a paint box for miles, or having to swat flies all afternoon while you search. He'd want to know exactly where he was going."

She opened a door at the top of the stairs, lighting more candles and a couple of lamps as Jenny and Will entered. Paintings leaped into light everywhere in the room, sitting on easels, hanging in frames, leaning in unframed stacks against the walls. The studio took up the entire top floor of the house; windows overlooked meadow, marsh, the smudges of distant trees, the village disappearing into night. Richly colored carpets lay underfoot; odd costumes and wraps hung on hooks and coatracks. A peculiar collection of things littered shelves along the walls: seashells, hats, boxes, a scepter, crowns of tinsel and gold leaf, chunks of crystals, shoe buckles, necklaces, swords, pieces of armor, ribbons, a gilded bit and bridle. From among this jumble, Alexa produced a lamp and studied it doubtfully. One end was pointed, the other scrolled into a handle. Gleaming brass with colorful lozenges of enamel decorated the sides. It looked, Jenny thought, like the lamp Aladdin might have rubbed to summon the genie within. Alexa put it back, rummaged farther along the shelves.

Will caught Jenny's eye then, gazing silently at a painting propped against the wall. She joined him, and saw his face in the painting, peering anxiously into a wild darkness dimly lit by the lantern in his hand. Alexa, a lock of red hair blowing out of the threadbare shawl over her head, stood very close to him, pointing toward the faint light across murky ground and windblown grasses. Her face, pinched and worried, seemed to belong more to a ghostly twin of the lovely, confident, easily smiling girl searching for a lamp behind them.

Something flashed above the painting. Jenny raised her eyes to the open window, saw the pale light in the dense twilight beyond the house and gardens. Someone out there, she thought curiously. The light went out, and her breath caught. She stepped around the painting, stuck her head out the window.

"Did you see that?"

"What?" Alexa asked absently.

"That light. Just like the one in the painting..."

She felt Will close beside her, staring out, heard his breath slowly loosed. Behind them, Alexa murmured, "Oh, here it is... A plain clay lantern Psyche might have used; no magic in this one. What are you looking at?"

"Jenny!"

She started, bumped her head on the window frame. Miss Lake stood below, staring up at them. Will drew back quickly; Jenny sighed.

"Yes, Miss Lake?"

"What are you doing up there?"

"I'm—"

"Come down, please; don't make me shout."

"Yes, Miss Lake. I'm helping Alexa. I'll come down in a moment."

"Surely you're not in Mr. Ryme's studio! And was that one of the village boys up there with you?"

Mr. Ryme appeared then, glanced up at Jenny, and said something apparently soothing to Miss Lake, who put a hand to her cheek and gave a faint laugh. Jenny wondered if he'd offered to paint her. They strolled away together. Jenny pushed back out the window, and there it was again, stronger this time in the swiftly gathering dark: a pulse of greeny-pale light that shimmered, wavered, almost went out, pulsed strong again.

"Oh..."

"What is it?" Alexa demanded beside her, then went silent; she didn't even breathe.

Behind them, Will said softly, briefly, "Jack O'Lantern."

"Oh," Jenny said again, sucking air into her lungs, along with twilight, and the scents of marsh and grass. She spun abruptly. "Let's follow it! I want to see it!"

"But, Jenny," Alexa protested, "it's not real. I mean it's real, but it's only—oh, how did my father put it? The spontaneous combustion of decayed vegetation."

"What?"

"Exploding grass."

Jenny stared at her. "That's the most ridiculous thing I've ever heard."

"It is, a bit, when you think about it," Alexa admitted.

"He obviously told you a tale to make you stay out of the marshes." Her eyes went to the window, where the frail elfin light danced in the night. "I have to go," she whispered. "This may be my only chance in life to see real magic before I must become what Mama and Miss Lake and Papa think I should be..."

She started for the door, heard Will say quickly, "She can't go alone."

"Oh, all right," Alexa said. Her cool voice sounded tense, as though even she, her father's bright and rational daughter who could see beneath the paint, had gotten swept up in Jenny's excitement. "Will, take that lantern—"

Will put a candle in an old iron lantern; Jenny was out the door before he finished lighting it. "Hurry!" she pleaded, taking the stairs in an unladylike clatter.

"Wait for us!" Alexa cried. "Jenny! They'll see you!"

That stopped her at the bottom of the stairs. Alexa moved past her toward the apple trees; Will followed, trying to hide the light with his vest. As they snuck through the trees, away from the tables, Jenny heard somebody play a pipe, someone else begin a song. Then Alexa led them through a gap in the wall, over a crumbled litter of stones, and they were out in the warm, restless, redolent dark.

The light still beckoned across the night, now vague, hardly visible, now glowing steadily, marking one certain point in the shifting world. They ran, the lantern Will carried showing them tangled tussocks of grass on a flat ground that swept changelessly around them, except for a silvery murk now and then where water pooled. Jenny, her eyes on the pale fire, felt wind at her back, pushing, tumbling over her, racing ahead. Above them, cloud kept chasing the sliver of moon, could never quite catch it.

"Hurry—" Jenny panted. The light seemed closer now, brilliant, constantly reshaped by the wind. "I think we're almost there—"

"Oh, what is it?" Alexa cried. "What can it be? It can't be—Can it? Be real?"

"Real exploding grass, you mean?" Will wondered. The lantern handle creaked as it bounced in his hold. "Or real magic?"

"Real magic," Alexa gasped, and came down hard with one foot into a pool. Water exploded into a rain of light, streaking the air; she laughed. Jenny, turning, felt warm drops fall, bright as moon tears on her face.

She laughed, too, at the ephemeral magic that wasn't, or was it? Then something happened to the lantern; its light came from a crazy angle on a tussock. She felt her shoulders seized. Something warm came down over her mouth. Lips, she realized dimly, pulling at her mouth, drinking out of her. A taste like grass and apple. She pushed back at it, recognizing the apple, wanting a bigger bite. And in that moment, it was gone, leaving her wanting.

She heard a splash, a thump, a cry from Alexa. Then she saw the light burning in Will's hand, not the lantern, but a strange, silvery glow that his eyes mirrored just before he laughed and vanished.

Jenny stood blinking at Alexa, who was sitting open-mouthed in a pool of water. Her eyes sought Jenny's. Beyond that, neither moved; they could only stare at each other, stunned.

Alexa said finally, a trifle sourly, "Will."

Jenny moved to help her up. Alexa's face changed, then; she laughed suddenly, breathlessly, and so did Jenny, feeling the silvery glow of magic in her heart, well worth the kiss snatched by the passing Will o' the Wisp.

They returned to find the villagers making their farewells to Mr. Ryme. Mr. Woolidge's carriage had drawn up to the gate, come to take Sarah and Jenny, Papa and Miss Lake to his house.

"There you are!" Sarah exclaimed when she saw Jenny. Alexa, staying in the shadows, edged around them quickly toward the house. "Where have you been?"

"Nowhere. Trying to catch a Will o' the Wisp."

Her father chuckled at her foolishness, said pedantically, "Nothing more, my dear, than the spontaneous combustion—"

"Of decayed grass. I know." She added to Mr. Ryme, "You'll have one less face to paint in the wedding party. Will won't be coming back."

"Why not?" he asked, surprised. His painter's eyes took in her expression, maybe the lantern glow in her eyes. He started to speak, stopped, said, "Will—" stopped again. He turned abruptly, calling, "Alexa?"

"She's in the house," Jenny told him. "She slipped in a pool."

"Oh, heavens, child," Miss Lake grumbled. "It's a wonder you didn't lose yourselves out there in the marsh."

"It is, indeed, a wonder," Jenny agreed.

She stepped into the carriage, sat close to Sarah, whose chilly fingers sought her hand and held it tightly, even as she turned toward the sound of Mr. Woolidge's voice raised in some solicitous question.

KNIGHT OF THE WELL

THE KNIGHTS OF THE WELL came last in the royal procession into Luminum. Their barge was pale green and ivory, the colors of the river; their standard was blue and stone gray, for water and for well. Their surcoats were cloth of gold, their cloaks white for foam, for the moon that drove the waters, bid them come and go. Their hoods were black for the secret dark from which the well bubbled out of the earth, also for humility. Their faces were all but invisible. The city folk crowding the banks of the Halcyon River to watch the parade of brightly painted boats carrying Kayne, King of Obelos, and his court to the summer palace in Luminum, cheered and flung flowers at the still, mysterious figures in the last barge. The procession heralded both the beginning of summer and the ritual, old as Luminum, which would honor and placate the waters of the world, most particularly the waters of the Kingdom of Obelos.

The dozen knights had been standing for hours, it seemed, though the procession had shifted from horses and wagons to boats just outside the city. No one dared move. The small, colorful barge was balanced to a breath, five men on either side plying their gilded oars, the oar master on his narrow perch keeping their time with a brass gong and hammer. The knights were supposed, by the city folk, to be contemplating their awesome function. Most were indeed contemplating water: the last one who had moved impulsively, at the nip of a bloodthirsty insect, had nearly thrown them all into it.

Mingling with the flow of water, the golden drip of sound from the gong, the drift of voices from the other barges, the distant roil of shouts, cheers, scraps of music from the crowds was the murmur of memory the knights passed to one another, trying, as they always did during this part of the journey, to pinpoint why the water-mage had chosen them.

"One of my ancestors was found floating among the reeds in a shallow pond just after she had given birth to a child with webs between its fingers... Family lore has it she fell in love with a water sprite."

"My grandmother flung herself over a cliff into the sea. Her body was never found, though she left her shoes at the place where she jumped. There were prints in the earth beside them that were not quite human."

"There is a lake on our land in south Obelos said to be inhabited by water creatures of a most extraordinary beauty..."

Garner Slade, who had been a knight of the king's for three years, and a Knight of the Well since the previous year, recognized most of the hushed voices that came from under the lowered hoods. Not all of the men were knights of the court; a few he only saw at this time of the year: those who left their lands and families at the mage's bidding. The young man who spoke next, Garner recognized as one of them only because he bore the standard that fluttered over their heads.

"I drink water," he said a trifle hollowly. "Sometimes I wash. Sometimes I just stand in a good rain instead. I don't know how to swim. I don't even like water. I'm afraid of it. I'd trade this standard for a beer in a moment. So why would the mage have picked me?"

He had a moment's sympathy. Summer was no further away than a change of expression on the moon's face, a richer hue in the gold that fell freely out of the blue. Even now, heat clung to them as heavily as cloth, beading their faces with the sweat that lured the tiny, malignant pests.

Then came the inevitable: "Clear your mind of such distractions or we will fail in our task. Contemplate water; allow it to flow into your thoughts, your blood. You will begin to know it instead of fear it. Take care what you say in the same breath as the word, for water will hear; you will offend."

And the crops, Garner thought, will wither on the vine. The sea will open the gates, plunder the ships in the harbor. He blinked salt out of his eyes and contemplated the floating market, the swift, narrow boats drawn close to the banks, decked with flowers and bright ribbons in welcome. The procession was passing through the heart of the city. Ancient stone river houses, interspersed with equally ancient thatched cottages whose garden walls were moldy with bygone floods, offered intervals of shadow cast by the sudden jut of high roofs. Then light, as the rooftops dropped. Then again the welcoming shadow.

Garner's cousin, who had been a Knight of the Well longer than any of them, and who liked the sound of his voice, was still proffering the benefits of his experience. "Our minds must be as waters flowing into one another, pellucid and free of the twigs and sodden leaves of earth. The debris of language. Water speaks; we must listen. Water hears; we must beware."

"I can't hear," Garner murmured finally.

"What?"

"Over the debris of language. A word the river is saying."

Edord paused. The pause was weighted with significance. Garner heard the standard-bearer's breath quiver with suppressed laughter. The oar master, reprovingly, struck the gong a sharp, meaningful stroke. Edord began another word. From the bridge arching across the river just ahead, someone tossed a handful of flowers into the boat.

Garner looked up. For that moment, his face was visible to the world: his dark hair and eyes, his restless, brooding, quizzical expression. He revealed himself as human within the hood, within the solemnity of his status. The young woman who had thrown the flowers flashed a surprised grin at him. The standard-bearer gave a sneeze of laughter, bending to conceal it. The barge rocked; the gong gave a hiccup between beats. For a moment oars flailed; the knights froze. The shadow of the bridge fell mercifully over them.

Then they slid again into light, water lapping with little, agitated river-words against the boat. Garner, standing stolidly, could feel it under the soles of his boots: the thin, thin boundary between wood and water, between dry and wet, between profundity and disgrace.

Even the standard-bearer was silent, the long pennant whipping reproofs into the air, which was stirring suddenly as the river quickened to meet the sea.

Edord opened his mouth.

Garner tried to shut him out, his fair-haired, handsome, humorless cousin with his irritatingly reedy voice that made Garner want to swat at it, as though it had wings and would bite. Edord was the oldest of the twelve, and entirely confident of the mage's choice of him to help balance the powerful, mysterious forces of earth and water. Her choices were varied; at times they seemed wildly arbitrary. Garner, for instance, would not have chosen himself. Despite his good intentions, he was more prone to muddying the waters than placating them. The standard-bearer, affected by nerves and fearful of water, seemed inexplicable. But the mage's ancient, sunken eye, weirdly nacreous, had seen in them both something she needed.

The blunt, craggy walls of the castle guarding the jut of land where the river met the sea revealed themselves above the houses, inns and warehouses along the tangle of city streets. The pattern of the oldest streets in Luminum resembled a wad of thread that had been shoved into a pocket and forgotten. Some said the early roads followed animal tracks, others that their loops and switchbacks were an attempt to confuse the floodwaters, the raging winter tides. Across the Halcyon, where land was diked and drained of marsh water, the younger city was flat as an anvil. Sea walls, gates and sluices, canals and locks, added over the centuries, had tamed much of the flow, trained it into fields, and, more recently, into pipes. But even on the most tranquil of nights, no one completely trusted water not to possess a will of its own. The impulses, secrets, history, the sprites and elementals who swelled beneath its surface, were understood most completely by the mage, who spoke all the languages of water. The rulers of Obelos would sooner have left a sea gate open to a wild winter tempest than neglect the Ritual of the Well.

There was a flourish of brass as the trumpeters in the high walls saluted the king. Edord fell mercifully silent. The castle walls were shrugging out of the city, growing sheer, stark against the blue sky and the sea. Garner could see the stone sea walls curving along the path of the river to front the tide. Tide was turning now, tugging the boats along with it. Ahead, the king's barge began to angle toward the royal dock, along which so many banners and standards and pennants flew that, in a better wind, they might have lifted the dock into the air.

The oar master spoke, slowing the ritual barge until it wallowed, waiting for those ahead to disembark. It took a while. The canopied stairway up the bank to the back of the castle was crowded with courtiers. The oarsmen plied oars expertly, pushing against the tide, then letting the boat creep a little closer as a barge pulled away. They emptied quickly; no one lingered on the dock after the long journey from the west, and all baggage had been left on the wagons coming down the coast road to the castle. Garner's thoughts drifted. He stared at the flowers at his feet, not daring to look up, knowing that his eyes would search for a phantasm, a dream. Petals the color of bright new blood reflected a sudden bloom of pain in his heart. She could have written, he thought. She could have sent word to him privately at the king's winter court, instead of word traveling carelessly from anyone to anyone before it reached him. He hadn't realized, until then, that in her eyes he was just anyone as well. In spite of himself, he raised his head slightly, looked up from under his hood to search the knots of courtiers along the stairs. The scallops along the windblown canopy hid too many faces; he could not find her. He lowered his eyes, found her face again in memory.

Much his return to the summer court mattered to her now, she with her betrothed with his great barking brass horn that bayed so deep it could have drawn whales to the surface to mate with it. She with her head full of water pipes and fountains. No room now for one who had loved her since she was six. Garner made an incautious, despairing movement. The barge shivered; an oar caught a crab, splashed.

"Peace," the oar master pleaded. "Peace. We're nearly there."

"Peace," Edord echoed abruptly, jarringly, "is what we must impress upon the waters of Obelos with our minds, our breath, the rhythms of our hearts. From us it will learn; from us it will—"

"Oh, give it a rest," Garner shouted, exasperated. Somehow he was facing his cousin, not an easy thing to do in a boat crammed with men. Turning, he had shouldered a couple off-balance; they reeled into others; the barge rocked one way and then the other. And then the great crowds on both sides of the river watched with astonishment as the Knights of the Well staggered out of the sides of their barge and tried to walk on water. The wallowing barge scattered its oars, then its oarsmen. The oar master, clutching his gong, fell in last and disappeared entirely as the barge flipped over on top of him.

Garner, descending among the riverweeds, thought he should just settle on the bottom with the snails and stay there. But someone was descending faster than he was within the streaming thicket of weeds. The standard-bearer, he thought in horror, and kicked hard upriver toward him, losing both his boots to the tide. A school of tiny fish flashed past his eyes; it was suddenly hard to see. What he thought was a cloak seemed darker, a cloudy gray shadow fading into the green. He pushed downward. Someone else's falling boot careened off his shoulder. The cloak, billowing and flapping in the current like a live thing, seemed empty as he grew closer, and it began to rise. So did he, with relief, tearing the clinging water weeds away as he pulled toward the light and air and churning bodies above him, beginning to hear his heartbeat in the surging wash of his blood.

He saw the cloak again, suspended in a long, motionless shaft of light. Still it seemed empty, his eyes told him as he passed it. It twisted slowly among the weeds, the hood turning, turning, until its limp emptiness, shaped by the current, opened to Garner's transfixed gaze.

He saw the face in it.

Breath bubbled out of him. He caught himself desperately before he took in water, felt the aching impulse all through his body. Still he hung there, treading water to keep from beginning the long, slow, irrevocable slide, unable to look away from the strange eyes, shell-white and expressionless in a shifting face as green as waterweed.

A struggling mass of boot and wool and limbs came between them. Garner, started again, lost the last of his breath. Then he recognized the standard-bearer, trailing bubbles and looking terrified. Garner reached out, grabbed his hood and drove them both, with a couple of furious kicks, to the surface. Coming up under the overturned barge, he bumped his head on the edge of the oar master's seat.

He held onto it, heaving for breath. The standard-bearer grabbed hold of an oarsman's plank. Garner, his vision clearing, found himself face to face with the indignant oar master. They were surrounded by the swirling cloaks and churning legs of men outside clinging to the bottom of the barge. The weltering tide pulling them toward the sea, the constantly shifting weight on the barge bottom, made breathing difficult for those caught under it. The oar master, gripping his gong with one hand and an oarlock with the other, looked as though he wanted to shove Garner back under the water himself.

"What," he barked, "possessed the mage to choose you?"

Someone outside hoisted himself higher up the barge bottom; the plank the standard-bearer clung to dipped abruptly. He inhaled water, coughing; flailing again, he seized Garner's hair, pushed him briefly down.

Garner hauled them both up again, answered between his teeth, "My cousin would say that I exemplify the chaotic aspect of water."

"Which it is your duty to guard us against!"

"Then the mage must have made a mistake."

"Impossible!" the oar master snapped unreasonably.

Garner rolled an eye at him, still grappling with the standard-bearer, whose sodden hood had slid over his eyes, blinding him. "Then she didn't," he said succinctly. He saw a pair of legs kick away from the side of the barge, and then another. The empty barges must have come to their rescue, he realized with relief, and added, "I might be your greatest hope."

The oar master snorted, inhaled a sudden splash as someone tried to turn the barge over and failed.

"Let go," Garner urged the standard-bearer, who had a death grip with one hand on an oarlock and with the other on Garner's hair. "They've come to help us."

The young man shook his blind head mutely, emphatically.

"Just leave him," the oar master suggested, and vanished under the side of the barge.

Garner treaded water and waited, wondering if the oar master would bother sending anyone to rescue the pair of them.

A little later, as he sat dripping in a fishing boat that had come out to help with the rescue, he saw Damaris finally, on the dock, talking to his sodden cousin, who was gesticulating forcefully. Green, she was wearing, the soft pale green of the waterweed dangling over Edord's shoulder. He would be making very clear to her exactly who had caused the Knights of the Well to become one with the river, of that Garner had no doubt. He sighed noiselessly, regretting the absurd incident, except for dunking Edord. Then, beneath the weave and break of light on the water, he saw the strange, rippling underwater face again, the pale eyes alone unmoved by currents, looking back at him within the waterweeds.

He blinked. The face or the memory of it vanished.

One of the water sprites, he guessed, drawn by the odd commotion in the river. The mage would know its name. He raised his eyes from the water again, and saw Damaris and Edord turned away from him, walking up the steps to the palace together. He watched that green until it disappeared within the walls.

In the small, private chamber allotted to him by his rank as knight both of the king and of the Well, he found his baggage and his young squire Inis, who had been attached to him, presumably to learn from Garner's knightly example and experience. Sweet-tempered and capable, he was too polite to comment on Garner's dripping garments, simply helped him out of them and handed him dry clothes. He looked more doubtfully at Garner's bare feet. Garner's family could trace its lineage, in the northern mountains, back past the naming of Obelos. But what with one thing and another, including some disastrous battles with a reigning monarch or two, whom Garner's ancestors considered usurpers, the family had lost its wealth over a century ago.

"Your boots, sir?"

"Water-logged," Garner answered tersely. "The river ate them."

"Your best boots?"

"Yes."

"Well," Inis said, rummaging. "There's your shoes in here somewhere. Ah, and here's your old patched pair of boots, right under them."

Someone pounded at the door.

It was not what Garner expected: his annoyed cousin, or worse, a summons from the king. It was the impossible, what he would have chosen if he had a say in the various possibilities knocking on his door. It was a request from the Minister of Water for his immediate presence.

Lady Damaris Ambre.

Dazed, he put on the boots Inis handed him and followed the messenger.

The minister was in her official chamber, a lofty corner room just beneath the battlement walls. The side casements overlooked the vast gardens behind the castle, the cobbled path leading down the back of the hill to the city below, with its eccentric tangle of streets cautiously edging closer and closer to the river where it curved around the sudden upthrust of land. From the adjacent wall, the view was of the harbor, the sea walls, the immense gates that protected the inner harbor, the brilliant, unending sea. An enormous table filled most of the room, covered with papers with seals and ribbons dangling from them, letters, lists, meticulous drawings of water projects, maps, schedules, sketches of everything from plumbing pipes to gargoyle-headed water taps. A tray holding pitchers of wine and water and cups stood swamped in the clutter like a drowning island.

Damaris had thrown a black work-robe over her gown; its sleeves were shiny with ink stains. The long, white gold coil of braid at her neck was beginning to sag, too heavy, too silken for restraints. Leaning over some paperwork on the table, she looked up as Garner entered. The sudden flash of green, the color of river moss, under her heavy, hooded eyelids and pale brows, took his breath away.

She gazed at him a moment, her ivory, broad-boned face the way he remembered it from childhood, open, curious, just beginning to smile. Then she remembered what he was doing there, and the smile vanished. She straightened to her full height, nearly as tall as he, slender and so supple her bones seemed made of kelp.

"Garner," she said in her deep, lovely voice that cut easily through any flow of water or words, "your cousin told me you nearly sank the ritual barge."

"I was told by rumor," he answered recklessly, "that you were betrothed."

"And that has what to do with half-a-dozen gilded oars that went sailing out to sea, and which must be replaced before the ceremony of the fountain?"

"Fountain?" he echoed bewilderedly, wondering how she could be thinking of such mundane details. "What fountain? Of course I didn't mean to overturn the barge."

"Then why did you?"

"I was provoked—"

She held up a hand before he could go on; helplessly he watched a familiar dimple deepen in her cheek as her lips compressed, then quickly vanish. "Never mind. I don't need to know. The water-mage wants to see you. You can explain to her."

Heat surged through him, then, as he remembered the precise moment. His mouth tightened; his eyes went to the sea, where a gull as white as Damaris's brows angled over the dark blue water.

"I was looking for you," he said bluntly, and felt her go abruptly still. "You drew my eyes. You always did. Since I first saw you coming so carefully down those same steps when you were a child, and so was I, come downriver to court in my uncle's company, just docking where you were about to step. You wore green that day, too, and your hair was in the same braid. We met there on that dock. Ever since, I have looked for you there. I was looking today, though I have no right." He looked at her finally, then, found her face as stiff, her eyes as distant, as he expected. "My cousin was lecturing. I lost my temper, and unbalanced the boat. For that, I'm sorry. Is this what I must tell the mage?"

Color flushed over her, swiftly and evenly, from collarbone to brow. "That it was my fault?" she asked with some asperity. "Because I forgot—No, because I didn't know how to tell you?"

"No. Of course not. Let's blame Edord."

"I don't understand. What has Edord to do with this?"

"He opened his mouth," Garner said dourly, "at the wrong time."

She studied him a moment, a line as fine as gossamer above her brows. "I love Lord Felden." Her voice had softened; her eyes shifted away from him briefly. "I discovered that he loves me, too. His music has always enchanted me. We have much in common."

"His horn and your pipes?"

She met his eyes again. "You and I have been friends for many years. Can we keep it that way? Or will you swamp boats every time you pass that dock?" He couldn't answer. The unfamiliar secrets within the green, the fine, clean bones beginning to surface in her face since he last saw her, rendered him wordless. She made a sudden, exasperated gesture, trying to brush away his gaze. "Stop that."

"What?"

"Stop looking at me like that. Just stop looking at me. Garner, just go away."

"Why," he asked her with simple pain, "could you not love me like that?"

She swallowed, whispered, "I don't know. I don't know. Maybe—you were too much my friend. My brother. Maybe nothing more or less than that."

"Damaris—"

"No," she told him firmly. "Go. The mage is waiting for you."

"How much of this do I tell her?"

She shook her head slightly, picking up a piece of chalk, worrying it through her long fingers. She didn't look at him again.

"I think she must already know. She sent for you through me. Now I understand why. Whatever she wants with you, it won't be about the mistakes and mysteries and messiness of love, but about the waters of Obelos. Go and find out."

So he did, feeling as shaken as if he had been bellowed at by the king.

Someone opened the door. Damaris, staring blindly at the chalk in her fingers and contemplating the messiness and mysteries, flashed a wide, incredulous stare at it. But it wasn't Garner back again with his obstinate, tormented eyes to demand impossible explanations from her. It was a stranger, gestured in by a footman.

"Master Tabbart Ainsley, Minister," he murmured.

"Yes?"

"The composer from Sucia."

She blinked. "Why didn't you take him to Lord Felden?"

"I couldn't find the musicians, my lady," the man explained apologetically. "Everything is chaos with the king's arrival. Master Ainsley said he wrote some water music, so I brought him to you."

Speechless, Damaris gazed at the composer, who looked miserably back at her. His face, framed by windblown chestnut hair, was colorless as curds; he swayed a little under the weight of her regard.

"You are welcome," she assured him hastily. "Please. Sit down."

"Thank you," he said faintly, and the footman closed the door. Master Ainsley crept into the nearest seat, which was her drafting stool, and dropped his face into his hands. Damaris, alarmed, poured a hefty cup of wine, brought it to him.

"Are you ill, Master Ainsley?"

He lifted one hand, eyed the wine glumly, covered his eye again. "I could be cheerfully dead."

"Ah," Damaris said, enlightened.

"In Sucia, I was dragged up a canal in a barge. And then floated down a river along with some goats and chickens and a great many noisy children. When we finally reached the ocean I thought, with all that blue space, it would be peaceful."

"But no?"

"But yes." He came out from behind his hands finally, and winced at the sight of the sea in the window. "But how could I enjoy it? The ship tossed me this way, threw me that; my bed fell down; my dinner came up. I was never so happy to see land. Your port looks so calm. It barely breathes."

"We struggle for that," Damaris told him a trifle grimly. "That's why we celebrate our victories so lavishly. And why you're here."

The young man reached for the wine, took a cautious sip. The damp fungal sheen on his face brightened to a healthier shade of white. He looked slight but muscular within his untidy traveler's garb; his eyes, going seaward again, had a blue-green hue much like it.

"Look at it," he said bitterly, nodding toward the spiky forest of masts rising over waters separated and calmed by sea gates and walls. "Somewhere among those stripped tree trunks is my torment. Now they hardly move. Like ships in a painting."

"Would you like to rest awhile?" Damaris asked him with sympathy. "Lord Felden is one of the musicians, as well as the director of the court orchestra which is to play your music. I'll find him; he'll know where you'll be lodged."

He smiled at her, a fleeting but genuine effort that brought even more color into his face. "If I'm not needed, I think I would like a walk first. I've been so confined, these past days. Perhaps you could direct me to the object of your celebration? I would like to be sure that my music is suitable. I've only seen and heard this wonderful fountain in my imagination. And you know how different they are, all the voices of water."

She found herself smiling back at him, and trying to remember what Beale had said about his music. She made a sudden decision, removed her work-robe. "I'll take you there. I want to be sure it will be finished in time, that there are no unexpected problems. I'm afraid you must continue to imagine the sound of it, since the water won't begin to flow until the day of the celebration. Nor has it been seen except by invitation. It's been shrouded in mystery for weeks."

The brisk walk through the royal gardens and out the back gate revived the composer even more. By the time they descended the gentler northern slope behind the castle and reached the streets he grew animated, viewing with energy and curiosity the flower boxes in the windows, the brightly painted doors of houses and shops, the costumes of other visitors. He brought to Damaris's attention tapestries from his own country in a shop window, and stopped now and then to exclaim over one or another of Luminum's renowned arts: delicate glass, lacework, water clocks of elegantly painted porcelain.

"You tell time by water?"

"Everything in Luminum is translated into water. It is the first and last sound we hear."

He made another of his fitful stops at the far end of one unusually straight street, glimpsing another blue horizon, another thicket of water traffic. He turned confusedly, walked backward a pace or two, gazing at the castle on the cliff around which the river curled. "Is Luminum an island?"

"Only on three sides."

He righted himself, gestured down the street. "And that?"

"The Halcyon River."

"More water," he breathed, making Damaris smile again.

"That, we worship. It waters our fields, our animals, our city. We dedicate monuments to it, build shrines, offer gifts to those who dwell in it. Your music will be among those gifts. It is finished, isn't it?" she asked practically, and was reassured when the composer nodded.

His eyes were on the concealed object in the square ahead of them, where four streets ended at a broad bed of cobbles. Flowering chestnuts shaded the people hurrying under them as intently and single-mindedly as fish pursuing dinner in the deep. It was a motley mix at this end of the city, where ancient cottages shared the waterfront with houseboats and barges flying pennants of laundry, and the market-boats darted and hovered like dragonflies over the water to sell a loaf of bread, a dozen oranges, before they flitted away to answer the next summons along the bank.

As they grew closer to the hidden object, Damaris heard the sound of hammering. The shrouds, great lengths of sailcloth, bulged briefly and oddly here and there, poked by mysteries within. The work must be finished, she realized, pleased. The scaffolding around the fountain was being dismantled.

"Minister," murmured the guard, rising from the stool on the cobbles where, with the aid of a book, he was defending the shrouds from entry. There was a shout from within; a sudden ridge in the canvas marked the path of a falling plank, which narrowly missed his head. He ducked, breathing a curse. "Are you sure, my lady, that you want to go in there?"

"You're wearing a helmet," she answered briskly. "Go in and tell them to stop for a moment."

The guard slipped between shrouds. Another plank clattered down; they heard laughter among indignant shouting. Then all was silent. The guard reappeared, held apart the shrouds for them.

"Be careful. There are perils everywhere."

There were indeed, Damaris saw: downed tools, swaying planks hammered half free, clinging to others by a nail, the rubble and dust of the sculptor's final touches to his masterpiece. He was still there, tinkering with the very top of the fountain, while he knelt in the basin below it. He grinned down at the minister, saluting with a brush, half his face masked with marble dust.

There were four broad basins, all scalloped and festooned with carvings. The largest, at the bottom, was a twenty-foot platter of pale yellow marble veined with cream. Three mermaids rose to their scaled hips out of the water in the center of the basin, their upraised arms holding the second basin, smaller by five feet. The exuberance of their poses, their alabaster breasts and dancers' arms, was mitigated by taut muscles the sculptor had chiseled to surface beneath the smooth skin. He knew how hard they worked to hold that ton of marble. Their serene smiles made nothing of it. The basin they held was sea green. Three porpoises, slightly smaller than the mermaids, danced upon the surface of the sea, balancing on their noses the third basin, a pale sky blue. A single rosy fish leaped out of its center, a carp by the look of the sinuous fins, standing on its tail and bearing the highest basin on its head. That carried the emblem of Obelos: the white fluted pillar with the water-blue orb upon it. The carp basin also held the sculptor, who was carefully cleaning the ring of holes in the orb, out of which water would rain in a perfect halo to overflow its basin and cascade into those beneath it.

Master Ainsley, who was staring at the massive stonework, closed his mouth with a click of teeth and lowered his head. The sculptor, blowing softly into the holes, had an ear cocked, Damaris noticed, toward their voices.

"Big," the composer pronounced finally, and added, after considering the matter, "Very big."

"As you noticed, we have a lot of water. Will your music be up to the task?"

"I think—" he paused again, finished cautiously, "I think so. I hadn't expected anything so ornate. I've seen such work in the courtyards and gardens of the rich in Iolea, but never so far north in a city square surrounded by chestnut trees.... The water will come from the river?"

"No. The source is the pure water of the Well itself. Water was guided from the underground river into a large holding tank; from there, pipes were laid across Master Greyson's hop fields, with concessions for use as irrigation, along a stone archway across the river, and then buried beneath the banks and run under various gardens and streets, and finally the square. Once the fountain is open, the water can be piped into houses all around the square. So you can see why we planned such an elaborate celebration. Many in Luminum still get their water by lugging a bucket down to the river."

She gazed at the great conduit head, the fountain, with satisfaction a moment longer, remembering months and even years of discussions, plans, legal contracts over property, endless papers she read requesting funds to pay for directors, engineers, pipe-makers, ditch-diggers, shovels and hoes and wheelbarrows, the ceaseless trail of problems into her office, annoyed citizens, leaky pipes, stolen equipment, miscalculations and miscreants.

All finished. Even the carp standing on its tail seemed to be smiling...

A halo of water shot out of the orb the carp carried. In a heartbeat, the sculptor's face and hair were drenched. A mask of wet marble dust opened its mouth in a silent, astonished O. Damaris, her own mouth open, noted dazedly the single clogged hole in the orb. The water, oddly striated, filled the smallest basin quickly and began to run over its scalloped edge in three orderly cascades around the frolicking carp and the sculptor.

The sculptor shouted an incoherent word that freed Damaris from her transfixed state. She drew a sharp breath and whirled.

"Where is the engineer?" she demanded of the staring workmen.

"What is it doing?" Master Ainsley asked confusedly. "Should it be running now?"

"He went up to the castle to see you," one of the workmen told her. "Said he needed to check something. I thought that's why you came here."

She was silent, pulling a vision of the project plans out of memory. The water had filled the carp basin and was flowing cheerfully down among the dolphins. The sculptor, on one knee in the water and clinging to the carp, was groping for a ladder behind him with his foot. It careened as he kicked. The workmen caught it, steadied it for him. He descended finally, cursing ceaselessly, wet as the carp.

"Go down to the river," Damaris said to one of the men. "Make sure no one is in the discharge drain, and that it is covered. When this starts gushing out the flow will be strong. And you—"

"Why," the sculptor demanded, interrupting his own steady stream, "is the water that color? It should be coming directly from the source waters of the Well."

It was, Damaris saw with horror, turning as brown as mud, or worse: as streams running beneath schools sometimes turned in summer when the water grew shallow and the waste from a hundred students tumbled into it from their simple wooden water-closets.

The guard was peering through the opening now, drawn by the noises of water and the sculptor. "Stay here," Damaris told him tersely as his eyes widened. "Don't let anyone in."

"What—"

"Don't say a word about this to anyone."

The composer asked helplessly, grimacing at the murk, "Should I revise my music?"

"Of course not." She seized his arm, tugged him away. "It's a temporary problem. A bit of soil in the water main. Most likely. The engineer will fix it easily. Come back to the castle with me; we'll find Lord Felden so he can begin practicing your music."

"I wrote water music, not mud music," he muttered with one last incredulous glance at it before Damaris pulled him out of the shrouds. "Maybe your Well is running dry."

Damaris closed her eyes briefly. Behind them, she caught an unexpected glimpse of the mage's eyes, the swirling hues of mother-of-pearl opening to look at her, and she felt the skin prickle painfully at the nape of her neck.

"Not possible," she told him adamantly, hurrying him along the ancient, colorful, bustling streets. "Human error. The engineer will find it. All will be well. You needn't mention the incident to the musicians. It might weigh heavily on their playing and your music."

"Water," he sighed. "It plagues me still, even on bone-dry streets. Is it cursed, this fountain?"

"I hope not," she breathed. "We would be forced to revise our lives."

"But it is possible?" he asked so shrewdly that she could not answer, only rush him even more ruthlessly uphill until he had no breath for words.

Within the castle, she delivered him gratefully into the care of her betrothed.

"I've been looking for you," Beale Felden told Master Ainsley. "They told me you had arrived and vanished."

"Lady Ambre kindly took me to see the fountain," the composer answered, and did not elaborate, to Damaris's relief.

"Ah." Beale smiled at her amiably but absently. She could almost see the notes and instruments, the faces of musicians crowded behind his limpid blue eyes. As he, if he noticed, might have seen the pipes and conduits in hers, as well as something of her terror. Fortunately for her, he was not particularly perceptive. That was one of the reasons, along with his fair hair, his amiable temper, his ancient title and wealth, that Damaris had permitted him to court her. He added to the composer, "The musicians are all eager to meet you, and see what you've brought us to play for the ceremony."

"I only hope it will be suitable," Master Ainsley sighed; his own eyes seemed to fill with visions of mud.

"I'm sure it will be wonderful," Lord Felden answered. "This will seal your reputation in Obelos." He bore the speechless composer down the hallway. Damaris watched them a moment; Beale seemed to be doing most of the talking. She turned away. She couldn't guard every word the composer said, and, anyway, Beale, if alarmed, would be convinced by the simplest of explanations. A little dirt in the conduit pipe. Easily flushed out. He wouldn't think to wonder who had started the appalling flow in the first place.

She found the engineer pacing as she entered her office; turning abruptly, he nearly bumped into her. They both spoke at once.

"Did you see—?"

"Have you heard—?"

They stopped, studied one another's perturbed faces. The engineer, a lean, muscular, balding man apt to grab a shovel and leap into a trench if work on a project seemed slow, asked tersely, "Is it about the fountain?"

"Yes. Yours?"

"Yes. I was at the river, early this morning, making sure the discharge drain was completely clear before the guard-gate was locked over it. You remember where it is? Parallel to the conduit at that point where it arches across the river near the central bridge—"

"Yes."

"It was just near my head, coming down off the stone archway. So I could hear what was going on inside."

Damaris blinked. "Inside."

"The conduit pipe."

"Nothing," Damaris said after a moment. Her voice shook. "Nothing should have been going on inside the conduit pipe. Why are you here? Why are you not checking the pipe at the source?"

He gazed at her, his brow furrowing. "For what?" he demanded. "What did you see?"

"A great deal of very murky water coming out of the fountain. Isn't that what you heard? Water in flow?"

"No," he said soundlessly. Then he cleared his throat. "I heard voices."

"What?" She stared back at him in horror. "Someone inside the pipe?"

"Singing."

"Inside the pipe?"

"And laughter. Some banging—"

"Children," she whispered, her fingers icy.

"They didn't sound like children. And I couldn't understand a word. Sometimes the pipes themselves seemed to sing. I sent one of the workmen to the Well to check the cap over the conduit pipe, make sure no one had broken the locks on it."

"If anyone had opened the cap to enter it, they would have drowned long before they crossed the river. No one would be laughing."

They were silent again; their eyes slid away from one another, neither wanting to glimpse the doubt blooming there.

"Mud," the engineer said heavily.

"Or worse. I couldn't tell. At least it didn't smell. But where could it possibly be coming from? What did the workman say?"

He shook his head. "The cap was sealed in the water as we left it. Nothing seemed amiss." He paused again, asked her diffidently, "Any word from the water-mage?"

"No. Not for me, at least."

His face loosened slightly. "An accident, then, along the pipeline. I'll have the workmen follow it, check for wet or sinking ground. I'll take a look at the source myself."

She nodded briefly. "And your voices?"

"Echoes from somewhere else, they must have been. The river was misty at dawn; I couldn't see clearly..."

She drew breath, loosed it silently, and met his eyes again. "That must have been it. Let me know immediately if you find anything."

He bowed his head, left her listening to the bewildering silence from the water-mage.

The water-mage stood listening as well.

In the rocky, sunken cave where the water ran up out of the secret earth, Eada was little more than a bulky shadow in her black skirts and the veil that hid her long silver hair. She might have been a boulder in the jumble of rock that had broken and cascaded down around the Well so long ago that the shards were growing together again, grain by grain, century by century. The water filled its ancient, rounded pool among the stones with only the slightest tremor at its heart, the little flutter in the center of the pool that spoke of the unseen treasure of water buried deep beneath, in perpetual night. Seemingly without end, it pushed itself up into this silent cave with its little circular roof of sky and light; it gleamed a greeting, then passed into darkness again, down a narrow, shallow bed of stones, pushing more quickly now through its ancient waterway to find the light again, beyond the cave, where it bubbled up and pooled beneath the open sky.

That pool was where the city dwellers came to worship. They brought gifts, dropped wishes into it in the form of coins or words written on thin strips of metal.

They crowded around it during the ritual, under the first full summer moon. The knights ringed the Well beneath the ground; the king stood on the earth above, drank water from a gold cup, and dropped coins and jewels the color of blood into the wellspring. Near the natural pool above, and fed by it, a great marble tank had been built, a pretty thing surrounded by broad walkways, flowering vines, fluted pillars with little fountains perpetually offering water to the worshippers. Beyond it, the water flowed free again, very briefly, offering itself to insects, mosses and reeds, birds and wild creatures before it dove underground again, vanished back into the dark. Around this open water, the city dwellers watched the ritual, flooding beyond their human boundaries once a year to honor the mysteries of the Well, and to drink, after the king, the pure water out of the earth.

The water welling up out of the underearth made no sound.

The water welling up out of the underearth should have made no sound.

The mage, standing in the shadows, kept listening for silence from the sunlit pool. An ancient, familiar silence, there should have been in that cave, as old and peaceful as the dark. Instead, there were half-words, like water emptying down a drain; there were hisses, a gurgle like a laugh that echoed against the walls, a sudden splash that left no ripple behind it. The language of water, she recognized. But who spoke? What was said?

She heard a step in the low passageway that led from the Well to her dwelling. The walls echoed suddenly, as though a stone had spoken. Eada looked quickly into the water, saw nothing but the insouciant reflection of the sky.

"Mistress, the knight is here," Perla said. She was a slight young girl, the daughter of a market-boater, used to the vagaries of water, who had come to peer into the cave one day and stayed to give the old mage a hand with this or that. She might have been part water sprite, Eada guessed. She feared nothing that poked its head unexpectedly out of the Well, and didn't mind running errands between the underearth and sky.

A hesitant step in the stone chamber beyond told Eada how far the knight had gotten. Her odd experiments, her trifles, had slowed him in her workroom. She played with water in all its forms, even ice in its season. In tanks, she kept strange fish and other river creatures Perla and her friends found; she studied most for a moon or two before she sent them back. Scholars and witches from all over Obelos sent her the odd instrument, the unusual crystal that might interest her.

Perla was hovering, looking, with her pale hair and scant, restive limbs, like she might sprout wings like a dragonfly if she touched the earth another minute. "Shall I stay, mistress? Or shall I go buy bread?"

"Go," Eada said, shooing the sprite away and found her slow way around the stony edges of the pool, and down the passage into her chambers. They were roofed above the earth by domes of stone and wood studded with crystals that caught the daylight and drew it underground in mellow, shimmering shafts. Entering her workroom, the mage found that the knight had indeed been slowed by her playthings; he was toying with a tiny windmill on the table, turning its blades with his forefinger.

"Better to blow it," Eada suggested, and he started.

"I wasn't sure it worked."

"Try it."

He blew gently. The slats turned; the mill wheel, driven by the cogs and pistons within, drew up water from a shallow pan, flicked it into a chute that fed it neatly into a pot of basil.

The knight grunted, almost smiled. But he wasn't in the habit of it; Eada could tell by the clouds that gathered immediately to engulf the simple moment of pleasure. The mage reckoned that she had not been that young in at least a couple of centuries.

He looked at her silently then, uneasily. Well he should, she thought. Living in the water-cavern, she had become a shapeless, bulky thing: a boulder with legs and great slab hands. Her neck had vanished somewhere; her white head balanced on her shoulders. Strange colors had seeped into her eyes from what she had seen. Witch-lights, Perla called them; they fascinated the child. But Garner Slade was not a child; he had a good idea of what was worth fearing.

"Did it speak to you?" she asked, and his eyes widened. He was quick, though; she'd seen that when she chose him.

"No. It only looked at me." He hesitated, ventured a question. "What was it?"

"Something that wanted you to see it. You," she repeated with emphasis. "Garner Slade. Your eyes."

"How did you—how did you know?"

"I was watching, in the Well. I'm mage, so I can do such things with water."

"And you saw—"

"Everything. I see through all your eyes." The knight opened his mouth, then closed it, a red tide rising in his face. "That's how I choose the knights," Eada continued. "I must be able to see. The young man who thinks he dislikes water sees it with such clarity.... And your cousin loves it, though he might have trouble loving anything human."

"I'm sorry," Garner blurted. "I'm sorry I lost my temper."

"Ah, but look what you found. Look what you saw. Something is wrong in the waterworld, and we need to know what. Since you were the one to look trouble in the eye, you're the one to help me. If we have offended the water realms, if some strange mage is churning up things better left on the bottom, if the kingdom itself is in danger, we need to know." She turned without waiting for him to answer. "Come."

Perversely, now that she wished to show, to illumine, the Well made no sound; not a ripple or a chuckle disturbed it. The bright face of the pool was blank and still. She waited, the knight a breathing shadow beside her. No one even glanced up from underwater to see who was there. Finally, without comment, she led him back into her workroom, where she rummaged through her books and manuscripts. The knight, looking confused, finally spoke.

"Was there something I should have seen?"

"I couldn't see anything either," she said absently. "They're teasing our eyes; they knew we were looking. They were whispering and laughing all morning before you came."

"Who?" he asked bewilderedly. "Who?"

She showed him.

"I drew these on my travels all around Obelos, when I was young," she said, turning pages slowly in the bound book she had made of her sketches. "I wasn't even a water-mage then. I didn't know that's what I wanted to be. I only knew that I never wanted to be far from water.... Some of these have been given human names. Others are seen so rarely they have no names in our world."

Many she had drawn from memory, a brief glimpse of the face within the waterfall, among the flowers along a brook, the shadowy creature swimming with the school of fish. Others she saw clearly;

they had human names: the kelpies, the water nymphs, the naiads, and nereids and undines, the mer-people. Some spoke to her in various ways, touching her with pale, webbed fingers, showing alarming teeth in warning, singing to her, beckoning. There seemed a different face for every stream, every pond and branch water. She drew as many as she could find. Some stayed to watch their own faces flowing out of her ink jars onto paper. They knew their human names, and had learned to speak to humans for their own purposes. They did not consider Eada entirely human. They didn't try to entice her underwater, or into their arms. They questioned her, gossiped about other water creatures, told her where to find the shyest, the most secretive, the wildest.

They spread her name throughout the water-web of Obelos. When the dying water-mage in Luminum searched for his successor, he heard the water speak Eada's name and summoned her.

"And that's when I finally realized what I am," she told the speechless knight, who was staring at the wide-set eyes and languid mouth of the face peering up from under a water lily. "Now you know what you'll be looking for."

He came to life again. "What?" he asked huskily.

"That one will make you forget your own name when you look at her."

"What is it you want me to do?"

"I need your eyes. I need you to follow the waterways of Luminum, looking for such as these. Look into every rivulet, every puddle, every rain barrel, every place where water gathers. See what you can see. You'll be my eyes; I'll be behind yours, watching, listening. I must know what is troubling the water creatures. Go swimming if you have to. That worked for you earlier."

"The creature seemed more inclined to let me drown than talk to me."

"Well, some are like that. Just do your best. I'll help you in any way I can. We need answers before moonrise tomorrow, or the Ritual of the Well will become the disaster your mishap on the river portended."

"That soon," he breathed.

"And let Damaris know what I've told you to do."

He gazed at her, seeing what she knew he would. "Must I?" he asked a little explosively. "I'm the last man she wants to see. She's the Minister of Water and you're the water-mage. Shouldn't you tell her?"

"I'm hoping you will," she only said. "Be careful of teeth, and don't fall in love with anything waterborn."

He drew breath, debated over any number of replies. Then he loosed it with a huff and a toss of his hands, and made his way back out of her caverns and across the threshold of day.

Faced with another encounter with the annoyed Minister of Water, Garner found the most labyrinthine path possible back to the castle. Follow the water, the mage had instructed. So he did, beginning with the irrigation ditches along the broad fields beyond the river. Seeing anything in them but gaudy insects and weeds seemed unlikely. The sudden glimpse of a splintered darkness beneath the surface made him start; his horse gave an uneasy snort. Then he saw the blackbird swoop past him, its shadow flying behind it in the ditchwater. The ditch ended at a canal with its sluice gate closed. He rode along the canal for a while. Nothing disturbed the water; nothing spoke. He watched it carefully, remembering that the mage watched as well. Remembering, too, the lovely eyes beneath the lily pad, he could not help looking for them among the clustering green on the still, sunlit water. But nothing beckoned; nothing lured; the only face he saw in the water was his own.

Nearer the river, he dismounted to thread his way at random through the streets of the city. On that side of the river, they fanned evenly away from the water toward the fields. The cross-streets, cobbled with fieldstones, were equally straight. Except for the ancient houses along the bank, this part of the city was newer, tidier, and, he discovered, eagerly awaiting the pipes that would connect it to the massive conduit from the Well, send its water flowing into the houses.

"The minister promised us water by the end of autumn," a tavern-keeper told Garner, who had stopped to peer into his rain barrel. It was positioned beneath a clay gutter-pipe; water poured out of the wide mouth of an ornate, hideous face that, despite its chipped nose, reminded Garner of one of the sprites in the mage's book. He gazed with interest into the water. But nothing gazed back at him, with or without teeth. "They have to wait until after harvest to go digging up the fields. I've waited years, but it's hardest to wait that one more season." He paused, watching Garner curiously. "Something your lordship wanted?"

Garner nodded, realizing what. "A dip into your barrel?"

"Help yourself."

Garner filled the cup dangling from its chain, drank, felt the sweet rain branch through him in all its secret rills. *How can I possibly?* he wondered tiredly. *How can I find what the mage needs? I might have just drunk the answer down.*

"They say the Well is as pure as rain," the tavern-keeper commented reverently. "We'll hear it singing from that fountain across the river in a day or two."

Damaris had said something about a fountain, Garner remembered. He let the cup drop. "Is it important, the fountain?"

The man cocked a brow. "Where have you been?"

"With the king at the winter court."

"Ah. Those with pipes and without take their water from the river, even the king. No telling what you might find in it, especially toward the end of summer before the rains come. The fountain will draw its water from the Well itself. Can't get much cleaner than that. Straight out of the bones of the earth...."

"Where is this fountain?"

"Just across the central bridge, up the street and in the square. Nobody's seen it yet. It'll be unveiled and let run after the Ritual of the Well. That'll be something to celebrate."

Garner left him gazing with anticipation in the direction of the square. He continued his meandering way through the streets until one led him to the river, ending at the dock where the market-boats loaded their wares. There he could see distant chestnut trees where the streets ended, and the smudged blur of part of some huge thing standing among them, the unwrapped gift to the city. He debated crossing for a closer look. Then he envisioned the Minister of Water with the same impulse at the same time, and the two of them running into one another under a tree. Not only would he be forced to give Damaris the unpleasant message from the mage, he must present her with the last thing she wanted to look at: his face.

He turned instead, went downriver toward the sea, and the place where he had seen the water creature.

That side of the river was wilder, thinly populated; the city tended to cluster around its stronghold and its bridges. Here the fishing boats docked, coming and going with the tide. Here the river quickened as it curved around the headland, broadened to meet the sea. A massive watchtower guarded the castle across the water. Garner had spent some months in it when he was younger, learning how to use his weapons. There was little river traffic now. The fishing boats were still out at sea. The royal dock where Garner had so ignominiously disembarked that morning still ported its pennants and scallops, but the few barges tied there were all empty.

Garner dismounted at the river, stood watching the water while his horse drank. The bank was low there. The water of the little inlet lapped softly along mossy tree roots and tangles of bramble and wildflowers. Afternoon sun lay gently on the shallows, a rumpled cloth-of-gold, stirring languidly in the backwash of deeper currents. The pennants fluttering like colorful leaves across the water drew Garner's eyes. He saw Damaris in memory, several years earlier, coming down those steps to welcome the returning court. Garner, who had accompanied one of the king's knights as his squire, had been transfixed by the sight of her. She had grown quite tall and slender over the winter. She moved like water, he thought. Like kelp, every frond graceful, swaying dreamily to the slightest touch of tide. He felt the moment when her eyes met his.

She laughed and waved; he could only stand there, forgetting to move even after the barge had docked.

He drew a soft breath, forced his eyes away. No one stood there now, and anyway, all her welcomes were for someone else. Lord Felden, with his wealth, his horn, his absent-minded humming, his amiable disposition. He gave all his passion to his music, Garner had heard, when news of the betrothal reached the winter court. His mother, who reigned in his rich house south of Luminum, must have reminded him that no amount of copious outpourings of beautiful music would transform itself into an heir to his title and fortune, no matter how hard he blew.

Her eyes met his.

Garner started, feeling the implosion like a silent lightning bolt all through him. Those eyes, as green as river moss, watched him just above the surface of the water. Her pale hair floated all around her like the petals of some extravagant flower. In the next moment he caught his breath. It was not, could not possibly be Damaris, silent as a wild thing, her nose under water, and from what he could see, naked as an eel.

A river creature, he realized, his pulse quickening again. Sunning in the shallows, breathing water like air as she gazed at him. He wondered whether, if he spoke, she would vanish with a twist and a ripple, like a fish.

But he had to risk it. "You startled me," he said.

She lifted her face out of the water then, revealing a familiar, charming smile, a slender neck, the curves and hollows of her shoulders. He wondered if her skin was that golden everywhere.

"I know," she answered. Her voice was light and sweet, a purl of water. She raised her fingers; he saw the webs between them, delicate, iridescent. She pushed lazily at the water, the light. "Come join me."

"I don't dare," he said somberly.

"Then I'll leave you."

"No—Don't do that."

"Then come in with me. We'll talk."

That face drew hard at him, so familiar, all its smiles for him, promising all he wanted.

"You're a dream," he breathed.

"So? Don't you take pleasure in dreams?"

Don't fall in love, the mage had warned him, *with the water-born....*
She was there, he remembered, starting again. In his head, watching
out of his eyes. He sighed noiselessly, relieved to have the choice made
for him.

"The water-mage sent me," he said carefully. "She wonders if we
have offended the water folk."

She flicked water toward him again, not answering, only looking
at him out of that face she must have pulled out of his thoughts. Was
her true face, he wondered, what he had seen under the water that
morning, watching him?

"If we have, tell us what to do to make amends."

She smiled, raising both hands out of the water, fingers stroking the
air like wings, beckoning.

"I'll show you..." he heard, but how he couldn't imagine, for she had
already vanished.

He stood a moment longer, waiting for her, feeling a curious
emptiness, as though it truly had been Damaris and he had turned
away from love.

Damaris, he reminded himself, or the mage did, urging him along.
Reluctantly, he mounted again, rode to the watchtower dock to
summon the ferryman.

A dozen market-boats had ventured down that far; they swarmed
around the dock, selling bread, strawberries, cheese, ale and savory
pasties to the men in the tower. Garner bought some meat and onions
skewered on a stick, and roasted on a little brazier balanced on a shelf
on the prow of the boat. It seemed precarious, but fire rode easily over
the swell and dip of water. The boatman, his face seamed with an
endless labyrinth of wrinkles, lingered at the dock to thread more meat
and turn his skewers.

Garner, watching him as he ate, asked impulsively, "Have you seen
anything strange in the water?"

"Strange? You mean like mermaids, such?"

"Anything out of the ordinary."

The man shook his head. But his mouth widened into a gap-toothed grin at the same time; he chuckled soundlessly, waving a skewer at the bees. "Only what everybody saw this morning."

Garner felt himself flush, but pursued the matter anyway. "What?"

"You didn't see? It happened near the bridge, where the market-boats are thickest. A man in one of the fancy houses along the river pushed his head out of the vent in his private water-closet, crying that something was in there laughing at him. Then the water-closet slid right down his wall and into the river. For a few moments, we all thought it would float at the head of the king's procession. But it stuck in the mud and got pulled ashore before the king had to see it. The man came out cursing his leaky pipes that had rotted the wood. But a water pipe wasn't what terrified him. You could see that in his eyes."

"What was it, then?"

The old man shrugged. "Water sprite, likely," he said calmly. "They get frisky sometimes just before the ritual. We make our living on the water; we've learned to placate them, leave gifts in the river—flowers, beads, floating candles, little carvings—so they don't toy with our boats. But I've never seen them go that far before. Up pipes and into someone's house."

Garner finished his meal hastily, disturbed, and rode to the shallows beside the dock, where the ferryman, a lean man with his head hooded against the wind, sat alone on his raft, watching the currents.

"Between tides," he remarked cryptically. "Easy journey."

Garner led his horse on; they were the only passengers. The ferryman glanced up and down for traffic, then gave a cry. High-pitched, inarticulate, it sounded across the river like some wild water bird calling to another. At the royal dock a giant spool began to turn. A pair of ropes attached to the front of the raft rose slowly through the water to the surface and tautened. Another spool turned on the watchtower dock, loosing the raft cables. Garner felt it begin to move.

The ferryman plied his pole, kept the raft from drifting. Garner stood stroking his horse, watching the great stone pile loom above them until it filled the sky. Its shadow slid over them, mid-river.

"She get the message yet?" the ferryman asked, shifting his pole.

"She—" His thoughts had strayed; he couldn't imagine what they were talking about. "The water-mage?"

The ferryman flashed him a glance. "The mage. The minister. Either." Garner stared at him. He looked back, long enough this time to give the knight a clear view of his spindrift face, his shell-white eyes. The ferryman smiled then, a quick, tight smile. "Guess not."

The cables on one side of the boat snapped, whipped the water with a vicious hiss. Garner ducked, clinging to his horse's reins. On the other side, the rope dipped underwater, pulling the raft down with it. He felt his boots fill again with water. The raft tilted like a door opening into the riverworld and he went through it for the second time that day.

Beale would not go away. Damaris, desperate to find her engineer again and inquire about the fountain, kept seeing her betrothed in her doorway, no matter how many times she paced around the table. His pleasant, thoughtful voice went on and on; his eyes, seeming to follow her spiral path, saw nothing disturbing in it; walking around and around a table must be simply what she wanted to do.

"Chairs," he said, "for fifteen musicians. The little gilt ones. To be placed, I think, beside the fountain and facing it. The music is, after all, a gift to the fountain. Don't you agree? The king, I believe, is planning to step out of the royal barge near the square and proceed up one of the streets to the fountain. I'm not sure who else will make up the procession. The musicians, of course, will not come down by water. The Minister of Ceremony has not yet decided exactly when to unveil the fountain: before or after the king's arrival. In either event, the musicians will already be there. I don't think I've told you this: Master Ainsley plays a very sweet flute and will be joining us to perform his own composition for the first time."

Master Ainsley, Damaris thought, chilled. Who must still wonder if he'll be playing mud-music.

"Beale," she said desperately.

"Not to leap ahead, since there are so many details to consider, but I am so much anticipating our journey after the celebration to my estate, where you will finally meet my mother. As I've told you, she's much too frail to make the journey to Luminum."

"Beale."

"She is eagerly awaiting our arrival. So is my sister, who used to be one of the king's musicians until our mother's health—"

"Beale!"

He stopped, seeing her finally, his fair brows raised. "What is it, my love?"

"If—if there should be—if something should go wrong—"

"What could possibly go wrong? You're intelligent, wonderful, young enough to bear twenty grandchildren for my mother, your family and history are impeccable, you look like a water nymph, my mother will adore you."

She closed her eyes, tried to keep her voice steady. "I meant with the fountain."

"The fountain. What could go wrong with the fountain? You let the water flow; it comes out the holes; we play. Simple as breathing."

She opened her eyes, saw, over his shoulder, a bad dream coming toward her down the hall, its bare feet squelching watery footprints on the marble. She gave a hiccup of astonishment, and closed her eyes again, hoping it might go away.

"Beale. Excuse me, but I must find my engineer."

"There is such a charming analogy between the holes in the fountain, and those in our instruments," he said with sudden enthusiasm. "Don't you think? One flowing water, the other music; both necessary for life, I would argue, though no amount of music would—Now, I wonder, could an instrument be fashioned that could flow with both water and music at once? What would it look like? Surely—"

The face of the nightmare was beside him now: the Knight of the Well running water like a leaky pipe. His dark eyes were furious, but that she understood. It was the fear in them that brought her fingers to her mouth. Be careful, she pleaded silently to him. Be discreet.

Beale turned; even he must have felt the exudations of emotions and dampness. He stared, amazed, at the knight. "You seem to be dripping."

"I fell in the river," Garner said shortly, and otherwise ignored him, holding Damaris's eyes with his disquieting gaze.

"Again?" she said through her fingers.

"The ferryman tossed me in. This was after I spoke to the nymph—"

"Stop," she said sharply, and, to her relief, he veered away from that.

"I have a message for you from the water-mage."

"Nymphs and water-mages and Knights of the Well," Beale murmured. "Sounds like a tale that should be set to music. Does it not? A small, perfect cycle of compositions—"

"Beale," Damaris interrupted explosively, "I must hear Eada's message in private. Please."

"Oh." He glanced with surprise at the doorpost against which he leaned. "Of course." He moved himself, but only to advance with a touch of deliberation into the room, where he positioned a kiss firmly on the cheek of his betrothed. "Come and tell it to me when you're finished here." He left finally, passing Garner with a careless nod and a laugh. "You must tell me your nymph story in more detail later. Don't forget."

"Come in and close the door," Damaris said tightly. "Don't drip on my papers. Tell me what the mage said."

"Something is wrong in the waterworld. She sent me searching everything from ditchwater to the river to find out what. She told me to tell you this."

"She did."

"Do you think I wanted to come back here?" he demanded. "To interrupt your intimate conversation with Lord Felden? To make a fool of myself drenched and barefoot in front of you both?"

"No," she admitted. "Anyway, it wasn't very intimate. Anyway," she said more firmly, "what did you mean about the ferryman? He had an accident, taking you across the river?"

"It wasn't an accident, and he wasn't human."

"Oh," she whispered.

"He sank the ferry deliberately. I nearly got kicked by my horse flailing in the water before I could grab its mane. We swam across together. I didn't have a chance to question anything among the waterweeds. I lost my boots. Again. Whatever is going on among the water people is becoming dangerous to humans."

"Well, did you find anyone to ask?"

"I asked the water nymph. She just looked at me out of your face and refused to answer."

Damaris felt behind her for the edge of the table, held on. "My face," she said faintly.

"You had been on my mind," Garner sighed. "I think she—whatever it truly was—must have seen it in my thoughts."

"I see." She chose words carefully, as though they were stones across a swirling current. "You didn't—I've heard such nymphs are—are difficult to resist."

"Of course she was," he said bluntly. "But I also had a water-mage looking out of my eyes, and after this morning, I was wary of going anywhere near you. Or anything that looked like you. I didn't want to come here now. But I'm beginning to be afraid for Luminum."

"Yes." Her fingers tightened on the wood. "So am I. We had what looked like muddy water coming out of the fountain earlier today. Before anyone had uncapped the conduit pipe at the Well."

He gazed at her silently, some of the anger in his eyes yielding to bewilderment. "Do you have any idea why?"

"Because we have run pipes out of the Well itself?" she guessed. "But we began the project years ago, and nothing has bothered us until now." She paused, eyeing his plastered hair, his sodden clothes, his naked feet. "Garner, be careful. They seem to be using you as a—a conduit for their messages."

"Yes," he said quickly. "The ferryman asked me if you had gotten it."

"What?"

"The message."

She felt the blood leave her face. "He said that. If I had—"

"The mage or the minister," Garner amended himself. "I assumed he meant the Minister of Water. Maybe not." He moved restively. "I need to get out of these wet clothes and continue my search. Do you have any suggestions? You know the waterworld as well as any human can."

"I'm beginning to feel that I don't know it at all... I may understand more after I speak to the engineer. But, Garner, what will you do for boots?"

He shrugged. "Steal a pair from my cousin."

"Be careful," she said again, and he looked at her a moment, silently.

"You be careful, too," he warned, and followed his own soggy path back out.

Soon after that, she received the first message from the engineer. He had checked the conduit line from fountain to Well, and seen nothing amiss. But something, he assured her, was. On that disturbing note, he ended, but she didn't have long to wait before the next messenger came, and the next. Garner's was not the only sodden body to appear in her office. Sprites had invaded the water pipes of Luminum, and they showed no respect, not even to the king, whose luxurious water-closet, fitted with cushions, scented linens, and bowls of flower petals, had somehow popped its ornate taps completely off to spew river water all over the carpets. There were similar disasters throughout the city, in those houses and inns fortunate enough to have private systems. The harassments extended beyond pipes, Damaris learned. Fishers found their boats immobile in mid-current, or completely overturned. Sluice gates between canals and irrigation ditches were randomly opened or shut, causing herds of pastured animals to find themselves shank-deep in water. Mill wheels ground to a halt for no reason anyone could see. Damaris, fearing for the dikes, sent riders out to check for breaches. The harbormaster came himself to tell her that a dock had floated out to sea.

"Why," she demanded incoherently of him, "can't they just put it into words? Why must water speak for them?"

"I don't know, Minister," he sighed. "I'm only hoping the sea gates don't start talking."

Beale wandered back in the midst of all this to invite her to the rehearsal, after supper, of Master Ainsley's music. She stared at him incredulously, then remembered what he was talking about.

"Music. Yes. For a little while. But Beale—"

But he was already leaving, trumpeting, in his resonant baritone, what must have been the horn section to Master Ainsley's piece.

She saw Garner again finally, taking his place belatedly among the knights in the hall for supper. He was still alive, and he looked dry; other than that she couldn't draw conclusions. She watched him, hearing Beale only when he stopped speaking. Then she would shift her attention quickly back to him.

"Beale," she said carefully, during one of his brief silences. "Are you aware of the water problems in the city?"

He shook his head. His eyes, she realized suddenly, were on the knights' table also. "You seem distracted," he murmured, in a rare moment of discernment she could have done without.

"I am," she said quickly. "I have been hearing all day long about disturbances, restlessness in the water."

His face cleared; he asked with a sudden chuckle, "You mean the king's water-closet?"

"Yes, that, too. And—"

"I heard they had to bail out the royal bedchamber before the water was stopped. You keep staring at that knight. The morose one with no manners."

"He's a Knight of the Well, on the water-mage's business. I need to talk to him after supper. I'm beginning to be very worried."

"Oh," he said complacently. "Is that all. I was beginning to think— No matter. It's probably just a storm."

"What?"

"The weather seems to be changing. I heard the wind rise as I came to supper. An early summer storm, nothing more; it will no doubt blow over by morning." She opened her mouth just as he pushed back his chair and stood up. "I beg your pardon, my dear, but we have so little time to practice. You will join us, won't you, before too long? You must hear Master Ainsley's composition; it is wonderful. The voice of water itself..."

She had to wait for Garner until the king and his nobles rose from the dais table; then the knights were permitted to leave. Garner, watching for her, came to meet her as the elegant court swirled around the king to welcome him. He looked exhausted, she thought, as well as a bit wild-eyed, haunted by sprites.

"Anything?" she demanded.

He shook his head. "Nothing that makes any sense. Fountains refused to flow, or poured like waterfalls all over the streets. Rain barrels overflowed as though they were fed by secret springs. Public water-closet doors stuck fast; I helped tear several open to free those trapped inside. Pipes leaked; people were chased out of their houses by water."

"Did you meet any other water creatures?"

"I heard them singing out of buckets people dropped on their way back from the river. I searched along the river, and on my way to the Well. But, perversely, they hid from me."

"You saw Eada again?"

"I tried to, but she was nowhere to be found, either. I saw your engineer."

"More than I did," she said grimly. "Did he have any messages for me?"

"Only that he could find—"

"Nothing amiss," she guessed, and he nodded.

"He told me to tell you that the fountain was clean, completely dry. The scaffolding is down; the debris cleared; the work is ready to be unveiled."

"If we dare," she sighed. "Well. That's something."

"A trick," he suggested somberly.

"Maybe. But if anything goes wrong, it will go wrong first tomorrow night at the Ritual of the Well. They won't wait for the water music the day after." He was silent, so completely baffled, she saw, that he had forgotten to be angry. She added, "At least you didn't fall in the river again."

"Maybe I should," he murmured. "Maybe I should go back, find that nymph with your face and listen to what she has to tell me."

"Lies," Damaris said succinctly. "Like her face."

He was silent again, blinking at her out of heavy, blood-shot eyes, as though he couldn't remember the difference between the minister and the nymph. She shifted abruptly; he raised his hand to his eyes, rubbed them wearily.

"I'm too tired to think. I'm going to rest a little, for as long as the mage will let me."

"Let's hope the night will be more peaceful than the day."

She went to the music room, where the musicians, Master Ainsley, and Lord Felden sat on their gilt chairs in ranks according to their instruments. Beale smiled at her, pleased.

"Welcome, my lady. We are just about to go over it again."

Damaris sat down. He lifted his horn and nodded his head. As they played the first light, charming flurry of falling water droplets, she heard the storm begin.

A summer storm, Beale had said. Warm, noisy, clearing by morning. But nothing was predictable that day, not even water coming out of a tap. Damaris left as early as she could, throwing Beale an apologetic smile without quite meeting his eyes. In her office, she studied the tide tables. Rare for a summer storm to be destructive. As rare, she thought dourly, for a water bucket to sing. And that night the moon was nearly full, the tide would be high, and late, and everyone would be sleeping as it rose...

She made her decision, wrote a note, affixed her seal of office, and sent it to the harbormaster.

Close the sea gates now.

The mage heard the first falling notes of rain on the river, on the sea. She was a shadow beside the Well, night-dark, motionless as the ancient tumble of stones around her. Her blank gaze was fixed upon the water. She saw nothing; she saw everything. Her mind was a fish, a ripple, a current running here, there, everywhere: through pipes, along ditches, in ponds, canals, down the river flowing to the sea. She listened, wondered, watched.

Snatches, she heard: underwater whisperings. Brief as the gurgle of water down a drain, some were, and as coherent. But she had been water-mage for many decades. She understood the ways of water creatures, and many of their words. When she didn't understand, she went farther, her mind seeping into another like water, filling every wrinkled crevice of it until she saw, she spoke, she understood.

What she guessed at last amazed her.

Her surprise cast her thoughts back into the still old woman she had left at the edge of the Well. For a long time she sat there, contemplating the fragments of this and that she had pieced together. A word repeated many different ways, an odd detail washing up against another, an underwater face seen through as many kinds of eyes as were in the water, now a colorless blur, now a bright, startling mosaic of itself repeated in a single eye, now as nearly human as it could get...

"Well, I never," the mage said in the dark, and, a little later, "All this fuss..."

The Well turned suddenly vivid, bone-white, as though the moon had fallen into it. The mage gazed at the water, astonished again. Then the thunderbolts pounded all around her, trying to shake apart the boulders. She drew fully into herself for a moment, hearing the rain hiss down through the open roof onto the Well; then she felt it. She grunted; her thoughts slid back into the water. She rode the river current down until down became up as the salt tide pushed upriver. She borrowed bodies, then. There were many, she realized, and all swimming against the tide, making for the sea.

She saw it as they did: the massive gates across the harbor, sluice gates lowered, hinged gates fashioned to open outward with the outgoing sea and close fast when needed, with the help of the incoming tide. The tide had barely begun to turn, but they were already shut.

She came slowly back to herself, feeling as though, between rain and river and sea, she must be wet as a puddle. She whispered, as she pulled herself to her feet, balancing on one stone, then another, "Good girl."

She moved through the torch-lit cavern of her workroom, into the chamber beyond, which had a bed, and a hearth, and warm, dry clothes. She put them on, and moved into the tiny kitchen. She found Perla there, windblown and barefoot, stirring something savory in a pot over the fire.

"The knight came, mistress."

"Did he?" She warmed her hands, remembering him like a dream: the knight looking into her cave, she seeing nothing out of his eyes. "Did he leave a message?"

"No."

"What are you doing here, child? Didn't you see the rain coming? You should have scampered home."

Perla answered only with a brief, wild grin at the thought that a storm should be something to avoid. She brought Eada a bowl of stew, bread, and some late strawberries. The mage ate absently, mulling over what she had glimpsed underwater.

"Who's to say?" she inquired finally, of nobody, she realized. The child had gone somewhere, maybe home, maybe out to watch the lightning. "Not I," she answered herself, and rose with sudden energy to clear the table. "Not for me to say..."

For a long time then, she sat beside the Well, half-dreaming, half-dozing. She heard rain dripping off reeds and waterweeds, dimpling ponds, sighing in gusts over the restless sea. In her thoughts, or her dreams, she allowed herself to be carried along by impulses. They went against the tide, she realized: push against flow, drive against mindless drag. Mute and innocent as a polliwog she went along, seeing little beyond a silken, singing dark running against the tide. Then the tide caught the shadowy travelers, sent them swirling, tumbling in its grasp, flung them toward stones, toward the moon. They melted down, fingering themselves between stones, slithering, flattening themselves, easing around, sliding under vast slabs of wood, finding ways through the heave and swamp of tide, clinging, climbing, up and over, into the calm on the other side.

And then they began to push back at the tide.

Eada woke as though she had heard, across the city and river and fields, the sound of moored ships banging recklessly against the wharves, straining at their cables, masts reeling drunkenly, swiping at one another.

She opened her eyes, just as she felt Damaris, in her own bed, open hers, stare into the suddenly chaotic night.

Damaris, the mage said to her. *They have opened a gate.*

"I can hear it," Damaris said aloud. The mage, riding her mind, looking out of her eyes as she sprang out of bed, felt the cold stones under her feet, and the slap of wind and rain as she pushed a casement open.

In the harbor ships and boats heaved and tumbled on a tide that was trying to tear away the wharves. Some, anchored in deeper water, had already begun to drift, meandering a choppy, heedless path toward other ships, toward warehouses and moored boats. Little rain-battered blooms of fire moved quickly along the harbor's edge; some met to confer, parted again; a few vanished, doused under a wild burst of tide.

The great harbor bell in its massive tower began to boom a warning, accompanied by the high, fey voices of ships' bells careening madly in the waves.

I'll be right there, Eada told the Minister of Water, and was, quick as a thought, far more quickly than any of the Knights of the Well her thoughts had galvanized awake along the way.

The tide was still dancing its way into the open gate, which trembled mightily under the onslaught, but couldn't bring itself to close, locked, as it was, in the grip of many invisible hands. The sprites recognized the mage, who was barely visible, and who looked more like a battering ram than herself. She wedged herself against the gate and pushed back at them: an enormous snag caught against the gate, her feet its root ball in the sand, her head and shoulders its broken trunk rising above the weltering. She could hear the hisses and whispers in the rain, the spindrift.

"You'll have to sort things out another way," she told them. "Drowning Luminum will not explain anything to humans."

The longboats were casting off from the wharf, rowing against the tide. Some of her knights were among them, the strongest, the most fearless, straining against the surge to reach the gate. Their boats rode low under the weight of huge chains, which they would lock into the iron rings on the inner side of the gate, so their pulling could help the tide push it shut.

If the water-mage could only coax it free from the stubborn grip of the waterworld.

She saw, in a vivid flash of lightning, the world out of Garner's eyes as he rowed.

The sprites have gotten hold of it, she told him. *That's what you must pull against.*

She gave him a crazed glimpse of the formless swarm inside the gate jamming it open. Eada felt their strength pitted against her power. The power of persuasion would be even stronger, she thought, if only she could think of what to say.

And then she knew.

How they understood something shaped like a battered old tree trunk, she wasn't sure. Maybe they just picked the impulse and the image out of her head. *Take what you want at the Ritual of the Well*, she told them. *Until then, let the city be.*

The gate shifted; the tree trunk slid. They were gone, she realized. Vanished like the last thinning rill of a wave into sand. Water pushed the gate; the men pulled their chains, plied their oars. The trunk, angled sharply now, and underwater, prodded at the gate as it moved a few more feet. The gate closed finally; tide built against it, but could not enter. The tree trunk, finally level, floated to the surface and vanished as well.

Garner, standing at the prow of one of the longboats, struggling with wet, numb hands to unhook all the chains from the ring, nearly fell overboard yet again when the mage appeared beside him. She freed the chains easily, and passed them back into the boats alongside them. Garner stared at her, worse for the wear, she noted, thoroughly soaked again, and just waking as from a nightmare.

"What happened?" he asked hoarsely. "We couldn't budge that gate."

"I made a bargain."

The boat lurched, turning; he tumbled into a seat, took up his oars. Eada sat in the prow on the pile of chain; the knight's incredulous eyes were telling him there was no room, between him and the pile of chain, and the sea, for anything bigger than a broom straw.

"Or a shadow," she told him.

"What?"

"I need you to do something for me."

"Now?"

"Well, no, not exactly at this moment. When it seems appropriate. You know far better than I how these things go."

He pulled his oars, blinking rain out of his eyes, as though, if he could see her more clearly, she might make more sense. "Exactly what kind of bargain did you make?"

"We've got something they think is theirs. I told them they could have it back at the ritual."

"And you want me to—"

"Find it." She put a weightless hand on his shoulder, patted it. "Don't worry. Just go along as you do. How do humans put it? Follow your heart." He stared at her, his mouth hanging open to any passing wave, as she nodded. "Oh, and tell the Minister of Water what I've just told you. That's all."

Above his head, she saw that the winds were busy shredding cloud, uncovering stars, and then the glowing moon, which illumined the tattered roil, turning cloud to silk and smoke before everything blew back into black.

"But I have no idea—"

"Magic," the mage breathed, enchanted, and vanished.

Garner fell into the sea and woke.

He pulled himself out of the dream of dark, cold, weltering water, and blinked at his squire, who was reverently examining the ceremonial garb.

"For tonight, sir," he told Garner, who needed no reminding.

He sat up, holding his head together in both hands, while pieces of the extremely early morning's adventure came back to him. What had the mage said to him? Something he was supposed to find? Something he was supposed to tell Damaris.... He groaned softly.

Inis murmured sympathetically, "A short and noisy night, sir.... At least you didn't lose your boots this time. My boots." He brought Garner a cup of watered, spiced wine, and added, "Your ritual tunic has a couple of stains on it, but only in the back, and your cloak will cover them. Everything's dry, now."

"Let's hope it stays that way," Garner muttered. "See if you can get me a pair of boots made by this evening, and you'll have yours back."

"Yes, sir," Inis answered simply, having grown used to the vicissitudes of knightly endeavor, especially Garner's.

"Do I have anything decent left to wear? I have to talk to the Minister of Water." He saw the rare trace of anxiety cross his squire's face. "Have you been hearing tales?"

Inis nodded. "From everywhere in the city. And even in the palace. Your cousin, Sir Edord, was found climbing into the well near the stables yesterday. He said a woman was calling to him, and he had to rescue her. He fought, but they managed to pull him out before he got far."

Garner, musing over possibilities, breathed, "Pity..."

"Sir?"

"The mage spoke to the water creatures last night while we were having a tug-of-war over the sea gate. She made some kind of truce with them. Things will be much quieter today."

"And the ritual?" Inis prodded shrewdly.

Garner shook his head, completely mystified. "All we can do is trust that the mage knows what she's doing."

He couldn't begin to guess what Eada wanted him to find. All he could do was send a page ahead to request an interview with the Minister of Water, and hope that the mage had revealed a few more details to Damaris. The Minister of Water, summoning him immediately to her office, seemed neither surprised nor displeased to see him. She hadn't slept much, either, he guessed; her braid was becoming unraveled and her eyes seemed huge, luminous.

"Eada told me to give you a message," Garner said.

"Another one?" she marveled. "Why doesn't she speak to me?"

"I have no idea."

"She wants you to speak to me," Damaris answered herself promptly. "But why?" She gazed at him, as perplexed as he; he restrained himself from taking the braid she was picking apart out of her restless fingers, and folding her hands in his own to calm them.

"I don't know. She said that we have something the water creatures think belongs to them. She promised that, if they left Luminum in peace until the ritual, they could claim it then." He paused. She was absolutely still now, her eyes lowered, her fingers motionless. "Oh," he added, remembering, "and she wants me to find this thing. Whatever it is. Do you have any idea what she's talking about? Where do I begin to look for this nameless, vital thing?"

She raised her eyes finally. "Why you?" she asked again, her brows crumpled, her tired eyes trying to look so deeply through his that he wondered if she were trying to find the mage in his head.

"Because we have known each other most of our lives? Because I can hide nothing from you, so if I know something that will help us, you will know it, too? Because despite all my blunderings and rashness, there is nothing I wouldn't do for the Minister of Water? I don't know. Is any of that likely?"

She swallowed, looked down again, quickly. "As likely as it is unlikely."

"What should I do?" he pleaded. "Where do I begin? It must be something that the water creatures want badly, judging from the ways they have been harassing us."

"And why now?" she wondered. "What's different now?"

"You're betrothed." She stared at him. "I'm sorry," he said hastily. "I'm sorry. It was the first thing that leaped into my head. Of course, that has nothing to do with water."

"Garner—"

"You have every right to please yourself, and I have no right to torment you about your decisions. I promise I will stop. Just tell me where to go, what to look for—"

"I don't know!" she cried, so fiercely that he started. "I don't know. Garner, just go away and look for something. Anything. I have to think." He opened his mouth. She shook her head wildly and he closed it. "If I think of anything useful at all, I will send for you, I promise. I promise. Go."

So he went, following the paths of water as he had the day before, hoping at every moment for a whisper from the mage, a message from the minister. Both were silent. So were the water people, he realized as the day passed. Water behaved like water in pipes and buckets, stayed mute and did not sing. Fountains splashed with decorum; sluice gates remained as they were set; mill wheels turned placidly. Everyone waited, Garner felt.

But for what?

At dusk, he returned to the palace to dress. Inis gave him new boots, buckled his sword belt and brightly polished spurs, pinned the bright silver disc of the moon that drew all waters onto his cloak. They joined the other knights and squires in the yard where the procession was forming behind the king.

The townspeople lined the streets, carrying torches and drinking vessels. They were subdued, murmuring, laughing only softly, for the ritual was ancient, vital, and, the previous day had warned them, by no means predictable. After the king, his consort, his courtiers, the royal knights and the Knights of the Well with their torch-bearing squires had all passed, the townspeople fell in behind them. The procession grew slowly longer and longer, a river of people flowing down the twining streets of the old city, past the shrouded fountain in the square and across the bridge to the broader streets that changed, beyond Luminum, into the wide, rutted, uncobbled wagon roads between the fields.

Garner rode silently, his eyes on the gentle uprise ahead, already marked by torches thrust into the earth around the opening above the

Well. It was growing very dark. The pillars and walkways of the outer pool were lined with fire as well, where the city folk would gather to drop their gifts and wishes, and dip their cups to salute the moon. The full moon, rising in leisurely fashion out of the sea, had been following the procession for some time, arching higher and higher among the stars. By the time the king and the knights gathered around the Well itself and began the ritual, the moon would already be regarding its own perfect reflection in the water beneath the earth.

The king reached the hillock finally and drew aside. Courtiers, warriors and city folk all waited, while the Knights of the Well dismounted and filed underground through the mage's doorway. Eada drew them one by one to their positions around the Well. No one spoke, not even Edord, who usually had some appropriate exhortation ready for the occasion. Even he looked apprehensive, Garner noted, after his adventure with the nymph in the stable well. Garner himself wanted nothing more than to drown himself in the nearest tavern until dawn. He had found nothing; neither mage nor minister was speaking to him; he foresaw nothing but disaster.

The king's face appeared in the water beside the moon. He stood above them on the stony crown of the hill, alone between water and moon; torches on either side of him illumined his face. He would address the Well, giving thanks for the generosity of its waters, pay tribute to the moon that drew such pure waters out of the earth. Garner heard a quick intake of breath beside him, from the newest of Eada's knights. He was seeing for the first time the gathering faces of the underwater creatures, blurred, distorted, many of them paler than the moon, or tinged the colors of water.

Garner looked down at them morosely. They didn't look happy, either, the way they milled and turned in the water, flicking so close to the surface that they left ripples in the peaceful pool. If they had been human, he would have said they were pacing.

Eada murmured something incomprehensible. Water splashed back at her, an unprecedented occurrence. The king had just begun the traditional phrases, which had lengthened, like the night's procession, through the centuries. Along with dropping the first words into the Well, he dropped a handful of gold coins, and a carefully faceted jewel. They fell in a rich little shower, lightly pocking the water.

The jewel shot back out of the water, smacked him on the shin.

He stopped mid-word, dumbfounded. His face, above his golden beard, grew bright, somewhere near the color of the jewel. He looked torn between continuing the ritual, and fuming at his water-mage, who was just standing there, as near as Garner could tell, doing nothing. A gold piece ejected next from the water, struck a rock beside the king with a tiny, musical clang. Another, cast higher, was caught in mid-air. It seemed as though the moon itself had reached out long white fingers to claim it.

It was the Minister of Water, moving into the torchlight. The king stared at her, as did the knights; even the moon seemed to take more than a passing interest in the proceedings.

The king found his voice first.

"Lady Ambre," he said brusquely. "Why are they rejecting our gifts? Can you explain?"

She nodded. Garner, seeing again the green-eyed, foam-haired nymph in the river, felt his heart twist like a fish in his chest.

"My lord," she said ruefully, "I believe they want your Minister of Water to acknowledge her heritage." The king's brows tangled; his mouth dropped. "I don't," Damaris continued, "entirely understand the disturbance, but if it will ease the tensions between our worlds, I will claim my connection with both. My mother is human. My father, evidently, is some kind of water creature. Since I have no markings of the waterborn, only a fascination with water-works and an ability to spend an impossible amount of time under water, I was able to conceal that side of me. Until now. Now, before you all, I claim the waterborn as my kin."

The king closed his mouth wordlessly, looked again into the Well, where the accumulated coin of countless rituals, tossed lightly out of the water, caught fire as they fell, and were tossed again, as quickly as they hit the water, like a little golden rain of cheers.

"They seem," he observed cautiously, "to be pleased with that. But why now? Why disturb the entire city of Luminum over this? Why ravage my water-closet?"

"My lord, I do not know."

"Eada?"

She shook her head. "Nor I. Shall I ask them?"

"Please," said the king. But it was not his answer she wanted. The water-mage gazed at the Minister of Water, one sparse brow cocked questioningly. Damaris looked down at her silently, her face as expressionless as the moon watching over her shoulder. They were speaking to one another again, Garner realized. And about time.

Damaris came to life again, answered the water-mage with a little, decisive nod. "I'll go to them," she said. "I owe them that courtesy."

Then she was gone, gliding down a shaft of moonlight, it seemed, to fall with scarcely a ripple into the water. The king gave a cry; Garner managed to swallow his. He froze, his eyes on the thin, fading ripples crossing the moon's reflection. Nothing, he decided, could make him move; he would stand there, watching the dark water, turning himself to stone if need be, until she returned to earth.

"Where did she go?" the king demanded. "She'll drown!"

Eada patted the air, as though his head were beneath her hand. "Hush, my lord," she said. "I'm listening."

"To what?"

"To them talking. She doesn't understand their words; I must translate what I can."

"But—"

"Shh."

The king was silent finally, staring into the Well, as they all were, and then at the mage, then back at the water, trying, as they all were, with his fixed attention to raise a sign of life from it. Garner, unblinking and scarcely breathing, grasped at what he could understand of the mage's language: her quick nod of comprehension, followed by suddenly raised eyebrows, and then a mew of surprise. *What?* he shouted silently. *What?* But nothing. Yet. The knights waited soundlessly beside him, as though if they listened hard enough they might hear, within the trembling waters of the Well, the language far older than their own.

Finally, a pale, wet head appeared above the water. Damaris drew herself out onto the rocks with such ease and grace she seemed scarcely human. Garner saw the water nymph again, and felt his own powerful urge to walk across water to join her. Shifting around him, unsteady breathing, told him he would not be alone.

Then she shivered slightly and turned human in his eyes.

"Well?" the king asked harshly, unsettled himself, it seemed, by this vision of his capable Minister of Water.

"My lord," Damaris began, then gave up, gesturing helplessly to Eada. "I understood so little. Except that they were pleased that I had come to meet them in their own world."

"Yes, they were," the water-mage answered. "Very pleased."

"What did they say?" Damaris and the king asked together.

"They told Damaris that her father has found his way back to the great deep from which all things flow and to which all return."

"I guessed that," she said softly. "I am sorry. I would like to have known him. I was never brave enough to admit his existence before."

"Well, it seems that he was the powerful ruler of the realm beneath the river. He has many children, and since such water creatures like their rulers to live a long time, it is the youngest child, not the oldest, who inherits the realm. That would be you."

"Me," Damaris said blankly.

"Yes."

"But I can't—I could never—"

"Of course not. You'd not last a day under water, which would surely defeat their intentions. But by their own customs, and out of honor to your father's wish, they were duty-bound to ask you first. To do that, they had to get your attention."

"Which I never, ever wanted," she breathed. "I only wanted to be human."

"Yes."

"So they tried to speak to me in the only language we have in common. Water."

"Yes."

"But the mage understood them," the king interrupted. "Why could they not just explain all this to Eada, so that she could tell you?"

The mage was silent, letting Damaris answer, which she did, drawing herself to her feet so that she could turn and look up at him.

"Because, my lord, they were angry with me. They wanted to do me this great honor, give me this gift from my father. But I refused to hear them. I made use of their water realm, but I gave them no honor, not even the simplest courtesy of recognition. I rejected them, pretending to everyone that I am only human. I ask your forgiveness for the deception, and for being the cause of all this trouble."

"You are more than human," the king amended gruffly, and raised his voice, to make her status very clear to those courtiers who might be forming doubts about the matter. "You do us honor to refuse a kingdom for the sake of Luminum. I would hate to lose our dear friend, and our very gifted Minister of Water."

"Thank you, my lord."

"Is that all, then?" he added with a touch of anxiety. "Can we get on with it?"

"You may continue the ritual," the water-mage told him. "They are content."

After the king and his knights had drunk from the Well, and then from the pool, Garner looked for Damaris. She was nowhere in the crush of city folk and courtiers filling their cups around the pool and drinking vociferously to the moon, the Well, to Luminum and to the eagerly awaited water pipes. He found her sitting where the king had stood, well away from the noisy crowd, gazing down at the Well. Someone was with her, Garner realized, just before he walked into the torchlight. He recognized the light hair, the deep, easy, unruffled voice, and stopped, trying, for once, to be courteous, to turn and disappear.

But Lord Felden's words unraveled his good intentions.

"Of course we cannot marry," he was saying. "You understand that,

I'm sure." Damaris's answer was inaudible, even to Garner's straining ears. "I can't risk having an heir with webs between its fingers who might spend all its time in the fish pond."

"Of course not."

"My mother will understand completely."

"Yes."

There was a short silence, during which Lord Felden refused to take his leave.

"I wish I could," he admitted unexpectedly. "I've grown very fond of you. If only I were not the eldest, with the title and responsibilities—"

"But you are," the naiad on the rock at his feet said firmly. "You must do your duty. Besides, our marriage might interfere with my work, and you heard what the king said." She lifted a hand to him. "Let us stay friends."

"You're not—ah—offended?"

"No. You will continue to enjoy the benefits of my work, and I the beauties of yours. Which should not be troubled tomorrow by so much as a misplaced drop of water from the fountain."

Still he paused, for which Garner had to give him credit, much as he wished him gone. "You almost make me fall in love with you all over again," he said huskily.

"It's the water nymph in me," Damaris said evenly. "Don't take it seriously."

He went off finally, a little hurriedly, after that. Garner, motionless and awkward in the shadows, wondered if he should as well; he had no reason to suppose she would be grateful for his presence. But he took a step toward her anyway. She turned, and he watched her expression change as he emerged from the night.

"Garner," she sighed.

"I don't want to disturb you if you would prefer to be alone."

She shook her head, gesturing him to join her. She was still wet, he realized, and trembling a little in the midnight air. He took his cloak off, put it over her shoulders.

"Thank you," she said, huddling herself into it. "Thank you for noticing that I am cold. I wanted to see you."

"Really?" he marveled, sitting down beside her.

"To apologize. Did you hear any of my conversation with Lord Felden?"

"Enough," he admitted. "Are you sorry?"

"Beale offered me everything I thought would make me completely human. The wealthy noble, the title, his children—I could hide safely behind him for the rest of my life."

"Are you sorry?" he asked again.

She stared down at the reflection of the moon, which was beginning to disappear as it drifted toward the underground stream.

"I would have wronged us both," she said simply, "if I had married him. I didn't understand that until tonight. I didn't understand how little in love I was." She looked at Garner then, wryly. "You saw how wrong it was, I think. That's why you were so angry with me."

"You were angry with me."

"For seeing far too much."

He was silent, gazing into the pool. Somewhere in his idle thoughts a child with Damaris's eyes and fingers webbed with dragonfly-wings dove without a ripple into a sunlit pond.

Damaris tossed a tear of gold into the Well; the image in his head blurred, faded.

"What was that?" he asked.

"One of the king's coins. I found it in the grass."

"Did you make a wish?"

She smiled at him, untangling her feet from her wet skirt, shifting to rise. "You can have the wish. All I want now is a drink of water."

So he took it, tossing his heart into the Well after the coin, and walked with her to join the celebration.

NAMING DAY

AVERIL ASHE STARED dreamily into her oatmeal, contemplating herself. In two days it would be Naming Day at the Oglesby School of Thaumaturgy, the midpoint of the three-year course of study. Those students who had gotten through the first year and a half with satisfactory grades in such classes as Prestidigitation, Legendary Creatures, Latin, Magical Alphabets, the Uses and Misuses of Elements, and the History of Sorcery were permitted to choose the secret names they would need to continue their studies. Averil had achieved the highest marks in every class, and she was eager to investigate more widely, more profoundly, the mysterious and wizardly arts of Thaumaturgy. But under what name? She couldn't decide. What would best express her gifts, her potential, the wellsprings of her magic? More importantly, what would she be happy calling this secret self for the rest of her life?

Think of a favorite tree, Miss Braeburn, her counselor, had suggested. An animal, a bird. You might name yourself after one of those. Or one of the four elements of antiquity. Some aspect of fire, perhaps. Water.

Averil stretched her long, graceful spine, thought of her pale hair and coloring. Swan? she mused. Or something with wind in it? I'm more air than fire. Certainly not earth. Water?

"Mater," she began; she had to start practicing her Latin, which half the ancient Thaumaturges had written their spells in. "What do you think about when you think about me?"

Her mother, turning bacon at the stove, flung her a haggard, incredulous glance. She was pregnant again, at her age, and prone to throwing up at odd times. An unfortunate situation, Averil thought privately, since they had moved from a house in the suburbs to a much smaller apartment in the city for Averil's sake, to be as close as possible to Oglesby. Where, she wondered, were her impractical parents planning to put a baby? In the laundry basket? In the walk-in closet with Felix, where it was likely to be shoved under his bed along with his toys and shoes? Her brother chose that moment to draw attention from her compelling question by banging his small fist on the tines of a fork to cause the spoon lying across the handle to go spinning into the air.

"Felix!" their mother cried. "Stop that."

"Bacon, bacon, I want bacon!" Felix shouted. The spoon bounced on his head, then clattered onto the floor. He squinted his eyes, opened his mouth wide. Averil got up hastily before he began to howl.

"Averil—wait. Stop."

"Mom, gotta go; I'll be late."

"I need you to come home right after your classes today." A banshee shriek came out of Felix; their mother raised her voice. "I want you to watch Felix."

Averil's violet eyes skewed in horror toward her squalling baby brother, whose tonsils were visible. He had just turned four, a skinny, noisy, mindless bundle of mischief and energy who Averil seriously doubted was quite right in the head.

"Sorry, Mom." She grabbed her book bag hastily. After all, her mother had nothing else to do. "I have group study after school."

"Averil—"

"Mom, it's important! I'm good at my studies—one of the best in a decade, Miss Braeburn says. She thinks I can get a full scholarship to the University of Ancient Arts if I keep up my grades. That's why we moved here, isn't it? Anyway, my friends are waiting for me." Something in her mother's expression, not unlike the mingling of admiration and despair that Averil's presence caused in less gifted students, made her round the table quickly, trying not to clout Felix with her book bag, and breathe a kiss on her mother's cheek. "Ask me again after Naming Day. I might have time then."

She discussed the situation with her friends, Deirdre and Tamara and Nicholaus, as they walked to school.

"My mother should understand. After all, she almost graduated from Oglesby herself. She knows how hard we have to work."

"She did?" Nicholaus queried her with an inquisitive flash of rimless spectacles. "Why didn't she graduate? Did she fail her classes?"

Averil shrugged. "She told me she left to get married."

"Quaint."

"Well, she couldn't stay in school with me coming and all the students' practice spells flying around. I might have come out as a ruffled grouse, or something."

Deirdre chuckled, and made a minute adjustment to the butterfly pin in her wild red hair. "Baby brothers are the worst, aren't they? Mine are such a torment. They put slugs in my shoes; they color in my books; they're always whining, and they smell like boiled broccoli."

Tamara, who was taller than all of them and moved like a dancer, shook her sleek black hair out of her face, smiling. "I like my baby brother, but then he's still a baby. They're so sweet before they grow their teeth and start having opinions."

Averil murmured absently, her eyes on the boy with the white-gold hair waiting for her at the school gates. She drew a deep, full breath; the air seemed to kindle and glow through her. "There's Griffith," she said, and stepped forward into her enchanted world, full of friends, and challenges within the craggy, dark walls of the school, and Griffith with his high cheekbones and broad shoulders, watching her come.

Someone else watched her, too: a motionless, silent figure on the grass within the wrought-iron fence. An intensity seemed to pour out of him like a spell, drawing at her until, surprised, she took her eyes off Griffith to see who the stranger was.

But it wasn't a stranger, only Fitch, who blinked at the touch of her eyes, and drew back into himself like a turtle. She waved anyway, laughing a little, her attention already elsewhere.

In her classes, Averil got a perfect score conjugating Latin verbs, correctly pronounced a rune which made Dugan Lawler believe he was a parrot, and, with Griffith, was voted best in class for their history project, which traced the legendary land on which Oglesby stood back through time to the powerful forest of oak trees under which early students were taught their primitive magic. She and Griffith pretended to be teacher and student; they actually reproduced some of the ancient spells, one of which set fire to Mr. Addison's oak cane and turned on the overhead sprinklers. Averil suspected the ensuing chaos was responsible for the popularity of their project. But Mr. Addison, after mending his cane and drying the puddles with some well-chosen words, complimented them on their imaginative interpretation of ancient history.

After school, she and Griffith, Nicholaus, Tamara, and Deirdre went to Griffith's house to study. The place was huge, quiet, and tidy, full of leather-bound books and potted plants everywhere. Griffith had no siblings; his parents were both scholars and understood the importance of study. His mother left them alone with a tray of iced herbal tea and brownies in the dining room; they piled their books on the broad mahogany table and got to work.

Later, when they had finished homework and quizzed each other for tests, talk drifted to the all-important Naming Day.

"I can't decide," Averil sighed, sliding limply forward in her chair and enjoying the reflection of her long ivory hair on the dark, polished wood. "Has anyone chosen a name, yet?"

Tamara had, and Nicholaus. Deirdre had narrowed it down to two, and Griffith said he had had a secret name since he was seven. So they could all give their attention to Averil.

"I thought: something to do with air?" she began tentatively. "Wind?"

"Windflower," Griffith said promptly, making her blush.

"Windhover," Tamara offered. Averil looked blank; she added, "It's a falcon."

"I don't think I'm a falcon. More like a—well, something white."

"Snow goose?" Deirdre suggested practically. "Nobody would ever guess that."

"Swan, of course," Nicholaus said. "But that'd be too obvious. How about egret? Or I think there's a snowy owl—"

Averil straightened. "Those aren't really names, are they? Not something really personal that defines me."

"What about a jewel?" Tamara said. "A diamond?"

"Pearl," Griffith said softly, smiling a little, making Averil smile back.

"Something," she agreed, "more like that."

It was all so interesting, trying to find the perfect name for Averil, that nobody remembered the time. Griffith's mother reminded them; they broke up hastily, packing away books and pens, winding long silk scarves around their throats, prognosticating cold suppers and peeved parents.

"Stay," Griffith said to Averil, making a spell with his caramel eyes so that Averil's feet stuck to the threshold.

"Well—"

"Stay for supper. My parents are going out. I'll cook something."

"I should call—"

"Call your mother. Tell her we're working on a project."

"But we're not," Averil objected; true wizards did not need to lie.

"We are," he said, with his bewitching smile. "Your name."

Averil got home later than even she considered marginal for excusable behavior. Fortunately, her father was already being taken to task for his own lateness, and Averil only got added to the general list of complaints. Still enchanted, she barely listened.

"You don't realize—" her mother said, and, "No consideration—"

"Sorry, dear," her father said soothingly. "I should have called, but I kept thinking we'd get the work finished earlier."

"Stone cold dinner—"

"Sorry, Mom," Averil echoed dutifully.

"If I don't get a moment to myself, I'm going to—"

"After Naming Day, I promise."

"Now, dear, he's barely four. He'll settle down soon enough. Take him to the park or something."

Her mother made a noise like cloth ripping, the beginning of tears.

Her father opened his arms. Averil let her book bag fall to the floor and drifted away, thinking of Griffith's farewell kiss.

She escaped out the door without breakfast the next morning after allowing her mother, who was on the phone pleading with a baby-sitting service, a brief glimpse of her face. At the table, Felix was upending a cereal box over his bowl.

"Bye, Mom."

"Averil—"

"See you, but don't know when. There might be a celebration later. It's Naming Day."

"Av—Felix!"

Averil closed the door to the sound of a gentle rain of Fruitie Flakes all over the floor.

She was halfway down the block, already searching the flowing current of students for Griffith's white-gold hair, when she remembered her book bag. It was still on the living room floor where she had dropped it; escaping the morning drama in the kitchen had taken up all her attention. She turned back quickly, trying to make herself invisible so that her mother wouldn't start in again at the sight of her. I am wind, she told herself, pulling open the apartment building door. I am... spindrift.

Spindrift! There was a name, she realized triumphantly, running up the two flights of stairs rather than wait for the elevator. White as swans' feathers, a braid of wind and wave and foam, always graceful, never predictable.... She flung the door open, leaving it wide for a hasty escape, and as she rushed in, something shot past her so fast it left only a vague impression of gnarly limbs and light in her eyes before it vanished out the door.

"My wand!"

The screech hit Averil like a spell; she skidded to a stop. This wasn't her apartment, she saw, appalled. She had barged through the wrong door. And there was this—this huge, ancient and incredibly ugly thaumaturge-thing, a witch or crazed wizard, seething at her from behind a cauldron bubbling over a firebed on her living room floor.

"You let my greyling out!"

"I'm sorry," Averil gasped. Plants crawling up the walls, across the ceiling, whispered with their enormous leaves and seemed to quiver with horror.

"Well, don't just stand there like a gape-jawed booby, get it back!

Averil closed her mouth, tried to retrieve some dignity. "I'm sorry," she repeated. Her voice wobbled in spite of herself. "I have to get to school. I just came back for my book bag, and I must have gone up an extra floor." She took a step, edging back toward the door. "I'll just— Your greyling is probably downstairs; I'll just go see. I won't let it get out of the front door, I promise."

Up the stairwell behind her came the distinct rattle of a heavy door fitting its locks and hinges and frame back into place as it closed. The old witch seemed to fill like a balloon behind her cauldron. Her tattered white hair stiffened; her eyes, like thumbprints of tar in her wrinkled skin, slewed and glinted.

"You get my greyling. You get my wand."

"I haven't time!"

"You let them out. You bring them back."

"I have classes! It's my Naming Day!" Even a senile old bag like that must have anticipated her own Naming Day once. If things had names that long ago. "You must remember how important that is."

"You. Get. My. Wand."

"All right, okay," Averil gabbled; anything to get out the door.

The witch's murky eyes narrowed into slits. "Until you bring me back my wand and my greyling, you will be invisible. No one will see you. No one will hear your voice. Until you bring me my greyling and my wand, even your own name will be useless to you."

"I don't have time." Averil's voice had gone somewhere; she could barely whisper. "I have to get to school."

"Then you'd better start looking."

"You can't do that!" Her voice was back suddenly, high and shrill, like a whistling teakettle. "I'm at the top of my class! My teachers will come looking for me! Griffith will rescue me!"

"Go!"

She couldn't tell if she moved, or if the word itself blew her out the door; it slammed behind her, echoing the witch's voice. She stood in the hall a moment, trembling and thoughtless. Then she took a sharp breath—"The greyling!"—and precipitated herself down the stairs two at a time, on the off-chance that the witch's familiar still lurked in the hallway below.

Of course it was nowhere in sight.

Averil plunged out the door, trying wildly to look every direction at once. What exactly was a greyling? She racked her brains; nothing leaped to mind from her Legendary Creatures class. Did it like water? High tree limbs? Caves? Could it speak? She hadn't a clue. A jumble of pallid, root-like limbs and a sort of greeny-yellow light were all she remembered. The one must be the greyling, the other the pilfered wand. She hoped desperately that the greyling wouldn't have the power to use it.

A familiar figure crossed the street toward the school. "Tamara!" Averil shouted with relief. Tamara's long stride didn't falter. She called out to someone herself; her voice seemed small, distorted, like words heard from under water. Ahead of her, a dark head turned; spectacles flashed. "Nicholaus!" Averil cried, hurrying toward them. "Tamara!"

Neither of them heard. They greeted one another, and then Deirdre caught up with them, red hair flying. They chattered excitedly, finally turning to survey the street where surely they would see, they must see Averil running toward them, yelling and waving her arms.

Their faces grew puzzled. A bell tolled once, reverberations overlapping with exaggerated slowness. It was the warning bell; those outside the gates at First Bell would be locked out. The three moved again, quickly. In the distance, Averil could see Griffith, just within the gates, waiting for them, for her.

However fast she followed, they were always faster. As though, she thought, breathlessly sprinting, they were always in the next moment, a slightly different beat in time; she could never quite catch up. She stopped finally with a despairing cry as her friends passed through the gates; they seemed farther away than ever. They spoke to Griffith; he shrugged a little, then pointed toward a high window, where their first class would begin. Maybe Averil's there, his gesture said. First Bell tolled three times. The gates began to close. As the last students jostled inside, Averil noticed one face still peering through the bars, searching the streets. Fitch, she recognized glumly. And then even he turned away, went up the broad stone steps into the school.

Behind her, something crashed. She jumped, then whirled in time to see the greyling balanced on the side of a garbage can it had overturned. Among the litter, a cat puffed itself up twice its size and hissed furiously. The greyling opened its mouth and hissed back. Averil finally saw it clearly: a grotesque imp with big ears and a body so narrow it seemed all skinny limbs and head, like a starfish. It held a stick with a dandelion of light at one end. A cartoon wand, Averil thought disgustedly. More for the goopy Tinker Bell fairy than for an evil-tempered, snag-toothed old hag who had stopped Averil's world.

The greyling leaped, clearing the spilled garbage and the cat. Averil moved then, faster than she had ever moved in her life.

The greyling rolled a huge, silvery eye at her as she gained on it, seeming to realize finally that something was after it. It increased its pace, blowing down the sidewalks and alleyways like a tumbleweed. Averil followed grimly. Nobody else saw it. Other people walked in a tranquil world where bus brakes and car horns made noises in miniature, and the shrieks of kids in the school playground sounded like the distant chirping of well-behaved birds.

Averil pursued the greyling across the park. It skittered up a tree and made faces at her until she drove it out with some well-placed pinecones. It led her up one side of the jungle gym and down the other, then disappeared completely. She found it in the rose garden, with roses stuffed in both ears and its mouth, trying to disguise itself as a bush. It waved the wand at her, shaking a sprinkle of light between them which Averil ran through before she could stop. But nothing happened. She heard several deep, familiar booms, then; the sounds echoed and rippled through the air with viscous slowness, melting into

Averil's heart, which grew iron with despair. Second Bell. The Naming Hour itself. And where was she? Chasing an imp through a world where nobody who knew her name could even see her.

A thought struck her. She missed a step, stumbling a little, so that the greyling leaped ahead. It veered into a small forest of giant ferns and vanished.

You're a student of magical arts, the thought said. Do some magic.

She slowed, panting. Eyes narrowed, she searched the stand of ferns for a single quivering leaf, the slightest movement among the shadows and shafts of mellow light. Nothing. She listened, tuning her ears the way she had been taught, to hear the patter of a millipede's feet across a leaf, the bump of a beetle's back against a clod of dirt. She heard the faintest of breaths. Or was it a butterfly's wings, opening and closing in the light?

She drew the rich, dusty light into her eyes and into her mind, where she focused and shaped it into a brilliant, sharply pointed letter of an ancient, magical alphabet, and let it loose in a sudden shout, hoping she was pronouncing it correctly.

The fern grove lit up as though someone had set off fireworks in it. Within the glittering, spinning wheels and sprays of light, the greyling exploded from behind a trunk and scrambled to the very top of a fern tree. It dangled there precariously, wailing at her, its eyes as huge as saucers.

She yelled back at it, "Ha!" and ran to get the wand.

She found it easily as her own fires died: the only glowing thing left on the ground. She studied it curiously, then carefully touched the puff of light. It didn't burn her, or change in any way; she didn't even feel it. She smelled something, though, that seemed peculiar in the middle of a fern grove.

Vanilla?

She looked up in time to see the greyling gather its spidery limbs and rocket off the fern head in a desperate leap that sent it smack into someone who had emerged out of nowhere to stare up at it. They both tumbled to the ground. The greyling wriggled to its feet, but not quickly enough. A hand shot out to grab its skinny ankle; a voice shouted breathlessly, "Gotcha!"

Averil blinked. The newcomer transferred his grip to the greyling's wrist as he got up off the ground. He smiled crookedly at Averil, who finally found her voice.

"Fitch!"

"Hey."

"What are you—why on earth did you—" The color was pushing so brightly into his face it seemed to tinge the air around him, she saw with fascination; he would have glowed in the dark. Only his fingers, wound around the hissing, whimpering, struggling greyling, hadn't forgotten what he was doing there. Averil's brows leaped up as high as they could go; so did her voice. "What did you do? Did you follow me?"

"Well." He swallowed with a visible effort. "I could see you, but I couldn't reach you until you made that magic. Then that weird spell forcing the jog in time pushed our moments back together, at least long enough so that—so—"

"Here you are."

"Yeah."

"On your Naming Day."

"Well," he said again, his face growing impossibly redder. "You were in trouble. I don't think real wizards get to choose a convenient time and place to do what they think they have to."

Averil studied him speechlessly. He was taller than she expected; he always seemed to shrink into himself when she was around. His brown, floppy hair did a good job of hiding his face; what she could see of it looked interesting enough. Between his hair and woodsy skin, she'd just assumed his eyes were dark, too. But he'd scarcely let her meet his eyes before, and now she saw the glints of blue within his hair.

Her voice leaped up a few notches again. "You saw me!" He gave a brief nod, dodging the kick the greyling aimed at his shin. "Nobody else could see me! That was part of the spell."

"That's what I thought, when I saw you calling your friends and they didn't notice you."

"Then how could you see me?"

His mouth curled in a little, slantwise smile. "It's one of the things I happen to be good at. Recognizing magic when it's around. Also." He stuck there, picking at words, ignoring the greyling jumping up and down on his toes. "You might have noticed. I watch you."

"Lots of people do," Averil said hastily, afraid that if he blushed any harder he might hurt himself.

His eyes came back to her. "You know what I'm saying. I've always wanted to talk to you. But I never thought you'd be interested."

"So you snuck out of school on Naming Day just to talk to me while I was alone for once?"

His smile flashed out at that, changing his entire face, she saw with surprise; it looked open now, and unafraid. "Right. I thought we might have a conversation while you were chasing this little goblin around garbage cans and up trees."

"Then why didn't you just tell one of the teachers?" she demanded bewilderedly. "You wouldn't have missed your Naming."

"I know my name," he said simply. I don't need to write it in ancient letters on a piece of tree bark and burn it in an oak fire. That's just a ritual."

Averil opened her mouth; nothing came out. The greyling showed teeth suddenly, aiming for Fitch's fingers. She rapped it sharply on its head with the witch's wand. "I'd better take this thing back, before it gets away from me again," she said, as the yellow-green fairy light shaken off the wand dazzled and glittered in the air around them.

"Where does it belong?"

"To a gnarly old warthog of a witch who put a spell on me when I accidentally let her greyling out."

Fitch grunted, watching the sparkles sail past his nose. "Funny light. Doesn't seem to do much, does it?"

"No. And it smells odd. Like—"

"Vanilla."

Averil shook her head, puzzled. "Bizarre... "

"Do you want me to help you take it back?"

She considered that, tempted, then shook her head again; no sense in introducing the witch to more opportunities for mischief. "No. It's my problem...but now you won't be able to get back into the school."

She saw his slanted smile again. "I have my ways."

"Really?"

"Doesn't everyone?"

"No," she said, amazed. "I always follow all the rules. At least at school."

"Well, of course, there's something to be said for that." He paused; she waited. "I just said it."

"You made a joke," she exclaimed. "I didn't even know you could smile, before." She took the greyling's skinny wrist out of his hold, wondering suddenly what else went on in that obscure realm under Fitch's untidy hair. "I always get perfect grades. How can you know things I don't?"

He shrugged. "I don't know. You're brilliant. Everyone notices what you do. So you have to watch yourself. I get to do things nobody notices."

She mulled that over, while the greyling tried to run circles around her. "Maybe we could talk?" she suggested. "Some time soon?"

He blushed again, but not so much. "I'd like that."

"I think I would, too." The greyling nearly spun her off her feet, then tangled itself around the foot she stuck in its path. "I'd better finish what I started with the witch," she said grimly, hauling the greyling up. "Thanks for helping me. That was really nice of you."

"You're sure—" Fitch said doubtfully, walking backward away from her.

"I'd like to think all my studying is worth something."

"Okay, then. Good luck with the witch."

"Thanks," she said between her teeth, and dragged the furious greyling the opposite direction.

The greyling finally stopped struggling when the door to the apartment building closed behind them. It trudged upstairs quietly beside Averil, only muttering a little now and then, its ribbony arm dangling limply in her hold. She scarcely heard it; she was trying to figure out how Fitch was getting back into school without being caught. Did he already know how to turn invisible? What other things might he have learned on his own, while she was only learning what was required? Would breaking rules make him a better wizard? Better than, say, Griffith, who would surely have skipped his Naming Day to come and help her, if he had been able to see her. Or would he? More likely, he would have done the practical thing and simply told one of their teachers that she seemed to be in trouble. Try as she might, she couldn't imagine Griffith missing his Naming to sneak out of school and help her catch some witch's demented familiar.

She was thinking so intently that she had opened the door of her own apartment out of habit. Her mother, sitting on the couch and reading, lifted her head to smile at Averil, who remembered, horrified, what she was holding.

"Hi, Mom," she said hastily, backing out before she had to explain the greyling. "Oops. I'll just be a—"

"Thanks, Averil," her mother sighed. "That's the most peaceful morning I've had in years."

The greyling broke free of Averil, ran to the couch, and climbed up beside their mother. "I'm tired," Felix groaned, falling sideways onto her lap. "Really, really, really—"

"Oh, that's wonderful, sweetie."

Averil, frozen in the doorway, remembered finally how to breathe. Her eyes felt gritty, as though fairy dust had blown into them. With great effort, she swiveled them toward the witch's wand in her hand.

Wooden mixing spoon.

"Mom—" Her voice croaked like a frog; she still couldn't move. "How did you—how could you—?"

"Well, you saw what I was turning into. Nobody was listening to me."

"But how—"

"I learned a few things at the school before I left to have you." She stroked Felix's hair gently; he was already asleep. "Peace," she breathed contentedly.

"Mom. It was my Naming Day."

Her mother just looked at her. Averil saw the witch in her eyes, then, shadowy, shrewd, filled with remnants of magic. "And did you finally choose a name?"

Averil looked back at the Averil who had been so blithely trying on lovely names and discarding them just that morning. She moved finally, closing the door behind her. She dropped down on the couch next to Felix.

"No," she admitted, twirling the spoon handle through her hair. "And now, nothing seems to fit me."

Her mother said after a moment, "I have a name that I haven't used since I left Oglesby, until today. You can have it, if you want."

"Really?" Averil studied her mother, suddenly curious. "What is it?"

Her mother leaned over Felix, whispered it into Averil's ear. The name seemed to flow through her like air and light. Her eyes grew wide; visions and enchantments swirled in her head. "Mom, that's brilliant," she exclaimed, straightening with a bounce. "That's amazing!" Felix stirred; they both patted him until he quieted. "How did you think of it?" Averil whispered.

"It was just there, when I looked for it. Do you want it?"

"Are you sure? You really want me to have it?"

Her mother smiled wryly. "I really don't want to be tempted to use magic on my children again. Anyway, ever since you became interested in the wizardly arts, I dreamed of giving it to you. Of it meaning all the wonderful things you could do." She paused, shifted a strand of Averil's shining hair back from her face. "Lately, I haven't been sure that you'd want it."

"I want it," Averil said softly. "I want it more than any other name. I never would have thought of it, but it's perfect. It feels like me."

"Good." Her mother rose then, took the spoon from her. "I'm glad you brought this back; it's my favorite mixing spoon."

"You didn't give me much choice." Averil watched her walk into the kitchen to drop the spoon into the utensils jar. "You made a pretty fierce witch."

"Thanks, sweetie. Are you hungry? Do you want a sandwich before you go back to school?"

"You know they won't let me in after First Bell."

"That's what they say," her mother said with a chuckle. "But once you find your way in, they always let you stay."

Averil stared at her. She glimpsed something then, in the corner of her mind's eye; it grew clearer as she turned her thoughts to contemplate it. Her mother, giving up all the knowledge she had acquired at Oglesby, all that potential, just to go and have Averil and take care of her. And now that incredible name...

She drew a sudden breath, whispered, "I didn't miss it."

Her mother, who had stuck her head in the refrigerator and was searching through jars, said, "What?"

"My Naming. You just named me."

Her mother turned, embracing mayonnaise, mustard, pickles, cold cuts and a head of lettuce. "What, sweetie? I didn't hear you."

"Never mind," Averil said, and summoned all her powers to speak words of most arduous and dire magic. "I'll-watch-Felix-for-the-rest-of-the-day-if-you-want-to-go-out."

Her mother heard that just fine.

BYNDLEY

THE WIZARD RECK wandered into Byndley almost by accident. He had been told so many ways to get to it that he had nearly missed it entirely. Over a meadow, across a bridge, through a rowan wood, left at a crossroads, right at an old inn that had been shut tight for decades except for the rooks. And so on. By twilight he had followed every direction twice, he thought, and gotten nowhere. He was trudging over thick oak slabs built into a nicely rounded arc above a stream when the lacy willow branches across the road ahead parted to reveal the thatched roofs and chimneys of a village. *Byndley*, said the sign on the old post leaning toward the water at the end of the bridge. That was all. But the wizard saw the mysterious dark behind the village that flowed on to meet the dusk and he felt his own magic quicken in answer.

"You want to know what?" had been the most common response to the question he asked along his journey. An incredulous snort of laughter usually followed.

How to get back again, how to get elsewhere, how to get *there*....

"But why?" they asked, time and again. "No one goes looking for it. You're lured, you're tricked there, you don't come back, and if you do, it's not to the same world."

I went there, he thought. I came back.

But he never explained, only intimated that he was doing the king's bidding. Then they straightened their spines a bit—the innkeepers, the soldiers, those who had been about the world or heard travelers' tales—and adjusted their expressions. Nobody said the word aloud;

206

everyone danced around it; they all knew what he meant, though none had ever been there. That, Reck thought, was the strangest thing of all about the realm of Faerie: no one had seen, no one had been, no one said the word. But everyone knew.

Finally somebody said, "Byndley," and then he began to hear that word everywhere.

"Ask over in Byndley; they might know."

"Ask at Byndley. They're always blundering about in magic."

"Try Byndley. It's just that way, half a day at most. Take a left at the crossroads."

And there Byndley was, with its firefly windows just beginning to flicker against the night, and the great oak forest beyond it, the border, he suspected, between here and there, already vanishing out of day into dream.

He stopped at the first tavern he saw and asked for a bed. He wore plain clothes, wool and undyed linen, boots that had walked through better days. He wore his face like his boots, strong and serviceable but nothing that would catch the eye. He didn't want to be recognized, to be distracted by requests for wizardry. The thing he carried in his pack grew heavier by the day. He had to use power now to lift it, and the sooner he relinquished it the better.

"My name is Reck," he told the tavern keeper at the bar as he let the pack slide from his shoulder. "I need a bed for a night or two or maybe—" He stopped, aware of a stentorious commotion as his pack hit the floor. The huge young man standing beside him, half-naked and sweating like a charger, his face flushed as by his own bellows, was rubbing one sandaled foot and snorting. "Did I drop my pack on you?" Reck asked, horrified. "I beg your pardon."

"It's been stepped on by worse," the man admitted with an effort. "What are you carrying in there, stranger? A load of anvils?" He bent before Reck could answer, hauled the pack off the floor and handed it back. Reck, unprepared, sagged for an instant under the weight. The man's dark, innocent eye met his through a drift of black, shaggy hair as Reck balanced his thoughts to bear the sudden weight. The man turned his head, puffed one last time at his foot, then slapped the oak bar with his palm.

"Ale," he demanded. "One for the stranger, too."

"That's kind of you."

"You'll need it," the man said, "against the fleas." He grinned as the tavern keeper's long gray mustaches fluttered in the air like dandelion seed.

"There are no fleas," he protested, "in my establishment. Reck, you said?" He paused, chewing at his mustaches. "Reck. You wouldn't be the wizard from the court at Chalmercy, would you?"

"Do I look like it?" Reck asked with wonder.

"No."

Reck left it at that. The tavern keeper drew ale into two mugs. They were all silent, then, watching the foam subside. Reck, listening to the silence, broke it finally.

"Then what made you ask?"

The young man gave an astonished grunt. The tavern keeper smiled slowly. His fatuous, egg-shaped face, crowned with a coronet of receding hair, achieved a sudden, endearing dignity.

"I know a little magic," he said shyly. "Living so close"—he waved a hand inarticulately toward the wood—"you learn to recognize it. My name is Frayne. On slow nights, I open an odd book or two that came my way and never left. Sometimes I can almost make things happen. This is Tye. The blacksmith, as you might have guessed."

"It wasn't hard," Reck commented. The smith, who had a broad, pleasant face beneath his wild hair, grinned delightedly as though the wizard had produced some marvel.

"My brain's made of iron," he confessed. "Magic bounces off it. Some, though, like Linnea down the road—she can foresee in water and find anything that's lost. And Bettony—" He shook his head, rendered speechless by Bettony.

"Bettony," the tavern keeper echoed reverently. Then he came down to earth as Reck swallowed ale. "There's where you should go to find your bed."

"I'm here," Reck protested.

"Well, you shouldn't be, a wizard such as you are. She's as poor as any of us now, but back a ways, before they started disappearing into the wood for decades on end, her family wore silk and washed in perfumed water and rode white horses twice a year to the king's court at Chalmercy. She'll give you a finer bed than I've got and a tale or two for the asking."

"About the wood?"

The tavern keeper nodded and shrugged at the same time. "Who knows what to believe when talk starts revolving around the wood?" He wiped a drop from the oak with his sleeve, then added tentatively, "You've got your own tale, I would guess. Why else would a great wizard come to spend a night or two or maybe more in Byndley?"

Reck hesitated; the two tried to watch him without looking at him. He had to ask his way, so they would know eventually, he decided; nothing in this tiny village would be a secret for long. "I took something," he said at last, "when I was very young, from a place I should not have entered. Now I want to return the thing I stole, but I don't know how to get back there." He looked at them helplessly "How can you ever find your way back to that place once you have left it?"

The tavern keeper, seeing something in his eyes, drew a slow breath through his mouth. "What's it like?" he pleaded. "Is it that beautiful?"

"Most things only become that beautiful in memory."

"How did you find your way there in the first place?" Tye the blacksmith asked bewilderedly. "Can't you find the same way back?"

Reck hesitated. Frayne refilled his empty mug, pushed it in front of the wizard.

"It'll go no farther," he promised, as earnestly as he had promised a bed without fleas. But Reck, feeling himself once more on the border, with his theft weighing like a grindstone on his shoulders, had nothing left to lose.

"The first time, I was invited in." Again, his eyes filled with memories, so that the faces of the listening men seemed less real than dreams. "I was walking through an oak wood on king's business and with nothing more on my mind than that, when the late afternoon light changed.... You know how it does. That moment when you notice how the sunlight you've ignored all day lies on the yellow leaves like beaten gold and how threads of gold drift all around you in the air. Cobweb, you think. But you see gold. That's when I saw her."

"Her," Tye said. His voice caught.

"The Queen of Faerie. Oh, she was beautiful." The wizard raised his mug, drank. He lowered it, watched her walking toward him through the gentle rain of golden, dying leaves. "Her hair..." he whispered. "Her eyes... She seemed to take her colors from the wood, as she came toward me, gold threads catching in her hair, her eyes the green of living leaves.... She spoke to me. I scarcely heard a word she said, only the lovely sound of her voice. I must have told her anything she wanted to know, and said yes to anything she asked.... She drew me deep into the wood, so deep that I was lost in it, though I don't remember moving from that enchanted place...."

He drank again. As he lowered the mug, the wood around him faded and he saw the rough-hewn walls around him, the rafters black with smoke, the scarred tables and stools. He smelled stale ale and onions. The two faces, still, expressionless, became human once again, one balding and innocuous, one hairy and foolish, and both avid for more.

Reck drained his mug, set it down. "And that's how I found my way there," he said hollowly, "the first time."

"But what did you steal?" Tye asked breathlessly. "How did you get free? You can't just end it—"

The tavern keeper waved him silent. "Leave him be now; he's paid for his ale and more already." He took Reck's mug and assiduously polished the place on the worn oak where it had stood. "You might come back tomorrow evening. By then the whole village will know what you're looking for, and anyone with advice will drop by to give it to you."

Reck nodded. His shoulder had begun to ache under the weight of the pack despite all his magic. "Thank you," he said tiredly. "If you won't give me a bed here, then I'll take myself to Bettony's."

"You won't be sorry," Frayne said. "Keep going down the road to the end of the village and you'll see the old hall just at the edge of the wood. You can't miss it. Tell Bettony I sent you." He raised a hand as the wizard turned. "Tomorrow, then."

Reck found the hall easily, though the sun had set by then and near the wood an ancient dark spilled out from the silent trees. Silvery dusk lingered over the rest of Byndley. The hall was small, with windows set hither and yon in the walls, and none matching. Its stone walls, patched in places, looked very old. The main door, a huge slab of weathered oak, stood open. As he neared, Reck heard an ax slam cleanly through wood, and then the clatter of broken kindling. He rounded the hall toward the sound and came upon a sturdy young woman steadying another piece on her block.

She let go of the wood on the block and swung the ax to split it neatly in two. Then she straightened, wiped her brow with her apron, and turned with a start to the stranger.

He said quickly, "Frayne sent me."

She was laughing before he finished, at her sweat, her dirty hands, her long hair sliding loosely out of its clasp. "He picked his moment, didn't he?" She balanced the ax blade in the chopping block with a blow, and tossed pieces of kindling into her apron. "You are?"

"My name is Reck. Frayne told me to find a lady called Bettony and ask her for a bed."

"I'm Bettony," she said. Her eyes were as bright and curious as a bird's; in the twilight their color was indeterminate. "Reck," she repeated. "The wizard?"

"Yes."

"Passing through?"

"No."

"Ah, then," she said softly, "you came because of the wood." She turned. "If you can bear carrying anything else, bring some kindling in with you."

Reck, wondering, gathered an armload and followed her.

"I'm my own housekeeper," Bettony said as she piled the kindling on the great, blackened hearth inside the house, and Reck let his pack drop to the flagstones with a noiseless sigh. "Though I have a boy who takes care of the cows." She flicked him a glance. "That heavy, is it? Shouldn't such a skilled wizard be able to lighten his load a little?"

"That's why I came here," Reck said grimly, and she was silent. She lit a taper from a lamp, and stooped to hold it to the kindling. He watched her coax flame out of the wood. Light washed over her face. It looked more young than old, both strong and sweet, very tranquil. Under the teasing flame, he still couldn't see the color of her eyes.

She gave him bread seasoned with rosemary, a deep bowl of savory stew, and wine. While he ate, she sat across from him on a hearth bench and talked about the wood. "My family wandered in and out of it for centuries," she told him. "Their tales became family folklore. Some were written; others just passed from one generation to the next along with the family nose. Even if the tales weren't true, truth would never stand a chance against them."

"Have you ever been—"

"To fairyland and back? No. Nor would I swear, not even on a turnip, that any of my ancestors had. But I've seen the odd thing here and there; I've heard and not quite heard...enough that I believe it's there, in that ancient wood, if you can find your way." He nodded, his eyes on the fire, seeing and not quite seeing, and heard her voice again. "You've been there and back."

"Yes," he said softly.

"That weight in your pack. That's what brings you here."

"Yes."

"What—" Then she smiled, waving away the unspoken question. "It's none of my business. I've just been trying to imagine what it must be that you want so badly to give to them."

"Return," he amended.

"Return." She drew a quick breath, her eyes widening, and he saw their color then: a gooseberry green, somehow pale and warm at the same time. "You stole it?"

"A more tactful innkeeper would have assumed that it was given to me," he commented.

"Yes. But if you wanted half-truths I could give you family lore by the bushel. I'm perceptive. Frayne thinks it's a kind of magic. It's not, really. It simply comes of fending for myself."

"Oh, there's some magic in you. I sense it. I think that if we picked apart your family folklore we would unravel many threads of truth in the tangle. That would take time, though. As you so quickly observed, what I carry is becoming unbearably heavy. Even my powers are faltering under it."

"Take it into the wood," she suggested. "Set it down and walk away from it. Don't look back."

"That doesn't work," he sighed. "I've lost count of the number of times and all the places I've walked away from without looking back. It always finds me. I must return it to the place where it will stay." She watched him, silent again, her eyes wide and full of questions. Is it terrible? he heard in her reluctant silence. Is it beautiful? Did you take it out of love or hate? Will you miss it, once you give it back?

"I stole it," he said abruptly, for keeping secrets from her seemed pointless, "from the Queen of Faerie. It was something she loved; her husband had his sorcerer make it for her. I took it partly to hurt her, because she stole me out of my world and made me love her and she did not love me, and partly because it is very beautiful, and partly so that I could show it to others, as proof that I had been in the realm of Faerie and found my way back to this world. I took it out of anger and jealousy, wounded pride and arrogance. And out of love, most certainly out of love. I wanted to remember that once I had been in that secret, gorgeous country just beyond imagination, and to possess in this drab world a tiny part of that one."

"All that," she said wonderingly.

"I was that young," he sighed. "Such things are so complex then."

"Do you still love her?"

"That young man I was will always love her," he answered, smiling ruefully. "That, I can't return to her."

"But how did you escape their world? And how can you be certain that this time you will be able to find your way out of it again?"

"It wasn't easy," he murmured, remembering. "The king and his greatest sorcerer came after me...." He shrugged away her second question. "One problem at a time. All I know is that I must return. I can't live in my world with what I stole from theirs." He set his plate aside. "If there's any way you can help me—"

"I'll tell you what tales came down to me," she promised. "And I can show you things my ancestors wrote, describing what stream they followed that turned into a path of silver or fairy moonlight, what rose bush they fell asleep under to wake up Elsewhere, what black horse or hare they chased beyond the world they knew. It all sounds like dreams to me, wishes out of a wine cup. But who am I to say? You have been there after all." She rose, lit a pair of tapers, and handed him one. "Come with me. I keep all those old writings in a chest upstairs, along with other odds and ends. Souvenirs of Faerie they're said to be, but none so burdensome as yours."

She told him family folklore, and showed him fragile papers stained with wine, half-coherent descriptions of improbable adventures, and rambling musings about the nature of magic, all infused with a bittersweet longing and loss that Reck felt again in his own heart, as though no time had passed at all in the realm of his memories. The writers had brought tokens back with them, as Reck had. Theirs were dead roses that never crumbled and still retained the faintest smell of summer, dried leaves that in the Otherworld had been buttons and coins of gold, a tarnished ring that once had glowed with silver fire to light the path of Bettony's great-great-grandfather as he stumbled his way from a tavern into fairyland, a rusty key that unlocked a door that had appeared in the oldest oak tree in the wood....

"Such things," Bettony said, half-laughing, half-sighing over her eccentric family. "Maybe, maybe not, they all seem to say. But then again, maybe."

"Yes," Reck said softly. He glanced out a window, seeing through the black of night the faint, haunting shapes of ancient trees. "I'm very grateful that Frayne sent me to you. This must be the place I have been searching for, a part of their great wood that spills into ours and becomes the path between worlds. Thank you for your help. I'll gladly repay you with any kind of magic you might need."

"There's magic in a tale," she replied simply "I'd like to hear the whole of yours when you come back out."

He smiled again, touched. "That's kind of you. Come to Frayne's tavern tomorrow evening and I'll tell you as much as I know so far. That's the debt I owe to Frayne."

She closed the chest and stood up, dusting centuries from her hands. "I wouldn't miss it. Nor will the rest of Byndley," she added lightly. "So be warned."

Reck spent the next day roaming through the great wood, hoping that his heart, if not his eye, would recognize the tree that was a door, the stream that was a silver path into the Otherworld. But at the end of the day the wood was just a wood, and the only place he found his way back to was Byndley. He went to Frayne's tavern, sat down wearily and asked for supper. The pack on the floor at his feet weighed so heavily in his thoughts he scarcely noticed that the comings and goings behind him as he ate his mutton and drank his ale were all comings: feet entered but did not leave. When he turned finally to ask for more ale, he found what looked like an entire village behind him, gazing at him respectfully and waiting.

Even Bettony was there, sitting in a place of honor on a chair beside the fire. She nodded cheerfully to him. So did the blacksmith Tye behind her. He picked the ale Frayne had already poured off the counter; the mug made its way from hand to hand until it reached the wizard.

"Where did we leave off?" Tye asked briskly.

There were protests all around him from villagers clustered in the shadowy corners, sitting on tables as well as benches and stools, and even on the floor. The wizard must begin again; not everyone had heard; they wanted the entire tale, beginning to end, and they would pay to keep the wizard's glass full for as long as he needed.

The innkeeper shook his head. "The tale will pay for itself," he said, and propped himself against the bar to listen.

Reck cleared his throat and began again.

By mid-tale there was not a sound in the place. No one had bothered to replenish the fire; the faces leaning towards Reck were vague, shadowy. As he began to describe what he had stolen, he scarcely heard them breathe. Deep into his tale, he saw very little beyond his own memories, and the rise and fall of ale in his cup that in the frail light seemed the hue of fairy gold.

"I stole what stood on a table beside the queen's bed. To prove that I had been in that bed, and that once I had been among those she loved. Her husband had given it to her, she told me. It was a lovely thing. It was fashioned by the king's sorcerer of a magic far more intricate than I had ever seen, which may have been why he pursued me so relentlessly when I fled with it.

"It was like a tiny living world within a glass globe. The oak wood grew within it. Gold light filled it every morning; trees began to fade to lavender and smoke toward the end of the day. At night—their night, ours, who can say? I was never certain while I was there if time passed at all within the fairy wood—the globe was filled with the tiny countless jewels of constellations in a black that was infinitely deep, yet somehow so beautiful that it seemed the only true color for the sky. In the arms of the queen I watched the night brighten into day within that tiny wood, and then deepen once again into the rich, mysterious dark. She loved to watch it, too. And in spite of her tender laughter and her sweet words, I knew that every time she looked at it, she thought of him, her husband, who had given it to her.

"So I stole it, so that she would look for it and think of me. And because I knew that though she had stolen my heart from me, this was as close as I would ever get to stealing hers."

He heard a small sound, a sigh, in the silent room, a half-coherent word. His vision cleared a little, enough to show him the still, intent faces crowding around him. Even Frayne was motionless behind his bar; no one remembered to ask for ale.

"Show it to us," someone breathed.

"No, go on," Tye pleaded. "I want to hear how he escaped."

"No, show—"

"He can show it later if he chooses. He's been carrying it around all these years; it's not going anywhere else until he ends it. Go on," he appealed to Reck. "How did you get away from them?"

"I don't think I ever did," Reck said hollowly, and again the room was soundless. "Oh, I did what any other wizard would do, pursued by the King of Faerie and his sorcerer. I fought with fire, and with thought; I vanished; I changed my shape; I hid myself in the heart of trees, and under stones. I knew that I only had to toss that little globe in their path, and they would stop chasing me. But I refused to give it up. I wanted it more than reason. Maybe more than life. Eventually the king lost sight of me, confused by all the different shapes of bird and animal and wildflower I had taken. But I could not hide the sorcerer's own magic from him. He never lost sight of the globe, no matter how carefully I disguised it. Once, in hart-shape, I wore it as my own eye; another time I changed it into the mouse dangling from the talons of the falcon I had become. He never failed to see it.... Finally, for no matter which way I ran I could not seem to find my way out of that wood, I performed an act of utter desperation.

"I hid myself within the wood within the globe. And then I caused everything—globe, wood, myself—to vanish."

He heard an odd, faint sound, as though in the cellar below a cork had blown out of a keg, or somewhere a globe-sized bubble of ale had popped. He ignored it, standing once again in the tiny wood inside the globe, among the peaceful trees, the endless, ancient light, feeling again his total astonishment.

"It was as though I had been in my own world all along, and I had mistaken all the magic in it for Faerie..." He lifted his glass after a moment, drank, set it down again. "But I could not linger in that illusion. It's not easy to fling yourself across a world when you are both the thrower and the object that is thrown. But I managed. When I stopped the globe's flight and stepped, with great trepidation, out of it and into my own shape, I found myself in the gray, rainy streets of Chalmercy."

He paused, remembering the grayness in his own heart at the sight of the grimy, cold, familiar world. He sighed. "But I had the globe, the world I had stolen out of fairyland. For a long time it comforted me... until it began to weigh upon me, and I realized that I had never been forgotten. It was what I had wanted—that the queen should remember me—but she began to grow merciless in her remembering. I had to return this to her or I could never live in any kind of peace again."

He bent then and untied his pack. The tavern was so still it might have been empty. When he lifted the little globe out of the pack, its stars spangled the shadows everywhere within the room, and he heard a sigh from all the throats of the villagers of Byndley at once, as though a wind had gusted through them.

He gazed into the globe with love and rue, seeing the fairy queen again within that enchanted night, and the foolish young man who had given her his heart. After a moment he blinked. He was holding the globe in his palm as lightly as though it were a hen's egg. The strange, terrible heaviness had fallen away from it; in his surprise he almost looked into the open pack to see if the sloughed weight lay at the bottom.

Then he blinked again.

It took no small effort for him to shift his eyes from the world within the globe to the silent villagers of Byndley. Their faces, shadows and stars trembling over them, seemed blurred at first, unrecognizable. Slowly, he began to see them clearly. The wild-haired maker with his powerful face and the enigmatic smile in his dark eyes... The tall, silver-haired figure behind the bar, gazing quizzically at Reck out of eyes the color of the tranquil twilight within the globe... The woman beside the fire....

Reck swallowed, haunted again, for not a mention of time had troubled that face. It was as beautiful as when he had first seen it, tinted with the fiery colors of the dying wood as she walked toward him that day long before.

She smiled, her green eyes unexpectedly warm.

"Thank you for that look," she said. There was Bettony still in her face, he saw: a glint of humor, a wryness in her smile. The faces around her, timeless and alien in their beauty, held no such human expressions. She held out her hand. Reck, incapable of moving, watched the globe float from his palm to hers under the sorcerer's midnight gaze.

"I always wondered," he told Reck, when the queen's fingers had closed around her globe, "how you managed to escape me."

"And I always wondered," the queen said softly, "why you took this from me. Now I understand."

Reck looked at the king among his mugs, still watching Reck mildly; he seemed to need no explanations. He said, "You have told your tale and been judged. This time you may leave freely. There's the door."

Reck picked up his pack with shaking hands. He paused before he opened the door, said without looking back, "The first time, I only thought I had escaped. I never truly found my way out of the wood."

"I know."

Reck opened the door. He pulled it to behind him, but he did not hear it close or latch. He took a step and then another and then did not stop until he had crossed the bridge.

He stopped then. He did not bother looking back, for he guessed that the bridge and every sign of Byndley on the other side of the stream had vanished. He looked up instead and saw the lovely, mysterious, star-shot night flowing everywhere around him, and the promise, in the faint, distant flush at the edge of the world, of an enchanted dawn.

THE TWELVE DANCING PRINCESSES

ONE DAY LONG AGO in a faraway country, a young soldier, walking home from a battle he had fought for the king, found himself lost in a forest. The road he followed dwindled away, leaving him standing among silent trees, with the sun just setting at his back, and the moon just rising ahead of him. Caught alone and astray between night and day, he thought to himself, there are worse things that could be. He had seen many of them on the battlefield. He was alone because he had watched his best friend die; he had given his last few coins to another soldier trying to walk home with only one foot. But he himself, though worn and bloodied with battle, had kept all his bones, and his eyes, and he even had a little bread and cheese in his pack to eat. He settled himself into a tangle of tree roots, where he could watch the moon, and took out his simple meal. He had opened his mouth to take the first bite when a voice at his elbow said, "One bite is a feast to those who have nothing."

He turned, wondering who had crept up so noiselessly to sit beside him. It was a very old woman. Her bones bumped under the surface of her brown, sagging skin like the tree roots under the earth. Her pale eyes, which now held only a memory of the blue they had been, were fixed on the heel of bread, the rind of cheese in his hand. He sighed, for he was very hungry. But so must she be, scuttling like an animal among the trees, with no one to care for her. There are worse things, he thought, than having a little less of something.

So he said, tearing the bread and cheese apart and giving her half, "Then feast with me."

220

"You are kind, young soldier," she said in her high wavery voice, and bit into her scanty supper as if it might vanish before she could finish it. After she had swallowed her last bite and searched for crumbs, she spoke again. "What is your name?"

"Val," he answered.

"A good name for a soldier. Did you win the battle?"

Val shrugged. "So they say. I could not see, from where I stood, that winning was much better than losing."

"And now what will you do?"

"I don't know. My younger brother has married and taken care of the family farm and our parents while I have been fighting. I will find my way back and show them that I'm still alive, and then find something to do in the world. After all, someone with nothing has nothing to lose."

"You have a fair and honest face," the old woman said. "That's something." Her pale eyes caught moonlight and glinted, so suddenly and strangely, that he started. "How would you like to be king?"

He swallowed a laugh along with a lump of bread. "Better than being a beggar."

"Then follow this road through the forest. It will take you into the next kingdom, where the king and queen there are desperate for help. They have twelve beautiful daughters—"

"Twelve!"

"None of them will marry; they will laugh at every suitor. The king locks them in their room every night; and every morning he finds them sleeping so soundly, they will not wake until noon, and at the foot of every bed, a pair of satin shoes so worn with dancing, they must be thrown away. But no one knows how the princesses get out of the room, or where they go to dance. The king has promised his kingdom and a daughter to any man who can solve this mystery."

"Any man," Val repeated, and felt a touch of wonder in his heart, where before there had been nothing. "Even me."

"Even you. But you must be careful. The king is half mad with worry and fear for his daughters. He will kill any man who fails, even princes who might one day marry his daughters."

The young soldier pondered that. "Well," he said softly. "I have faced death before. No one ever offered to make me king if I survived." He stood up. "There's moon enough to see by, tonight. Where is the road to that kingdom?"

"Under your feet," she answered, and there it was, washed with light and winding among the trees. Val stared at the old woman; her face rippled into a thousand wrinkles as she smiled.

"Two things. One: Drink nothing that the princesses give you. And two"—she touched the dusty cloak at his back—"this will make you invisible when you follow them at night. It pays," she added, as he slid his pack strap over his shoulder, "to be kind to crones."

"So I hope," he breathed, and stepped onto the moonlit road, wondering if he would find death at its end, or love.

Death, he thought instantly, when he met the father of the twelve princesses. The king, wearing black velvet and silver mail, was tall and gaunt, with long, iron-gray hair and a lean, furrowed face. His eyes were black and terrible with frustration and despair. He wore a sword so long and heavy, it would have dragged on the ground at Val's side. He kept one hand always on it; Val wondered if he used it to slay the princes who failed him.

But he spoke to the young soldier with courtesy. Val found himself soaking in a fragrant bath while a barber cut his hair. Then he dressed in fine, elegant clothes, though he refused, for no reasons he gave, to part with his torn, dusty cloak. He sat down to a meal so wondrously cooked that he could scarcely name what he ate. When night fell, the king took him to the princesses' bedchamber.

The doors to the long chamber opened to such color, such rich wood and fabric, such movement of slender, jeweled hands and glowing hair, and bright, curious eyes, so many sweet, laughing voices, that Val froze on the threshold, mute with astonishment that any place so lovely and full of grace could exist in the world he knew. "My daughters," the king said as they floated toward him, breasting the air like swans in their lacy, flowing nightgowns. "The queen named them after flowers. Aster, Bluet, Columbine, Delphinium, Eglantine, Fleur, Gardenia, Heather,

Iris, Jonquil, Lily, and Mignonette. She could not find an appropriate flower for K."

"Kumquat," one with long, golden hair giggled behind her hands.

"Knotweed," another said with an explosion of laughter into her nearest sister's shoulder. Then they were all silent, their eyes of amber, emerald, sapphire, unblinking and wide, watching Val like a circle of cats, he thought, watching a sparrow.

He said, scarcely hearing himself, while his own eyes were charmed from face to face, "There are folk names for flowers, sometimes, that queens may not know. Kestrel's Eye, farmers call a kind of sunflower, for its smallness and the color of its center."

"Kestrel," a princess with a mass of dark, curly hair and golden eyes repeated. Her beauty held more dignity and assurance than her sisters'; her eyes, smiling at the handsome young stranger, seemed full of secrets. "A pretty word. You might have been Kestrel, then, Lily, and Mignonette would have been you, if our mother had known."

She was the oldest, Val guessed, and was proved right when the youngest protested, "But, Aster, I am Mignonette; I do not want to be Lily."

"Don't worry, goose, you may stay yourself." She yawned, then, and stepped forward to kiss their grim father. "How tired I am, suddenly! I could sleep for a month!"

"I wish you all would," the king murmured, bending as one by one they brushed his face with kisses. They only laughed at him and vanished behind the hangings of lace and gauze around their beds; they were as silent then as if they had already begun to dream.

The king showed Val a small room at the end of the bedchamber, where he could pretend to sleep as he waited for the princesses to reveal the mystery of their dancing. "Many men have come here," the king said, "seeking to win my kingdom, thinking it a trifling matter to outwit my daughters and take my crown. They are all dead, now, even the jesting, lighthearted princes. My daughters show no mercy, and neither do I. But if you fail, I will be sorry."

Val bowed his head. "So will I," he answered. "How strange it seems that yesterday I had nothing to lose, and today I have everything. Except love."

"That alone drives me mad," the king said harshly. "They can love no one. Nothing. They laugh at the young men I put to death. As if they are spellbound...." He turned, begging rather than warning as he closed the door. "Do not fail."

Val sat down on the bed, which was the first he had seen in many months, and the last he dared sleep in. He had just pulled off his boots when the door opened, and the eldest, Aster, appeared, carrying a cup of wine. She handed it to Val. "We always share a cup with guests, for friendship's sake. My father forgot to tell us your name."

"My name is Val. Thank you for the wine." He pretended to take a sip while he wondered blankly how to pretend to finish the cup under her watchful eyes.

"A proper name for a prince."

"I suppose it is, but I am a soldier, returning home after battle."

Her brows rose. "And you stopped here, to try for a crown on your way. You should have kept going. There is nothing for you here but what you escaped in battle."

He smiled, holding her eyes, while he poured the wine into a boot standing at his knee. "There are better memories here," he said, and tilted the cup against his mouth as if he were draining it dry.

He stretched out on the bed when Aster left, and did not move when he heard the door open again. "Look at him," one of them mocked. "Sleeping as if he were already dead."

"I put a stronger potion into the wine," another answered. "His eyes were far too clear."

Then he heard laughter in the princesses' bedchamber, and the sound of cupboards, chests, and cases being opened. He waited, watching them while he pretended to snore. They dressed themselves in bright silks, and lace and creamy velvet gowns; they tied the ribbons of new satin dancing slippers around their ankles. They took rings and earrings and strands of pearls out of their jewel cases, and they spun one another's hair into amazing confections threaded with ribbons.

Val had thought them beautiful before; now they seemed enchanted, exquisite, unreal, as if he had drunk the wine and were dreaming them. He was so entranced, he forgot to snore. Aster came to look sharply at him through the open door, but another sister only laughed.

"He sleeps so deeply, he has forgotten how to breathe."

Aster went to a bed in the middle of the chamber. She knocked three times on the carved headboard, and the entire bed abruptly disappeared, leaving a dark, oblong hole in the floor. Like a grave, Val thought, feeling his heart beat at the strangeness of it. In a long, graceful line, beginning with A and ending with M, the princesses descended into the earth.

The wet pool of wine at the bottom of one boot cleared Val's amazed thoughts a little as he pulled them on; he remembered to fling his worn cloak over his shoulders before he left. He glanced into one of the many mirrors in the bedchamber as he hurried after Mignonette. *There is no soldier,* the mirror told him. *The room is empty.*

Fearing that the hole in the earth might close behind the princesses, he followed too closely. His first step down the broad, winding steps caught the hem of Mignonette's gown.

She said, startled, "Who is there? Aster, Lily, someone pulled at my dress."

All their faces looked back toward Val, a lovely, silent chain of princesses stretching down the steps. Aster turned away first, picking up her own silks. "Don't be a goose, Mignonette; you caught your skirt on a splinter."

"The steps are marble," Mignonette muttered. "And I have a bad feeling about tonight."

But no one answered her. Val saw a shining ahead, like a thousand touches of starlight. When they reached the bottom of the stairs, the princesses began to walk down a wide road lined with trees. The leaves on the trees were moonlight, it seemed to Val; they were silver fire. They were silver, he realized finally, with such wonder that he could scarcely breathe. He reached up to touch such beauty, and then, beginning to think again, he broke off a twig bearing four or five leaves to show to the king.

The tree gave a splintering crack as if a branch had fallen; Mignonette whirled again. "What is that noise?" she cried. "You all must have heard it!"

Val held his breath. Her sisters glanced indifferently around them. "It was the wind," one said. "It was fireworks from the dance," another offered.

"It sounded," Aster said lightly, "like a heart breaking."

They turned then onto another broad, tree-lined road. Val closed his eyes and opened them again, but what he saw did not change: All the leaves on these trees were made of gold. Like tears of gold they glowed and shimmered and melted down the branches; they flowed into Val's outstretched hand. Again he broke the slenderest of twigs; again the tree made a sound as if it had been split by lightning.

"Another broken heart," Aster said after Mignonette had screamed and complained, and her sisters had bade her to stop fussing so, they would never get to the dance. Only Val heard her whisper, as she trudged after them, "I have a bad feeling about tonight."

On the third road he broke off a cluster of leaves made of diamonds. They burned of white fire in the moonlight, a light so pure and cold, it hurt his eyes. Mignonette stamped her foot and wailed at the sound the tree made, but her sisters, impatient now, only hurried toward the lake at the end of the road. Only Aster slowed to walk with her. Her voice was as calm as ever as she spoke to Mignonette, but she searched the diamond-studded dark behind them now and then, as if she sensed their invisible follower.

"I have a bad feeling about tonight," Mignonette said stubbornly.

Aster only answered, "We are almost there. One more night and we will never have to leave again."

On the shore of the lake, twelve boats waited for them. Out of each boat rose a shadowy figure to take the hand of the princess who came to him and help her into the boat. Val paused almost too long, trying to see the faces of the richly dressed men who were pushing the boats into the water. He whispered, suddenly sick at heart, "I have a bad feeling about tonight."

He realized then that the boats were floating away from him. He stepped hastily into the last one; it rocked a little until he caught his balance. Mignonette, whose boat he had the misfortune to enter, promptly raised her voice, calling to her sisters, "I think someone got into the boat with me!"

Her sisters' laughter fell as airily as windblown petals around them; even the man who rowed her smiled. "Don't fret, my Mignonette. I could row a dozen invisible guests across the water." His mouth did not move, Val saw, when he spoke. His eyes were closed. And yet he rowed steadily and straight toward the brightly lit castle on the other side of the lake. Torches burned on all its towers and walls; its casements opened wide; candlelight and music spilled from them. Val, his heart hammering, his hands as cold as if he waited for the beginning of a battle, did not dare move until Mignonette left the boat. The man, pulling it ashore, commented puzzledly, "It does seem heavier than usual."

"You see!" Mignonette began. But he only put his arm around her as she stepped ashore, and kissed her with his mouth that never moved.

"Never mind, my smallest love," he said. "Tomorrow you will have nothing to fear ever again."

Val, following them into the castle, saw the light from the torches at the gate fall over their faces. He stopped abruptly, his bones turned to iron, and his blood turned to ice at what he saw. "This," he heard himself whisper, "is the worst thing that could be."

Still, he forced himself into the castle, to watch the dance.

In the vast hall where the music played, the walls glowed with rare, polished wood. Traceries of gold leaf outlined the carvings on the ceiling. Candles in gold and silver and diamond holders stood everywhere, illumining the princesses' enchanting, sparkling faces. They began to dance at once, smiling into the faces of their princes, who may once have been handsome but who, to Val's unenchanted eyes, had been dead a day too long. Their lips were grim, motionless gashes in their bloodless faces; their eyes never opened. The room was crowded with watchers, all holding empty wine cups and tapping a foot to the music. The music, fierce and merciless, never let the dancers rest; it sent them breathless and spinning around the floor. Ribbons came undone, hems tore, pearls broke and scattered everywhere. Still, the princesses danced, their smiles never wavering at the faces of the dead who danced with them. Their satin slippers grew soiled and scuffed; the thin fabric wore through, until their bare feet blistered against the gleaming floor. Still, they danced, driven by blind musicians who had no reason to rest; they had left their lives elsewhere.

"What a celebration there will be tomorrow night!" Val heard many times as he waited. "The wedding of twelve princesses, and a dance that will never end!"

As the lake grew gray with dawn, the music finally stopped. In silence, drooping with exhaustion in their boats, the princesses were returned to the far shore, where they kissed the frozen faces of their princes and bade them farewell until tomorrow. Val walked ahead of them this time so that he could reach his bed and pretend to sleep before they came back. He kept pace with Aster. She looked a wilted flower, he thought; her eyes seemed troubled, now, but by what she could not imagine. She stumbled a little, on pebbles or the bright, sharp metal of fallen leaves, wincing where her shoes had worn through to her bare feet. He wanted to take her hand, help her walk, comfort her, but he guessed that, in such a place, he could be less alive to her than the dead.

When he saw the stairs, he paused to take off his boots so that he could run up without being heard. As he passed Aster, a boot tilted in his hand, spilling a little red wine on the steps. He saw Aster's eyes widen at it, her step falter. But she did not speak to her sisters. Nor did she say anything when, moments later, she found him sleeping in his bed. Another sister said tiredly, "At least he'll die before we wake. And then no one will have to die for us again."

He waited until they were all hidden in their beds, and nothing moved in the room but morning light. Then he rose, and crept out, with his boots in one hand and the magical leaves in the other, to speak to the king.

The king was pacing outside his daughters' bedchamber; he had not slept that night, either. His hand tightening and loosening and tightening again on his great sword, he gazed wordlessly at Val out of his lightless eyes until Val spoke.

"They go down to the underworld," Val said. "They dance with the dead." He showed the king the three sprays of leaves, silver, gold and diamond, that could only have come from such an enchanted place. His hand trembled with weariness and horror; so did his voice. "Tomorrow night, they will wed their dead princes, and you will never see them again."

The king, with a shout of rage and grief, tore the leaves from Val's hand and flung open the bedchamber doors. Exhausted, astonished faces appeared from between the hangings in every bed. The king showed them the leaves; sunlight flared from them, turned gold and silver and diamond into fire. "What are these?" he demanded. "Where are they from? You tell me, daughters. Tell me where to go get them. And then I will know where to go to find you."

They stared at the leaves. Little by little, as if before they had only dreamed themselves awake, their faces came alive to terror and confusion. From beneath their beds came the sound of a great, splintering crack, as if a tree had been struck by lightning, or a heart had broken.

Mignonette was the first to burst into tears. "No, it isn't real," she sobbed. "It was a dream! You can't have taken those leaves from a dream!"

"Val followed you," the king said while all around him his daughters wept as if their hearts had broken. "He brought these back with him to show me."

"How could it have been real?" Aster whispered, shivering in her bed while tears slipped down her face. "We were—we pledged ourselves in marriage to—we danced with—"

"Dead princes," Val said. She stared at him, her face as white as alabaster.

"Which dead princes?" she asked him. "The ones our father killed because of us?"

"I don't know," he answered gently, though he shuddered, too, at the thought.

She closed her eyes against a nightmare. "You might have died, too, Val, if you had not kept watch."

"I knew someone followed us," Mignonette sobbed to her sisters. "I tried to tell you. And you would not believe me!"

"You were all enchanted," Val said.

Aster opened her eyes again, looked at him. "Did I know you were there?" she wondered softly. "Or did I only wish it?"

There was another sound, the clang of the king's great sword as he drew it from the scabbard and flung it to the floor. Then he took the crown from his head and held it out to Val. "Take my kingdom," he said with great relief. "You have broken the spell over my house, and over me. I no longer want to rule; there are too many innocent dead among my memories."

"Well," Val said uncertainly, turning the crown, which looked too big for him, over in his hands. "There are worse things that could be."

He lifted his eyes, looked at Aster, for comfort, and for friendship. She smiled a little, through her tears, and he saw that she agreed with him: There were worse things that could be than what he had: a kingdom and a choice of flowers from A to M.

UNDINE

ALL MY SISTERS caught mortals that way. I have more sisters than I can count, and they've all had more husbands than they can count. It's easy, they told me. And when you get tired of them you just let them go. Sometimes they find their way back to their world, where they sit around a lot with a gaffed look in their eyes, their mouths loosing words slowly like bubbles drifting away. Other times they just die in our world. They don't float like mortals anymore. They sink down, lie among the water weeds and stones at the bottom, their skin turning pearly over time, tiny snails clustering in their hair.

Easy. When it was time for my first, my sisters showed me how to find my way. In our deep, cool, opalescent pools, our reedy, light-stained waters, time passes so slowly you hardly notice it. Things rarely ever change. Even the enormous, jewel-winged dragonflies that dart among the reeds have been there longer than I have. To catch humans, I have to rise up into their time, pull them down into ours. It takes practice, which is why so many of them die.

"But don't worry," my sisters told me blithely. "You'll get the hang of it. When you bring the first one home alive, we'll throw a party."

I had to choose a patch of sunlight in my water and swim up through it, up and up in the light until it blinded me, while I kept a vision of mortals in my mind. What mortals I knew were mostly my sisters' husbands and some mossy-haired, frog-eyed women who had accidentally fallen in love with my snarky water-kelpie cousins as they cavorted among the water lilies in human and horse disguises. But, my sisters assured me, as I moved from our time into theirs my hunger—and my loneliness—would grow. I would be happy to see the human face at the end of my journey. I should not expect to be in the same water there, but it would not be hard at all, they promised, for me to find my way back. I had only to wish and swim.

They gathered so sweetly around me in the water, all languid and graceful, their long hair flowing as they sang me farewell. The singing helped shift me across time; I felt as though I were swimming through their voices as much as through water and light. When I saw the trembling surface of strange water, I could still hear them, the distant singing of water faerie, so lovely, so haunting.

I should have turned at that instant, followed it back. But I felt the odd, shallow depths I had reached. My face and knees were bumping stones and I had to break the surface. I stood up, awkwardly, trying to find my balance in the rocky shallows and pulling my hair out of my face so I could see. I took a breath and smelled it first.

"Yark!" I shrieked. "Gack! What is it?"

I finally untangled the hair over my eyes and shrieked again. Dead fish. I was surrounded by dead fish. Big ones. Hundreds of them, in various stages of decay, wallowing in the water and reeking. They bumped me as I floundered through the stink, their eyes filmy with death where they weren't covered with flies. I wanted to screech again, but I had to breathe to do that. I was panting like a live fish by then, taking short little breaths through my open mouth, trying to get out of the river as fast as I could. The stones were slippery with moss. I flailed, terrified of stumbling and falling into the dead fish. Wearing what I did wasn't helping much; my long dress sagged, wrapped itself around my knees, caught underfoot. At every step, flies swarmed around me from the fish, buzzed into my eyes.

So, half blind, cursing furiously and gasping like a fish, I rose out of the river, and a mortal caught me in his arms.

"What are you doing in there?" he shouted.

I could feel his startled heartbeat, his dry shirt rapidly dampening with me. I opened one eye cautiously. I stood in mud now. I could feel it oozing up between my toes, which didn't improve my mood, but at least I could catch my balance. The mortal I had snared was very cute, with straight golden hair that flopped above one brow, eyes the gentle blue of our limpid skies rather than of the fierce blue-white blaze above our heads. He wore a shirt with a frog sitting on a lily pad and unrolling its enormous tongue to catch a tiny flying horse. A conversation starter, that would have been, if I hadn't just waded out of a river full of one.

I had to answer something, so I said, "I got lost."

"In that dress?"

I looked at it. My sisters had woven it for me out of mosses and river grasses, decorated it with hundreds of tiny bubbles. In this world, it looked like some kind of shimmering cloth overlaid with pearls.

"What's wrong with it?" I demanded, trying to kick away the ribbon of greasy fish scales decorating the hem.

He stared at me, goggling a bit, like the fish. Then his eyes narrowed. "Did you—did you, like, jump off something? After a party? Like a bridge, or something? And instead of drowning you came to in all this—this—" He waved at the appalling river, which was making a sort of gurgling noise as it drained through the fish jammed across it. "What was it? Some guy made you do this?"

I nodded cautiously after a moment. Some guy, yes. I pushed at my hair, trying to make it more presentable. A nasty odor wafted up from it. I couldn't cry—why bother with tear ducts if you are born in water? But I had seen mortals do it, and now I knew why. My first human, and here I was, sinking in mud and stinking while vicious little flies bit my ankles.

Extremely sorry for myself, I sniffed and whuffled piteously, "Yeah. And now I don't know my way home."

"Don't cry—"

"What did you do to all these fish?"

"Me?" he said incredulously. "I just came out here to throw a line in the water. Fishing's great here when the salmon are running. I could smell this all the way out to the highway. I've never seen anything like it."

"Fish can't run," I said crossly; he seemed more interested in them than in me.

"It's an expression," he explained with exasperating patience. "It's what they call it when the salmon swim upriver trying to get back to the waters where they were born so they can spawn."

"Spawn?"

"You know—lay their eggs and fertilize them. Propagate. That's when they're supposed to die." I nodded. That happened to mortals often enough where I lived. "Not like this," he went on. "Not halfway upriver before they've gotten home. And look at this water! It should be deeper and fast-flowing. It's like they couldn't breathe or something in this shallow water. This is all wrong."

He was still fixated on them, staring over my shoulder. I saw his point, though. I could never have dragged him under those pathetic shallows. I sniffed again, to reclaim his attention. His eyes came back to me; he touched my bare arms lightly with his fingers. "Ah, poor kid. What a nightmare. Where do you live? I'll take you home."

I had to think, then, which is not something my sisters warned me would be necessary. "Farther upriver," I said, pleased at my cleverness. I would make him take me to some deep pool where I could lure him under, steal him away from his world, take him back into mine. "But I can't go home like this. Reeking and covered with fish scales. Do you know a place where I can swim it off?"

He considered, torn between me and the dead fish. I rolled my eyes in mortification, hoping none of my sisters had followed to watch. But then, considering myself, I could hardly blame him.

"Sure." He bent down to collect his fishing gear. "I know just the place."

He took me in his truck to his home.

It was a little cottage not far away beneath some immense trees. His dog came out to greet us, wagging its tail politely until it caught a whiff of me. Then it bounded into my arms, howling joyously, nearly knocking me over.

"Whoa!" my mortal said. "Down, Angel. She loves company." Angel was big and golden, with a stupid grin on her face; she acted like she wanted to roll around on the ground with my dress. "Down! My name's Mike, by the way. Mike Taylor. What's yours?"

"Undine." At home we have our private names of course, but to mortals we are all Undines. "Ah—what are we doing here?"

"Undine. Pretty. Come on in. You can wash off in the bathroom; I'll give you some dry clothes to change into. Then I'll take you home. Okay?"

But he wasn't thinking about me as he led me into his house. It was sunny, cluttered and full of dog hair. He waved me into a tiny room which contained a tank, a basin, and a big porcelain mushroom. I had never seen anything like it. Luckily, he turned the water taps on himself. Some gunky water spurted out. And then it ran clear, so clear I had to reach out and touch it, smell it.

"Sorry I don't have a shower, just this tub. The pipes pick up dirt sometimes," he said unintelligibly. "You have to clear them out. There's lots of hot water though. I'll bring you some clothes in a minute. First I have to make a phone call."

I filled the tub to the top, managing to stop the flow before I made a waterfall over the side. As it was, I slopped plenty on the floor when I pulled my dress off and got in. I submerged myself completely, rolling and rolling in the warmth, my hair growing silky again, coiling around my naked limbs. I heard Mike's voice now and then when my ears came out of the water. Fish, he was talking about. Not the mysterious, enchanting young woman he had met on the river's edge.

Dead fish.

"I called the Forestry Department," he announced, breezing in with his arms full of ugly clothes. "And the Fish and Wildlife Department. And—" He stopped abruptly, the absent look fading from his eyes as I stood up in the water. "Oh," he whispered. "Sorry." He didn't move. I hummed softly, lifting my streaming hair away from my neck with upraised arms. The clothes dropped onto the floor. I held out my hand. He stepped into the water, forgetting even that he was wearing boots. The splash we made as I pulled him down hit the ceiling and pretty much emptied the tub, but neither of us cared.

But there was nowhere for me to take him except down the drain. He lay in my arms afterward, spellbound, contentedly talking, even though he had to balance his drenched boots on the faucets and he was squashing me. I let him ramble, while I tried to think of a way out of our predicament.

"I don't make much," he said, "at the Sport 'n Bait Shop. But I don't need much to keep up this place, and my truck's paid for, and there's just Angel and me... I hunt and fish whenever I can. I love the outdoors, don't you?"

"Water," I murmured. "I love water."

"Yeah... That's why this thing with the fish is so upsetting. Turns out it's all political, that's what Fish and Wildlife told me. The water that normally comes downriver got diverted fifty miles upriver. Can you believe that? To water crops in the Saskill Valley, which got hit by drought this summer. Dead crops or dead fish, take your pick. Well, fish don't vote." He had begun to fidget; in another moment he would realize he was lying with his pants down and his boots on in a bathtub with a stranger.

I kissed him, felt his muscles slacken. He babbled on, his voice dreamy again. "You don't have to go home right away, do you? I'll take you home later. We can build a fire, grill some burgers, go for a moonlight swim...."

"Moonlight swim, yes."

"Well, we could have anyway, except that I doubt there's enough water anywhere along the river around here to do much but wade in." He was beginning to brood again. Then this noise rattled through my spell, some kind of weirdness clamoring for attention that made all his muscles tense. His boots jumped off the faucet; he rolled and floundered clumsily against me, groping for balance.

"Sorry, babe, gotta get that. It's probably Sam. She's always on top of stuff like this."

He sloshed out of the bathroom to go talk about fish again, leaving me in a puddle on the bottom of the tub.

That was the last I saw of water until dawn.

Another shrillness woke me when it was still dark. I didn't remember where I was, and something moist was prodding my cheek and panting dankly. Then Mike switched on a light, and Angel, her grin inches from my eyes, licked my face.

"Garf," I said, wanting to cry again because this was not supposed to happen.

"Sorry, babe. Gotta go." Mike pulled a shirt over his head, popped out again, looking hopeful. "Come with me?"

"Will there be water?"

"Oh, yeah."

Which is why, an hour later, I was back with the dead fish, wearing Mike's clothes, standing on the riverbank with a sign in my hands that said PROTECT THE WILDERNESS IN YOU along with dozens of other dour, cranky humans, some wearing badges, others watching us through one-eyed monsters on their shoulders from a big truck labeled KXOX NEWS TEAM.

Mike keeps promising me that soon, soon, we will go out and find that moonlit pool, or that deep, deep sunlit lake, and we will float together, locked in one another's arms, our breaths trailing bubbles behind us as we kiss, and then we will swim beyond the boundaries of mortal love. Soon. But then, on our way to that magical place, the truck will suddenly detour to follow a creek that's turning all the colors of the rainbow and smelling like garbage. Or it will find the lake with the signs along its shores Warning of the Dangers of Swimming Here. Then he spends hours on the phone with Sam or Kyle or Vanessa, and then wakes me at dawn to walk in circles carrying a sign. And I still hope, because what else can I do?

But I am beginning to wonder if I'll be stranded here like a fish out of water for a mortal lifetime with this human, sweet as he is, before I can ever swim my way back to that deep, sun-stained pool where I was born.

Xmas Cruise

It was one of those "Rediscover Gaia" cruises, with forty-four cabins, fourteen lecturers, bars fore and aft, a swimming pool, views of quaint towns, icebergs, whales. I gave the cruise to Alex for Christmas. On Christmas day we sailed south from the tip of South America. I found Alex studying her short black hair for gray and her green eyes for wrinkles in a hand mirror by the light of the porthole, and murmuring dreamily, "Strait of Magellan. Tierra del Fuego. Cape Horn. I'm o-o-old, Jeff."

"You'll never be as old as the world," I said.

We ate cheese Danishes and drank coffee on the deck, shivering in the bite of breeze off the ice floes. Other passengers sat inside the big dining room, eating scrambled eggs and sausages at tables surrounding a huge old-fashioned tree decorated with colored balls and popcorn and topped with a golden star. They couldn't smell the cold fishy brine in the air, or see the distant feathery puffs the whales blew just before they sounded. I didn't know what they were; I didn't know where we were. We were somewhere on a planet covered three-quarters with water, and the water was wrinkled like a rhinoceros hide, and a blue that must have been the first shade of blue in the world, because I don't think it had a name, and I never saw it again.

We kissed a while; whales dove around us and gulls like chips of white iceberg flashed low over the blue. Then we went into one of the lectures. Alex consulted the program guide; I just followed her, not caring, just wanting to be told anything—the names of birds, or icebergs, whatever—as long as it connected me with that blue.

Skin, the lecturer talked about. The skin of the ocean. The lecture room had no corners; the chairs were soft, the floor carpeted with patterns of scallop shells and undulating kelp. The soft lights dimmed to a friendly underwater dark, that special, moneyed museum dark, where nothing bad can ever happen to you, and you get lulled into thinking that thinking is easy.

The ocean's skin, which was where water touched air and turned that blue, was more than just a color. Living stars, glass-blown eggs, garish snowflakes, strips of light with transparent digestive systems appeared on the viewing screens. "Protozoans, microalgae, minute snails, jellyfish, shrimp, literally thousands of strange, colorful species inhabit this rich, fluid, constantly moving sheen that is at once delicate and enormously flexible," the lecturer said. He was small, dark, with a voice like a sea lion, and one of those faces that seems to generate light. "Whale sharks feed on it." He showed a slide of a monster vacuum cleaner inhaling fish bouillon along the surface of the sea. "It's the incubator for billions upon billions of eggs, which grow up to be the fish fillet on your plate." He chuckled. We chuckled back. Billions of eggs, blown by Tiffany and Lalique. Billions of fish fillets. I glanced at Alex. Like the lecturer, she was rapt. Rapture of the blue. When the lecture was over, we went out to look at it again. But it was gone. The water was glittery now with sunlight glancing off ice. We joined a group by the rail, not knowing why, just that they were people gathered together and all looking the same direction.

Then we saw the glittering surge sleekly upward, and break, and roll back into the sea.

"Whales," someone breathed, like God was walking on the water. Faces vanished behind cameras and camcorders. Things clicked.

"I wonder," Alex said softly as we hung our naked faces overboard, "what they see of us."

Click, click, click.

"How many people know a walrus can sing?" the next lecturer asked. "Not your Uncle George, I mean a real walrus?" He showed us a slide of a rotund, whiskery animal perched on ice, looking, in spite of the enormous tusks hanging out of its face, like Uncle George might look bundled up in mink and smoking a cigar, if I had an Uncle George. Alex giggled.

We heard the walrus sing. And then the humpbacked whale, and the beluga whale, the sperm whale and the killer whale. They sang like ships' masts swaying in the wind, like a jungle forest whooping and whistling, like a barnyard, like birds, like the earth might sing just before it split in two. Alex took my hand. In the blue light from the screen, I saw a tear run down her face. So I knew her Christmas gift was a success. After the lecture we went back to the tiny cabin and imitated whale noises on the skinny bed. The ship heaved once; I fell off and got wedged between the side of the bed and the bathroom door. The porthole swung open; above Alex's laughter I thought I heard the deep, private moaning of the whales.

The next afternoon we found the saunas. Everyone was at the bars, or on deck watching the bone-white line of the distant southern horizon come closer and closer. We went into the men's sauna together, and in the dark, we found another couple, who had left the light off for privacy.

We pulled our towels up and introduced ourselves. Paolo was getting an advanced degree in paleontology. Sharon taught violin and composed. I asked her if she had heard the whales sing.

"Wasn't it amazing?" she said. By the pale light from the changing room, I saw her eyes widen and gleam; I couldn't see their color. Her long hair was the yellow-white of the walrus's tusks. "And what do you do, Jeff?"

"He's a composer, too," Alex said proudly. "He has a contract with Oak Hill for three CDs. His first one is called *Concerto for Moon and Three Planets.*"

"I also play lounge music at an airport hotel," I said. "I spent the contract advance on this trip. It's a present for Alex. And an inspiration for my second album."

"Is it?" Sharon asked.

"Oh, yeah. So far I've written a whole cocktail napkin full of song titles."

They laughed. Paolo, who had, as far as I could make out, a couple of inches and a few more muscles than me, aimed his white smile at Alex. "What about you?"

Alex taught first grade. School was out for the Christmas season. She was also trying to be a writer. Paolo, when he wasn't digging up mastodons, liked to read mysteries. So did Alex. They got so busy swapping titles, while Sharon and I talked synthesizers, that we all forgot we were on a ship bound for the South Pole, until the changing room door opened and a man entered and undressed.

All he wanted to do was swim. We waited until he went out to the pool before we emerged. Alex looked at the clock on the wall and gripped my arm.

"We missed the penguin lecture!"

"Penguins," Paolo said. "Aerodynamically challenged birds wearing tuxedos." His smile, in his dark face, was friendly. But Alex shook her head, oddly upset.

"I wanted to go to all of them," she said. "I wanted to learn everything. Otherwise what's the point? We might as well be on the Love Boat."

"There's another after dinner," Sharon said. "There are three a day for the next ten days."

But Alex was unappeased. "We won't miss another," she insisted. "I want to hear them all."

"It's your present," I said.

"Do fish sleep?" the lecturer asked. In the first row, dimly, I saw the smooth ivory-yellow of Sharon's hair, the color of an old piano key, and beside it, barely visible, Paolo's curly black head. Alex's fingers made a tense bracelet around my wrist. She tended to be moody, passionate, driven by obscure desires. This was one of them, I felt, but I was also intrigued by the question. The sleep of fishes. They weren't human. They weren't even mammals. They didn't need to dream. They didn't have eyelids. How do they sleep?

"Like humans, there are day fish and night fish. And even sharks sleep. As the light fades in the upper regions the patterns on bright butterfly fish change. The parrotfish spins a cocoon of mucus around itself to shield its scent from predators. Crevices in coral reefs begin to fill with small fish finding their safe haven against the hungers of the night. Wrasses bury themselves in sand. As the fish sleep, the coral colonies wake and open their polyps. The shark and the eel move from their resting places to feed. The dark sea becomes full of the tiny luminescent organs, the living lights, of hunting fish."

The black screen filled with eyes. Alex's fingers loosened. I heard her take a soft breath; she was absorbed, contented again. I watched the eerie, glowing, hungry dark and waited for the music in me to begin.

We sat through another lecture after dinner, watching sea horses with huge bellies and huge eyes and delicate, elongated faces off a medieval chessboard, court and mate. Their bellies touched. The female deposited eggs into the male and he became pregnant. His body took charge of changing those eggs into tiny seahorses. Labor, which looked like a serious case of hiccups as he pumped and thrust the younglings into the sea, took days. We were too mesmerized to laugh. I tried to imagine what it would feel like having something inside me change my body, rearrange its chemicals, take room for itself to grow without even knowing that it took its life from me. And then to hiccup it out of me, and watch it swim away, tiny as a nail-paring, perfectly formed, completely free, never knowing, as it rose up to the blue skin of the sea...

"Jeff?" Alex whispered. "Are you sick?"

"I'm bonding," I said. I was clasping my stomach. Alex made a noise somewhere between understanding and a snort.

"Don't worry. It will pass."

"Wasn't that incredible?" Sharon said, as we wandered onto the deck. Paolo didn't look entirely comfortable, either. He murmured something in Spanish. Sharon tossed her incredible hair and took his arm.

"Moon's full," she said. "Let's get drinks and watch for whales in the moonlight."

The ship was moving through a dream, between two converging planes so black, so fiery white it was hard to tell where the stars fell into the black sea and froze and floated. We listened for whales' voices. I kept hearing music, vague, distant, as if walruses were playing rock and roll on an iceberg somewhere. Sharon heard it, too.

"There's a band somewhere," she said abruptly. "Let's find it. Let's dance."

The ship seemed bigger than I remembered it. We climbed stairs to an upper deck I hadn't noticed, and the music grew louder. We opened some doors with stained-glass mermaids on them and found an underwater cavern. Kelp swayed behind glass walls; bright fish darted in and out of the leaves. Musicians with mermaids' hair, pearls in their ears, in penguin tuxedos, played raucous blues. Screens above the bar and near the band gave us underwater views of coral colonies, and giant clams, worms that looked like chrysanthemums and starfish that looked like feathers. I don't remember what we resembled in that dim blue light. The Christmas tree, fake pine sprayed with fake snow, looked as if it had floated down from a sinking cruise ship. After a while, after enough beer, we started inventing fishy courtship rituals on the dance floor. Then I found myself out on the deck, blasted by an icy wind. Alex was laughing or crying; I couldn't tell which. I didn't remember going to bed.

We made the morning lecture, just barely; Paolo and Sharon didn't. Alex looked puffy-eyed and grim, her normal hangover expression. I kept hearing "mermaid," and staring at the screen and seeing a mournful, fleshy, snub-nosed face with big, gentle eyes. A hyacinth eater, the lecturer said. Suckles its young. A docile herbivore. Slaughtered in certain countries for its porklike meat. Ability to recognize, remember. Accident-prone. Keeps bumping into propeller blades on speedboats, and slaughtering itself. Too slow to live in modern times. Order Sirenia. The siren, the mermaid. Globally endangered.

"How was the lecture?" Paolo asked at lunch. I shook my head, still groggy.

"Mermaids are an endangered species."

"It's not a joke," Alex said crossly. Sharon pushed her hair out of her eyes and blinked at her salad: a docile herbivore.

"What did we do last night? What did we say? Oh, God, I need a weight room. I need a Jacuzzi. Anyone want to help me look for a Jacuzzi?"

"There's a lecture," Alex said. We all looked at her blearily. She looked bleary, too, but somehow still rapt. "Killers and Healers."

"Fish?" Paolo asked. "Or us?"

She gave him a smile. He had asked the right question; he was still paying attention. He flashed teeth. Sharon poked at her lettuce, wide-eyed. "I still need a Jacuzzi," she said softly. "Something. You go to the lecture, Paolo. You and Alex. And Jeff."

Alex gave me a look. It wasn't easy to interpret; I had a feeling it referred to something hazy in the previous evening. I stuffed my mouth with endive and mandarin orange, and said, after I chewed a bit, "Of course I'm going to the lecture. Killers and Healers. A subject in its way analogous to music. If you get my drift."

They didn't. Neither did I. They looked at me, fishy-eyed. Sharon consulted her watch. "Jacuzzi, a swim and then a nap. I'll meet you in the bar before dinner. The one on C Deck."

"I thought," I said stupidly, "there was only one deck. And a poop deck."

Sharon only laughed, as if I were either remarkably obtuse or joking. Paolo said, "I'll go to the lecture. At least part of it."

So I got to catch his profile along with Alex's, against the pale light of the projector. After a while I stopped looking at her. I was too busy learning how to die by eating pufferfish, by bumping into a Portuguese man-of-war, getting stung by a sea wasp, bitten by an octopus, barbed by a sting ray, stabbed by a stonefish, poisoned by a lionfish, eaten by a shark, or sat on by a whale. I could, on the other hand, discourage a shark with a Moses sole, treat a throat infection with coral, herpes with sea sponges, cancer with a sea cucumber, and heart attacks with a hagfish. When the lights went on, and I looked at Alex again, Paolo was no longer beside her.

"Where's Paolo? Did he get discouraged by a sole?"

She didn't get that either. "You're punchy, Jeff. Let's go for a swim."

But we never made it into our suits. I was getting used to the bed; it seemed big enough to accommodate an orgy. By the time we left our cabin, it was nearly dinnertime. We climbed the stairs to C Deck, which seemed made entirely out of tinted glass, so we could see, in any direction, the tinted ocean, the line of the polar icecap, passing islands and ice floes bright with sunlight, dotted with birds and seals, too far to be seen clearly, but there as promised. There was an indoor pool on C Deck, surrounded by exotic tropical plants; there were shops, salons, game rooms, a couple of fast food restaurants, one selling carrot juice, the other French fries. Alex said incredulously, "It's like a mall up here. Oh, look, Jeff, there are aerobics classes."

"There's the bar," I said. It was full of wooden figureheads, sea captains, and mermaids smiling cheerfully. Ashtrays were clam and abalone shells; table lamps had shades made out of scallop shells. Tiny cowry shells, butterfly shells, baby sand dollars, checkered snail shells were scattered across the table tops and preserved in an inch of acrylic. Tiny trees made of gold tinsel, topped with plastic starfish, stood in the middle of the seashells.

We found Paolo and Sharon sipping drinks with plastic penguins skewered onto their stirrers. "Isn't this wonderful?" Sharon sighed, gazing at the bottom of the world, which had been approaching for days, it seemed, without getting much closer. "I could live like this forever. I sat in the Jacuzzi and then went for a swim, and by that time I felt so good I went on deck and thought up some themes for my next piece, which will incorporate some of the whale songs we heard. I have a synthesizer that can do those sounds. I thought about references to Bach, and maybe U2—like the whole planet making music."

She glowed, ivory and sunlight. Paolo glowed bronze. I glowed fungus, the way I felt. But Alex gave me a little private smile, as if I had done something right. I picked a plastic seahorse out of a drink called an Ice Breaker, and drank half of it. It was salty and so cold my facial bones ached in the aftermath. Alex, who seemed to carry the lecture schedule with her even when she was stark naked, pulled it out of the air and consulted it.

"Lights in the Abyss," she read. "Luminosity in Fish."

I dropped my head in my arms, groaning. My nose bumped against the plastic seahorse; it smelled oddly dank and briny. "I can't."

"Yes, you can," Alex said calmly. "We'll go dancing again afterward. I promise. We'll find every band on the ship."

"It'll be better," Sharon sighed, "when we reach the pole. They'll take us out on boats to see the penguins and things."

"How can this ship have so many bars?" I asked the seahorse. "I swear it wasn't this big when we got on it."

But they only laughed. Alex finished her drink and went for a swim; Sharon went to buy a tape of the whales' songs. That left me with Paolo, who excused himself and headed after Alex. I ordered another Ice Breaker and watched an enormous ice cube in the distance. It looked delicate, ethereal, a floating palace rising out of the glittering blue. I watched it a long time; it never came any closer.

Much later, I contemplated the luminosity of Sharon's hair on the dance floor of yet another bar, and wondered where we were all going, and if we would ever get any closer.

The next morning, in the lecture room, I stared at something huge, alien, with a metallic mouth that kept taking bites out of a fossil reef on some sunny island. It kept eating as, on another screen, the lecturer showed us brilliant branches of coral colonies, and the tiny polyps opening on them like night flowers to feed in the dark, while the parrotfish, who also ate coral, slept. The monster machine kept grinding away at the reef as she spoke. Finally, one of the three other people who had made it out of bed that morning asked.

"A resort," the lecturer said without expression. "The island is owned by a very poor country. The government is trying to create jobs and to increase its revenues."

I heard Alex take a breath, then loose it slowly. Polyps or poor people? The lecturer showed us another coral colony. The metallic monster kept soundlessly chewing.

So did we at lunch. In apology for something I didn't catch, they served mountains of lobster tails, crab legs, shrimp. A boat trip, Sharon sighed, to take a closer look at the iceberg. I watched, mesmerized, as her full lips, the red-pink of coral, closed and sucked.

"What's the matter with the boats?" Alex asked, peeling a shrimp.

"Nothing," Sharon said, swallowing. "There's something wrong with the water."

"Too choppy?" I guessed, though I hadn't felt anything. Paolo said something, then translated it.

"A tanker hit the iceberg last night. They're having trouble containing the oil."

Alex got up wordlessly; I followed her to the glass walls of the restaurant. But they were tinted; the water looked normal, full of ice floes, sea birds and light. The ice palace had floated past us during the night; it seemed farther away now. One end of the tanker stuck out from behind it, on its side and bleeding. Small boats, trawlers, Coast Guard cutters hovered around it, like gulls around a dying shark. I expected Alex to be upset; she only said absently, "There are other boat trips planned."

Maybe, I thought incredulously, I had eaten the wrong side of a flounder under a full moon in a month with the letter "K" in it. I was hallucinating the entire cruise. Alex drifted back to the table. She didn't look at Paolo. He didn't look at her. Maybe I was hallucinating that, too: the effort they made not to look at each other.

"Don't you find this inspiring?" Sharon asked, as I sat down again. "I mean, musically? I've been dreaming music." She cracked a lobster claw, and squirted lemon on it, catching me in the eye with acid. "Oh, Jeff, I'm sorry."

I blinked away lemon tears. I had lost my napkin on the way to the window. Alex stared at me, then passed her napkin over. But it was too late; my other eye had started tearing in sympathy. I couldn't stop it. I stood up finally, red-eyed, trying to laugh, while Alex kept staring, and Sharon kept making musical noises, and Paolo looked at his plate. I left them there.

I missed the afternoon lecture, and dinner. I roamed around trying to find the deck in the complex corridors, wanting to hear gulls, waves, wind. Arrows pointed every direction but out. I gave up finally, after climbing up more stairs than I thought the ship had decks for. I found a quiet bar with small tinted portholes covered with plastic green wreaths. A tape kept playing five Christmas carols arranged for synthesizer and marimba over and over. I drank beer and ate cold shrimp, tuna sushi and caviar, and watched trawlers on a screen spread nets that scraped the ocean bottom clean of fish, coral, sponges, sea squirts, urchins, starfish, beer cans, broken bottles, torn sails, and spilled them all onto the deck. The fishers picked through the dying animals, threw out everything but shrimp.

I drifted out finally, to find Alex at the evening lecture.

She wasn't there.

But I was, so I stayed and watched whales sounding, dolphins leaping, orcas spy-hopping, coral polyps and anemones blossoming, bright reef fish cavorting, kelp swaying. Every now and then something the lecturer said penetrated.

"We have so thoroughly decimated the population of whales on this planet that only five percent remain alive…. More than thirty percent of the fish in every ocean…six million tons of fish per year…everywhere in the open sea we find oil, garbage, toxic chemicals…over one hundred million barrels of oil per year…. Heated wastewater from manufacturing processes provide false signals in the wrong season for spawning to begin…. Lobsters and catfish acquire a taste for oil…. Shorelines are dying…. Coral reefs are dying…. Over one thousand species since the century began…."

Someone sat down beside me. I looked at the trail of smooth ivory hair over my hand. Sharon put her lips to my ear, whispered, "We were worried about you."

Her mouth lingered; I felt her breath. I stirred a little. No one else was in the room; the lecturer spoke grimly, her eyes wide, gazing at the empty chairs. If she spoke with enough passion, enough love, enough fear, people would materialize on them, begin to listen. Sharon rubbed my hand gently beneath her hair.

"Come on."

I shook my head, stayed to the end. The lights went on. The lecturer rewound her video silently, collected her notes. I followed Sharon out. Everywhere in the vast and complex ship sailing to the end of the world, people congregated, talking, drinking, dancing, swimming, shopping, eating. Sharon led me up, continually up. I heard music at every turn of the stairs: rock bands, jazz bands, classical quartets, Christmas choirs, jukeboxes, waltzes, whale songs. I couldn't see out anywhere. It was too dark. Or maybe the ship had sealed itself up because what was out there we didn't want to see. We kept going up, passing elaborate rooms full of oak and gold leaf, decorated with enormous, beautiful, unreal trees, and gardens under glass. We walked on carpets an inch thick that changed colors like certain fish. After a while, I got used to Sharon's slender, tense fingers holding mine. On every screen I glimpsed, whales surged upward blowing spume; seals clapped; penguins waddled; all the children of the sea played in the sea while we sailed serenely into the dark.

A GIFT TO BE SIMPLE

I RECEIVED THE VISION as I danced. I was the turning auger, the wheel spun around its center, the end of the circle moving to meet its beginning, to complete itself, without beginning and without end. I remember speaking of what I saw; sounds like shining gold bubbled up in me, floated out of my mouth. Across the room, in the light, I saw her, our divine Teacher, Mother Ann, the Word Incarnate, Daughter of God, in Whom He was well pleased. She smiled upon me, well pleased, and spoke. *Yes,* she said. *Do this in memory of me.*

And I turned and I turned in the glory of her light.

The next morning I was awakened before dawn, as always, by the rumbling motors of the delivery trucks in the A&P parking lot. The lot was on the other side of our pond and beyond the thicket of wood surrounding it, but I always heard them. I never minded waking then. The rest of the world was quiet, as it must have been in Mother Ann's time over two centuries before. Darkness hid the malls and offices and houses; our community might have been surrounded by dreaming farms again, with only a sleepy cricket still singing, and a bird beginning to rustle in a tree. In those peaceful moments I thought about my vision, the way I thought about something made with my hands: testing the design I had chosen, the material, making sure they conformed, with proper strength and simplicity, to the purpose I had in mind. Before long our cocks cried awake the sun, and the cows in the barn, and the traffic on the thruway, which began its morning flood toward the city. The soft chime that Brother Michael had programmed into the system above our doorways sounded for morning prayer. Sister Lisa and Sister Tiffany stirred in their beds, yawned. We all got up silently, knelt in prayer in our nightgowns until the chime sounded again. Then we rose and bade each other good morning. We turned our backs to one another and dressed quickly, talking about the household chores and who would do what.

"I need to change the oil in the truck this morning," Sister Tiffany said. "Brother Greye wants to pick up lumber later on, for his chests."

"Then I'll help him with the milking," Sister Lisa said. I heard her snapping the bib onto her denim milking skirt. Turning, I saw her flex her knobbed, reddened hands experimentally, as if they were stiff.

"I'll do the beds," I said. "And the dusting. And take the laundry down." I opened a window wide to let the brisk autumn air in. The light was lovely, the color of old gold, from all the yellow yarrow and the dying leaves. Sister Lisa stepped to a mirror, began to pick her white braids apart. She grimaced once, absently, as at a sudden pain in a joint. I wondered if she saw herself anymore in the mirror; if any of us had seen ourselves for years. We were so used to our faces, we never saw the changes in them. There were no changes in our lives, so why should there be in our faces?

"I'll make bread this morning," Sister Lisa said, "after milking and breakfast. I think Sister Jennifer wants to work in the wood shop all day."

I combed my own hair, a short and simple task. For some reason I remembered vividly what shade of red it had been when I was younger. I realized then how it had faded, day by day, year by year, since—when? When had it begun to turn? What year, what day had I begun to turn from young to old?

Sister Tiffany grunted suddenly. A button popped out from under her hands, spun across the floor. She gazed at me, flushed and wide-eyed. "It wouldn't close," she said of her skirt band. I retrieved the button from under a chair.

"I'll mend it," I promised. "Leave it here."

"But it won't close. It must have shrunk."

"It's all right. I can put a panel in it."

"A lot of things have been shrinking lately."

"Maybe it's the laundry soap."

She gazed down at herself as she reached for a skirt with some give in the band. "Is it," she asked with wonder, "what they mean by middle age?"

We both looked at Sister Lisa, still so thin she wore the skirts and blouses of the adolescent girls we had cared for, before they left us. But her hair had no color left at all; it was ghostly white. Along the center of her head, where she had parted her hair in the same place every morning for decades, I could see her scalp.

The discovery reinforced my vision, gave it purpose and intensity. "Yes," I answered Sister Tiffany. "But it will be all right."

She blinked at me. "You mean my skirt."

"That, too."

We had had children, years earlier. In those years, we scarcely noticed our dwindling numbers. God would replenish them, we thought, for we had made the transition across the millennium, and had once again found our place in the world without sacrificing our beliefs. Our families had tried to escape it in earlier years, as Mother Ann had wished. But there was no place left unchanged, at peace, in this busy, noisy century. No matter where we went the world followed, leaving its huge dinosaur footprints: a shopping mall where we had last worshiped, a hotel where we had planted crops, a small airport in what had once been our apple orchards. The world shaped its houses with our circular saw, harrowed and threshed its vast fields with other designs, hung its clothes, pared its apples, and shelled its peas with our ideas. It would not leave us alone, and we could not survive the century without it. So, desperate, we had prayed and danced and sung, until it was revealed to us that if we could no longer separate ourselves from the world, we should transform it and make it our own.

We began to patent all our inventions. We shared them, as we had always done, but no longer as freely. The money we earned with our discoveries and our designs, we used for the work that we had done since the beginning: sheltering and feeding the needy, the homeless. By the dawn of the millennium, we had 196 shelters all over the country, many of them run by those who had once been homeless. We could pay them well. Brother Brian had sold his unguent of beeswax and herbs to a pharmaceutical company; that had paid for all the land we now owned. Sister Jennifer's designs for wood-handled flatware and carving knives had remodeled the first five battered old hotels we turned into shelters for the poor. Sister Tiffany's hand-loomed weavings of carpets and quilts found their way into boutiques and major department stores. They bought our cars and trucks and kept them running. We built our own factory for packaging our seeds, and printed our own catalogues for seeds and furniture. Brother Michael, who loved animals, experimented with breeding, and produced a strain of sheep whose wool was multicolored and soft as silk. He told us what methods he used in breeding them, but I don't think any of us quite understood that language. And I never thought of it again, until my vision.

We had everything we wanted and we were dying.

We had children, years earlier. Kyle and Carmela had come to us from the homeless shelter in the city near us. Megan had been left on our doorstep. Stephanie had run away from her parents, wearing nothing, in midwinter, but a thin dress and the burn marks on her arms. We took them in, fed them, taught them our ways. "Hands to work and hearts to God" as our precepts instructed us. "Excel in order, union and peace, and in good works. A place for everything and everything in its place." So they learned to milk a cow, make a chair, mend a tool, to weave a hat to protect them in the garden, draw a perfect circle on the computer, print out a catalogue page, raise a chicken, roast it, and fire a platter to serve it on, then to wash the platter and put it in its place, all for the glory of God.

They were good, dutiful, gifted children. When they became adults, we gave them the choice to stay with us or leave. They all left. They chose the world that Mother Ann had sheltered us against, and they did not return. We ran our shelters, our factories, our stores, with those who were honest and gifted, but who did not believe. For a while, we scarcely noticed. Others would come, we thought. Our faith could never die with us. Instead came the evening, after the meal had been cooked and eaten, the table cleared, the prayers spoken, and the permitted number of us had sat down to talk about the day, brothers and sisters separated and facing one another in our solid, worn rockers, when I saw with the sudden clarity of revelation how old we had all gotten.

Brother Michael's hair had turned completely white, the color, appropriately, of a fine sheepskin. Sister Tiffany's bright cinnamon hair was shading into sage; her chipmunk's face, with its big, inquisitive eyes, was lightly lined. Brother Bryan's chestnut hair stubbornly refused to turn, though he had to reach back much farther to comb it now. Sister Jennifer, always thin and energetic, had grown pear-shaped in the past year; I could hear her wheeze as she climbed the stairs. Brother Greye, who had gone bald early, had grown a set of turkey-wattles under his chin. My own face, I noticed that morning, was beginning to resemble an apple that had sat too long in the bowl. Other members of the family, quietly busy in the house around us with late evening tasks, had also faded, the way dried flowers will grow pale, sitting for too many seasons in the light.

There was no one else. A couple of families, one in California, one in Nebraska, had survived gracefully and successfully for nearly two decades into the new millennium. We received notice from our lawyers three years ago that the last of them had died, and that the check from the sale of the property would be in the mail. Even then, we did not worry. God the Father and Mother Ann would see to our future.

It was revealed to me that night that I should worry. I brought up the subject at a tangent, as I squinted to thread my needle; I was cross-stitching a pattern for the seat of a chair. I wished aloud for younger eyes, quick, flexible fingers that never cramped.

"We had them once," Sister Tiffany said calmly. Children, or vision, I wasn't sure which, until she added, "Everything fades. Maybe you need glasses, Sister Ann. I think I finally do."

"I think I need an apprentice," I said. "Like Megan. Remember Megan?"

"How could we forget her?" Sister Jennifer asked. "Such a sense of design she had. I used to drive her to the malls so she could study fashions. She could take the oddest pieces of clothing—a lime green shirt, a skirt made out of glitter—add a bit here, take away something there, sew the two together, and sell it for ten times what she paid for it."

"Such a sweet girl," Sister Tiffany added. "But I don't think she ever understood why we couldn't let her wear what she made."

Brother Bryan murmured assent, rocking gently. "That must be why she left."

"And Kyle," I persisted.

"And Kyle," Brother Michael echoed. "He had such a God-given gift for computer art. But what he wanted to use it for—"

"Action comics," Sister Jennifer said reminiscently.

Brother Greye scratched a tufted eyebrow with his thumb. "I never understood what they are, exactly. So much color, so much violence. Children sit and look at these?"

"It was most likely a passing fad," Sister Jennifer guessed. "Though perhaps not for Kyle."

Kyle still wrote to us, now and then, from southern California, where, it seemed, he kept getting paid for his strange art. I stirred, anxious in spite of the peace of the house. They were the last we had cared for, and they were no longer children.

"I think—" I began. But I did not know what to think, then, and Brother Greye was filled, suddenly, with the spirit.

He said sonorously, "Everything must be done to perfect this world on earth, with perfect love, and in preparation for the Day of Judgment, which will close the perfect circle of our days. Of course we could not have encouraged Kyle, even to keep him with us. He made his choice. 'Do all your work,' Mother Ann taught us, 'as though you had a thousand years to live, and as you would if you knew you must die tomorrow.' It is difficult for children to contemplate their death. They would rather read action comics."

"But Carmela," Sister Tiffany remembered, "was different. She was not brilliant, but she did the things she could with a simple perfection. I really thought she might have wanted to stay with us."

Their voices were filled with the past, I thought; a comfortable past, not a threatening future. They added to one another's memories of the children who had grown and gone; they found the flaws in faith that made them leave, but no terror in their absence. I said nothing more that night, but prayed and danced over my own fears, in our next evening service. Even dancing, I couldn't transcend the world. It frightened me, how my heartbeat became tangled in the rhythms of Brother Greye's heavy, clumsy tread; how I could not hear the familiar, bliss-filled conversations from the next world, only our thinning, wavering voices singing and chanting, like lonely children comforting themselves in the dark. Even that fear, I saw days later during our long Sunday service, was a gift. It led me to my vision.

I saw as I turned and turned in the light of Mother Ann's love, how God Himself had become human. He had come among us not through any human intercourse, as we were of course forbidden; not even by any human touch. He had made an announcement, and it became the Word. He had cloned Himself, using a pure, perfect, human tool. We also were known for the purity and perfection of our handiwork, and for our love of the best tools. We led our lives by His teachings, and by the example of our Mother, who had lost four infants before she understood that she was to be a vessel of God, and not of the whims of her own body. The vessel is filled; it does not fill itself. Emptied, it remains in perfect stillness and submission, waiting to be used. It does not use itself. So it was revealed to me, we would find the perfect tools, the flawless vessels for God's Word, and fill them.

I was moved to speak sometime later, after we had filled endless hot and steamy vessels full of the season's pears, tomatoes, cucumbers, grapes, blueberries, cherries, and crabapples. In the fields, the cornstalks had been cut and mulched; the apples picked and stored; the potatoes and onions, squashes and peppers packed for market. We were all grateful, that evening, for our rockers. Outside, the cold rain tapped against the windows; a dark wind harvested the few leaves still clinging to the trees. How many more autumns would we all see, I wondered, before we wore our winter faces? Which of us would outlive the rest, to die among strangers in an unfamiliar place?

The distant sound of a jet coming in to land in the municipal airport inspired me; I found the place to begin. "Do you remember," I asked the others, "when Orville and Wilbur Wright made their first flight—"

"No," Brother Michael said with some amusement. "We have a few gray hairs, but we can't be that old, Sister Ann."

"We're not that young, either," I answered softly, and they were silent, wondering where I was taking them. "Anyway, do you remember the story of how our family in Ohio decided that since we had learned to master the automobile, we should buy an airplane? It was the newest and best tool, then. We have always loved the finest things."

"So," Sister Tiffany said, pulling thread; she was quilting a case for her new bifocals. "Where does all this take us, Sister Ann—the Wright brothers and airplanes and the best of things? Do you think we need a private plane?"

"No. I think we need children."

They were silent again. We could hear Sister Lisa above our heads, at the linen closet where she was mending seams and patching holes in our winter quilts and sheets. Brother Patrick was in the kitchen, tottering dangerously on a stool, sharpening knives. People who live together for decades grow to know each other's voices and expressions, their thoughts, whether they want to or not. My brothers and sisters knew mine; they heard what had never been there before. Nobody bothered with words like adoption, homeless, celibacy, faith. We had adopted the homeless; they did not stay. We were forbidden by our faith to touch one another unless it was absolutely necessary. We were forbidden even to pet a cat. We were the last of our faith; we would die without heirs. Sister Jennifer, her rocker twitching a quick, agitated little rhythm under her, said simply,

"How?"

I leaned back, rocking myself now, in a slower, even measure, like a pendulum. I looked at Brother Michael again. "From airplanes to sheep," I murmured. He blinked. "You told us how, once. Tell us again. How you did it with sheep, so that the strain was always pure, unchanging."

He drew breath. "Sister Ann. That may get us around the necessity for sex, but there is still the physical matter of birth." He had been an Elder, briefly, before our dwindling number made such distinctions moot. But he still spoke like one, sometimes. "You are all young enough for that, but I don't think you would be here, if you wanted to be pregnant. Even if it did not cut too close to the boundaries of our Mother's tenets. If she could have conceived of the idea, two centuries ago, she would have considered it part of the evils of the world, for no other reason than that all the babies she gave birth to died."

"But she didn't conceive of the idea," I answered calmly. "So it was never forbidden in our laws."

Sister Tiffany had stopped sewing; her needle glinted between her fingers as she rocked. I knew her expressions, even beneath her new glasses: the bright, intense interest in her eyes. "Then you had better explain," she breathed. "Sister Ann. How we are to give birth without sex."

"God showed us," I said. I rocked harder now, my whole body trying to dance without rising, my thoughts swooping through me like a flock of white doves turning and turning in the summer light. "He cloned Himself. We'll find a virgin. The perfect, unfilled vessel. As He did. We'll make children from ourselves, from our own cells. We all have something in our makeup that wants this life, this work. We will make children who will not leave us, because they will be born with all our faith. If we don't do this, we will die, and there will be no one in the world to remember the name of Mother Ann."

They were all silent, gazing at me. Every rocking chair was still. Then Brother Michael cleared his throat, and I saw the light in his eyes as if a door had opened and our future shone out of it.

"Let us pray over this," he said, and we did, then and there, with such inspiration and enthusiasm that the house itself seemed to dance on its foundations around us.

So we found a virgin. They still exist, though finding one without some odd brand of religion attached is not easy, and the proof is even harder to obtain. And then we spent days in prayer, chanting and dancing ourselves into trances, so that our Mother's instructions would be revealed to us. Her name, we heard again and again, in many different tongues: Ann, Ann, Ann... We followed her instructions. In a year we had our child, and the ironclad documents that said she was ours from the day of her birth. I left her naming to the others. They called her Ann, after our Mother, of course. We live without possessing; we share everything equally. The child, like the idea, was something that came from me, but she was not mine, any more than she belonged to the woman who bore her. But she had my red hair, and when I sang or danced, I felt her in me like light, as if I had truly given birth.

Two years later, she said her first prayer, and five years after that, she had her first brother, James, named after Mother Ann's successor.

She harries us, the child does: she demands more children, more dancing, more singing and devotions. She has designed her own line of toys, and has specific ideas about how to market them. She herself dances like the wind and speaks in her trances, to a woman she calls Mother. Her dark eyes see beyond this world. She foretells things, in ways our Mother did, at the unlikeliest times. She gazes through the open doors at the fields as Sister Tiffany rocks the butter in the churn on the porch, and Brother Patrick strokes the crabapples into his basket with the picker he invented. "They will flock to us like doves," she says, as if she sees the multitudes pouring through the wood, surging around the pond, to come to us. We have cloned the Word, we know now. I was simply the instrument of her creation. She is the second coming of Mother Ann. We keep all things in readiness for her flocks. We watch the empty fields with her, and wait.

THE OLD WOMAN AND THE STORM

THE SUN ROSE, as it did every day, making the birds squawk, painting the world. But this rising was different. Arram sensed it as he stepped out of his house. His bare sole felt a newness. His eyes filled with a memory of light. He stood still, watching the night melt away, and for just a moment, time enough for the first warmth to touch his face, he knew that this was also the First Sunrise, when the Long Night had ended and the world began to form. The sun had risen so. The earth was old-new underfoot. Dreams and memories stirred in a breeze through the trees. Arram went for a walk in the new world.

The Sun, the painter, got out her paintbrushes of light. She drenched a bird in red and yellow as it swooped by. She spattered purple among the berry bushes. She painted stones and reflections of stones in the river. Arram passed his favorite rock, where he himself had painted his First Name. The Name had come to him in a dream: the First Name which the being that breathed through his body and saw through his eyes had called itself. Now it had Arram's name and voice. Arram had made a gift of the Name to the rock. It slept so calmly in the water, massive and yellow, a dreaming giant. Other people had liked it also: many pictures, gestures of affection, patterned its weathered sides.

Arram filled his belt-skin with water and turned away from the river. The flat earth, the Sun's domain, spread before him in a thousand shades of brown. He faced the Sun, felt her pour hot dark color into his hair, his body. Far away, another stone, huge and rounded with age, smoldered in the morning with a glow like fire. It caught his eye, greeted him with the common greeting: the languageless, timeless memory of the First Morning. Arram walked toward it.

A lizard scurried away from his foot. A hawk circled above him, then hurtled down, a fist of brown plumage. It rose again with a snake in its talons. Minute red flowers swarmed across Arram's path. Animal bones slowly buried themselves in the earth. Tracks of a live animal came across the desert, crossed Arram's tracks, and went their own silent way. A cloud smudged the sky, and another. The Old Woman who hated the Sun was smoking. The distant rock moved slightly closer to Arram. It had changed color: the fire had melted into brass. Have I been to that rock before? Arram wondered. Or do I only remember it from another time? Thoughts rambled pleasantly in his head; the world constantly changed under his eye. Is this walk mine? Or am I remembering an earlier walk? He stopped for a swallow of water. The ground simmered around him, blurred with light. The air droned and buzzed with invisible singers. A shadow passed over him, and he looked up. The Old Woman was puffing clouds all over the sky.

Arram walked on. When he grew hungry he killed a lizard and roasted it. The soul of the lizard went on its own walk, searching for another container. The rock began to loom across the horizon, bigger than Arram had thought. It darkened; the clouds were draining the Sun of color. The air was motionless, moist-hot. If I remember the rock, I should remember reaching it, Arram thought. But I don't. So this must be my own walk. There was a fragment of red cloth on a thorn. Someone else had come that way and gone. In the dim, steamy afternoon, the voice of the desert was a vibrant bass hum. The Sun managed a final angry shower of light. She burned the cloud-edges silver, struck sweat from Arram's face, turned the great wall of rock orange. A shadow, black as night, fell across Arram's path and he stopped, as though he had caught himself from stepping into a rift. He glanced up. Then down and up again. Someone lost a shadow, he thought surprisedly. There was nothing, even in the sky, that it belonged to. As his eyes fell again to the earth, a wind came up tasting of dust and rain, and sent the shadow tumbling across the desert like a leaf.

Now that's strange, Arram thought.

He continued his walk. The rain fell, drenching, warm as a lover. He opened his mouth and drank; he walked through water as through air, for who could know how many times his soul might have been a fish? He had dwelled in water, under the earth. He had died again and again, and been reborn to the same earth. Now he was a man, with a head full of misty memories. Dreams of other lives. There was nothing in the world to fear; he had been, or he would be, every shape in the world. But still, when two boulders crashed and split over his head, and the sky flashed a frosty color that was no color, the man decided it was time to run.

He reached the lacework of caves in the rock just as eggs made out of ice began to fall out of the sky. One struck him, a hard blow on his shoulder that drove him to his knees. He crawled the rest of the way into the cave, sat against the wall in the dim light, rubbing his shoulder and wondering at the force of the storm. The rock above his head seeped into his awareness. It had been battered times past counting, nothing could destroy it. I would like to be a rock now, Arram thought. A puff of smoke made him cough. A stone-painting on the cave wall was no longer a painting. It was the Old Woman. She lifted her pipe, made lightning flash and Arram saw her face.

He stopped breathing. She was the ugliest woman in the world, as well as the meanest, and he wasn't sure what to say to her. He wanted to move very quietly and take his chances with the ice-eggs. But he hesitated, and as he sat motionless, the Old Woman passed him her pipe.

He took a puff, not knowing what else to do, and passed it back to her. "So," she said in her croaky voice, "you want to be a rock. Go ahead. Walk outside. You won't be a man very long. You won't be anything recognizable." She laughed a reedy, insect-laugh. Her hair was white as river-froth, her nose humped and battered like the rock they sat under. She was shriveled, light as a bundle of twigs. She was crazy with jealousy of the Sun, and she was dangerous. Her eyes were the color of lightning.

Arram sighed. He thought with longing of the butterflies along the river, of his love putting her hands on his bare skin. Who would have thought a walk in the morning would have led to death? "The storm will end," he said softly, and she answered,

"I am the storm."

His eyes flicked at it. The sky was growing darker, the ice was still falling constantly as rain. His throat closed suddenly. He wondered how far it could spread. It could batter homes to the ground, it could kill children....

"You're so angry," he breathed. "Why are you so angry?"

"You made me angry!"

"Me? What did I do?"

"I saw how you looked at the Sun this morning! She rose and touched your face and you followed her without a thought...."

"No, that isn't the way it was! She—I—"

"How was it? You looked at her as if she had never risen before. I saw you."

He nodded, confused. "That's the way it was. She was—But I—I was only remembering, the way I must have seen her first. When I was a child. Or in another time. The world—"

"Could you ever look at me like that?"

He leaned back, sighing again. He was silent, drawing his name on the ground in the dust, feeling the air in his lungs, the blood beat in his fingertips. "All right," he said after a while, his voice detached, faraway. "You can kill me now. But first stop the storm."

She only growled something and the thump of ice in the dark sounded louder. Many living things would be left looking for shapes that night. He gazed at her, bewildered.

"Then what do you want?"

"Well, look at me! I am rain! I am thunder, I am lightning, I am bitter, bitter winds—I never have choices! Make me another shape. One that will move you to look at me the way you look at the Sun." She waved her pipe again, and the lightning swam over Arram's amazed face. "Do that, and the storm will stop."

"I'm only a man," Arram protested. "I walk naked in the world. I kill lizards and paint rocks and then I die. I have no power."

"But you don't know what power you might have had. In another time." She snapped her fingers impatiently and thunder rolled. "Think! Remember."

Arram tried to think. But each time he tried, the thunder snarled and the lightning spat. He could only think of the quiet river with ice-eggs smashing into it, the forest bruised and broken by the storm. He couldn't remember a life of magic power. He didn't even know anyone who could remember. The Old Woman herself was the most powerful being he had ever seen. More powerful it seemed, even than the lovely Sun, who had fled from this storm. Maybe, he thought suddenly, the Old Woman is so strong, so angry, that she never sees the simple world. How can she? She throws fire at it, she rains on it. Maybe if I tell her what I see she'll believe that I will have to die to make the storm stop, because I can't help her.

So he said, "In my forest there are red flowers, so big they overflow two hands. They are very beautiful, with many petals reaching toward the sky." The Old Woman was beginning to look annoyed. Her white brows flew together and a boulder crashed down the cliff outside. Arram cleared his throat and continued hurriedly, "They weren't always flowers. Once they were all young women who had no lovers. They cried and pleaded for lovers, but all the young men had died in a battle, and no one knew what to do. One day the great black Hunting Beetle came to them and said, 'I'll be your lover. The only lover all of you will ever need.' And of course they laughed and threw stones at him, making him scurry into a hole so he wouldn't get squashed. That night he crawled back out and looked wistfully over all the arms and legs and breasts of the sleeping women, all of whom he loved at once. He wished for them, and wished, and they sobbed in their sleep for the young men who would never come. And his desire and their sorrow kindled a magic between them, for all things are connected and the earth takes care of its own. In the morning, where the young women had lain, grew the loveliest flowers in the world. The beetle had his wish. And so did the young women: for even today the Hunting Beetle roams over all the flowers in the forest, feeding on their honey and freeing their seeds to the wind."

He stopped, feeling a little confused. He had meant to tell the Old Woman a simple story, but this had a magic in it he had never noticed. She was watching him puzzledly, puffing brief puffs on her pipe. The terrible sound of the ice storm seemed to have lessened a little. The Old Woman said finally, "That's no use to me. I wish and I wish, and nothing ever listens to me. But tell me another one."

Arram drew breath soundlessly, and decided to tell her about the rock in the river, which surely had to be the simplest thing in the world. "In the heart of the river beside my home there is a great rock. It is very old, old as the First Morning. It is very peaceful, so peaceful sometimes you can hear it dreaming."

"You can?"

"Yes. It is hard and massive, so hard the river itself scarcely wears away at it. Only one thing ever came close to cracking that rock, and that thing was light as a breath. A butterfly. You ask me," Arram said, though the Old Woman hadn't, "how such a light thing could—"

"Get on with it."

"It's a simple tale."

"It doesn't sound simple."

"It's just about an old rock in a river. Anyway, one day the rock decided it was tired of being a rock."

"How do you know?"

"How do I know? I don't know. Someone told me the story. Or else I heard the rock remembering. It was very young then, and many things were still new. Caterpillars were very new. One big purple caterpillar fell out of a tree onto a leaf floating on the river. The leaf carried it downriver, where it bumped against the rock and the caterpillar crawled off with relief, thinking it had found land. But it toiled up a barren mountain instead. The hairs on the caterpillar's body tickled the rock, waking it, and it wondered what strange little being was trudging up its side. After a time, the little being stopped trudging and started spinning, for its time for change was upon it. The rock went back to sleep. For a long time there was silence. A star shone, a leaf fell, a fish caught a fly. Then one morning, the shell that the caterpillar had spun around itself broke open. The rock felt feet lighter than bubbles walking about on the warm stone. Their dreaming merged, for the butterfly was half-asleep, and the rock half-awake. And the rock realized that the purple hairy being which had crawled up its side was now a fragile, gorgeous creature about to take to the air. And the rock was so moved, so amazed, that it strained with all its strength to break out of its own ponderous shell to freedom in the light. It strained so hard that it nearly cracked itself in two. But the butterfly, who felt its longing, stopped it. 'Rock,' it said gently, 'You can live, if you wish, until the Final Evening. You saved my life and sheltered me, so I will give you a gift. Since you can't fly, I will return here on my Final Evening and bring you dreams of all the things I have seen along the river, in the forest and desert, as I flew. And so will my children. You will not need to fly, and you will not need to die.' And so, even to this day, butterflies rest in the warm light on that rock and whisper to it their dreams."

Arram stopped. They were both silent, he and the Old Woman. She puffed her pipe and blew smoke out of the cave, and far away a forest fire started. "I don't know this world," she said slowly. "This is the world *She* knows. The Sun. The world I know is harsh, noisy, violent. Tell me a story with me in it instead of her. And make me beautiful."

Arram accepted another puff from her pipe. His ears hurt from the thunder, his voice ached from his storytelling. He couldn't remember whether it was day or night; he couldn't guess whether he would live or die. He supposed he would die, since there was no way in the world to make the Old Woman beautiful. So he decided, instead, in his last moments, to tell her about the one he loved most in the world.

"The woman I love is not very beautiful either," he said, seeing her face in his mind. "She is very thin, and her nose is long and crooked. When she was younger, the other children called her 'Crane' because she grew so tall and thin she stooped." He paused to swallow, no longer caring if the Old Woman were listening, for he wanted to spend those last moments with his love. "She thought no one in the world would ever love her. But I did. She was light, like a bird, and shy like a wild thing, and full of funny movements. When I told her I loved her, though, she didn't believe me. She thought I was making fun of her and she hit me. The second time I told her, she threw a pot at me. So I had a sore ear and a sore shin. I went down to the river and sat wondering what I was doing wrong." He heard an odd, creaky sound, but he was too engrossed in his memories to wonder at it. "I decided to bring her all the beautiful things I could find and pile them at her door. I brought her flowers. I brought her bright snakeskins. I brought her feathers, colored leaves, sparkling stones. I fell on my head out of trees collecting speckled eggs for her; I roasted myself in the desert to find purple lizards for her. And you know what she did with all those treasures? She threw them, she walked on them, she gave them away—every single thing. Finally, one day, I brought her the fattest fish I had ever caught, all roasted and ready for her to eat—and she burst into tears. I didn't know what to do. I wanted to cry. I wanted to pull her hair. I wanted to shake her until her teeth rattled. I put my hands on her shoulders, and a madness came over me, and I kissed her so long we both ran out of breath and fell on the floor. And when I looked at her, she was smiling." He paused. "Like you are now." He laughed himself at the memory, and at the shining in the Old Woman's face. "Look at you. You look just like her. Look—" His breath caught. He stared out at the quiet sky, at the blazing colors that arched from one end of the world to the other. The Old Woman's smile. He stood up, watching it, marveling, his face a lover's face, until the smile melted like pipe smoke, and the Sun burned away the clouds.

He went back home. His tall, shy, crooked-nosed love saw him as she filled the water-skins, and came to meet him, smiling. He took the skins from her; she tucked her hand in his arm.

"Where have you been?"

"For a walk."

"What did you see?"

"A rock. A shadow. A rainbow."

THE DOORKEEPER OF KHAAT

THERE WERE KHAATI everywhere in Theore, those days, refugees from the war on the other side of the planet. There were Meri in the city also, but Meri had been moving into Tatia for a hundred and fifty years. There were Datu, but the land the Tatians had civilized had been theirs once, anyway. Now they ran restaurants in one side of the city, and in the other, they stole transport parts or painted huge bright murals on tenement walls and called themselves artists. There had always been Tatians in Theore but not as many now, Kel noticed, as there used to be. As the Khaati and the Meri moved into the city, Tatians moved out to the country, to the northern cities, to the sea-colonies if they could afford it. For a while, before he decided to become a poet, Kel had lived in one of the tiny, white-domed spaces in a sea-colony. His father had bought the space for him as a reward for finishing his engineering studies. Kel spent afternoons swathed in light, swaying gently to the movements of tide, listening to words well up from some shadowy, unnamed river running through his brain, fit themselves together as neatly as molecules. One day he left the sea-colony full of golden faces like his own and went to live on the oldest street in the oldest city in Tatia.

A hundred years ago, the street had been famous for its passionate, impoverished poets. Now it was populated mostly by Khaati. Kel, intoxicated by the past, saw pale, aqua-eyed faces so constantly that he forgot his own was different. The odd singsong language he heard on the street formed an undistracting background for thoughts. He drank their alcoholic teas, bought steaming, spicy fish from their shops, nibbled it as he walked down the street in the evenings. From behind paper curtains, he heard their odd, tuneless, meandering music told of places no boat could sail to, of thresholds no shod foot cou. cross.

There were rules on that street. He couldn't remember learning them, he just knew them: rules his poet's eye observed while he himself was doing nothing much. Do not look their maidens in the eye, the rules said. Do not compliment the babies or lay a hand on the young children's heads. Never step on the shadows of the elderly. Do not whistle in their shops. Never point at anyone, you could lose a finger. Be careful what small, amusing, tourist trinket, pin, or jacket you buy—you might find yourself wearing the emblem of the latest street gang, and unlike Tatians, they did not discriminate. And don't call them gangs. Clans, they were. Clans.

He lived from hand to mouth there, from moment to moment, as a poet should live. Or at least as he understood them to have lived on that street in Theore a hundred years before. He tracked down their forgotten poems, read voraciously, and tried to imitate them in his writings. They had written of everything, they valued every word, for each word, each experience, was equally sacred, equally profane. His Tatian lover, who had come with him from the sea-colonies, bore with his obsession for a couple of months. Then she realized that he was absurdly content in that neighborhood among the Khaati, that he had no inclination to take a job from his father, live in the great light-filled high-rises mid-city that strove like gargantuan plants toward the sun. She left him, disappeared into the Tatian heart of the city. The shock of her leaving and for such reasons fueled much articulate and bitter poetry. Sometimes, sobering up and rereading his work, Kel felt almost grateful to her for the experience of pain.

Around the time that brooding over his lost love was becoming habitual rather than unavoidable, Kel met Aika. He sat down beside her in a Khaati bar one afternoon. The scent of her mildly intoxicating tea wafted toward Kel as he chewed over his loss. Sometime during the next couple of hours, he found talking to Aika more interesting than getting drunk. She neither laughed nor sighed when he said he was a

a thin white eyebrow and told him she was going to

that H

said blankly. He had been wondering why her eyes— clear blue as every other Khaati he had ever seen—were y beautiful. Then he blinked. "Khaat?"

"Yes.

"Khaat is not a place. Khaat is a war."

"I was born in Khaat." She sipped tea delicately; her fingers were long, tapering, ringed. "My parents escaped just after I was born. So I have lived in Tatia all my life. I know two languages, I have a Tatian education. But Khaat is still my country, even at war with itself. My heritage."

"Your heritage—the best of it—is on this street," he argued. "There can't be much left in Khaat. It's been tearing itself apart for so long nobody remembers who's fighting who or why."

She smiled after a moment, a thin-lipped, amused smile. "Just Blues fighting Blues in one of their interminable clan wars."

"No. Clan wars I understand. But Khaat seems intent on destroying itself. What do you think you'll find there but a dying country with nothing left of it but a name?"

Her level gaze did not falter at his glib bluntness, but her eyes seemed to grow enormous, luminous. She only said dryly, "You want to be a poet. Read Coru."

He sat up until dawn reading Aika's copy of Coru's poems, while she slept beside him. The poet-shaman had lived two thousand years before in a Khaat that Kel had not realized was so old. Coru had spent his life wandering down farm roads, through jungles, into villages, bringing both practical and mystical remedies for everything from hangnails to impotence. He wrote of everything: fish soup, morning dew, sex, starving children, clan battles, and white tigers. Words kept the world orderly, he believed, kept the past from vanishing.

> *Soul, like butterfly, has no language.*
> *We who walk from moment to moment,*

Must say where we have been
Moment to moment,
Or we disappear.
So, like rice pickers,
We harvest words out of our mouths,
To feed ourselves.

Aika made an irritated movement in her sleep at Kel's voice. He stopped reading, blinked gritty eyes at the dawn. Strange images prowled in his head like ghosts of somebody else's relatives: the white tiger that appeared sometimes ahead of the poet to lead him to a place where he was needed; monkeys and teal-eyed birds screaming at one another in different languages; noon sun on a chalk-white road; the stout, broad-faced, sweaty farmer's widow whose lovemaking Coru compared to every natural disaster he could think of; the Doorkeeper, the mysterious, many-faced woman who carried the keys to the Doorway of Death on her belt.

"Yes, but," Kel, his eyes closed, heard himself say, "that was two thousand years ago. The shelf-life of a country's soul is two generations after the revolution that formed it."

Aika, waking, snorted sleepily. "You Tatians. How would you know? Everyone knows you are born lacking souls."

"Maybe. But whatever soul Khaat has, it's tearing into bloody pieces now."

"Maybe," she said softly, turning away from him, "that's why I want to go."

If he didn't talk about it, he figured later, maybe she would forget. He began to know her, the way her pale hair fell across her brows to snag her eyelashes, the way he could change her habitually brisk, humorless expression, the way her eyes caught light sometimes and turned so clear they held only the memory of color. Her white skin smelled of almonds; the perfume she sometimes wore smelled of apricots. She had a lovely laugh, like water running in a forest on a hot day, like distant bells of some unknown metal. He loved to hear her laugh. But no matter what he did to distract her, the thoughtful, distant look would return to her eyes, and at those times she would not hear him say her name.

"But why?" he asked helplessly. "It would be like going into a burning house when it's simply too late to rescue anything."

She sighed. "If there was a child in the burning house?"

"If it's too dangerous even for that?"

"Suppose this happened in Tatia—you had such a civil war. At what moment would Tatia no longer be Tatia? And you no longer be Tatian?"

"That's different. You want to go back and rescue something that might have existed in a poem. Tatia can be rebuilt. Tatians grow anywhere, like grass or mold. They don't worry about carrying their souls with them."

She propped her chin on her hand, sighing. "Do you know what the Khaati word for Tatian is?"

"I can guess."

"Cloud."

"What?"

"You are cloud people, we reach right through you. You have no past."

"Sure we do," he protested. "Everyone does."

"You have no gods, no magic. No myths, no shadows."

"We had myths. We never liked shadows."

"You don't like secrets. You don't like anything you can't take apart, put back together. You explore everything, try to know everything. If you know everything, where is the shadow to rest in?"

"What shadow?"

"The shadow you need crossing the desert of knowing everything. The shadow behind the language." But she was laughing at herself, now, or at whatever he had been doing to her.

"I know enough," he said, "to get along."

But her words clung to him; he considered them at odd moments. Past was only a way of getting to the present, myth and magic were a pair of shoes too small to walk in any longer. Learning everything was a busy-minded civilization's way to survive. It was a road that increased in proportion to its traveled part. Still, he wondered, what in Tatian culture made its people seem like clouds? Insubstantial, always changing form... They were thinkers, creators, they built roads across deserts, they did not waste time sitting under shadows. They pushed back the night; it was busy with artificial lights blazing against the background of stars. They even counted stars, they were so busy. They counted everything: people, nuclear particles, cold viruses, board feet, time.

You have no past.

Sure we do, he thought, and it's as bloody as everyone else's.

The shadow behind the language...

Aika left him finally, as he knew she would. She did not ask him to come with her.

He missed her sorely. He watched endless news-holos of the distant war, hoping and fearing for a glimpse of her face on some schoolteacher, soldier, nurse. Gradually the ache lessened, became bearable. He pursued his fragmented, kaleidoscope existence; he cooked soya-chili at a restaurant, tended bar at another; he cleaned floors at the Aquarium at night and watched the octopus brood. He drank wine sitting on the curbs with wizened Khaati grandmothers, who needed to get away from their bustling families. They taught him a few Khaati words, he taught them a little Tatian.

Then he received an order from his father: Come home.

Home was a city in the north full of Tatians, a structure of glass and steel and light, light everywhere, always. We landed in the desert, Kel thought, confused, as he stepped off the air-shuttle. But it was only the Tatian preference for sun in the chilly north. The golden, hairless faces, his own face, after a street filled with Khaati, startled him.

"I'm dying," his father said abruptly, when they were settled in the vast apartment overlooking out of all sides most of the north end of a continent. Kel took a large gulp of brandy, opened his mouth; his father continued without letting him speak. "It's a congenital virus. My mother had one of the first known cases of it. There's no cure yet, it hasn't been around long enough. You show no signs of it in your system, I had them check. They would have found the virus in you by now, if you were going to get it."

"I—" Kel said, and coughed on brandy fumes.

"Let me talk. You have this thing about being a poet."

"I—"

"So you go and live on a street full of Khaati. I don' know you too well, but you're one of three people I trust, and the other two don't have your connections. One's dead anyway," he added surprisedly. "There's a drug the Khaati make. It's lethal, but in my case it doesn't matter. It will kill the pain, which does matter. They give it to their old people when they don't want to live anymore. I want you to get me some. Will you?"

Kel was still swallowing brandy fumes. "You want me—" His head finally cleared, along with his throat. "You want me to give it to you because you don't want to live anymore."

"I do want to," his father said. There was no expression in his big, stolid, golden face. None in his voice. All in his words. "I do," he said again. "But I won't. And this will give me some hours, days maybe, without pain. Then pouf. Finish." He added, with a shade of amusement in his voice, "Anything else I take they can cure me of. But not this. That's why it's illegal. Do it for me? You can write a poem about if afterward, I don't mind."

"If I don't wind up in jail," Kel said. He was regaining control; his hands were trembling but he kept them locked around the brandy glass. "How'd you know about that stuff anyway?"

"Dr. Crena told me," his father said. His face seemed more peaceful, less implacable, now that he knew Kel wouldn't fuss, need things from him. He smiled slightly at Kel's expression. "He's known me since I first swore at him coming out of the womb. He has a right to advise me how to go back in. He knew I'd never betray him. And I know you won't."

"I'm just surprised," Kel said, and swallowed more brandy. "How does he know about it?"

"It's no secret, it's just illegal. It's not a street drug or a party drug, it's what you take to die. There's no popular demand for it."

Kel shifted. He felt, suddenly, intensely uncomfortable, as if his head were the wrong size, or his bones were trying to outgrow his skin. It was an idea forcing itself into him, he realized; he had to chew and swallow and make it part of himself. It was like trying to eat a stone.

"How can you be so calm?" he burst out finally, furiously. Again the expressionless, tawny gaze, reticent, impersonal.

"Don't shout," his father said mildly. "Doesn't do any good. I know. I've told you what will help me. Will you help me?"

Kel stared back at him. He could feel it then: shadow between his bones and his skin that had been there since the day he was born. "All right," he said, thinking of clans, the Khaati grandmothers, the thin, thin secret paper walls. "All right."

Bu. That was what the drug was called. Just that. *"Bu?"* he said to one of the grandmothers or great-grandmothers who had come out in the night to get a moment's peace, look up at the three stars showing above the city, smoke a cigarette smelling like ginger. She said nothing, stared at him as she drew in smoke, her cheeks hollowed. Her blue eyes looked sunken, pale. He repeated the word; the cigarette was replaced by a very old finger pressed against her lips. "For my father," he explained. *"Na babas."* But she was gone, she was a trail of smoke and a shadow, motionless, inside the open door.

The next evening, as he walked late through the quiet streets after sweeping the Aquarium, he was jumped.

He hit the pavement on his back, too surprised for a moment to realize what had happened. Then he saw the silver sun, looking like a demented sunflower, dangling from a chain in front of his nose. He saw the Khaati face above it. He felt the hard street pushing at his back, his skull.

"You want Bu, Tatian?" the young man murmured. He had a drooping white mustache and a tic near one eye. Kel remembered seeing him pulling down the awnings at one of the shops. He slid one hand around the back of Kel's neck, tightened his fingers. Stars, more than were ever seen in the night sky above the city, roared down around Kel. He tried to see, tried to scream, could do neither. Someone said something; the stars dulled, a thick night faded away like fog.

"Aika knew him," he heard. The name echoed: Aika, Aika. He could finally see. The fingers were still there, feather-light. The blood sang in his ears. Behind the Khaati bending over him, he saw others: one watching, smoking, one with three suns in one ear, one smiling a thin, crooked smile.

"That's the poet," he heard and someone laughed. Poet, poet. He tried to speak; a thumb licked his throat slowly and the words froze.

"Aika said he reads Coru."

"Who is Coru?"

"Ignorant Sun. You dumb kid." There was a brief dance, flashes of knife-light, a good-natured laugh. Someone else said:

"Why does he read a Khaati poet?"

"Ask him."

"Why, Tatian?"

"Why do you read poetry?"

"Why do you want Bu?"

"For my father," he said through the ice-floe in his throat. There was silence. His head thudded back on the pavement; he closed his eyes, seeing stars again. "For my father," he whispered. Then the silence became empty; he opened his eyes and saw no one.

He tried to write a poem about that: about the dancing suns and the wild stars and the hard, cold hand of the world against the back of his head. But the memories kept intruding between him and the words. I saw the dead-end of time, he thought. I nearly died. On an empty street in a Khaati neighborhood. Died of not being able to speak. I would have been a body and a stack of poetry. They would have put the body in the ground and the poetry in the garbage. That's it. End. Finis. Poof. He couldn't sit still, he was too aware of his body, the amazing, continuous beating of his heart despite all odds against it. I should be able to write this, he thought. But he couldn't.

Poet, poet.

Give it up, he thought the next morning. You don't have to get Bu. You don't have to kill your father.

But that evening, as he walked home from a bar, a woman stepped out of a doorway and beckoned to him. She was back-lit, a sketch of a woman, a seduction of familiar lines: long, long hair, no face, a lithe body stylized as a cave drawing, to be recognized until the end of time. She lifted a slender hand; rings flashed. He turned mid-step, followed her. He heard the silken whisper of the traditional tight-fitting sheath that covered her from throat to ankle. Birds flew across it, spiraled around her body to hide within her hair. When she finally turned, he was startled at how old she was.

She smiled slightly, young-old, knowing. They were in a small room behind a restaurant; he smelled spices, heard plates clatter, meat sizzling. Her face was very delicate, paper-pale, a country of small, secret roads. Her eyes were outlined in black, her hollowed cheeks flushed with pink powder. She smelled of ginger cigarettes and the perfume Aika wore. The perfume and her graceful, tapering fingers confused him. She was Aika, she was not Aika. She was young, she was old. Birds circled her. Her hair was dead-white, her eyes were beginning to sink a little into her head. Her body looked supple as a child's. He wanted her, he did not.

The smile-lines deepened under her eyes, beside her mouth. "Do you know," she asked him, "how much death costs?"

"No." He had to say it twice before he could hear himself. "No."

"It is not cheap."

"No," he agreed, though privately he considered death the cheapest thing in the universe. Hell, it was free. It handed itself out to anybody, anywhere. He cleared his throat again. "How much—" He thought of his meager salaries and shook his head. "I mean, it doesn't matter. My father will pay. There's nothing else he wants to buy."

"He wants it? Or you want it for him?"

He stared at her, then realized what she was asking. "Do I want to murder my father, you mean? No, not really. Do you want me to bring you a note from him?" He felt himself trembling and wished he could sit. But it was like sitting in front of a goddess. The goddess pulled a battered chair out from the table and gestured. She sat across from him and lit a cigarette. She narrowed her eyes, at her smoke, or at something she saw in the smoke. She no longer smiled.

"This is business," she said. Her voice was low, slightly grainy from the smoke; if he closed his eyes she would be the faceless woman in the doorway, eternally young, beckoning with her voice.

"Would they have killed me?" he asked abruptly. She looked at him, a face without an answer anywhere in it.

"Khaati have customs, as you do. We, perhaps, are more practical. You regard death as an end. We see it as a doorway. If someone wishes to enter that doorway, we are not so reluctant, so terrified to let them. You Tatians do anything to avoid entering that doorway. You see only a wall. So. Things that are illegal for you may be overlooked for us. As long as we keep certain rules. As long as we do not provide death for the wrong reason. Once that happens, once we have that reputation, of selling death for the wrong reason, we will be subject to your rules. We must be very careful. Especially of Tatians. They do not buy death for good reasons. I must know that you are buying death for a good reason. Your father is rich?"

He nodded, mute.

"You live among us, not among wealthy Tatians. You eat our food, read our poets. Perhaps your father will not share his wealth with you now. If he dies you will be very rich."

He blinked. "Not very rich. Rich."

"Then you will no longer have to live among the poor, eating our food, listening to our music."

He shrugged, not answering. He smelled the perfume again, but he did not want the woman who said those things. She only wanted to be safe; she could never understand. He said finally, "I chose to live here. I could kill my father and be rich, yes. But then I would not have my father." He was silent again, while she watched him. His mouth shook; he lifted his hand, hid it. "He is dying, anyway."

"That can be cured by Tatian ways. They always want to cure the dying."

"And they always die. This can't be cured. It's a recent, very rare virus. He will die in pain."

She said, "Ah," very softly.

"So his doctor told him about the—About death. Khaati death. And he asked me to get it for him. He'll pay. Whatever you ask, he'll pay. If you want to get rich yourself."

Something flickered in her eyes; she smiled fully then, showing blackened, broken teeth. "Money cannot buy death from me."

He drew breath, suddenly bewildered, depressed. "He'll die anyway," he said, more to himself than to her. "I don't have to do this. But he asked me to. He asked me. I can't remember the last time he asked me for anything. He always tried to give me things. A job, a trip, my own private air-shuttle. He never asked me before for anything that I might be able to give him. And now he asks this. So." He looked at her wearily. "It's not important how much."

Her terrible smile had gone; she watched him from behind her smoke. She put out her cigarette slowly, in an ashtray full of butts. She was looking beyond him again, her face thoughtful, absent; looking at her past, he realized, as he saw the ghost of her youth fly out of her face.

"I gave Bu to my mother," she said softly. "You are Tatian and I tell you that. A moment of peace, a dream, a doorway—that is what you will buy from me for your father. Not a wall, a doorway. You are Tatian, but you have found your way to me. You may have what you want."

"Thank you," he whispered.

"For my price."

"What is your price?" She told him.

He flew north three days later, carrying a very old, very expensive bottle of brandy for his father. His father met his flight. He looked shrunken, and very tired, though he moved and spoke as stolidly as always. His vigor required more effort; his face glistened constantly with a sheen of sweat.

"I brought you brandy," Kel said when they were safely in the apartment.

"Thanks," his father said, and Kel gave him the box. He seemed to sense something, holding it. His eyes went to Kel abruptly, wide, and with more expression in them than Kel had seen in a long time. He lifted the bottle out of the box; both hands closed around it. He sighed, his eyes closing, opening again, and Kel's throat burned at the relief in them. "Thanks, Son."

"You can take a few days to drink it. It won't make you drunk right away."

"It's all right," his father said. "This place is private as a tomb. You can say what you want."

"They just—" He stopped again, rubbing his eyes. "I'm used to talking about it that way. They said you'll have three or four days free of pain. Then you go through the doorway."

"Through the doorway."

"That's what they say. It's not a wall but a doorway. Not an end. Just a path through to someplace else."

His father grunted. "They say where?"

"No."

He smiled. He put his arm around Kel's shoulders. "I never read any of your poetry. Send me some."

"I will. When—how long—"

"Dr. Crena says I'll need to go into the hospital soon. He says I won't come back out. I'd rather not go in."

"So—" He was breathing shallowly, not finding air. "So—"

"So you should go back home."

"No." He drew breath with his mouth open, finally found air. "You shouldn't drink this alone. I want to stay with you."

"You do?"

"Keep you company. Is that all right?"

"Oh, yes," his father sighed. Kel moved closer to him, just to feel his big, sagging body, his breathing, his hold. "I didn't want to ask you. I'd never have asked. I've done a lot in my life, but I never cared much for the thought of dying alone." Kel's face turned, burrowed against his shoulder a moment. Then he straightened, thinking: a doorway. That's all it is, a doorway. "One thing I learned about life," his father added, patting him awkwardly. "It wins all the arguments. Sit down, I'll get a couple of glasses." He loosed Kel, turned to a cupboard. "You didn't say what this is costing me."

"Not much," Kel said. His father turned to look at him then, with the direct, opaque look that he used like a microscope to examine things he was given and wasn't sure he liked. Kel met his gaze, shrouding himself with visions of rain forests, white tigers, old women with long white hair and beckoning hands. When he was sure of his voice, sure of tranquillity, he continued, "What do you care, anyway? You're opening the door and leaving me the rest. Unless you've written me out of your will. What kind of poet am I going to be, surrounded by all this?"

"Ah." His father waved a less costly bottle of brandy, reassured. "You'll get used to it." He handed Kel the bottle and a glass. He touched Kel's glass very gently with the bottle Kel had brought. "Cheers."

Two weeks later, Kel sat on a shuttle heading east. A book of Coru's poems lay open in his hands. But he no longer had to read it. He was about to travel into those words: into Coru's land of dusty roads and green rivers, children hungry for rice, for souls.

Find Aika, the old woman had said. Find Aika and bring her back. For your father I open the door. For Aika I close it. She is my daughter. Bring her back.

That is my price.

He waited, his blood singing in terror, to enter Aika's land, where the children cried as they had never cried in Coru's time, and where poems awaited him, and everywhere every door was open.

WHAT INSPIRES ME

Guest of Honor Speech at WisCon 28, 2004

A friend asked me recently, "What inspires you to write?"

She is a writer herself, so I knew she wasn't asking me, "Where do you get your ideas?" She would know that ideas are as random as shooting stars; they come while you're cleaning the bathtub, or watching *Four Weddings and a Funeral* for the ninth time, or in the morning when the last bit of your dream is fraying away, just before you open your eyes. You see it, then, what you've been searching for all these weeks or months, clear as day; you look at it and think, "Oh. Yeah," and open your eyes. That wasn't what she was asking. And that was why I couldn't answer; I could only sit and stare at her with my mouth hanging gracelessly open, because all the answers that sprang immediately to mind answered the question she hadn't asked.

Such as, well, money. Money is an enormous and entirely respectable source of inspiration when writing is your sole means of support. I did the math recently and was astonished. I've been writing for forty-two years, since I sat down one morning when I was fourteen and wrote a thirty-page fairy tale. I sold my first novel when I was twenty-three, so I've been published for thirty-three years. Which means I've been supporting myself by writing for over three decades. My agent swears that I'm most inspired when I'm broke. As when, during one financially dicey period, the cesspool of the 130-year-old house I had bought in the Catskills gave up the ghost one spring on the first day of May. It is a day indelibly etched in memory, because I had a guest with whom I was trying to kindle the fires of romance, my cesspool was backing into my bathtub, and I remembered then that my plumber and his wife, who threw a Kentucky Derby party every year, and everyone who worked for him would be three sheets to the wind by the time the horses galloped out of the starting gate.

After the race was won and my guest had gone home, and I finally got someone interested in my problem, I had something else to worry about. My next-door neighbor, the minister for the elegant stone Dutch Reform church across the street, had walked over a mossy patch of my back lawn when I moved in, and told me that was where my cesspool was. I expressed mild interest and then forgot about it. Before that I'd lived for a quarter of a century in California, where nothing much was older than the Gold Rush. I understood apartments with white walls and shag carpets, or apartments that had done a little dance with the 1906 earthquake and refused to fall down. I had never needed to know what a cesspool was, or how it might affect my life. That morning I stood in the back yard and watched half a dozen hefty young guys unbury my cesspool, and I wondered uneasily how personal was this going to be, exactly? Would they, for instance, see my tampons floating around in the murk? What they unearthed first caused them all a great deal of interest. It was the passenger door to an ancient pickup truck somebody had laid down to cap the cesspool. There seemed to be a ritual involved here: the men could not lay the door aside until they had first figured out the make and model of the pickup truck. I waited; they sorted it out to their satisfaction, and moved it to uncover the source of my problem.

To my surprise, I saw a very neatly constructed little fieldstone well, a perfect circle of stones running down into the earth, holding, to my relief, what seemed nothing less innocuous than the average mud-puddle. It was a gorgeous day in early spring, with lots of blue sky and budding leaves, and a good strong, sweet wind that probably saved the day. A shovel, inserted into the puddle, only went down a few inches. The well was pronounced dead, and was buried again. Being, as I said, temporarily out of funds, I borrowed money from my mother and repaid her a couple of months later for my new system with what was probably the delivery payment for *The Book of Atrix*.

A steady accumulation of detail over a length of time is also a good source of ideas. For instance: music. I had followed it across country: friends who had played in a band in and around San Francisco also moved to the Catskills and played there in homespun places called the T-Bar, the Pine Hill Arms, Larry's Place. I sat on maple barstools drinking whatever passed for white wine, and thought about all the variations on the theme of relationships a band and its groupies go through in time. Outside, a snow squall might be covering the country road, making the night seem very dark and very old. Left to my own devices, I was more inclined to blunder my way through Bach and Chopin on the piano. I learned soon that if you tossed a stone in pretty much any direction in those small mountain villages, you would hit a piano player. Or an aging fiddle-player, keeping up the traditional tunes of the region. A friend down the road played all of those things—Bach, rock, and fiddle. He also played recorders and from him I learned how much fun it is to play music with someone else. We played recorder and keyboard sonatas by Handel and Telemann. I took a fiddle class briefly, and met the wife of a missionary of some brand of faith I never quite figured out. She and her husband had traveled widely in Eastern Europe; she had once danced in a nightclub with a Russian general; she gave me a piece of the Berlin wall for a wedding present. We played sonatas of violin and piano, and actually performed, during one fiercely hot summer day when my fingers felt like sausages on the keys, for the residents of the village retirement home. Which had once been the country home of the railroad baron Jay Gould's daughter. Who had built the elegant Dutch Reform church with the Tiffany windows next door in hope that the gesture would somehow ease her father's way into heaven. Whose pulpit was graced, each Sunday, by the minister who had told me where to find my cesspool if I ever needed it. Who, later, scandalized the village by having an affair with—well, never mind. Music. I don't know if the residents of the rest home were impressed by our performance or not, but I was certainly grateful when it was over.

In a crying need to get out of those mountains for a bit, I registered for a music class offered at Julliard to the community at large. To this day I wonder if Julliard realized that the Catskills was part of its local community. The subject was World Music, which I didn't know much about. It was held every Thursday evening from seven to nine, from late September to early December. To get to it, I would drive for an hour and a quarter out of the Catskills, across the Hudson River, to another tiny village called Rhinecliff, which boasted a little train station with two tracks. I would board an Amtrak train there. After an hour and forty minutes, the train would pull into Grand Central Station, and I would step into an entirely different planet. The huge buildings, the noise, the smells, the languages, the music, as varied as the languages, offered at every street corner were mind-boggling, intoxicating. By day, I explored the city; in the evening I sat in a classroom listening to weird instruments, exotic music. Afterwards, I would reverse the journey, moving farther and farther out of the enormous, intense hothouse of civilization until the roads became narrow and solitary, mountains hid the river and the city lights, and I reached the strange point in my drive home where I felt that I had somehow traveled so far that I had left the real world, real time behind. I had passed into the realm of Sleepy Hollow, the Otherworld, which was just a little farther than anyone should go.

The final class was held in the Indonesian Consulate so that we could learn about the Gamelan. I had also learned, on those Thursday explorations, enough about the subway system to find my way there and back again, which gave me no end of satisfaction. Later, I would put that journey from one tiny world into a huge, complex and noisy world, those details of bar and classroom and my amateur efforts at music, into a fantasy novel: *Song for the Basilisk*.

A Looming Deadline can also be a galvanizing source of inspiration. I got married for the first time at age fifty-three, which is statistically highly improbable or maybe even impossible, but what the hey. It seemed like a good idea at the time, and still does. Because it was easier for me to plan a wedding 3000 miles from where I lived than it was for my mother, in a wheelchair with Parkinson's, to get on a plane, and because both our families were for the most part scattered between San

Francisco and Puget Sound, Dave and I got married in a small town on the Oregon coast. Over the internet I found the only department store in the town of Bandon that hadn't burned down in the devastating fire of 1936, and which had been turned into a charming guest house, with five bedrooms, a hot tub that didn't leak into the living room unless you filled it too high, a potbellied stove for an altar, a big kitchen, and enough space for seventy-five chairs. Since JPs don't travel in Oregon, I commandeered a good-natured Presbyterian minister to marry us, and asked my dearest friend along to cater. Meanwhile, Dave started to dismantle his own life of thirty-four years in New York, pack up the house and the memories for our trek west. This was the summer of 2001.

We flew out a week before the wedding to prepare. Preparation involved things like cleaning the scales with a garden hose off five huge salmon a fisherman friend of my mother's had given us, driving the byways to gather wild sweet pea vines along the roadside for decoration, peeling enormous quantities of potatoes while my siblings, who came from Puget Sound, and Reno, and Coos Bay, unpacked guitars and flutes and tried to remember the words to "The Wedding Song" which they had played for one another's weddings way back when we were all young.

The day itself was quite delightful. During the month after the wedding, we spent a week looking for a house to rent, flew back to the Catskills to close up my house and say goodbye to friends, get Dave's possessions into a moving van, and then took off back across country in separate cars—Dave in his sleek black jet-propelled Talon, and me in my gerbil-driven Chevy Metro, with two cats in the back who were so totally not amused. We couldn't dawdle; the moving van was somewhere on the road with us, making for the rental house. As with the wedding, most memories are blurred. Others are indelible. The rear end of the Talon. The tornado in Iowa. The rear end of the Talon. The eerie badlands of South Dakota, full of ancient, sleeping gods. Losing sight of the rear end of the Talon on the empty, rainy highway across Wyoming. Realizing that I had been married for scarcely three weeks and I'd already misplaced my husband. The devious places the cats found to hide themselves every morning in motels—under blankets, under beds that seemed riveted to the floor—to avoid being put back into the cat-carrier. Driving up a gentle slope in Montana and finding myself at the top of a dizzying mountain in Idaho, with nowhere to go but down, and the rear end of the Talon so far ahead of me I thought it would be in Oregon a day before I got there. Driving from the gentle, tangled woods of the Catskills, with their modest slopes of 3000 feet, into the spectacular vastness of the west, where mountains look down at you from 10,000 or 14,000 feet, shrug a few boulders, and ask, "What did you expect?" A friend, visiting me once in the Catskills, commented of them: "Mountains higher than these are unnatural." But I'm half-Swiss; my forebears came down out of the Alps to settle in Oregon, and I knew why: they felt at home.

Another indelible memory: waking very early on the last morning of our journey, our first morning in Oregon, turning on the news while the coffee brewed, and watching the twin towers fall.

Later that day, stunned and groggy, we reached the town where we would live, tracked down the key to the rental house, and settled in to wait for the moving van, which we had managed to outrace. I'm not sure how long it was afterwards—I think it was after we finally got a bed and pots and pans—when I began to consider seriously the Looming Deadline.

It had been a year away when I began searching for a place to get married. It had been over six months away when we got married. When I looked again, it was four months and small change away. I had thirty-nine typed pages and a contract stating I would send the completed manuscript in by February 1, 2002. I knew where I wanted the novel to go, but I couldn't seem to shove it past page 39. I couldn't find the point of view I needed to examine the life and motives of a man who wanted to conquer the world. I did the usual: sacrificed small rodents to the moon, offered my soul to demons in exchange for inspiration, did some research. Nobody wanted the rodents or my soul, and the research into ancient conquerors seemed barren. Finally, out of the blue, a young girl stepped into my head, opened her mouth and told me where that part of the story began. I finished *Alphabet of Thorn* in three and a half months, the fastest book I'd written in thirty years.

Certainly the Looming Deadline provided the crucible in which inspiration and imagination fused to give me what I needed. But none of these things—money, experience, deadlines—answers the question I was asked, because the question was not about inspiration or ideas at all.

The question was about drive, motivation: What possessed you to write eight or ten entirely different fantasies in ten or twelve years? What compels you? How could you? Why would you want to? Ever since I was young, the imagination, like the raw stuff of magic, has seemed to me a kind of formless, fluid pool of enormous possibility, both good and bad, dangerous and powerful, very like the magma in a volcano. And I envisioned myself sitting on top of this mountain of magma, spinning it into endless words, visions, imagery, controlled and useful, to keep it from bursting out in its primitive shape to devastate the landscape. At first, I felt very precariously balanced on top of my private volcano, spinning word and image into tales as quickly as I could to keep up with the unstable forces I was trying to harness. Lately, I've been feeling rather at home there. The magma level has gone down a bit; I've done some satisfying work. I can slow down, maybe, take a longer time to think what I want to make now. What I set out to do about fifteen years ago was to write a series of novels that were like paintings in a gallery by the same artist. Each work is different, but they are all related to one another by two things: they are all fantasy, and they are all by the same person. That's all I wanted to do. And now I'm reaching the end of that series.

I have no idea what will come next.